DECALOG 3 CONSEQUENCES

DOCTOR WHO

DECALOG 3 CONSEQUENCES

TEN STORIES
SEVEN DOCTORS
ONE CHAIN OF EVENTS

Edited by
Andy Lane
&
Justin Richards

DOCTOR WHO

First published in Great Britain in 1996 by
Doctor Who Books
an imprint of Virgin Publishing Ltd
332 Ladbroke Grove
London W10 5AH

ISBN 0 426 20478 6

Cover illustration by Colin Howard
Internal artwork by Richard Atkinson

Typeset by Mark Stammers Design, London

Printed and bound in Great Britain by
Mackays of Chatham PLC, Kent

CONTENTS

Illustrations by Richard Atkinson

...And Eternity In An Hour

By Stephen Bowkett

He had slept for three days. It was that strange and rather disturbing sleep into which the Doctor sometimes sank when he needed to draw on the deepest resources of his being: not a human sleep, though Jo knew that for him it was completely natural. Even so, she could never get used to the utter stillness of his body – not even the slightest flicker of an eyelid or the twitch of a finger; nor the alarming drop in the Doctor's body temperature, or the cadaverous whiteness of his skin.

She checked on him every four hours, day and night in the TARDIS, looking for some change in that uncanny changeless state, pressing her ear to his chest to hear the reassuring dull double drumbeat of his hearts – the only sign that life continued there. She draped a blanket over him, talked to him when her anxiety grew a little too overwhelming, and made him regular cups of tea, which she poured away again four hours later, when the liquid had turned as cold as the Doctor's icy skin.

Three days. And on the fourth day she found him awake and smiling, his gaze as clear and mischievous as she had always known it. The relief squeezed hot tears into her eyes.

'Oh, Doctor – you're...' She'd almost said 'alive again', but caught herself in time and chuckled self-consciously. 'You're back.'

'This tea's cold, Jo.' He grinned at her, put the cup and saucer delicately down on the side-table by the bed and took trouble to pick a fleck of lint from the red velvet of his jacket: it was an affectation he exaggerated when serious matters were troubling his mind.

Jo knew him well enough by now to realize this. Her sunny expression clouded.

'Doctor, there's something wrong, isn't there?'

His smile did not diminish as, once again, the Doctor took pleasure from the innocence, the simplicity and directness, with which Jo summed things up. The Universe trembled sometimes, shuddered under the force of evil that threatened to shatter it – and Jo would try so desperately hard, and so earnestly, to understand and to help. He admired her for it more than he could ever say.

The Doctor stood, stretched, and picked again at his jacket, thinking that he should have hung it up before entering the state of hyper-meditation. Velvet did rumple so.

'To tell you the truth, Jo, yes. I think something is terribly wrong…'

'What? Can you explain it to me?'

He stared beyond her into the distance, wondering how best to communicate ideas the merely human mind was never designed to embrace.

'I believe I can. But first I'll need another cup of tea – hot this time, please – and at least five hundred dominoes.'

It was a few hours later. The Doctor had busied himself preparing the TARDIS for what Jo described to herself as 'a long flight', knowing full well that any description of the journey would prove totally inadequate. Then he'd set up the domino-push on a huge table in one of the side-chambers she rarely entered.

The dominoes, standing carefully on end, formed a tree pattern, the 'trunk' splitting into two, each branch itself subdividing, on and on until the dominoes were used up.

'If you were doing it for charity, you'd make a fortune,' Jo commented, using watery humour to hide her unease. She knew what would happen when the Doctor toppled the first domino, and couldn't understand why he'd bothered, when this was something she could easily imagine.

'Let's pretend,' the Doctor began, his mildly patronizing

lecturer's tone making her smile. 'Let's pretend this is a game of cause-and-effect. I push the first domino and – '

'It knocks down the second, which knocks down the third, and so on.'

'Excellent, Jo!' he said, with genuine joy.

'I did pass science at school, you know!'

The Doctor held up a cautionary finger. 'But not pandimensional unified metaphysics.'

'Actually,' she admitted, 'it was domestic science...'

'Now, let's further pretend that we know that the dominoes are toppling only because we're looking through a little window at two or three of them. This means we don't know where the toppling began, or where it will end – '

'Or *if* it will end,' Jo added, as a chill deep inside her made her shiver.

'Or if it will end...But we do know that if we can remove one strategically placed domino, then we might limit the damage, and possibly halt the chain reaction entirely.'

'You're talking about the time rift!' Jo interrupted with sudden insight, shocking herself as the dominoes became populated worlds in her head. He had spoken to her briefly about it, before dropping into that strange unfathomable state he had called his 'learning sleep'. ' Oh Doctor – you mean...'

He nodded gravely. 'This is something even the Time Lords don't know quite how to handle...' And he smiled wryly at his use of the word 'even'. Again the strange paradoxical relationship he shared with his kind had prompted them to ask for his help, and compelled him to offer it; though deep in the Doctor's heart of hearts he wondered what even he could do about it this time.

Temporal rifts were the multidimensional equivalents of earthquakes: vast maverick outpourings of chronotronic energy rippling like seismic waves across the fragile space-time cobweb of the Cosmos. And the one to which the High Council of Gallifrey had alerted him was bad – very bad: eight-plus on the galactic Richter scale.

So, for his own sake as much as for Jo's, the Doctor tried not to dwell on the overall picture, that bleak scenario the Gallifreyan Chronologists had painted for him, instead focusing on his little parlour trick and the faint possibility of hope it implied.

'The trick is, if we can't see the whole picture, how do we decide which domino to remove? Which world do we travel to? And when in its history do we choose to arrive?'

The Doctor was speaking intensely, not really to her. And Jo wondered if he was pleading with the core of his mind where he went in sleep, or to the spirit of great Rassilon, or to whichever ineffable god he and his kind had once perhaps worshipped.

'Is there an answer?' she asked him, almost brusquely.

His expression lightened and he beamed at her. Though somehow she wasn't entirely convinced. 'Why, Jo, there's always an answer! Let me show you something else. Come on!'

Jo frowned as the Doctor pushed the first domino, then turned his back on the experiment. She leant over the table, snatched a domino from the path of its tumbling fellows, and was gratified to see the toppling halted.

She carried the domino away with her as she followed the Doctor, noticing with the merest of frowns that, quite by coincidence no doubt, it was the double blank.

Jo had thought the Doctor's assertion that the TARDIS was as big as a town an apocryphal tale. But now she was not so sure. They walked for twenty minutes before reaching a darkened chamber of indeterminate size. The Doctor stood aside to let her enter first…And Jo found herself standing in the centre of immensities, clouds of stars and swathes of interstellar gas spreading above her head, beneath her feet, and on every side of her. She gasped at the beauty and splendour.

'Doctor – it's a planetarium!'

He tutted, his voice close beside her as velvet soft as his jacket.

'Shame on you, Jo. It's a holographic representation of the galaxy – '

'Of course…Pandimensional, naturally.'

'Naturally. And it's connected to a complex neural net which forms part of the TARDIS's AI fuzzy logic circuitry, allowing right-brain metalogical algorithms to work alongside standard reasoning programs.'

'I knew that.'

'I call it the "intuition circuit".'

'And...' She chuckled delightedly, like a child. 'It comes up with an answer without working things out! Doctor – you're telling me the TARDIS relies on hunches!'

He shrugged. Jo felt the faint movement of the gesture against her elbow.

'How do you think I get to be in the right place at the right time so often?'

'And it will tell us how to stop the damage caused by the time rift?'

'Hmmm. Maybe in a later model. The intuition circuit can indicate where and when to go, but we need to work out for ourselves what to do when we get there.'

Because all of the preparatory work had been done earlier, the Doctor was able to engage the TARDIS main drives from a tiny console in the projection room itself. Jo actually cried out in awe as the jewelled panorama of galactic space swirled wildly around her, stars suddenly streaking past in their millions, lensing into scintillant, expanding rainbow circles as they spun past.

'We're not actually moving through the fabric of space-time,' the Doctor explained casually, 'but, rather, we're exploiting the spaces between the threads of physical reality...'

Jo was hardly listening, and the Doctor smiled warmly at her pleasure, briefly enjoying the bright theatricality of his little illusion.

They waited inside the room, inside the place that was all places in one, until a certain pattern of stars spun up out of the far distance and seemed to slow as it approached. One particular yellow star grew from among its neighbours, unfolding like a vaporous flower until it loomed large in Jo's field of vision.

She could even make out the tiny specks of its retinue of planets, circling.

'Iota Ophiuchi,' the Doctor said, relishing the words. 'And that violet planet, just there Jo, the world of Alrakis, and our destination…'

'How do you know that?' In the starlit darkness he could not see her frowning, but the puzzlement and even a mild frustration were clear in her tone.

'I recognize the star patterns,' he said. 'And besides…' The Doctor touched Jo's elbow and pointed away towards one invisible corner of the room. There, sigils and letterlike shapes flickered in and out of existence, the celestial coordinates by which the Doctor knew at once, and precisely, where and when in the known universe he had landed.

Now the galactic display was fading and a soft lambent glow replaced all.

'Let's get back to the main control room and take a look at the scanners.'

Jo nodded and followed him, saddened somehow that she must leave this cocoon of delicate beauty; afraid now to be going once more into the real universe of life and of death, of terror and nightmares and despair…

The TARDIS databanks offered up what information they possessed – both historical background and raw material gleaned from the sensors – skimming it across a screen more quickly than Jo was able to follow.

The Doctor let out a slow deep sigh as the extent of the temporal damage became obvious.

'Is it that bad?' she wondered, knowing the answer by the way his expression had darkened.

'I'm afraid it is, Jo. Although in local real time the effects of the rift spillage reached Alrakis just a few months ago, because the planet has been exposed to unmodified chronotronic energy, drastic time-distortion will have occurred, and – '

'Uh, Doctor…Plain English, please.'

His mouth tightened with irritation – a sign of his worry – but then he relaxed, realizing he was translating his apprehension about Alrakis into frustration directed at Jo.

'Simply put, time has gone haywire. Certain areas of this world will have experienced accelerated time, where years fly by in moments. Elsewhere, a state of "slow-time" or even total temporal stasis will have occurred. Imagine a child on a swing, Jo, trapped for ever at the top of the arc. Or a bee poised at the flower's lip, waiting for eternity to taste its nectar. Or the sun, perpetually hidden by a passing cloud that never passes...'

'Doctor, that's horrible!'

'It's worse. Because the "stray time" pouring from the rift will surge unexpectedly, throwing whatever bizarre state already exists into utter chaos. The consequences are thus completely unpredictable, and, for anyone left alive and sane on this planet, utterly terrifying.' He looked at her ambiguously. 'Which is to say, it's dangerous out there, Jo. And I'm wondering whether you shouldn't stay and –'

'Oh no, you're not pulling that one on me!' There was wry laughter in her voice, but anger too, that after so long he should still want to keep her safely tucked up in the TARDIS. She became quietly serious. 'I mean it, Doctor. I may not always be useful in a crisis, but I'm no liability.'

He knew it to be true, but to hide his unease over her safety, he made a small bow of acquiescence and beamed at her brightly.

Jo said, 'But I don't understand why the TARDIS brought us here now. Wouldn't it have made more sense to have arrived on Alrakis before the rift energy reached it?'

'Common sense would say so.' The Doctor snapped off the scanners and activated the great double doors. 'But the intuition circuit moves in mysterious ways. All I can say for certain is that these space-time coordinates were picked for a reason.'

He smiled wanly. 'Though it's a confounded nuisance when that reason remains completely unfathomable to the logical mind...'

Jo drew her coat more tightly around herself and shivered in the wind that swept along the rain-lashed alleys of Almaraqq, the city where they had materialized. The Doctor had briefly explained to her that the dominant race on Alrakis, the Tonska, were a humanoid species whose technological capabilities had far outstripped their capacity to nurture and care for their world.

'A bit like our lot, really,' Jo commented, her mood matching the weather.

'At least your lot, in being a confused bundle of contradictions, produce souls able to appreciate beauty, cherish the weak, look up at the night and ask, Why? But the Tonska have become grey and mechanical, just like their machines. They're a sad chapter in a tawdry tale that's told all across the Cosmos, Jo. But, despite what I think of them, they still need our help.'

'How do we give it?'

'They are a spacefaring people, highly developed, and know that the Time Lords exist. We must go to the highest authority on Alrakis – to a person known as the Yed-Prior – introduce ourselves, and explain that it may be possible to reverse the devastation of the rift spillage.'

They had walked to the end of the filthy alley, emerging at the head of a wider, busier street that dropped ahead of them down towards a bleak esplanade stretching towards the vast outer ramparts of a Babel-tower whose granitic peaks and pinnacles were lost among the streaming clouds. Jo traced its solid, desolate lines upwards, lifting her gaze beyond the huge edifice to the purplish sky, wherein floated an enormous cratered moon. Even from here, Jo could make out the scars and pockmarks of mining activities on its surface, and suddenly felt a fierce revulsion for the Alrakian people, who were eating away at the magic of the heavens, day in, day out, without pause.

'The Citadel of the Yed-Prior,' the Doctor explained, nodding towards the immense building which dominated the horizon. 'That's where we need to go.'

'Do you suppose there's a cab?'

The Doctor laughed brittlely. 'It's Shanks's pony I'm afraid. Still, if we put our backs into it, we should be there in a couple of hours!'

Jo glanced at him to see if he was serious. The Doctor's mass of white hair seemed to flame around him, halo-like, in the strong, chill, metallic wind. She felt desperately grateful he was with her.

But then he shuddered, his form rippling as though under water. He staggered, turning towards her and speaking from far, far away.

'Jo...Time dis-tort-ion...No – way – to...'

She shook her head, both to clear her senses and indicate she could no longer understand what he was saying.

'Doctor, what's going on?' She almost shrieked it, for to herself she seemed normal. But now powerful siren notes were lifting themselves to a high drone above a confusion of screams and running figures. For the first time, Jo set eyes upon the Alrakian race and, even in the midst of this crisis, was moved by the look of tragedy and loss stamped on the faces of the people, whatever beauty and hope now lost beneath the grey patina of too much terror.

She turned back to the Doctor, who appeared to be reaching out through twisted distances towards her. His eyes held a look of fear she had never seen in them before. Beyond him and around him, drably clothed Alrakians were pushing and bustling in a panic; a herd of dumb creatures stampeded by the great predator, Time.

One man spun round as though something was at his shoulder. He looked up into it and the lines and wrinkles of his face, carved by a half-century of squalor, melted like hot wax and oozed back to a child's innocence. Then, as the temporal breaker crashed over him fully, even the child was gone and a speck of blood and plasm dropped from the air to be trampled by the oblivious crowd.

Someone barged heavily into Jo's left side, even as the scream was ripping up from her throat. She stumbled, was struck hard in the right temple by an elbow, and sprawled helplessly to the ground.

Now came a greater horror, spurring her to action where the

sight of the retrogressed man had paralysed her with disgust. Jo
knew that if she didn't regain her feet, she'd be trodden to a pulp
inside seconds. She looked wildly through a moving forest of
legs and flapping coat hems, using them to claw herself upright
with a yell of sheer determination.

A woman of about her own age paused and held out a hand.
Jo gasped and reached thankfully, lifting her face to look at her
rescuer...

But the face was already crumbling, flesh falling sloppily
from the bones to splash in the roadway. The woman tried to
speak, but the word died in a throat rotted instantly by the years,
the eyes giving up their spark of life to take on the pale opacity
of stone.

The skeleton toppled in a cascade of bones as Jo pushed
herself clear, backing away, turning to let the nightmare take
her wherever it wished.

Darkness had swept across the sky like the beating of a vast
black wing. A few lamps flared on automatically, some burning out at once with the greater forces tearing through them;
others guttering fitfully in the chaotic dark, showing the frightened faces of the soon-to-be dead.

Jo numbered herself among them, even as she watched a
large armoured vehicle grind rapidly along the street from the
esplanade, casting the crowd aside with some kind of invisible
energy field. It moved directly towards her like a steel arma-
dillo, swung side-on in a clever half-track manoeuvre, and
stopped.

A door-ramp slammed down and two people bulked up in
grey body armour ran towards her. She was grabbed before
there was time to gather her senses, hustled towards the vehicle
and hurled inside...

While beyond the window the full force of the timestorm hit
the streets, and living beings were tossed like burnt-out ashes
into the howling hurricane of the future.

What grieved the Doctor more than the thought of Jo's death
was that he had brought her unerringly here to suffer it. He had

known the risks, and they were terrible risks; yet Jo had placed her full faith in him, secure in the illusion of her knowledge that he would see her safe, as he had always done before.

He barely saw the people dying around him, as the outriders of the temporal disturbance gathered and washed through the city. Men and women were transformed into dust, or reduced to tiny fragments of latent life, all tossed away on the wind.

He hardly noticed, allowing himself to be carried along by the crowd, through a stout-portalled doorway and into a huge shelter that was already heaving with humanity – or what passed for humanity on Alrakis.

A great metal door was closed and the Doctor laughed weakly, realizing that these people had found the simplest way possible of protecting themselves: by using the sheer durability of granite and steel. Except under special and quite infrequent conditions, the energies of the time rift would not appear here within the chamber. Instead, a whirlwind of centuries hurled itself against the redoubt, eating away at the metal and stone until the timeforce was spent and what mortals took for reality returned.

Leaning tiredly against the wall, the Doctor prepared to bide his time. His exhaustion was not simply a response to the rigours of the situation, but also the result of despair. He guessed it was possible that Jo, too, might have found shelter and survived. But the chances were slim and the likelihood was that she had been consumed by the timestorm like a moth shrivelled in a flame.

A grief that was sharp as a blade cut through him – until the Doctor chided himself that, after everything he had been through in all his adventures, he should have forgotten on this occasion that hope could outlast even the stubbornness of stone.

The air in the armoured vehicle smelt stale, rich with a disconcerting background aroma of chemicals which Jo found unnerving. Her rescuers, or perhaps captors, struggled out of their heavy protective outer clothing, ripped off their visors and

hoods and slumped down onto a plain metal seat. They stared
at Jo with open hostility, and Jo stared back, shocked at the sight
of the man whose face on its left side was barely out of
adolescence, while on the right the skin hung in the wattled
folds of an eighty-year-old.

'Take a good look, girl, at what your meddling has caused.
Do you like Arkab as he should be' – the man tilted his youthful
face towards her – 'or what the Time Lords have made of him?'

Jo's shock was tempered with the need for extreme caution.
'What have the Time Lords got to do with this?' she bluffed.

Arkab sneered, the paralysis of age twisting half his face into
an even grotesquer grimace. Jo saw that his jaws and teeth on
the right side had been heavily reconstructed using a blend of
crude metalwork and sparkling microelectronics. Circuitry
glittered delicately as Arkab broke into derisive laughter.

'You're telling me there's another explanation for this
carnage! Well perhaps when your kin hear that we –'

Jo interrupted him sharply, her face flushing with anger,
impatience and a sudden pity that rushed through her at this
ruination of a man.

'Wait a minute, Arkab. There are a few things you should
know – No, you listen to me now!'

He had leant forward to brush aside her excuses, but now
found himself taken aback by this slight, rather youthfully
pretty girl whose initial meekness obviously belied the strength
of character within.

He smiled at her then, his temper fading somewhat. The
woman who was his companion in the rear of the vehicle
grinned too, at seeing Arkab's ferocity subdued.

'First,' Jo said, ticking off the points on her fingers like a
teacher sternly explaining to a child, 'I am not a Time Lord –'

'But –'

'I *travel* with a Time Lord, the Doctor. And we've come here
to try to undo the damage caused by the rift. We want to help
you, Arkab, believe me.'

'Belief, trust – these are difficult concepts in a world that's
insane.'

'The insanity is not of the Time Lords' doing, I'm sure of that. They do not believe in meddling with the temporal affairs of other races.'

Arkab could not withhold his bark of cynical laughter.

Jo shrugged, disdaining his reaction. 'Neither is the Doctor here to meddle. We have calculated that now, in Almaraqq, is the point at which we can do the greatest good.'

'How?' the woman asked.

Arkab chuckled. 'Good question, Saiph. How, girl? Tell us that.'

'I don't know how,' Jo said quietly. 'All I do know is that the computers in our vehicle, the TARDIS, gave us these co-ordinates.'

'But why here, why now?' Arkab demanded pompously.

Jo sighed. She was tired, drained by the shock of her ordeal, wearied further now by the prospect of giving long explanations to these people. Now that she felt her life was not in imminent danger, all she wanted to do was eat and sleep, then set about looking for the Doctor. If he had survived.

She said as much to Saiph and Arkab. The woman's expression softened and she nodded, turning to her friend.

'We are forgetting our manners. Whether the girl's story is true or not, she's no use to us in this state.'

'Jo. My name's Jo...And I have as many questions for you as you have for me. But please, just an hour's rest...'

Her eyes were closing even as she spoke, the harsh grey confines of the vehicle fading as her consciousness ebbed away. Saiph caught her as Jo slumped forward, lowering her onto the hard pallet and covering her over with a rough-woven blanket which was itchy, smelly – and the warmest, most comfortable bedding that Jo could possibly imagine.

Night remained once the timestorm had passed, having wrenched the daylight out of the sky. The planet's huge companion moon hung low in the west, its nether rim below the horizon, as the Doctor left the bunker and moved purposefully among the dispersing crowd towards the Citadel.

As he walked, he could not help but be moved by the devastation all around him: human remains scattered over the pavements and roadways; piles of rubble, dust and rusting, aged metal; children crawling in the remnants of their adult rags, some of them crying, some moving in silence – all with fear and incomprehension large in their eyes...

The Doctor looked away, forcing his mind to tackle the complexities of his mission here on Alrakis. There was nothing he could possibly do to save more than a handful of these poor pathetic individuals, hurled back into innocence by the vicissitudes of the storm, doomed to slow death in this uncaring, decimated society. No, any help the Doctor might offer would need to be on the large scale, using his abilities to manipulate time so that the fearsome energies of the rift might be diverted harmlessly into some sterile sub-universe, or...

'Or by harnessing the cold-fusion power plants of Alrakis, create a seamless temporal feedback loop as a space-time containment vessel for the spillage...'

He walked on, his mind locked into the details of the strategy, oblivious now of the anonymous grimy faces that stared stupidly as this strange, colourful figure passed by, before returning to gaze at the twinkling lights in the sky that looked so beautiful, but meant as much to them as to the unheeding sheep in the fields.

Jo passed over the double-blank domino at Arkab's request. She had been toying with it casually as he'd talked.

Arkab glanced at it, then at Jo. 'What is it?'

'Oh, er, a lucky piece...Go on with what you were saying.'

'Despite all of this' – he opened his arms to include the city and beyond – 'we believe that the Universe is unfolding as it should. Whatever happens, it must be for a purpose. People fear the unknown simply because they don't understand how it operates. But beneath what seems to be random, a deeper organizational force must be at work.'

Arkab tossed the domino; it clattered to the floor, face down. He picked it up, flipped it again, and this time the blank face landed uppermost.

'It's impossible to predict how this amulet will fall. But don't you see, Jo, that's all engineered into the basic structure of the Cosmos!'

Jo avoided Arkab's eyes, staring instead at the domino. She had heard the Doctor speak like this about deep structures of space-time: and indeed, the very notion of a fabric to the Universe implied a weaver. Or was it, she wondered, just making meaning out of chaos? Could it all be simply self-delusion, the pretence of prescience in a purposeless void?

'Arkab,' Jo said slowly, 'I don't know how to answer you.' She was rather frightened by the man's evangelical zeal, together with the dawning realization that Arkab and Saiph and the others aboard the vehicle represented some kind of rebel splinter group, an anarchic force determined to destroy structures more than philosophize about them. 'All I understand is that we've got to find the Doctor. He's the one who can help you.'

'No problem.' Saiph had been operating a scanner system, and now directed Jo's attention to a number of flickering screens, most of which were incomprehensible to her. But a couple showed the Citadel, quite close up, a façade so vast that it seemed to fill the entire sky.

'As you might imagine, we have become very adept at detecting temporal anomalies. We picked up the arrival of your craft – which is why we were able to reach you as the timestorm struck – and have traced your friend the Doctor through the residual chronotronic energy surrounding him.'

Saiph tapped the glass of the screen with a bitten fingernail.

'He's in there, Jo, inside the Citadel of the Yed-Prior – probably talking to her right now.'

'Her?'

'Yed-Prior simply means "The Foremost". The current Yed-Prior is a woman named Zaniah,' Arkab added. 'An evil bitch if ever one existed! Zaniah came to power, the rumour goes, by eliminating her opposition. At least, nothing has been heard of her rivals for months – if I can speak of "months" on

Alrakis!'

'There's no doubt she's a megalomaniac,' Saiph went on. 'And an incredibly clever one, too. She managed to exploit the panic caused by the opening of the rift, consolidating the weaker members of the Senate, wiping out the stronger, taking full control of Government even while she launched a powerful propaganda campaign to swing the people round to her side.'

Jo thought secretly that, under the circumstances, Zaniah seemed to have done a reasonable job. At least the city was still functioning after a fashion, and though people were dying in their hundreds owing to the rift spillage, the majority had survived because of the building of the bunkers, of which Saiph had earlier spoken...

And perhaps the woman traced the flow of Jo's thoughts in the cast of her eyes, for now she leant forward and talked very earnestly.

'Jo, you don't fully understand what Zaniah intends, the true horror of her plan. We have accused the Time Lords of interference, but Zaniah's scheme goes much further. She is determined to harness the rift energy for her own ends. She has promised the people that she can grant them full and comfortable lives – lives that will span just an hour of local real time. Alrakians will be born, breed and die within sixty minutes. But for herself, Zaniah will engineer just the opposite; extending her own lifespan indefinitely, safe from the timestorms inside the Citadel. Practically speaking, she will rule Alrakis for ever.'

'That's why we've got to stop her,' Arkab explained. 'And we will succeed, Jo, with or without the Doctor's help.'

Reading the puzzlement in Jo's face, Saiph said, 'This troop carrier is loaded with a fusion device. Our aim is to break into the Citadel and detonate it. We thought that, in one fell swoop, we could end Zaniah's terrible reign, and wreak revenge on the Time Lords for their intrusion into our lives...'

'You mean by making sure the Doctor and I were aboard?'

Saiph nodded slowly. 'That was and is our plan – though we accept now what you say, and believe that the Doctor has come to help us.'

'But he will fail,' Arkab added with certainty. 'Once Zaniah realizes who he is, and *what* he is, she will force him to work towards her own ends. He will have no choice: no one can withstand her tortures.'

'And that's why, Jo,' Saiph went on, 'whether you choose to come with us or not, we are proceeding with our mission. We are going to breach the Citadel's outer barriers and set off our nuclear device. With a little luck, Zaniah and her evil will be blown to atoms!'

Arkab hefted the domino in his hands and tossed it lightly to Jo.

'Because,' he said, 'the Universe always unfolds as it should.'

She was as cold and beautiful as a marble sculpture, the Doctor thought, contemplating her beauty in a distant and rather cerebral way, and finding it tainted by the single-minded passion of her purpose. Zaniah, Yed-Prior of Alrakis, in seeking to dominate her people, had grown away from them and become something quite alien.

She leant forward now and filled the Doctor's tall-stemmed glass with a reddish-purple wine which, to be truthful, he thought rather cloying.

The woman smiled at him seductively, letting her rich auburn hair fall across her shoulder in a full spill of colour. ' It's the best on the planet,' Zaniah told him, rather arrogantly. 'Untainted by temporal contamination, naturally matured. What do you think?'

The Doctor swirled some across his palate and tongue and swallowed it with a neutral expression. 'Sardonic,' was his opinion, 'without being impertinent.' He might have been describing his own attitude towards this dangerous borderline-psychotic, whose clumsily feigned ignorance of his origins belied to him her deep knowledge of the Time Lords of Gallifrey and the nature of the power with which she was tampering.

The Doctor had had no difficulty in entering the Citadel to its deepest levels, speaking the appropriate words of admission and validation at each gatehouse, until, very quickly, he had been escorted to the inner sanctum of the Yed-Prior, there to be introduced to the woman before whom he now sat, exchanging pleasantries. He smiled inwardly and bitterly. Exchanging pleasantries while this world and how many others became cinders!

'You have an unusual way of judging a vintage, Doctor.' Zaniah chuckled, as though she herself might have enjoyed a sip too much. 'But your assessment is elegant and stylish. I like that.' She lifted the decanter, offering more. The Doctor held up his hand to forestall her.

'Thank you, but no, Yed-Prior. Good wine, like time itself, is best taken in moderation.' And his own smile was as generous and as deceptive as her own.

They had been talking for an hour, each probing for information without wanting to reveal too much; verbally circling like opponents beneath a façade of urbane politeness and etiquette. During this time, the Doctor had formed an opinion of more than the woman's fine wines. She was obviously unbalanced, perhaps because of the power of the stray time she had brought under partial and precarious control; perhaps for reasons he would never understand. It hardly mattered. What fragments of Zaniah's plan he had gleaned from her chilled his blood. This talk of redesigning timeframes so that generations lived for only an hour was madness – and not just the madness of tyranny. She and her technicians had grasped the possibility without comprehending the implications. Didn't they realize that the fundamental forces of the Universe were not separate components, but an irreducible Whole wherein one primary influence could never be modified without affecting the others? Time, Space, Gravity, Life: tamper with one and all are changed.

Zaniah's beaming smile remained, though the light in her eyes shifted subtly, like lucent ice transformed by a setting sun.

'You speak of time as though it is something that can be

squandered, Doctor.'

'It can indeed be squandered, Yed-Prior...'

'Your formality is flattering, but unnecessary. If we are to work together, I much prefer you to call me Zaniah.'

The Doctor made the smallest bow of acknowledgement, his fury rising at the need to engage in such hollow diplomacy.

She went on with velvet remorselessness: 'We have too much time here on Alrakis, Doctor, as you have seen. The rift has already caused great devastation, and its chaos is not yet at an end. I find it imperative that my people should be given every chance to live out lives that are as normal as possible – as fulfilling and rewarding as I can make them.'

'Yes, but I don't think you understand –'

He paused, cursing himself. It was a clumsy mistake to have made. Already the sting of his words had caused the woman's face to flush angrily and her eyes spark with indignation. Around her in the imposing crystalline room, the armoured representatives of the Yed-Prior's personal guard stirred in anticipation of her temper.

'I understand that I have offered you hospitality, an explanation and the chance to save a population on the brink of oblivion. And yet, Doctor' – the slightest frown of puzzlement creased her brow – 'you seem to be disdaining my proposition.'

'I will do all I can to help your people, Yed-Prior,' the Doctor replied, wearying now of these razor-barbed niceties, 'but I have to say that I think your scheme to meddle with the morphogenetic templates of life is both ill-considered and extremely hazardous.'

He had expected an outburst – some kind of catlike refutation of his criticism. Instead, and to his mild surprise, the woman eased back into her luxurious silken couch, picked up her wineglass and sipped at the liquid very delicately.

'You strike me as a man who relishes hazardous situations, Doctor,' Zaniah told him, noting that the *double entendre* had not been wasted. 'And I believe that you are also capable of minimizing the dangers, which is why I insist you meet my scientific team and –'

'Yed-Prior, I have to tell you that –'

'*And* assist them in bringing my programme to completion.'

The Doctor sighed with impatience, and with a certain intimation of doom. The Yed-Prior's mask of urbane sophistication bored him now, and having nothing to lose, as he judged, he let his anger surface.

'Your scientists are like children playing in a minefield. And you, Zaniah, are no better. Indeed, your insistence on success, even when every instinct I possess screams out that you will find nothing but failure, speaks of a pride and a narrow-mindedness that I find both astonishing and intolerable –'

'Take care, Doctor,' the woman said with a dangerous purr in her voice.

'No, Yed-Prior, *you* take care. For, when you have brought upon your world the disaster which I predict, the powers of a thousand other planets, mightier and more terrible than your own, will seek their revenge. And it will be a just revenge, one that will see Alrakis reduced to a burned-out boulder in space. I will not mourn the passing of this madness,' the Doctor went on, as Zaniah's face became white with fury. ' What does grieve me deeply is the witless destruction of other worlds and other civilizations that your ill-conceived dreams of power will perpetrate.'

The Doctor rose, replacing his wineglass on the jewelled table before him.

'Kill me if you will, Yed-Prior. But I shan't help you in this. That's my final word.'

Zaniah nodded slowly, and, by some subliminal gesture that the Doctor failed to catch, summoned her guards to surround him.

'I admire your stubbornness, Doctor – although you seem to think it's something else. Nobility, perhaps. But what you haven't realized is that only the Yed-Prior can have the final word in her own domain.'

Zaniah stood and faced the Doctor brazenly, touching the red velvet of his jacket with a long fingernail dusted with a million microscopic diamonds.

'You would sacrifice yourself to thwart me, I know that. But I also know that your pretty young companion is out there in the city, together with several billion Alrakians who, one way or another, will die unless you intervene. You speak truly when you accuse my scientists of ignorance. But they will proceed anyway, because I have ordered it. So, Doctor, your choice is to allow them to fail, with unimaginable consequences, or to assist them and salvage what you can from your impossible dilemma. Guards! Escort the Doctor to the laboratory complex.'

The Doctor allowed himself to be led, but turned as he neared the door, and pointed a steady finger at the Yed-Prior.

'Tyranny will always be defeated by persistence and intelligence. You will not see your ambitions flourish.'

Zaniah smiled, and in reply toppled the Doctor's discarded wineglass, shattering it, spilling the contents like wasted blood across the table.

They were more than determined. Jo found herself cowed before the stark single-mindedness with which Arkab and Saiph had delineated their plan. She didn't doubt for a moment that these terrorists would fail: because they were terrorists fighting an infinitely greater terror, it seemed, and believed with a fundamental passion that losing a life was nothing when set against losing the Cause.

As the armoured vehicle lumbered through the poorly lit streets, avoiding the random and rather cursory militia patrols, Jo tried to plead for the Doctor's safety.

Saiph shook her head, and with a touch of humanity that Jo found profoundly moving on this bleak, dark world, she explained why a rescue would be out of the question.

'Our life expectancy once we are within the Citadel can be measured in minutes. The Doctor will have been taken to the laboratory complex where work on modifying the population is being undertaken. This area lies at the centre of the building, and is as secure and well-protected as Zaniah's own inner sanctum. Only sheer force – the sheer force of a nuclear explosion – will allow us to achieve our aim. We do not anticipate that anyone caught unprepared within a wide radius will survive the blast.'

'A secondary unit,' Arkab continued, 'will arrange for the sirens to sound shortly before we detonate the device. People will hurry to the bunkers, thinking they are seeking shelter from a timestorm. We hope, and foresee, that the loss of life in this case will be minimal.'

'But the Doctor…' Jo said again, her voice catching like a burr in her throat.

'I'm sorry,' Saiph replied, and meant it.

'There is,' Jo whispered, herself caught unawares by the audacity and unexpectedness of her thought, 'another way.'

'What other way?' Arkab leant back against the metal bulkhead, digging in the pocket of his untidy, baggy overjacket for a smoke.

Jo's heart was beating furiously as she reached behind her neck and unclipped the clasp of a silver chain, drawing it out to hold the timekey of the TARDIS in front of the others. It had been the Doctor's greatest gift to her, the most complete and sincere symbol of his trust and affection that she could ever imagine.

Arkab sniffed disdainfully and carried on searching for his smoke. Saiph raised an eyebrow quizzically.

'With this,' Jo said, putting more conviction into her voice than she felt, 'I can get you right into the heart of Zaniah's Citadel…'

The laboratories were vast: a complexity of towering metal and crystalline structures built around a series of gleaming pits sunk deep into the bedrock beneath the city. The Doctor and his escort emerged on an upper gallery, where, for a moment or two, the sheer scale of the machinery in that immense panorama took the Doctor's breath away.

'Fondly do we hope, fervently do we pray,' he thought, recalling Lincoln's famous phrase, before an unsmiling guard nudged him roughly and indicated the way to the elevators.

He was taken to a workplace set close to the central pit. A

metal guardrail circled it at chest height, and, despite the wishes of his watchmen, the Doctor paused to peer over, his gaze dropping down and down for many hundreds of feet, before the scene became clouded over with shrouding mists – illuminated dazzlingly every few seconds by strange blue flashes of light of incalculable voltage.

He edged away, appalled. 'But this is monstrous! Somehow you have channelled the rift energy and attempted to contain it here. What are you using to bottle up these incredible forces? Surely not electromagnetic fields?'

The guards looked at him stupidly. 'Ask Sabik,' one of them told him, the small cadre stepping away as a diminutive and rather nervous-looking man strode up to the Doctor, his face tense and anxious.

'I am Sabik, Coordinator of the Project.' He made a small agitated bow, which the Doctor ignored. 'The Yed-Prior has advised me of your expertise, Doctor – and warned me too of your refusal to help.'

'Do you realize...' the Doctor said by way of reply, his voice rising. 'Do you realize the incredible foolishness of what you are attempting to do?'

'What was foolish to initiate would now be foolish to terminate,' Sabik told him, almost apologetically. 'Can you not see that the emergence of the time rift on Alrakis forced desperate measures upon us?'

'I see that you are tampering with the primary forces of Creation! You have "succeeded" in containing, in a very limited capacity, a stream of raw chronotronic energy from the rift spillage. Are you seriously contemplating using it to manipulate the life-fields of the Alrakian people – to condense their existence down to mere minutes? Would you play God with the lives of these millions of beings?'

The Doctor's outrage and sheer fury made Sabik cower before him. And, while the Doctor felt a towering anger against this pathetic little man, he also found himself moved to pity at the vicissitudes of destiny that had brought Sabik to this sorry and degenerate state.

'I simply follow the commands of the Yed-Prior...' Sabik

began. Then his eyes filled with something more, a profound sadness of loss that gave the Doctor pause.

'And,' he admitted, 'because a father will always do whatever he can for his son…'

The Doctor opened his mouth to demand explanation, but Sabik had turned away and walked the few steps to the safety rail at the edge of the central pit.

He stared into the depths, the Doctor following suit, a terrible suspicion dawning that the Yed-Prior's programme of experimentation was further advanced than he'd suspected.

'Menkib was the first, and so far the only, volunteer to subject himself to the unrefined energy of the timefield,' Sabik said, speaking as though to himself. 'I was confident, so confident, just a few short months ago… The computer-guided quark-drivers we used epitomized the sophistication of our technology. There was no way we would not be able to access the morphogenetic templates and re-form the specific field-flows that defined Menkib's form – and duration.'

'You got more than you bargained for,' the Doctor said simply. His gaze was fixed on terrible lightnings far below, which seemed, like living things, to be rising in excitement as something even deeper down disturbed them.

'We accessed the life-templates,' Sabik confirmed, the words breaking up into a burst of insubstantial laughter. 'Oh yes, we laid bare the circuitry of mortality itself – and how supremely conceited we were to think we could wire it differently…Menkib! Menkib!' Sabik was suddenly shouting, startling the Doctor. 'He still knows! He still loves me as his father!'

The Doctor looked, and was horrified, at the twisting, churning, transforming thing that was ascending from the depths: an amorphous mass that changed second by second with a hideous flowing motion which seemed to liquefy the form – now into an egg-shaped monstrosity with a multitude of limbs; now into a creature that had several heads and limbs growing from its trunk where no limbs should be…The Doctor reeled as he caught sight of one of those heads. It was startlingly human, but the expression in its eyes held such agony and such fierce horror that it was almost enough to freeze the blood in his veins.

And, despite the shifting, surging multiplicity of shapes that the passage of seconds brought closer, the Doctor recognized the leviathan as the focus of the dark archetypal nightmares that haunted the minds of people on a thousand civilized worlds. Deep mythologies across the galaxy spoke of this monster – one that had perhaps existed in the Dawn Time, or maybe only in twisted nightmares. Doubtless the minds of the Alrakians had been touched by the name and nature of this beast, even before they had begun to experiment. But now, from primeval chaos, recreated anew and with astonishing stupidity, Sabik and his team of technicians had called forth the Cerunnos.

Jo was exhausted by the time she, Arkab and Saiph had hurried to the TARDIS, leaving the others to drive the halftrack to its destination. There were no words she could have used to divert these people from their plan: the Citadel would be destroyed, and soon. All that was in Jo's power to do was use the TARDIS to reach the Doctor and rescue him before the situation resolved itself – as it did so depressingly often – in fire and blood and devastation.

The gleaming key seemed to guide itself into the subtle locks of the TARDIS. Attuned to her brainwaves and aura patterns, the ship admitted Jo quickly, as though welcoming an old friend to its embrace. Saiph and Arkab were suitably impressed by the spatial dislocations as they stood, mouths agape, gazing around the glowing control room.

The double doors hummed closed behind the three and Saiph was prompted to ask, 'What next?'

It was a moot point. While the Doctor had made provision for Jo to enter the TARDIS (in times of crisis, she mused, when she would otherwise 'just be in the way'), he had never shown her how to operate any but the simplest of the ship's controls. It was something that had worried her as she'd first put forward this alternative...But then she recalled what the Doctor had said earlier, about always being in the right place at the right time – and remembered the intuition circuit that had brought them so surely to Alrakis.

'Now,' Jo said, loudly and clearly, speaking both to Saiph and Arkab, and to the TARDIS itself, 'now we go and find the Doctor.'

The grinding throb of the engines, and the rise and fall of the glowing central column of the console, surprised Jo as much as it did her fellow passengers. But she was instantly reassured, as though by a comforting inner voice, that somehow the TARDIS had understood her intention and would take her surely to her appointed destination.

She turned and grinned, thinking that, for a machine, the TARDIS was pretty wise. Sometimes, she reflected, rather wiser than its master...

So absorbed and horrified was the Doctor by the manifestation in the pit, that he failed to hear the distant dull rumble running through the fabric of the building. Around him, banks of monitors registered the shockwave. An alarm siren sounded far away in the outer reaches of the Citadel.

Sabik had moved away to check on the status of the containment vessel, which held in precarious balance the rogue energies of the rift spillage. Now he hurried back and grabbed the Doctor by the elbow.

'The Citadel is under attack! Did you not feel it – the exterior barriers have been breached! Doctor, if the vessel is damaged –'

'The chronotronic energy will flood out through the rupture. You will have succeeded in creating your own artificial timestorm, Sabik – yet another little side effect you failed to foresee.'

'But the consequences –'

'Will be ferociously destructive...But, perhaps ultimately, just.'

The Doctor saw the bright glitter of panic overlying the dull mask of fear on Sabik's face. He could not bring himself to feel sorry for the man, nor ever to forgive him; but to rant from the high ground of hindsight was profitless. And there was also, he considered, the small matter of saving his own skin.

'Possibly if we reposition the flux foci and retroprogram the vessel-defining software...' the Doctor began, speaking initially to Sabik, but then to himself as the intricacies of the problem unfolded in his mind.

He walked with the scientist towards the primary console, which controlled the field manipulation computers, admitting mentally that Sabik's team had accomplished a great deal: first harnessing the erratic flow of stray time in this locality, and then holding it in stasis long enough to overwrite the morphogenetic templates controlling the vital aspects of Menkib's being...

But of course, the creature in the pit was Menkib no longer. It was nothing in particular – or, more precisely, everything in general. The Cerunnos, madness made flesh, had the capability to assume all and any forms – and possessed the primal urge to do so. Having been freed from the constraints of one form, it sought stability again, and would attach itself to whatever living beings wandered near.

The Cerunnos, in myth and now in reality, was the ultimate parasite in the living flesh of the Universe.

As the Doctor's fingers flickered over the nexus-boards that controlled the field computers, further explosions boomed through the Citadel. High up in one of the topmost galleries, vast windows and towers of crystal shattered with the shock and cascaded down. The cacophony of sirens increased. Sabik clapped his hands to his ears and let out a moan of utter despair.

'Pull yourself together man!' the Doctor snapped, flinching as a lightning flash seared from one field-node to another nearby. Out of the pit, the roaring of the Cerunnos from its hundred malformed mouths rose in volume and pitch.

'It feels the change in the flux energies!' Sabik wailed. 'It knows it can break free!'

If the Doctor had had more time, he would have been interested to discuss the concept of whether the Cerunnos could in fact 'know' anything. But Sabik was right about one thing: the flux energies were shifting rapidly now, and in unexpected directions. The carefully balanced lattice of forces containing the frightful chronotronic power of the rift was breaking down. And although the primary computers employed tachyonic circuitry, which operated faster than the speed of light, the temporal distortions inherent in the system were causing a slowing effect, such that the Doctor expected an imminent and disastrous collapse.

'Sabik, can you arrange to have more power boosted through the –'

There was a scream. The Doctor glanced up in time to see one of the technicians spinning to the floor in a shower of his own blood. Beyond him, a number of black-clad guards had appeared, flanking the icily regal form of the Yed-Prior herself.

'He was trying to escape,' Sabik whispered. 'He was just trying to save himself.'

'Too late for either, I think,' the Doctor whispered.

He lifted his hands from the nexus-boards and stood away from the console.

'Do something!' Zaniah shrieked, her voice cracking like a whiplash through the vast spaces and galleries of the complex. Now they could all hear the sounds of destruction growing closer – a background percussion to the higher, more immediate noises of the containment vessel's implosion.

Zaniah caught sight of the Doctor and rushed forward, clawing at him, all pretence of calm authority gone.

'You've got to do something, Doctor,' she chattered, breathing wine fumes up into his face. 'The terrorists are inside the Citadel – some kind of bomb – they have positioned their vehicle, and now…' She laughed, a brittle shriek of hysteria. 'You've got to do something!'

With great dignity the Doctor disengaged Zaniah's hands from his clothing. There was a strange expression on his face. He said, very quietly, 'All through my life I've thought exactly the same thing. On a thousand worlds, from the hot primeval morning of the Cosmos to its dark and lonely twilight, I have journeyed in search of answers. Invariably I have encountered beings in danger, societies in crisis… And I always thought, I have got to do something.'

'But you must!' she interrupted. The Doctor looked beyond her, as if into the light of revelation.

'But who am I to say what must and must not come to pass? I am one individual, mortal, frightened, sometimes lost. Perhaps there are no answers: perhaps there is nothing to be done. For the Universe unfolds as it should, whether by design or random circumstance. Things are never finished – because they are always finished...'

Zaniah stared hard into his eyes for a moment longer, judging his madness. Then her lips curled back and she lifted her hand to strike him blind.

A sudden hurricane of gunfire forestalled her. Most of the guards were running, though a few stood their ground as the Cerunnos rose above the lip of the pit and reached out its multitude of limbs to claim them. One man, squeezed in a vast reptilian claw, burst like soft fruit. Another was entangled in a red appendage that might have been a tongue, and whirled into a lipless, anemone-like mouth fringed with undulating cilia. A third guard raked high-velocity shells across the flank of the monster, failing to move in time as a talon scythed his body, splitting him from chin to groin.

Zaniah gave a choking gasp as she beheld the results of Sabik's labours. Her head began shaking to and fro, to and fro, in finding herself unable to grasp the enormity and grotesquerie of the leviathan before her.

She ripped her gaze free momentarily, as though to acquiesce to the truth of the Doctor's words.

Then she snatched a weapon from one of her men and swept it backwards and forwards across the body of the Cerunnos, the scattering scientists – anyone who happened to stand in her way.

The Doctor made a grab for Sabik. He was running, not towards the Yed-Prior, but into the arms of his child. He was calling out, 'Menkib! Menkib!' making a mantra of his son's name. But Menkib was as good as dead, the Doctor knew; utterly absorbed, totally lost within the matrix of the creature.

The Cerunnos caught sight of Sabik, this particle of life approaching, and failed to recognize his face. It mantled above the man, and dropped, engulfing him in an instant.

The Doctor ducked, then took his opportunity to hurry back to the computer console. There was one chance, one slim possibility – not for himself now, but for the swathe of worlds in this part of the galaxy. If he could draw off just a little of the chronotronic energy and use it to form a stasis-field around the Citadel, then he might trap the Cerunnos, maybe even the nuclear blast – all of this chaos – in a frozen moment for ever.

He reached the console, in time to see Zaniah raise her weapon in his direction.

There was a staccato spurt of gunfire – and the Yed-Prior's shoulder vanished behind a spray of shattering tissue. She was hurled back and spun round by the impact, flung towards the grasping limbs of the Cerunnos.

The creature was already embedded in the tidal pull of the pit's temporal field, but its lifespan was vast and the stray time flowing around it harmed it little. However, Zaniah was simply mortal, and, as the Doctor watched aghast, the woman aged as she writhed in the All-Consumer's embrace, becoming bones and blood and dust within moments.

He turned away in disgust, and found Jo standing at his side.

'Jo – how…?' Pleasure and surprise passed quickly across his face, which immediately darkened again with concern.

'Explanations later, Doctor,' she told him, looking quickly around. Her face was white and taut with shock. 'Maybe you'd better get busy sorting out this mess.'

Saiph and Arkab came barging past, cutting into the dwindling cadre of guards who, leaderless now, were torn between retreat and decimation.

Catching some glimpse of these tiny deaths, the Cerunnos howled and hauled itself further out of the pit, slopping the bulk of its torso mere yards from where Jo and the Doctor were standing.

The Doctor laughed briefly and bitterly. So much for the intuition circuit that had brought him, not to the pivotal point in time and space where he might have been of some use, but instead to this instant of disaster where the Cerunnos was unleashed into the physical realm.

He hesitated as Jo stared at him in bewilderment. She touched his arm, disturbed by the look in his eyes.

'Doctor...?'

Arkab turned, distracting himself momentarily from the slaughter.

'Get back in your machine, Jo – and take your companion with you. The nuclear device is set to detonate! There is nothing more for you to do. We will cover your retreat.'

Jo needed no second telling. She knew the critical moment had come, leaving no time even for goodbyes.

Grabbing the Doctor, she pulled him unresisting into the TARDIS, which, prompted by her subconscious wish, began the dematerialization process.

With tears in her eyes, Jo watched the monitor as Saiph and Arkab were cut down by retaliatory fire. She saw the Cerunnos create a plethora of eyes and distorted heads, the better to see the curious timecraft waver and fade...

And then all was obliterated by a scalding wash of light as the Universe dropped from view.

The wall of flame, unimaginably hot and blindingly brilliant, flashed towards the Cerunnos – and then slowed. Encountering the expanding ripples of chronotronic energy from the rupturing containment vessel, the nuclear blastwave was delayed just long enough to give the creature time to drop back down into the pit.

But now the incredibly complex web of energies there looked different – torn and ravaged, like a shredded net, beyond which lay the boundless ocean of the Cosmos. There were a quintillion directions the creature might have taken, but only one that was obvious – along the fading afterglow of a timetrail between a planet called Alrakis, and a world known to some as the Earth...

'Thousands of years,' the Doctor muttered, studying the readouts on the TARDIS console. 'The force of the explosion, and the subsequent tidal surge of rift energy, have hurled us thousands of years into Alrakis's future...'

He activated the outer doors and they stepped out into a sunny late-summer afternoon.

The sun hung low on the horizon, like a great orange hull, sinking through the haze and down beyond the hills. The world's great moon, drawn closer now by the gravitational pull of the parent world, occupied half of the southern sky. Its inexorable orbital decay, and eventual collision with Alrakis, would most likely see the destruction of both, further aeons ahead in time.

But for now, tiny creatures like iridescent green bumble-bees hovered at the seductively exposed throats of violet flowers. Tall feathery grasses the colour of amber waved languidly in a warm wind. Farther off, the ancient hills dropped towards a lush river valley. There was no sign of habitation. The grim megalopolis of the Alrakian people, and the immense hulk of the central Citadel, had long ago been weathered down to dust.

The Doctor picked one of the beautiful violet flowers and arranged it in the buttonhole of his jacket. He smiled. ' "All through history the great brush has not rested," ' he said quietly, ' "nor the paint dried; yet what eye, looking coolly, or as we now, through the tears' lenses, ever saw this work and it was not finished?" '

And Jo returned his smile and nodded. 'The universe unfolds as it should, Doctor,' she said, and he raised an eyebrow in mild surprise that she should so quickly have learnt a lesson it had taken him this many centuries to understand.

They did not linger. The Doctor made his way back to the TARDIS as Jo drew the blank-faced domino from the pocket of her jeans and, in a symbolic gesture, tossed it high into the air as she turned her back and followed the Doctor inside.

The domino spun, reached the apex of its flight, and began to fall...slower, slower, as the sunlight rippled and froze, until it hung motionless in a sky that was now utterly silent.

Moving On

By Peter Anghelides

YESTERDAY, she knew she hated Scott Wojzek. She hated his mean self-interest, his Vauxhall Vectra, his easy familiarity with complex technology. She hated his phoney sincerity and long lunches. She hated his male-pattern baldness. And when he had died in a traffic accident, and she felt no different about him, she felt no guilt either. So, when she saw him walking towards her across Kensington High Street, she knew at once what had been happening to her for the past eight weeks.

TWO MONTHS AGO, she'd been sitting in her cold study, finding faces in the pattern of her new cotton curtains. The coffee remained cold and congealing in her Nescafé mug, untouched since she'd poured it forty minutes ago. 'What are you sounding so pleased about?' she asked her laptop, which hummed smugly.

She looked up at the plastic wall clock: 7:35, it blinked back. She was going to be late again. With a little hiss of disappointment, she swept the printouts into an open desk drawer, and pushed. The drawer clunked shut with a solid sound.

She left the study and locked the door carefully behind her. 'Another waste,' she said to her mug, pouring the coffee into the handbasin and swilling it away with water as she brushed her teeth again. She frowned into the mirror, wiping away the condensation from her earlier shower. In the unkind light of the bathroom, she could briefly see more white hairs protruding from her brown bob before her reflection misted over again. 'Men don't stay if they see grey,' her aunt always said. Her maiden aunt. As she stepped into the hall, the phone was ringing.

'Katy? It's the crack of dawn – is everything all right?'

'Of course,' said Katy's voice in a hurt tone. 'I was just on a break, and wanted to check we were still OK for our regular lunch date.'

'Katy, if I had a penny for every time you'd checked this week, I could *pay* for lunch.'

'You *are* paying. And we are eating at the *Gens du Monde*, as usual?' A pause. 'Are you OK? You sound a bit down.'

'It's the novel I'm working on – *Unforgiving*.'

'Put it back in the drawer and forget about it.'

'I did. Am I becoming predictable?'

'First sign of senility, my dear. But that's enough about you; let's talk about me.'

'Katy, I thought that talking about yourself was the first sign of old age.'

'Talking *to* yourself, darling, talking *to* yourself. Now don't be late, will you? It won't do to keep Claude hopping from foot to foot.'

'Why the sudden interest in the serving staff, Katy?'

'It's a waiter thing. See you at twelve.'

She put the phone down. 'She'll be there at quarter to,' she said wearily, as she brushed her hair in the hall mirror.

She had known Katy since they were both students, though for the past eighteen months Katy had been appearing on *Wake Up! with Tom and Katy*. She sometimes found it hard to connect implausibly cheerful, impossibly composed and impeccably attired Daybreak Television Katy with dizzy, disorganized 20-year old Katy whom she had first met at a freshman party, scrounging a light for her clumsy roll-up.

She had, however, come to expect infuriatingly early phone calls from Katy, checking minute details. A brief undergraduate affair with a business studies senior had turned mousey Katherine Smith-Pickering into controlled, synergistic Katy Pickering, whose first step on the stairway to Broadcast Heaven was to tidy her possessive, dominating boyfriend out of her life and take charge of her own ambition.

One outcome of this reincarnation was Katy's fanatical attention to detail, the effect of which on her friends was that a phone call from Katy always left them with the sneaking suspicion that their own lives, homes, or relationships were a thoroughgoing mess. With a sigh, therefore, she now looked around the bomb-site of her living room, and reluctantly began to return books to shelves and magazines to racks.

As she was constructing a leaning tower of magazines against the wall behind the sofa, she felt a sharp pain through her tights and, giving a little cry, lifted her foot. She knelt down, and ran her fingers through the pile of the rug, finding a purple plastic dinosaur with spines on its back. She recognized it at once. Joshua, her editor's toddler son, had brought it when he and his mother had visited at the weekend. She remembered how pleased Andrea had been when the two-year-old had described the 'Stegsus' and the 'Rex' to them.

'Better take the Stegsus to work today, then,' she said, stepping over a bag of washing and into the hallway.

'Mistress?'

'Nothing, K9. I'm talking to myself again.' She was stuffing her laptop into its case, and watching as K9 made his way unevenly across the carpet tread from the dining room. 'The first sign of senility.'

'Senility,' said K9 helpfully. 'State or quality indicative of old age, characterized by loss of reasoning faculties, mental and physical infirmity –'

'Thank you, K9,' said Sarah, pulling the front door sharply closed. 'I can always rely on you to cheer me up.'

Sarah stepped briskly towards her yellow Metro, her feet scrunching and skittering the loose gravel on the drive. She unlocked the rear door, and popped the laptop case onto the back seat. Then she opened the driver's door, and tossed the purple dinosaur toy onto the dashboard and her handbag onto the passenger seat. As she slid into the driving position, she spotted a yellow Post-it on the steering wheel. She let out a long groan, knowing what it said before she read it – her own handwriting: *Wojzek/Tonska, 8:45am (don't be late!!).*

She looked at her watch grimly. Twenty past eight, it read accusingly. No time to go into the *Metropolitan* offices – she'd need to drive like a bat out of hell straight to the Tonska offices.

Sarah fumbled with her car phone, cursing quietly as she struggled to obtain a dial tone. When the Doctor had returned her to Earth, only a few years had elapsed since she had originally left with him, but it might as well have been a decade for Sarah. To her friends and colleagues, consumer electronics were the indispensible accoutrements of modern living. For Sarah, they formed a series of baffling tests, a constant source of potential embarrassment as she tried to slip back into her old life and career as a *Metropolitan* journalist. She had assumed it would be like putting on a pair of comfortable old shoes, but it turned out that her feet were a different shape and she couldn't remember how to tie the laces.

For a while, before he had gone to university and she had moved from her country home back to London, Sarah had relied on her irritating nephew Brendan to explain, in the patronizingly minute detail that teenagers reserve for their older relations, how to use a microwave oven, what a barcode was, the mysteries of VideoPlus. In a world still strangely familiar to her, she was not in synch. Like the soundtrack on a badly-dubbed video she had hired, her thoughts seemed just a little out of step with whatever she saw. Brendan had explained that, too.

She phoned the office, and left a short message with her editor's secretary, Belinda, to say that she was going straight to Tonska. When she tried to phone Tonska Industries, she accidentally used Number Recall and found herself unexpectedly talking to Belinda again. On the third attempt, she managed to dial the correct number.

'Thank you for calling Tonska Industries,' said a calm woman's voice.

'Oh, hello, I wonder if…'

'To find out more about our products and services,' interrupted the woman, 'press one.'

'I just want to…'

'To speak to one of our members of staff,' continued the voice, unperturbed by Sarah's tut of annoyance, 'press two. For other functions, press three.'

Sarah chose two with an irritated jab of her forefinger.

'To connect to a member of staff, please tap in their surname on your alphabetic phone keypad.'

'My what?' said Sarah, looking at the handset on her car phone. No matter how long she stared at it, she couldn't see any letters. She could hear the infuriatingly calm woman's voice repeating the instruction.

'Oh, just put me through to Scott Wojzek,' snarled Sarah.

'You have waited too long,' said the woman's voice, its inflection unchanged. 'Goodbye.' Then the line went dead.

'Damn,' said Sarah, putting the Metro into gear.

'My head teacher wrote on my last school report: "He'll be good at something. But not anything we teach here".' Scott Wojzek peered at Sarah from the depths of his swivel chair with his swivel eyes. 'D'you know, Miss Smith, he was completely correct. What was your strong point at school. Attendance, perhaps?'

She knew he could see that her HB pencil had stopped making notes on the pad, that he could see his comment register. So she doodled conspicuously at the bottom of the sheet before flicking it over the wire binding. She watched Wojzek lean forward, placing his thick arms on the solid, pedantically tidy metal table which separated them. 'Do you feel secure, Mr Wojzek?' she asked.

He paused to push his heavy black-framed spectacles back up his nose once again. Then he smiled. 'You've seen our security systems here, Miss Smith.'

'That wasn't really what I meant.' When she had at last found the Tonska Industries car park, Sarah had suffered several indignities with video cameras and badge-locked doors before a secretary had finally ushered her with bad grace into Wojzek's clinical third-floor office. 'You're at the top of the heap here at Tonska, and your business is based on high-risk innovation. If a project fails, your job disappears.'

'I prefer the view from the top,' said Wojzek. 'When I was a research scientist, I found I trod on too many colleagues' toes. I've never been very good at the office waltz.' He was clearly pleased with this phrase, as he repeated it for her benefit. Sarah made a show of writing something down, and looked up at him again. Early thirties, but it was evident he mistook expensive dressing for taste. His Ralph Lauren suit was grey Prince of Wales check with a subtle red stripe, but his green YSL shirt fought with that and the steel blue of his piercing, ever-moving eyes. Now he was rubbing a forefinger lazily at one temple, just where his fine blond hair was starting to recede.

'So it's not just independence. You enjoy controlling people, too?'

'Do bears shit in the woods?'

Sarah coughed to hide her surprise at his answer. He was amused by the effect, and pushed his heavy glasses back up his nose with the middle finger of his left hand – a languid, affected gesture.

Sarah tried not to look at her watch. She remembered writing a *Metro* profile of the chairman of the CBI, who had observed that in one-to-one meetings he consciously never checked the time, because it was discourteous, suggested he wanted to be somewhere else. She must have been talking to Wojzek for their agreed half-hour already, but he showed no signs of wanting to finish the interview. 'Where does that leave ambition?' she asked at last.

'Oh dear, a journalistic cliché,' said Wojzek immediately. 'Serendipity. Feminine intuition. Mad inventors with the crazy idea of running the company. Plain secretaries with glamorous dreams of marrying their bosses.' He made a nasal sound which Sarah realized was supposed to be a short laugh. 'Thin journalists with fat books inside them struggling to get out. Invariably, that's where they should stay.'

Sarah had put her pad and pencil down on her knee. 'Those are very human aspirations, don't you think? Do you sometimes feel that Tonska's work makes people's lives less human? Your life?'

'Sentimental claptrap.'

'Your phone system, for example.'

Wojzek laughed again, and placed his big hands flat on the desk, palms up. 'Miss Smith, that system doesn't lose an incoming call by pressing the wrong button, or sound morose on a wet Thursday afternoon. To my knowledge, it has never once called in sick.'

'And your customers all complete their calls?'

Wojzek squeezed his hands together and leant forward. 'Do I want to deal with stupid people?' His eyes darted to and fro as they scanned her face. 'Do I want a hole in my head?'

Sarah thought back to her initial discussions with Andrea, and found a phrase. 'There's a difference, surely, between naive users, poor enabling technology, and poor implementations of good technology.'

Wojzek was studying her thoughtfully now. When he flicked over his arm suddenly to look at his watch, Sarah thought he was about to dismiss her abruptly. But instead he said, 'I think we should see some of Tonska's technology, Miss Smith.'

After the claustrophobic series of third-floor offices, it was a shock to be shown into a huge open-plan room on the floor above. Sarah stared across a 90-metre expanse, which was broken only by supporting pillars and clustered groups of strange equipment.

To one side, cables stretched sinuously between power points and a squared-off white cubicle the height of a telephone box. Opposite, a dress shop mannequin sat incongruously at an empty desk, bare-chested and wearing a 1970s wig slightly askew. Its arms were giant meccano-set replacements, ending in five-fingered clamps; one clamp touched the 'wrist' on the other, and, where the metallic limbs joined the torso, filament wiring sprouted like multicoloured underarm hair. Further across, a little island of office furniture was surrounded by fake walls, doors and windows which reached only halfway to the actual ceiling.

Looking around, Sarah realized that there were no views to
the outside of the building anywhere in the enormous room. All
the illumination came from a formidable array of strip tubes,
with sharper pools of tungsten light slanting down in random
areas. And, apart from Sarah and Wojzek, the room was
completely empty.

'Would you like to play with my toys?' asked Wojzek.

He tugged at one button on his left sleeve, and then arched
his arms above his head like some plump ballerina. With a
buzzing hum the mannequin's hands rose in an arch above its
unmoving head. Sarah let out a little gasp, and Wojzek smiled
unctuously.

'Remote manipulation,' he said, reaching for a cuff button
again. The mannequin's arms reflected the movement until the
right fingers touched the left wrist and the machine hummed
into silence once more.

They moved to the office area, and Wojzek demonstrated a
video conferencing system with tiny cameras that tracked them
as they moved around their respective desks. On top of another
desk, an arrangement of lasers generated hologram scale images of car engines, and Wojzek picked up a letter-opener to
point out details within them. Sarah was less amused when he
called up moving holograms of a medical operation, and
counterpointed the invasive surgery with the letter-opener
again.

She was also aware that he was studying her reaction when
he displayed a view of her own face, which had apparently been
recorded while she was talking with the Tonska receptionist on
her arrival. With feigned nonchalance, she walked around as if
to examine the rear view of her own head, quietly irritated to see
how much grey hair was visible from that angle.

Her hologram head faded, replaced by a scrolling list of text
and the occasional two-dimensional photograph, which rolled
effortlessly from the centre of the desktop to vanish into thin air
two feet above its wooden surface. She struggled to read the
words, and it was a moment before she realized that she was

seeing the text from behind as it displayed to Wojzek on the other side of the desk. She recognized the *Metropolitan* logo reversed, then a photo of herself. These were replaced by more rows of text, and then a photograph of K9. She opened her mouth to comment, but stopped herself as she caught sight of another familiar logo. But Wojzek had already jabbed a fat thumb on the corner of the desk, and the image fizzed and faded immediately. As the lasers cut out, the UNIT symbol vanished abruptly.

'It's amazing the information one can glean from public domain sources, isn't it?' he said with smug satisfaction. 'Your publisher's database on the World Wide Web. The NUJ membership lists. Hackers driving their spy vehicles down the information superhighway and posting what they find.'

Now she looked at him, searching for words to make his thin-lipped smile disappear. 'This technology is certainly impressive, Mr Wojzek. But it does seem to make my point: it's designed to eliminate human contact, not to make real communication easier.' She looked steadily into one pale blue eye. 'They're marvels of human ingenuity, but designed to dehumanize.'

He steepled his plump fingers. 'Designed to *enhance* human experience,' he noted, as though correcting a junior-school grammarian. 'You clearly believe that technology which humanizes is virtually impossible. Would you like a demonstration of the virtually possible, Miss Smith?' He guided her towards the tall white box surrounded by cables.

On the door to the cubicle, someone had blu-tacked two dog-eared cardboard notices. *You don't have to be mad to work here, but it helps!* read one. The other said *Warning: Do Not Look into Laser with Remaining Eye*. Sarah reached for the handle, determined not to be intimidated.

'Outside, there's a lot of talk about VR,' said Wojzek, opening the door for her. 'A lot of smoke and mirrors, plenty of vaporware, and bugger all to show for it in terms of practical applications. But while those smart-talking shysters from our US competitors are still talking about empowerment, Tonska has already produced this working product. There's nothing like it anywhere on Earth,' he concluded emphatically.

Sarah had stepped into the cube, surprised at how little hardware it seemed to contain and yet how bright it was inside. 'Empowerment sounds like a business buzzword. Or claptrap.'

Wojzek stared at her intensely. 'Imagine giving a paraplegic the experience of running a four-minute mile. A blind man the view of his first sunset. Playing Schubert to a deaf person.' Sarah must have been staring at him blankly. 'Those transatlantic greenhorns are still in the Dark Ages, with helmets and gloves and worrying about taste-scent applicators.' He narrowed the door to a crack. 'Your favourite film is *ET*,' he said, apropos of nothing.

'How…?' she began as the door shut with a soft thud. She expected the room to be soundproof, but she could still clearly hear Wojzek's nasal drone outside.

'The *Media Weekly* Questionnaire, last June I think,' he said. 'Enjoy.'

Before she could reply, Sarah heard the rapidly building hum of power building around her. Now she was alone, unsure whether Wojzek could see her, but beginning to experience the sort of nervous sensation that came just before a job interview. And then…

…an impossible sensation. She is flying. Wind-chill. Darkness. The whirring hum of bicycle wheels, and then the clicking ratchet sounds as she stops pedalling. Her hands gripping the handlebars too tightly as she leans tentatively to one side. The bike scooping up further into the night sky, and her feeling the rollercoaster sensation in her stomach again. Achingly far below, the trees are lichen pieces on a model railway, effects of light and shadow below a brilliant full moon. She hauls herself straight again, and the bike rights itself in the rushing air with a giddy new motion, charging through the icy night towards destiny. She dares to release her small white child's hand from the rubber grip, and brushes back the hood on her kid's coat. In the basket hanging from the handlebars in front of her, the white blanket is sliding back, and she can sense rather than see the improbable combination of huge baby-blue eyes in an ancient wizened face, as...

...she reeled against the wall of the white box, and for some seconds her eyes refused to focus on the soft-white surface ahead of her. Just as they made the connection, Sarah sensed the door opening behind her, the machine's power draining away to a low purr. She practically fell out into the big demonstration room, to find Wojzek's secretary studying her with grim disdain.

'Mr Wojzek's schedule is overrunning,' said the secretary accusingly. She gestured towards the exit. 'Allow me to show you to reception.' It was clearly not a request. Sarah looked towards the main doors, still disorientated. As her whirling thoughts settled into a familiar pattern, she recognized the portly grey shape of Wojzek vanishing through the exit.

'Miss Smith?' The secretary was taking her by the elbow.

'Is he all right?' asked Sarah, gently disengaging her arm from the secretary's grasp.

'This way please.' Sarah thought that her question had been ignored, until she saw a doubtful, worried look in the secretary's face. It had not disappeared by the time they both reached reception in silence.

She found her Metro, and reversed it out of the Tonska car park. She was relieved to find that there was no traffic coming down the sidestreet to witness or complicate her inelegant five-point turn. She drove along the road between the rows of meter bays, which had been fully occupied on her arrival that morning. Never one spare when you needed one, she reflected, and now every single space was available.

As she continued around the block, she tried to work out what seemed different about Wojzek as he was leaving the demo room. Then she realized: the confident swagger was no longer in his gait – there had been a hesitancy, almost a stumble as he had disappeared out of sight into the corridor beyond.

She had expected that the lunchtime traffic jams would be building up as she drove away, but now she noticed that there were no vehicles as she turned into a main road. In fact, there was no sound above the noise of her car engine. Ahead of her, the traffic lights at a major junction were out. But there were no snarl-ups, no bad-tempered scenes and arguments about priority. And no pedestrians. She shifted down into second, and peered down Tottenham Court Road. Litter blew fitfully along the pavements and into the gutters, but there was no sign of any current human activity. She parked on a double yellow line, and stepped out slowly.

The electronics shops all along the street had chipboard covers nailed over them. Sarah held her breath, as if to listen more attentively for any sign of life. Far away, she could hear the faint, trilling insistence of an ignored burglar alarm.

She was putting her keys into the car door, and laughing at the incongruity of locking the vehicle in a deserted street, when a shattering bestial ululation reverberated from far behind her. She whirled around with a scream, and gaped incredulously at the dead traffic lights.

The creature dwarfed them by a clear ten metres. Its reptilian head swayed to and fro, pinched nostrils sniffing the air along the building line, ropes of saliva strung between rows of sharp teeth in its enormous jaws. Tyrannosaurus rex.

Sarah choked back another scream, and scurried around to the other side of her car. The dinosaur seemed to sense the movement, and, as it moved one enormous hind leg, the foot swatted a traffic signal aside like a straw.

'Oi, lady, you can't leave it there!' Sarah slewed round, panicked by the man's sharp tone. She stared disbelievingly at a London traffic warden, who was indicating her Metro with a flicking gesture of his ballpoint pen. 'Are you serious?' he was continuing, stepping towards her. 'Can't you see the road markings?' It was like surfacing from water: the air was suddenly alive again with the noise of pedestrians marching anonymously past them, diesel engines, tyres on tarmac, the dull distant roar of the rest of London. A squeal of brakes in the middle distance and a throaty roadhorn.

And she could feel her heart thudding, a percussive rhythm she could almost hear despite the overwhelming street noise.

'I'll move the car now,' she stumbled out, and was fumbling for the keys in her brimming handbag when she realized that the traffic warden had already lost interest and was walking away from her and towards a gathering crowd. Two hundred metres away on the other side of the street, right in front of the steel-grey exterior of the Tonska building, a crowd of pedestrians was knotting closer together in front of a red double-decker, spilling individuals into the carriageway. Sarah recognized the developing hubbub that characterized any press of people drawn together around an inventive shop display, or a cajoling street vendor, or an accident.

She hurried after the traffic warden, aware as she drew nearer to the scene that some people were negotiating routes out of the throng, ashen. A woman in a shiny mackintosh tugged firmly on the arm of her five-year-old daughter, unmoved by her increasingly tearful pleas to see what was happening. Sarah slipped into the gap that this created in the wall of overcoats, and looked towards the centre of the crowd, towards the front of the bus.

It was Wojzek. She recognized his thick black spectacles, the crazed glass of one lens still impossibly fixed in the frame. They were clutched in the balled fist of a sprawled arm, the other projecting from beneath the Prince of Wales check as though it must belong to someone else. The bottom half of Wojzek's squab body was beneath the nearside wheel of the bus, and blood ran glutinously over the grit in the gutter.

'He jumped out of the building. Bloody near killed me,' a news vendor was saying, his voice high, babbling, anger masking the shock. His fingers clenched and unclenched around the *Evening Standard* early edition. Sarah looked up with the others at a white net curtain, flapping through an open window three floors above them like a flag of surrender.

The crowd was still evolving, shedding individuals and luring in their substitutes to mesmerize with repulsion, as Sarah returned to her Metro. The plaintive wail of an ambulance siren strengthened in the distance. She found her keys in the top of her handbag, and opened her door on the second attempt. Then she sat heavily in the driving seat, and reached instinctively over her shoulder for the safety belt. As the buckle clicked shut, she spotted a purple shape on the dashboard in a nest of old parking tickets and boiled sweet papers. Joshua's stegosaurus.

She let go of the steering wheel carefully, and stared through the dirty windscreen for fourteen minutes until her hands stopped shaking.

LAST MONTH, Sarah was struggling with the fusebox in her cellar. The previous owner of her house had had the bright idea of replacing the fuses with a modern board, but had chosen to leave it in the gloomiest corner of the dank basement room at the bottom of the building. Now Sarah stood in the cold, her towelling dressing gown over the top of her jeans and T-shirt in an attempt to stay warm and fend off the permeating odour of damp plaster, and gazed at the baffling array of coloured switches.

'Shwr,' she read. 'Uplit, Dwnlit... Ah.' She spotted one switch that was flicked down, and pushed it back into place. Immediately, a faint gurgle and hum filtered down the concrete steps of the cellar and over the damp carpet as the washing machine started up again in the utility room. 'Dwnplg,' she said. 'Obvious.'

Back in the kitchen, she surveyed the sad array of electrical equipment on the counter. Her grotty old toaster; the cordless kettle; the slow cooker, with whose pre-fitted plug she had struggled briefly before tripping the switches.

'Apologies, mistress,' said K9 quietly. 'Perambulation via staircase or stairwell is beyond my current operational capacity.'

Sarah studied K9 thoughtfully as she plugged in the kettle. 'Current operational capacity?' she mused aloud. She had noticed the robot taking longer to recharge recently, and lately he also seemed more reluctant to follow her around the building. Early on, she had soon tired of lifting him in and out of her small car, so he had been effectively housebound. But now he seemed satisfied to remain in one place for whole days, rather than contend with the deep-pile carpets that were a feature of all the downstairs rooms.

She had once struggled for hours to replace his tickertape. Eventually, after she had growled that it was completely typical that the Doctor forgot to enclose a user manual, K9 had helpfully provided what he described as 'on-line documentation and operational schematics' to assist her, which he displayed on his flank monitor. Only then did Sarah recognize the problem she had with K9's maintenance: while the firm that made her vacuum cleaner had long ago stopped manufacturing the dustbags for that model, a company making replacement parts for the robot had yet to come into existence. K9 was slowly becoming obsolete before his time.

Sarah drew the curtains in her study, and waited for the screen on her laptop computer to fade into existence as the machine powered up. She put down her cup of coffee with an exasperated noise when the familiar set of icons did not appear. Instead, a pulsing array of stroboscopic lines washed across the screen, first vertically, then horizontally, then vertically again. She shut down the machine and rebooted. Within a minute, she was squinting balefully at the same image. She snapped the case shut, and stamped into the living room, uttering imprecations against the absent *Metropolitan* youth trainee, who had installed the operating system for her and promised that the machine was virus-free.

She drew the heavy curtains to block out the strong, bright sunlight which spilt like a splash of paint across the room. Then she placed her coffee onto its familiar ring on a side-table, and slumped into her favourite chair. She reached for the remote control, and switched the television from standby. As the television tube flickered a chiaroscuro across the furniture in the darkened room, Sarah scanned through the *Radio Times*. When she looked up at the screen, she frowned resentfully. The chequerboard interference pattern was there too.

'K9?' she called into the kitchen. 'Can you detect any unusual transmissions in this area which might be...'

'Mistress?' The robot's metal nose had appeared at the

doorway. Sarah studied the steady reflections on K9's burnished casing, and realized that the dancing lightshow from the television had stopped. An Australian soap soundtrack was playing quietly from behind her. When she turned back to the television, the picture was clear.

'Lunch appointment at twelve hundred hours with Ms Pickering, mistress,' said K9. 'You instructed me... me... to remind you, mistress.'

'Darling, you look simply awful,' said Katy Pickering briskly, waving a languid hand towards the empty seat beside her. 'Like shit warmed up.'

'And *bon appetit* to you, Katy.' Sarah sat down heavily, and picked up the *Gens du Monde* menu. She peered around the gloom of the restaurant, letting her eyes adjust from the bright sunshine outside before she riffled through the starters. 'I've had a week of early nights, and I still feel exhausted.'

'It's that wretched novel, SJ. It's draining you. I can remember when we spent the whole night in the college bar, and could still write and deliver our assignment paper first thing the next morning.' Katy smoothed a wrinkle out of the damask table-cloth.

'Writing it is hardly exhausting me. I can't get past page five. Mmm, *cuisses de grenouilles*. You've already been here for twenty minutes, I suppose.'

Katy smiled primly. 'To catch Claude's eye. What about all this *fabulous* material I'm throwing at you? My life is an open book to you. All you have to do is transcribe it in your impossibly beautiful prose style, for which I hate you of course.'

Sarah fiddled with her silver cutlery. 'You should write *Unforgiving*, then. You're the one with the fund of irreverent stories about breakfast television. You're the one bonking the producer. And your co-presenter. You're living it. I'm just observing.'

Katy slapped Sarah's wrist. 'Stop fidgeting. You're getting your forks out of order. I may be indiscreet, SJ, but I'm not

irrational. And you're a much better writer than I am, I already
knew that when we were cub reporters. That's why I work in
television. And why I left Boris.'

'Is that a TV thing then, Katy?' asked Sarah.

'Out of sight, out of mind,' replied Katy, closing her menu
with a slapping sound.

Claude sent a thin, melancholy eighteen-year-old to take
their order. Katy puckered her mouth in disappointment, and
chose lobster.

'I'm a "sinky",' said Katy later, pouring a large glass. 'Single
Income No Kids Yet. I want the career and the sex, not the
Volvo and the school run.' The gazpacho had arrived. 'Look at
this lot,' she said, with a gesture that encompassed the room.
Sarah slid lower in her seat as Katy's voice rose. 'The best is a
seven, and he's the waiter at the next table. Pretty in a pointillist
sort of way.' Sarah looked blank. 'From a distance,' said Katy.

'Definitely a Seurat,' said Sarah pensively. 'Not my type at
all.' She chased a slice of pepper around her bowl. 'Wouldn't
you prefer someone more mature in his attitudes? Someone
you could, um, talk to?'

'Someone to debate with,' teased Katy. 'Someone intellec-
tual. Someone I can trust, someone exotic... Someone to watch
ov-er meee,' she trilled. 'Oh really, SJ, you might as well have
dated one of my overseas uncles. Or your college tutor, "The
Foreign Correspondent". I seem to remember you liked the
father-confessor type.'

'That's not quite what I mean,' said Sarah, reddening as
Katy's giggles filtered across the quiet restaurant and to the
neighbouring tables.

'Besides,' said Katy, 'if I wanted to date an illegal alien, I'd
go and work on our travel series.'

They were drinking their second cup of coffee at Katy's flat
before Katy stopped talking about her new arts series for
Carlton. 'After the third offer,' she concluded, 'I thought I
couldn't refuse it.'

'Typical,' said Sarah briskly, looking around the sitting room at the impossibly clean surfaces. 'You wait for ages, and then three *Omnibus* programmes come along at the same time.'

'Ha ha,' reprimanded Katy, frowning at an invisible spot on her coffee table. 'That's very droll. Well, if you can't write my life, why not write your own? You're a journalist, darling. Doesn't anything bookworthy happen to you? Anything odd?'

Sarah gazed distantly at the large Toulouse-Lautrec print on the wall opposite, and was on the verge of dismissing the thought. Then she remembered her previous day's meeting. 'I met Wojzek's family, you know.'

'The technocreep had family? I thought he was popped out of a high-pressure mould.'

'No,' said Sarah, leaning forward, serious. 'It was... unnerving. I'd located them through Barney at the *Mirror*. They were hiding from the London press, but, when they found out I'd been talking to Wojzek just before he died, they agreed to see me. Barney was spitting, of course.'

'Poor Barney,' mouthed Katy.

'The mother told me that Scott Wojzek's business partner, a young man called Kendrick, had also died in a similarly unexpected, similarly strange way. Their son – they called him Scottie...'

'Beam me up...'

'No, it was too bizarre to be funny.' Sarah could remember the old woman who was Wojzek's mother, her shoulders slumped in grief, her hands fidgeting at the armrests of her arch-backed chair as she spoke about her son. She had worn a high-necked black dress and a broad hairband. When Sarah had asked her about Kendrick's death, she stopped picking at the fabric of her chair and sank back against the antimacassar, steepling her fingers, a figure from a Plantagenet tomb.

'Scottie was never the same,' she had said in a whisper half remorse, half accusation. 'Dad and I never understood Scottie's work, though he wanted us to. He wanted us to share in his love of it. His infectious enthusiasm. His wonder and ambition. He was full of that when Kendrick joined him, and they set up

Tonska together.'

Sarah remembered how she had jumped, despite herself, when the old woman's husband cleared his throat with a rumbling sound. She had looked across to where he sat, hunched on the fading sofa, and she strained to hear his faltering, accented words. 'Scott told us that Kendrick had brought him all this fantastic technology, "leading edge", he called it. Leading edge: that was always the way I knew Scott was impressed.'

He had spat the words with heavy irony, his thick dark eyebrows bunching together over deep-set, angry eyes.

'Kendrick was a "leading edge" authority on robots, and something he called imagining – no, *imaging* technology. I wish I'd paid more attention. I sometimes wonder if our indifference...' He lowered his head, and the words trailed off into his chequered wool shirt.

'No Dad.' The old woman's voice had been steadier. 'It was Kendrick's death. From the moment that man killed himself, Scottie worked like a man possessed. He was in the office all hours. It was as though he was frightened. Frightened that it would all slip away from him.' She had tugged a crumpled, lace-edged handkerchief from the cuff of her dress while Sarah listened to the *tok-tok* rhythm of the grandmother clock. 'He had no time for anything else,' she said at last.

'We didn't see him after that,' said her husband. 'We were on better speaking terms with his answerphone.'

Sarah had said gently, 'Kendrick also... Kendrick killed himself?'

'Threw himself under a tube,' said the old man gruffly. ' "Passenger action", as they say.' The euphemism seemed to give him some grim amusement, until he coughed into silence again.

'And Scottie...' Mrs Wojzek had touched her nose with the handkerchief. 'We spoke to him on the phone twice in three months. We heard about his... his accident from the police.' At this point, she had started to cry softly, and Sarah had looked at her own hands, awkward at the grief. 'He hadn't even spoken to his friends in all that time.'

'Work changes you,' said Katy brusquely. Sarah abruptly surfaced from her memories. Katy was reaching over the table, collecting the crockery and placing it with exaggerated precision onto a bronze tray. 'It changed me, SJ. I used to go home from college every weekend, d'you remember? Now, I haven't seen my parents in months.'

Sarah snorted. 'If I remember our earlier conversation, you're never off the phone to your mother.'

'Work changed you, Sarah,' Katy continued regardless, moving into her kitchen. Sarah could hear her loading the cups into the dishwasher. 'You never talk much about your time abroad, after all. Except to say how coming home had brought you down to Earth with a thump. A hell of a bump, if you ask me. For months, it was as though you'd had the stuffing knocked out of you.'

Sarah doodled with the toe of her shoe in the carpet pile. 'I'm not so sure,' she called back.

'I'm *damned* sure,' continued Katy, her voice echoing from the other room. 'What did you leave back there? Hell, you hardly ever talk about back *where*. Have you put the coasters away?'

Sarah grinned. 'I'm rearranging the contents of all your drawers in here.' She made a shuffling sound with her feet on the carpet to suggest activity.

Katy appeared immediately, drying her hands carefully on a small towel. 'SJ, I know you're only joking. And I'd laugh myself if I didn't know that, as soon as you've left, I won't be able to stop myself checking every cupboard. Just in case...'

'You're so anal,' said Sarah rudely, smiling. 'Maybe you *would* make a good character.'

'And you're *not* obsessed, of course. No dark secrets in your past,' Katy replied tartly. She studied her Swatch, and looked meaningfully at Sarah. 'Time we were off.' Sarah recognized the cue.

Katy helped her on with her jacket in the hallway, pausing briefly so that Sarah was held for a moment with her arms half in and half out of the sleeves. 'Perhaps you found your foreign mentor while you were away all that time,' pondered Katy. 'In which case, what are you doing here, mmm?'

Sarah made an excuse to pay a visit to the bathroom before leaving. While she was there, she noticed another of Katy's framed Lautrecs – a poster from the Aristide Bruant cabaret. She pushed it at one corner so that it hung slightly off square.

She listened to Classic FM all the way home to keep herself cheerful in the traffic. She was turning off Fauré's *Cinq Mélodies* as she pulled up in front of the house.

She hung her coat on the hall hatstand, realizing with a little shiver that the central heating had not yet come on. Sarah removed her gloves, and rubbed her hands together briskly to encourage the circulation. Then she opened the door to the living room.

'K9. Canine, geddit?' Brendan honked. He was kneeling down, and peering into a large cardboard box to see what else it contained. As he scrabbled around at the bottom of the container, a flurry of styrofoam chips spilt out of the top. 'I can't find an instruction manual.' He continued to rummage enthusiastically.

K9 was already out of the box, his burnished metal surface glowing softly in the light flickering from the hearth. Beads of polystyrene clung to him with static. In two easy movements, he reversed in front of where the fresh coal fire was sparking and fizzing, and then glided to Sarah's feet. His antennae quivered briefly. 'Mistress.' Sarah hunkered down to greet him, putting her hand to his side and feeling the warmth from where he had been standing near the flames.

'This is fantastic,' enthused Brendan, sitting back on his feet and looking across to where Sarah crouched in the doorframe. 'Who's it from?'

'It's a parting gift,' she said quietly. 'An affectionate gesture.' Or settlement, confirmation, a duty discharged. She smiled wearily at K9, flicking pieces of polystyrene from the side of his head with her folded gloves. There was a weight in

her chest, and she had to swallow before she could speak again.
She put her hands over her eyes, suddenly exhausted by the
day's events.

'I thought you'd gone to college,' she said to Brendan,
glancing up towards the fireplace. The hearth was cold and
cinereous. A vase of dusty dried flowers stood to one side, an
overflowing basket of sewing propped next to it.

K9 hummed uncertainly in front of her. 'Gone to college.
Gone to university. Serve an apprenticeship. Serve one's time.
Learn one's trade.' There was a longer than usual pause,
accompanied by an electronic click. His head drooped. 'Does
not compute.'

Sarah drew her jacket more closely around her. 'Sorry K9.
I was daydreaming.' She patted the drab metal of his snout
disconcertedly, noticing as she did so how the surface at the
corner was wearing thin.

LAST WEEK, Sarah sat on an airport courtesy bus as it jostled
its way through the early afternoon traffic to the long-stay car
park. She stared into space, wondering whether the herbs she
had planted in the back garden two weeks before would still be
alive when she got home. What had the British weather been
like while she was in Switzerland?

On the seat opposite, rocking back and forth with the motion
of the vehicle, a woman in late middle age and a heavy green
plaid coat squinted back at her through heavy lenses.

'We'll see how things have changed since we've been
away,' averred the woman, poking a frizzy piece of wispy grey
hair back under the control of her knitted hat. 'Just been away
for a few days?'

'Sorry?' said Sarah.

'You don't have much luggage.' The woman nodded towards Sarah's small travel bag, and then to her own two large
trunks. 'I've been away for three weeks. Oh, Mrs Goodson,'
she explained, offering a hand in a fingerless glove.

Sarah shook it, and said, 'I've been away for ten days. But
I got used to travelling light.' The woman looked puzzled. 'In

my… previous job,' Sarah added lamely.

Mrs Goodson nodded as though she understood. 'When travelling in foreign climes, I like to take lots of items which remind me of home. One feels so alienated, otherwise.' She leant forward conspiratorially. 'Even then, there are so many familiar things that seem wrong when you return, don't you find?' She sneezed into a grubby paper tissue. 'Driving on the left. No mountains in the distance. Policemen in tall helmets. Red telephone boxes…'

The colour of the sky, thought Sarah. The number of moons.

Mrs Goodson chattered on, seemingly unworried that the conversation became increasingly one-sided. Sarah allowed her attention to wander, the other woman's cheerful flow becoming a burr in the background. Just when Mrs Goodson was pulling family snapshots out of her handbag, the bus slowed as it approached Bus Point Blue 3. Sarah checked her parking ticket, quietly relieved to see her scrawled annotation confirming this as her stop. She stepped down into the aisle and picked her bag off the seat beside her, swaying as the bus came to a halt.

The exit door sighed open. Clasping the travel bag in front of her, Sarah stepped down from the bus.

But instead of stepping out to a row of parked cars, she was on a suburban high street. Momentarily thrown into confusion, she turned back to look through the bus doors. Instead, she saw the outline of a tall blue box shimmering away to nothing. And she recognized the fading sound of the TARDIS engine.

She could feel the knot in her stomach again, the familiar hunger pain of abandonment and loss. Her mind was a whirl. She hadn't wanted to leave, only wanted some attention. Ignored by the Doctor once too often she had, in a moment of adolescent pique that had surprised her even as it happened, gathered up a random handful of belongings from her room and stood in the console room, explaining that she was leaving right there, right then. She had peered accusingly at him over her hastily assembled box of books, clothes, a toy owl, working herself into a convincing lather of indignation, to which the

Doctor appeared to be only half listening. And then, with a suddenness that had knocked all argument from her, he had practically bundled her out of the doors.

The TARDIS was gone, leaving Sarah staring at the tall, untidy privet hedge. She looked around, disconsolate, her feelings disjointed. The roads seemed empty, apart from a golden labrador which trotted incuriously across the road towards her, sniffing at spots on the low curve of redbrick wall.

'This isn't Hillview Road,' she said to herself. Then she dropped to her haunches, and placed her battered box of sad belongings on the patched pavement so that she could fondle the dog's ears. 'I bet this isn't South Croydon, either.'

The dog's muzzle wrinkled into infeasible shapes. 'Lady, this isn't even Earth,' it said.

Sarah leapt to her feet, knocking over her box. The owl sprawled, its large cotton eyes staring blindly skywards. Sarah was still staring at the dog. 'No,' she said.

The dog blinked once. 'If you don't believe me, ask her,' it said, tossing its head in Sarah's direction.

'Hello?' said a woman's voice behind her. For a crazy moment, Sarah stared at her feet, thinking that she must be blocking the pavement with the spilled box contents. She turned with an apology on her lips; but she half stepped, half stumbled backwards as she recognized the woman. It was Mrs Goodson, standing by Bus Point Blue 3, her puzzled face peering at Sarah from beneath her woollen hat. 'Oh, here you are dear. For a moment, I thought you'd disappeared on me.'

YESTERDAY, Sarah sat in her kitchen and studied K9. The robot stood motionless beside the white front of the Belling cooker, humming a wavering note. Sarah thought about Rab, the pet labrador her father had given her for her fourteenth birthday. Rab was easy to read: feed me, chase me, tickle me were all telegraphed by the way he stood, the shape of his ears, his dark brown eyes. Sometimes, she would have staring contests with the dog, looking for as long as she could into Rab's expressive dark gaze to see who would blink first, always losing. Now she stared at K9's featureless visor, wanting the robot to lower its grey snout first.

For nearly a week, she had again been feeling tired and wretched, despite sleeping heavily every night. So this morning, she had come to a decision, and had been deleting files from her laptop. As she dragged the final WordPro icon to the trashcan, the familiar pattern of interference had sparked and flashed across the screen. But this time she had made a logical connection of her own: K9. And, after making herself a cappuccino so that she had time to think through what she was going to say, she had brought him into the kitchen and stared at him for this long moment. 'Why didn't you tell me sooner?' she said eventually.

'I cannot say, mistress,' whirred K9.

'No excuse,' muttered Sarah, stirring the remaining cornflakes in her cereal bowl. They swirled around in a puddle of semi-skimmed. 'Whatever's wrong with you is generating this signal. And that's what's causing all kinds of electrical interference. I don't know why I didn't ask you about it sooner.' She looked across to K9 again. 'Can't you fix it?'

'Not permitted... possible,' said K9 uncertainly. 'Repairs require facilities not yet available in this era. Technology not yet available on this planet.'

'Will it get worse?'

'Systems attrition exponential, mistress. Minimum performance capacity will be reached in...' His sensor ears twisted haltingly as the calculation took place. When they stabilized a few seconds later, K9 had not spoken again.

Sarah looked down beside the kitchen table. 'What is this signal you're transmitting, K9?'

'I cannot say, mistress.'

Sarah picked up the sheaf of pages that she had placed on the kitchen table. 'Unforgiving', said the top sheet in 36-point Helvetica 'a novel by S. J. Smith'. She riffled through the pages in a desultory fashion, and then carried them across to the kitchen sink, opening the cupboard beneath to reveal a bin half full of vegetable peelings. 'And Katy can write her own novel,' she said, rolling the sheets into a tube and shoving them firmly into the waste.

Sarah took her coat from the peg on the kitchen door, and started to pull it on. 'Without your cooperation, I can't help you either, K9,' she said, turning the chrome handle of the door and looking out into the hallway, away from him.

As she walked out to the car, the fallen leaves blew across the gravel drive in a flurry of browns and yellows. She remembered how cold it had been the last time her father had driven her with Rab into town, and found she was surprised by the details she could still recall. The crisp, cold air in which their breath hung in small, grey clouds. The clear marks her green boots made in the smooth white snow on their front lawn. The dirty grey sludge on the pathway leading up to the vet's surgery. The scuffed and chewed cardboard box on the back seat, empty on the journey home.

Kensington High Street was bustling when she saw Wojzek. For a moment, she thought that he had not seen her, and she was about to turn and retrace her steps before she realized that he was only looking down the street to find a gap in the traffic. When the red double-decker growled out of the way, Sarah could see that he was grinning straight at her as he crossed.

She started to cross towards him, bristling. 'I should have known,' she started.

Wojzek took her by the arm, steering her back onto the pavement and out of the path of a delivery bicycle, which sped past them in a blur of neon lycra. 'Do be careful, Miss Smith. You'll get yourself run over.'

'In a dream?' she snapped, shrugging his hand from her elbow. She studied his clothing in what she hoped would appear a disparaging manner, but the effect was spoiled by the way she was shaking. 'More a nightmare,' she was just able to add.

Wojzek refastened his check jacket, and brushed invisible dirt off one sleeve. He was smiling his patronizing smile again, looking her up and down like a sale item in Harrods. Other

pedestrians swirled past them in a steady stream, no one
jostling them, nobody even glancing at the pair, as though the
tension between them was a physical barrier. Wojzek pushed
his glasses back up his nose. 'You could do with a drink,' he
said, and with a casual gesture indicated a shop behind her.

She declined a brandy, but sat opposite him at a window
table, sipping apprehensively on a cappuccino. She focused
through the grey net curtains on the busy street beyond. A
woman in a heavy green coat eased a double pushchair through
the crush, a violin case incongruously slung over her shoulder.
'You died,' Sarah said distantly.

'So I did,' said Wojzek, running one fat finger around the
rim of his cup, gathering the chocolate powder on its tip. His
tone was amused.

'This is another dream, then? You're responsible.' She
watched for a reaction. 'Your technology is much more personal than I'd been prepared to believe.'

Wojzek tilted his head on one side, as though studying her.
'And yet, ironically, also much more alien than perhaps you'd
be prepared to believe.' He must have seen her eyes widen.
'I'm not from this solar system. Though,' he continued, 'I
know that won't surprise you.'

'You have me at a disadvantage. That won't surprise you.'
Sarah inhaled the cinnamon tang from her cup. 'Are you a long
way from home?'

Wojzek gave a short, sharp laugh. 'How pleasant, how
convivial. How very human.'

'We could talk about the weather, too.'

'I come from a race called the Tonska.' Wojzek pursed his
lips thoughtfully. He was leaning on the table, directly opposite
her, but his voice sounded as if it was drifting across the room.
'I don't know how far I am from home. My memories of
Alrakis are fragments, a handful of snapshots snatched ran-
domly out of an album. Single lines remembered verbatim
from a forgotten script I once performed.

'I can remember black moments of wretchedness and despair, trapped in a dungeon of failure not of my own making.

I have no memory of my father, yet somehow I'm aware of his belief that I could be whatever I desired, and his unwavering knowledge of my innate gift to accomplish anything.

'I recall with crystal clarity the instant when I could attain freedom from physical bounds. Above all in that one pellucid moment, when I was cast out at the moment of my apotheosis, I remember the man who ostracized me from all I had ever embraced and believed and desired. I will never mistake the one who banished me.'

Sarah smiled. 'You should stick to decaff, Mr Wojzek.' She looked away and through the net curtains again. Two women were peering at the menu, which was held in a brass frame in the window. A woman in a heavy green coat eased a double pushchair around the women and on through the lunchtime crush of pedestrians, a violin case incongruously slung over her shoulder. A delivery bike sped past in a blur of neon lycra. 'Is Wojzek merely a *nom de guerre*?'

'Very droll, Miss Smith. Of course, you haven't lost your schoolgirl French.' He leant forward, as though afraid the next table would overhear him. 'I can't remember my name. I was known as Cerunnos, but there was a name before that. I've been known by many names since that time, though. On Earth, I've been Scott Wojzek. And Jonathan Kendrick. And Jennifer Bendick. And Mary Jones. So many fascinating people. I've learnt a lot.' He stirred his coffee contemplatively. 'I've been trying to escape this dreary world for thirty years. I stumbled here after an aeon of incorporeal wandering, following a thread of meaning across the Universe, tracking a sense of belonging that wasn't mine. But which would bring me to the one who cast me into my eremitic oblivion.

'In my weak and delirious moment of arrival, I took on human form. And I stumbled around this pitiful backwater for years before recognizing that my tormentor was no longer here. I knew I must escape this primitive prison, and in stages took on the forms of others who could help me be free. I was able to adopt or adapt the archaic technologies of your planet to develop systems and minds which would bring me closer to a route home.'

Sarah turned her head away, and looked distantly through the shop window as she dabbed the corners of her mouth with a napkin. A thin boy wearing a blue cycle helmet sped past on his delivery route in a blur of neon lycra. 'You're a parasite.'

Wojzek gave a mock pout. 'Don't be insulting, Miss Smith.'

'I wasn't insulting, I was defining. How else would you describe it?'

Wojzek pushed his glasses back up his nose, and ran his fingers through his thinning hair. 'I recognize potential, my own and that of others. That is my gift. On Alrakis, I could be anyone, any *thing*. Bendick was a psychologist – as her, I learnt the potential of humanity. Kendrick conceived the VR technology, which I brought to Wojzek. And as Wojzek, I funded its development to capture minds and experiences.' He drank the dregs of his coffee. 'You have potential, Miss Smith. You have a vivid imagination, and a range of experience which would surprise even your closest friends. You don't use it of course, because you're constrained by your own little-minded English attitudes. Wasting your time on a novel you'll never finish, for example.' He studied her for a response. 'You don't seem surprised.'

'I'm not impressed, if that's what you mean.'

'I don't require your approbation,' he said quietly. 'I need your help.'

Sarah looked down at the spilt contents from her handbag on the paper tablecloth, and scooped them back before latching the strap over her shoulder.

'Not my help, Mr Cerunnos,' she said, and stood up. 'The Scott Wojzek remembered by his family and friends is not the self-serving boor I met. Whatever you are or were, you seem to be quite capable of ostracizing yourself.' She pulled her jacket closer around her, and walked to the door.

'I was banished by the Doctor,' said Wojzek, without looking at her.

Sarah's hand hovered over the shop door handle for a beat. Then she twisted the brass knob sharply, and stepped into the

noisy street past two women who were studying the menu in the
window.

Wojzek was hurrying through the doorway after her. 'Miss
Smith, I'd prefer your cooperation,' he called after her.

'Push off,' she retorted without turning round. Within
seconds she was at the first junction on the street, and turned
down it to escape from him. Then she stopped abruptly, her
handbag slapping against her side. Ahead of her was Wojzek,
his back turned to her and, beyond him, two women looking at
the menu in the window of the café. A thin boy on a delivery
bike sped past in a blur of neon lycra. Wojzek turned around
and spotted her.

He spread his hands in an open, pleading gesture. 'I knew
before we met that you were a colleague of the Doctor when he
was on Earth,' he was saying, his voice unnaturally clear in the
busy street. 'I thought you could help me reach him, help me
effect my escape.'

Sarah turned on her heel, and ran past the first junction to the
traffic lights at the next. She stumbled around the corner in her
short heels, almost running into a woman pushing a twin child
buggy. Incongruously, the woman was also carrying a violin
case. And beyond her, impossibly, Wojzek was standing outside the café. He turned to look at her, already knowing she was
there.

'When I used the VR machine, I discovered that he'd gone.
But I also learnt that he'd left you K9.'

Sarah barged her way through the unheeding stream of
passers-by. 'Since you know all that, then you'll also know he
abandoned me,' she shouted. 'That he's the last person on Earth
I want to see. Until now,' she added with a snarl.

Wojzek stepped closer, and held her gently but firmly by
both shoulders. 'Come on, Sarah. You know that K9 will
deteriorate until he's a write-off. And he's already told you that
no human technology can repair him. We need each other.'

She was standing close to him now, watching his ice-blue
eyes flicking rapidly from side to side as they searched for an
answer in hers. 'Why can't Tonska Industries provide what you

need?' she said. 'The technology you showed me seemed advanced enough.'

'*Omne ignotum pro magnifico*,' said Wojzek. When he saw Sarah's brow wrinkle, he added, 'Interesting what you know from O-level Latin. You just can't remember it at the moment.'

'Don't patronize me,' Sarah hissed, stepping back out of his grasp. And then she thought about what he'd actually said.

Wojzek laughed again. 'That would hardly be appropriate. In so many ways, I *am* you.'

When she awoke in that instant, she was screaming. Her hoarse cries filled the confined space of her car for only a few, ragged seconds, but when she had stopped her ears still sang with the sound of her own terror.

She stared through the misted windscreen at her own house, her eyes blurred with tears. K9 would still be inside, transmitting his erratic, unfathomable signal.

Sarah looked at the dashboard, and saw the crumpled yellow Post-it still reminding her of the original appointment. Wojzek was dead, she had seen that. He was gone. 'Out of sight, out of mind,' she told herself firmly as she twisted the key in the ignition and started the engine.

TODAY, Sarah sat in her sitting room watching her mug of coffee go cold on the table in front of her, and deciding that she would have to put it back into the microwave and reheat it.

With her index finger, she tapped an uncertain rhythm on top of the biscuit barrel in her lap, pondering the events of the previous day. What was K9 not telling her? During the first few weeks that she had known the automaton, she had tried to elicit information about what had happened to the Doctor since she had known him. It had soon become evident, however, that, much to her journalistic chagrin, no amount of ingenious interviewing, strategic questioning, or painstaking unearthing of clues by Sarah would produce fascinating new insights. It transpired that the reason for K9's initial reluctance to furnish information was that, after his construction and programming, he had hardly known the Doctor at all. He had been boxed up

and packed off before he knew where he was, a feeling that
Sarah recognized only too well.

But could the robot conceal information from her? Could
she trust K9? After her own recent behaviour, could she trust
herself? She considered her options, and wondered idly how
the Doctor would have approached the problem. Then she
angrily dismissed the thought, snapping, 'Damn it, K9, you're
no longer the Doctor's dog. You're here with me. I'm acting *in
loco parentis.*'

On the other side of the room, radar ears twitched. '*In loco
parentis,*' stated K9. 'Latin. Translated definition: in place of
parent. Etymology: adverbial usage in Earth English since
early nineteenth century...'

'Enough, K9. Are you going to tell me what's going on?'

'Mistress?'

'Why are you so obstructive?' She gathered her thoughts,
and took a deep, pensive breath. She had always treated K9
more as a peer than as a servant, so to give him an explicit
command was unprecedented. 'I demand that you tell me
what's going on. That's an order,' she added feebly.

K9 whirred forward across the carpet to stand beside her,
ticking quietly.

'You forbade me to reveal any details, mistress.'

She stared at the robot as though she had heard a short, tinny
expletive from it. 'I did what? Never mind, I'm changing my
mind. Tell me, why are you transmitting this signal?'

The robot raised its snout with a servo noise, which sounded
to her like a sigh of relief. 'Sub-space transmission on a
specimen range of distress frequencies, mistress. Initiated
when parameters for self-repair and regenerative replacement
became sub-optimal.'

Sarah peered at the dim lights behind K9's visor. 'A last call
for help, for when you can no longer help yourself.'

'Affirmative,' said K9. 'The program was incorporated into
this unit's design by the Doctor.'

'Lucky that didn't break down first, then.' Sarah watched
K9's tail antenna droop. 'All points broadcast to the stars, eh?

Which unfortunately has been ruining our neighbour's recordings of *EastEnders* for weeks.' She crunched on a bourbon
while she thought for a moment. And then she said, 'You'd
better play it to me.'

She had expected to hear K9's clipped tones speaking, like
a mayday message from a stricken vessel crackling through a
radio set. So she was quite taken aback when a spear of light
lanced from K9's blaster and across the coffee table. Her coffee
cup did not splinter and disintegrate, however. Instead, a
familiar distortion pattern started to display in mid-air.

'Decoding,' said K9.

The distortion jumped and shimmered, and a tiny, translucent figure resolved itself in the centre of the table. Sarah leant
forward and slid her coffee mug to one side. It was a woman,
stooping over as though switching on a television set. She
recognized the nightie first. Just before it started to speak, she
realized who it was. It was her. The diminutive facsimile spoke
in a lazy monotone, requesting the Doctor to come immediately
to K9's assistance, and quoting a variety of technical details
that Sarah did not comprehend from beginning to end. Then the
image jumped into its original position, and the message
replayed.

Sarah slumped back into her chair. 'Terrific,' she snorted
disgustedly, slapping the chair arm and producing a shower of
biscuit crumbs. ' "Help us, Obi Wan, you are our only hope."
Well not this time, Doctor.' She leant over the arm of the chair.
'Stop transmitting, K9. Now.'

The beam from K9's laser cut out abruptly, and the image
fizzed and died. 'When was this recorded?' she demanded. K9
quoted a date and a time. The middle of the night, several weeks
previously. 'Explain.'

She listened in growing confusion as K9 detailed more than
twenty similar occasions over an eight-week period. On each
night, she had attempted to effect repairs on K9, each time
reiterating that the robot was not to discuss the event with
anyone subsequently – including Sarah herself. Her repairs
were having quite the opposite effect from what she intended,

and over the previous two months K9's operational efficiency
had declined so significantly that the effects of long-term self-
repair systems were being slowly overtaken by the damage
inflicted by her tinkering. At which point, the Doctor's communications program had cut in. And, although she was una-
ware of it, the strictures she had placed on K9 about discussion
of the repairs meant that the robot would not volunteer information to her about the message.

'Repairs in my sleep? No wonder I've been so shattered.'
She leant heavily on the chair arm, looking for an explanation
in K9's blank expression. 'But the whole idea is crazy, K9. I can
barely program my video.' There was a long pause. 'What was
I trying to do.'

K9 gave a hum, changing key unexpectedly. 'Not necessar-
ar-ar-arily you, mistress.'

'K9?'

'Alien symbiosis,' said K9 cryptically. 'Tonskan host. Hy-
postatic osmosis.'

The telegraphese petered out into an electronic mumble, and
Sarah recognized the signs that K9 was shutting down to
conserve energy while recharging. 'Just when it was getting
confusing,' she grumbled, and was reaching for her cold coffee
when a sound to stop her heart echoed from the next room.

She stood in the kitchen doorway, gripping the jamb because she felt her legs would give way at any second. A tall blue
cabinet was crammed incongruously into the space between
the pine units that led to the back door and the garden beyond.
It was jutting out at an awkward angle, one narrow door ajar on
the side nearest to Sarah's washing machine, which was
gurgling in rinse mode. Across the dark quarry tiles of the
kitchen floor dangled a ragged gathering of wool tassles,
attached to an implausibly long scarf containing too many
colours. The scarf was unwound on the heavy oak table, and
looped around the neck of a lanky figure who was sprawled
across one of the four fiddleback chairs. The man's shock of
curls was nothing compared with the shock of recognition on
Sarah's face.

'Doctor,' she said in a hoarse whisper. 'What are you doing here?'

He beamed back at her. 'What, no tea, Sarah Jane?' He dragged the scarf towards himself and flung it over his shoulder in one fluid gesture. 'Never mind, I'm sure we can find something suitable in the TARDIS. Shall we?' He gestured to the open door.

Sarah hesitated in the hallway. 'Why are you here?'

'I got your message,' he said, and hopped through the police box doors.

Sarah tentatively stepped into the kitchen, as though breaking in a new pair of shoes. She stood before the TARDIS and looked it up and down, perhaps expecting the door to close in her face and its familiar contours to shimmer and fade in front of her eyes. When they didn't after thirty seconds, she stepped through the doors.

At once, she was enclosed in that too-familiar otherworld, aware once more that the purring reassurance of the TARDIS at rest somehow replaced any sound from outside, the grumbling roar of the washing machine's spin cycle now a world away.

She blinked as her eyes became accustomed to the day-bright lighting, and saw the familiar tall figure leaning casually on the nearest face of the six-sided control console.

'We have work to do,' he said.

'What about K9, Doctor?'

'Well, there's him to see too, of course. But first, I've a duty to discharge with our friend Mr Wojzek, wouldn't you say?' He was grinning at her, and his eyes were alive with the old excitement of a journey commencing, an adventure under way. 'Would you like to do the honours, Sarah?' He indicated the door control on the panel across from him, and Sarah walked over to operate it.

'Are we going back to his home planet to change things, so that he doesn't get banished?' she asked.

'Alrakis is rather nice this time of the century,' he replied.

Sarah took her hand away from the door control. 'You have

a good memory for planets, Doctor.' She looked around the transparent central column at him. 'Remarkably good, now I think about it. But how would you know about Mr Wojzek?'

'Well,' he laughed. 'You know, I get about a bit. People. Places.' He ran one long finger from the tip to the bridge of his nose in a casual gesture. 'Times,' he added. 'Aren't you going to close the doors?'

Sarah moved around the console to stand next to him. 'That's what you'd like, isn't it, Mr Wojzek?' Her voice rose in pitch and strength, and she ignored the frown on his face. 'You've been very clever. And you are obviously still inside my mind. Something tells me that closing those doors would effectively close your trap.' She looked up at the face she thought she'd known so well. 'Call it feminine intuition, if you like.'

'You're very clever yourself, Miss Smith,' said Wojzek in the Doctor's voice. 'It has proved much more difficult to control you than the dozen other humans of my acquaintance.'

Sarah could feel her stomach turn. 'You inhuman monster. You sussed me out from your information systems, and you polluted my mind with Kendrick's VR machine.'

Wojzek grinned the Doctor's grin. ' "Monster" is a value judgement, Miss Smith. And, since I learn something new and unique about human capabilities and aspirations with each person I possess, I'm not sure your insult applies at all.' He folded his arms and leant back appraisingly. 'You have taught me a lot about strength of spirit. I thought your experience of alien races would make you more receptive to my mental advances, but it has actually made matters considerably more complicated. Those others seemed only too happy to release their tenuous hold on reality and allow me to occupy their higher thought processes. Inevitably, of course, relinquishing my control subsequently has rather dramatic effects. As you saw when the unfortunate Mr Wojzek blundered to his death, like Kendrick and the others before him.'

Sarah's eyes burned. 'Then you've learnt nothing about humanity. It isn't enough to understand the mechanics of being human. You need to know about pity and compassion and individuality.'

Wojzek laughed at her passion. 'My few attempts to control your mind have provoked some fascinating dream responses, but these seemed only to strengthen your resistance. So I had to conduct most of my work when your mental defences were at their weakest – at night, as you slept. That's when I introduced the virus into K9 that would bring the Doctor back to Earth. And to me. Now, unfortunately, you've rather spoilt that. So I'll need to be more direct.'

'I won't help you to harm anyone. I won't let you harm the Doctor.' She screwed her eyes up tightly, balling her fists as she tensed her whole body. 'I won't let you control me.'

When she opened her eyes again, the TARDIS was gone. Wojzek stood on the other side of the kitchen table, still looking like the Doctor. 'Are you trying to impress me? You could do, if you accept that your strengths can combine with mine in a symbiotic relationship. Open your mind to mine; don't resist.' The silky, warm voice echoed in her ears as he leant across the table to her. He reached out a finger and touched her forehead. 'I've been living here for more than eight weeks. You don't fit into your old life, because the Doctor showed you there are worlds beyond this tiny outpost in space, worlds beyond imagining. But he tantalized and then abandoned you. You deserve better than that.'

'You're a parasite,' said Sarah with a quiet intensity. 'But you're a parasite which doesn't nurture its host, doesn't understand that being humane is part of being human. I can't trust you. I won't trust you.'

Wojzek shook the Doctor's head. 'I know your mind like I know my own.' He barked a short laugh. 'Soon it *will* be my own. You don't draw strength from your faith in the Doctor. He's the weak link in your life.'

'Not true,' Sarah shouted back, her fists clenched again. 'You don't know him. To you he's just some faceless nemesis.'

'I know him the way you do,' said Wojzek calmly. 'The Doctor dumped you when he tired of you. You could expect no better. What had you hoped for, what could you really expect? What can any companion of the Doctor expect? The nagging knowledge that you led a second-hand life, that's what. Shadowing someone else's needs and desires. Just another time groupie, grasping at anything which might fill the emptiness of your own paltry existence. And after all that, no thank-yous. No rewards. Except maybe an unheroic farewell, or a grave too far from home.'

Sarah slammed a fist on the table. 'And what is your alternative? You want to enforce an unequal relationship. You want power and control, not a partnership. You can't survive without controlling your companions completely. And when you have no further need for them, you discard them like a spent wish, without caring what happens.' Her voice cracked, and her hand beat the urgent message of her words onto the table, though she could not feel the pain of the blows.

'You didn't need me,' she sobbed, staring through a mist at the tall figure opposite. 'You abandoned me, Doctor, and I've just about learnt to live without you. I'm coping. I can manage. And I don't need you any more, so you can just piss off and leave me alone.'

A rustle of paperwork and letters on the dresser indicated a gust of wind building up in the room. Within seconds, it had built into a whirling vortex of noise and air which engulfed the whole room. Plates spun into fragments, and pans rattled off their hooks on the wall. The kitchen clock flew across the room and cracked against the cooker hood.

At the centre of the maelstrom, Sarah stared at the figure of the Doctor. They were in the eye of the storm, untouched by the swirling madness around them. As she watched, the Doctor's face froze into immobility, as though he were a wax model incapable of independent expression. Now he was Wojzek, with thinning hair and heavy spectacles and Prince of Wales check. Now he was a wiry redheaded young man with heavy freckling, a pink-faced old woman in a staff nurse's uniform, a young blonde girl with a milk-white complexion. And then the transformations were indistinguishable, changing with maddening frequency into a formless, featureless, faceless mass. After minutes, or hours, or seconds, all Sarah could see was an amorphous blur around which sparks crackled and spat as though around a spoon left in a microwaved coffee.

She felt a wrenching pain in the centre of her head. The roaring fury of the storm rose to its screaming crescendo, and Sarah cried out in pain and anger and despair.

She woke up to find she was slumped in her armchair in the sitting room, her head aching like a migraine. On the table in front of her, she could see a thick film on her untouched coffee. K9 was humming beside her, his recharge complete.

She put her hand out to touch the dog's head. 'K9, I want you to erase that emergency transmission.'

'Affirmative, mistress,'

'And I want you to delete the program that broadcasts the signal. Let me know when you've done that.'

She held one hand to her pulsing head. Then she slipped out of the chair, and folded her legs beneath her so that she could sit on the pile carpet in front of the robot. 'I've got the worst headache, K9.' She paused, almost too frightened to ask the question. 'Has it gone from my mind, K9? Am I free of it?'

K9 flicked his ears at her briefly. 'Affirmative, mistress. Program erased.'

TEN YEARS FROM NOW, Sarah will be sitting up straight in an arch-backed chair, a large bound volume in her hands, reading aloud in a firm voice. 'She hated Warren Fletcher. She hated his mean self-interest, his Nissan Karelia, his easy familiarity with complex technology. She hated his phoney sincerity and long lunches. She hated his male-pattern baldness. And when he had died in a traffic accident, and she felt no different about him, she felt no guilt either. So, when she saw him walking towards her across Hyde Park, she knew at once what had been happening to her.'

She reads confidently, naturally, a little proudly. When she speaks dialogue, she differentiates each character by inflection, not by performance. And when she finishes the passage, she closes the volume and places it on her lap.

'S.J. Smith, reading from her new novel *Moving On*, which is published in two weeks' time by Virgin. This is the latest in her series of novels featuring 'the Doctor', a mysterious figure of unspecified, possibly alien, origins. And it's her first new novel to be published in several years.'

A two-shot: Sarah sitting at a table with Katy Pickering, bookshelves ranged behind them.

'Sarah, welcome to *On the Books*.'

'Thank you, Katy. It's nice to be here.'

'Sarah, your publishers have made much in their advance press publicity that this will be the last in your very successful series of Doctor novels.'

'You can't believe everything you read…'

Katy smiles. 'I know I'm not giving too much away by saying that the Doctor is almost peripheral to this latest novel. That seems very different to your earlier books, which attracted criticism that the Doctor was a dominant male lead whose accomplices were feeble caricatures of helpless women.'

'I think they started out as confident, able women who were faced with challenges beyond their experience. And they coped as well as you would expect on that basis.' Sarah runs her fingers in an unconscious gesture through her short hair, pepper-and-salt. 'The Doctor doesn't react in those familiar, human ways, and that counterpoints the other characters' reactions. Towards the end of the series, I hope readers see that his accomplices have adapted their life skills by adopting some of the Doctor's. They could have let themselves be led, relied wholly on his character. But they choose instead to learn from his strengths *and* weaknesses. Human feelings, emotions, intuition and initiative, it turns out, are all strengths, some of which the Doctor himself lacks.'

'You talk about him as though he was real. Is that a writer thing?'

'I think it's important that a writer allows her characters a life of their own. Sometimes, when one goes into these adventures, one has literally no idea what to expect – not even if one will make it to the end. Nevertheless, it's also important to establish that, if there is a relationship of control, then it's the author who controls the character, not the other way round. I've lived with the Doctor now for many years, and I feel I've known him from long before my writing. We go back further than people would understand or believe.'

'But the Doctor has made you a bestselling author, and allegedly Amblin Entertainment have expressed great interest in financing one or more films based on the character. Why stop the series now?'

'From the process of writing about him, I know him and myself so much better. But sometimes I recognize that my connection with a character, a job, a house, a hobby is just like my involvement with those adventures, Katy – I can't know how they will turn out. For me, it's important to deal with those connections on my own terms. So no matter how fond you are of them, how familiar and comfortable you are, you have to make your own choice. You have to decide for yourself that it's time to move on.'

The attic room of a large Victorian town house in Islington, London, contains a large brown cardboard box, which is tucked discreetly into a gloomy corner. Inside, sitting quietly, is K9, his lights out.

Bibliography, S.J.Smith

Short stories (all published in *Metropolitan* Magazine)
'Irongron's Star' (#886, Aug 1995)
'Operation Golden Age' (#891, Jan 1996)
'Exxilon' (#892, Feb 1996)
'Return to Peladon' (#894, Apr 1996)
'Eightlegs' (#897, Jul 1996)
'The Destructors' (#901, Nov 1997)
'A Girl's Best Friend' (#965, Mar 2003)

Novels (all published by Virgin Publishing, London)
More than Human (1997)
Noah's Ark (1997)
Dalek Dawn (1998)
Return to the Ark (1998)
Terror of the Loch (1998)
Forbidden Matter (1999)
A Gift of Death (1999)
The Kraal Invasion (1999)
Solon's Brain (2000)
Terror Stalks (2000)
Death Masque (2001)
A Hand through Time (2001)
Moving On (forthcoming)

Tarnished Image

By Guy Clapperton

'Most disturbing, my dear, don't you think?'

'Them murders, you mean?' Dodo Chaplet said as the Doctor unlocked the TARDIS doors. 'Yeah, they was freaky.' She took one last look back at Rotar City, capital of the planet Tarron. The metal pyramids gleamed in the blue sunset. It looked like a perfect place to hang out, but appearances were deceptive. Tarron hadn't exactly been the ideal spot to land. With a shiver, she followed the Doctor into the warmth of the TARDIS.

'No, no,' he fussed, 'I mean the holoprobe. For a technical advance like that to be misused in such a way… Most disturbing, as I said, hmmm?'

'Er – yeah,' she said, glancing uncertainly at him. She hadn't been with the Doctor for long, but his dismissive attitude towards casual violence had already begun to worry her.

'What's that you have with you?' he asked sharply, activating the door control.

She glanced down at her hand. 'Just the weekly newspaper digest,' she said, holding the flimsy metal sheet up. 'After all, we did go down in Tarron history. I just wanted a keepsake. Something to remember the old place by.' She shifted her grip, touching an incised icon at the top of the sheet. The metal glowed briefly, and columns of text sprang into existence. 'Look – here's the stuff for the day we arrived.'

The Doctor walked slowly past the console to his ornately carved chair. Putting down the objects he carried, and supporting himself unsteadily, he lowered himself into it. 'Well bring it over here where I can see it, then,' he ordered, waving his hand.

Dodo walked over and handed him the sheet. He scanned the first page within a few seconds, and clucked disapprovingly. 'Dear me, what is humanity coming to?' he muttered. 'Such sensational reporting. This will never do. This will never do…'

MUTILATIONS LINKED TO ANCIENT CULT!

(From 'City Watcher': Calendar Ten, Issue Eleven)
Think of Rotar City, Tarron, and you think of sophistication, technical elegance and total civilization. You wouldn't tend to think of brutal ritual murders. At least, not until seven days ago. But in the last week the sheer barbarity under the surface of our grace in everyday existence has been much in evidence.

The so-called re-emergence of the Vorassan cult of killers is perhaps the most worrying single event to take place on Tarron since the colonists left Earth centuries ago. Every child will remember the story of these grim warriors from the dawn of our planet's history. Convinced that Tarron had been somehow violated by our forefathers' presence, a group of retrogrades led by Danta Vorass banded together to take revenge on its behalf. Some called it a religion, some called it space madness, everyone agreed it was bloody-minded murder.

Until this last week observers have found it easy to shrug off such grim elements of our heritage. All civilizations go through a barbaric phase in which mutilation and torture are pretty much the norm, and ours is no exception, said the self-forgiving scholars in later years. Critics said they were throwing a sop to the populace to allow them some complacency about the chaos in which our society started – but being academics they were themselves, of course, above criticism.

Still, even this complacency looked reasonably acceptable until the events of the last couple of weeks. Now, the Vorassans look as though they have returned in spirit through a series of copycat crimes too horrific to be anything other than the work of seriously ill minds.

First came the horrific murder of Jayspekt Payn, a young man for whom life seemed to hold a lot of promise. The Science Council spoke highly of his grading, while his conduct was agreed exemplary by all who knew him. Well-liked – admired, even – and dead from a series of savage blows to the skull. Then there was Student A. Female, about twenty. Nobody knows much more than that about her, and unless a relative comes forward soon, no one ever will.

The Vorassans' methods were not pretty. Using base methods based on the ancient Earth beliefs in trepanning, it was their belief that knocking a hole in someone's skull would rid them of the inherent 'Earth Spirit' and allow for their acceptance by planet Tarron. But this would only work if the subject could feel the spirits leaving him or her – the pain had to be real. Sick, but they believed it.

Two deaths in the last fortnight, each caused by a ritual blow to the skull, each body marked by the etching of a 'v' shape on the back by 'some sharp implement as yet unidentified', according to the pathologists. This mark was said to be the insignia of Vorass himself, reserved solely for those victims in whom he took some personal interest. His followers always maintained that he would return after a period of abeyance. And some one is trying to make out that he's done just that.

Our Enforcers have taken little interest so far. Has our society really become so aloof we deny the existence of serial killers when they emerge? Are we so sophisticated we consider ourselves above such events of actual violence? Regrettably it appears we do.

The Doctor's forefinger stabbed at the touch-sensitive icon on the metal sheet. 'Where are the facts, hmmm?' he snapped. 'Too much speculation and not enough concrete evidence!'

'Cool it, Doctor,' Dodo protested. 'They're just making a living.'

'If there's nothing to say then they shouldn't say anything!'

Dodo touched a second icon. 'Look,' she said, trying her best to short-circuit his tirade, 'here's a report on our arrival. Looks like we went down a treat at that party. There's even a photograph of you.'

The Doctor sniffed. 'The food was cold and the wine was warm,' he said. 'And I was cornered by some dreadful man named Juslan who seemed to think I was an actor of some sort. Imagine that – me, an actor!'

Dodo stifled a smile. 'Well it looks like he was more taken with you than you were with him,' she said, 'cos he wrote the report!'

ACTORS STEAL THE SHOW AT HOLOPROBE LAUNCH

A special report by our scientific correspondent Kronel Juslan

(From 'City Watcher': Calendar Ten, Issue Eleven)

Much as I hate to admit it, the launch of the holoprobe was as magnificent a piece of theatre as the Azmec Corporation has come up with in a long time. The gadget itself looked fairly impressive to start off with, but the show they put on was even better. Especially coming from the normally strait-laced organization whose mandate to run the planet may date back centuries but whose sense of humour seems yet to have developed.

The holoprobe is an upgrade to the well-established holoview, in that both are used to look at holovids. Not that there was anything actually wrong with the holoview for looking at pictures, but the resolution achieved on the holoprobe is really stunning. It truly makes the viewer feel as though they are part of the image rather than a simple onlooker.

Dar Katin, Azmec's science consultant, told me how the device works:

'It takes whatever is in the holovid in the first place and the software makes intelligent guesses as to what else might have been in the image when the picture was first constructed,' he said. 'So, if you had one of the holovids from Earth, even one of the antique holorelics from the ancient days, indistinct as they are, the holoprobe would be able to reconstruct the picture by using the history files resident in its software.'

Presumably then, I suggested, this technique could

be applied to enhance and clarify the oldest holovid – the one of Simvoa, founder of our Tarron civilization. As every schoolchild knows, the speech in which Simvoa assigns the rule of Tarron to the Azmec Corporation is audible but the picture is barely distinguishable due to its age.

Katin smiled at the suggestion, but declined to comment directly. 'You'll be suggesting we try to enhance the fabled image of the screaming woman that appears in the Jewelled Head-dress of Princess Maxtra next.'

Perhaps the Azmec Corporation's sense of humour *is* developing after all.

Mind you, having seen the holoprobe, most of our editorial staff agree about the stunning results achievable from even the most faded holovid. The prospect of reconstructing more accurate pictures of the Founder's face is incredibly exciting, despite Katin's apparent disinterest. An obvious demonstration to launch the device, you might think. But you'd be wrong. Instead, Azmec bewilderingly, but amusingly, decided to pepper up the launch with the appearance of a comic double act called Doctor and Dodo – a bit kitsch, but there you go.

Like everybody at the launch, I was expecting a standard product demonstration, and it looked like just that until the last minute. Katin took an image of an old woman from the archives, one of his ancestors apparently, and enhanced it so that it looked as though she was standing next to him. This in itself was very impressive and we applauded as he expected. Then suddenly there was a creaking, howling noise and a holovid of an upright blue box with some ancient inscription appeared as if from nowhere, complete with a light flashing on the top. The initial cacophony subsided and was replaced by a simple low-pitched hum.

We fell silent.

I'll be honest: I've written about Katin's product demonstrations for over five years now and I've never thought of him as a performer. But he changed my opinion within seconds by offering up the most aghast look and some of the most convincing spluttering I have seen since my days on the theatre pages. Incredibly, he made his eyes bulge even more when the elderly white-haired man and his young companion came out of the box, looking genuinely surprised to see such a crowd.

The applause, of course, was ecstatic. The older player made a lot of 'harrumph' and 'hmmm?' noises, which the audience loved, while the young woman exuded a quieter interest in what everybody was doing there. Born stars if ever there were any.

Then the fireworks really started. The old man introduced himself as the Doctor and demanded to know who Katin was. Katin prides himself as being one of the most influential and recognized people on the Ruling Council, so predictably he did some more spluttering. Audience participation being the order of the day, some of the onlookers started throwing answers at the new arrivals, after which the young woman – calling herself Dodo – managed to arouse Katin's ire by referring to the holoprobe as a 'gimmick', that sounded 'a bit of fun'.

A hysterical bit of visual business followed in which the Doctor tried to wrest the holoprobe control from Katin's grip, succeeding eventually (of course) and commenting that he had something similar in a locker somewhere 'in the ship'. Katin was as good as foaming at the mouth by this stage. 'What are you doing to my exposition?' he shouted, to raucous laughter from the audience. 'Well I don't think much of it, you know,' the Doctor replied. 'It's a bit, ah, cumbersome, don't you think?'

All in all the launch offered some of the best value for money we have seen from Azmec for some time.

But the attitudes of the visitors became a little obsessive afterwards, bordering on the disturbed. Far from taking their money and going home like any other performer might, the Doctor stayed resolutely in character. As an acting method this is one of the very best, but when I spoke to him at the subsequent buffet reception, he seemed more interested in our murders than in the holoprobe. 'Dear boy,' he said to me, 'this device is interesting, certainly very interesting, but how does it extract things from the past without actually having been there? It can't, you see, it just can't.' As a publicist, he would be bound to stress the impossibility of his product – thus making it seem all the more brilliant – but he did seem to press his case just too hard.

And more than that, why express more interest in the murders than the holoprobe? 'Murders in the style of history and a machine that re-creates images from the past. I really do think that deserves some investigating, don't you agree?' He begins to sound less and less like the simple-minded, elderly performer he at first appeared, I think, as I reach for a passing vol-au-vent.

As I left the buffet reception, slightly the worse for wear, I reflected that the launch of the holoprobe had been a lot more innovative than I had expected. It remains to be seen whether the same can be said of the product...

'So this entire civilization was settled from Earth,' Dodo said, 'and run by this Azmec Corporation? That's a bit weird, isn't it?'

'Perhaps.' The Doctor settled back in his chair and steepled his fingers. 'Someone has to lead a colony – as this was when the first ships landed. The Tarronians believed – based on this one indistinct holovid – that the leader of the colonists had handed the colony over to the rule of the Azmec Corporation, although nobody quite knew who the Corporation were or what they had to do with the colonists. A pity I was not there at the time.' He gazed at the news digest again. 'Hmmm, not a terribly flattering picture. And this Juslan misquoted me. Still, at least he realized the significance of the ritual murders before anyone else did. Anyone else besides myself of course.'

'Of course,' Dodo said. She knelt beside the chair so she could see the metal news digest more clearly. 'In fact, I'm not entirely sure I understand their significance myself. Things moved so fast towards the end that I kind of missed the explanations. What was it about the murders that was important?'

'It wasn't the murders that were important, my child,' the Doctor chided. 'I keep telling you that. It was the ritual that was important. Look –'

He touched an icon, and the sheet filled with an article concerning the murders dated the day after they arrived.

'THE VORASSANS': OUR HISTORY CORRESPONDENT CHARTS THE GROWTH OF AN ANCIENT CULT

(From 'City Watcher': Calendar Ten, Issue Twelve)
The alleged return of the Vorassans after so many centuries is highly disturbing, but it is not wholly clear how many non-specialist citizens have truly grasped what the cult of Vorass truly was in the first place. Far from being brainless thugs colouring themselves in vegetable dye, history now believes they were the victims of a virus that attacked their central nervous system and drove them to their brutal pursuits.

It started, so legend has it, when Akha Vorass, the colony leader, went into the wilderness for fifteen days. It is not known why he left the early settlers, only that he moved about in the jungles on the surface and returned just over two weeks later carrying 'branches from the trees'. Every schoolchild knows there are no trees on Tarron, but presumably he had some sort of vegetation samples with him. He may well have been a hydroponicist; there are no records to confirm or deny this. Nonetheless, he returned. It is at this point that stories surrounding Princess Maxtra's head-dress first appear in our legends, and it is possible that he also brought this when he came back.

It was a further fifteen days before the first murder took place. Vorass had fashioned himself a primitive adze and made a loincloth from his polyfibre pressure suit, then dyed his skin with some sort of vegetable resin. He killed Marran, the wife of the then leader Garva, but instead of grieving the records show that Garva joined Vorass. It appears that everyone touched by the vegetable resin joined him in his belief that Earth men had no place on alien planets and the murders continued. Vorass would disappear frequently and return, claiming to his disciples – as he thought of them – that he had seen the future.

It was in this chaos that the infrequently seen Simvoa took power and handed the care of our civilization over entirely to the Azmec Corporation, which provided an infrastructure. No mention of the Corporation had been seen in the records up to that point, but peace was restored and the murderers disappeared. It is now believed that the vegetable resin with which they came into contact carried some sort of parapsychotic drug that turned otherwise rational people into deeply disturbed killers.

'Spooky!' Dodo exclaimed. 'How long ago did this cult do their stuff?'

'Hundreds of years,' the Doctor said, closing his eyes briefly. 'Yes, hundreds of years. If not longer. Yes, quite possibly.'

He appeared to be drifting off. Dodo quickly touched another icon. 'Hey, look Doctor! Here's us again!

KRONEL JUSLAN'S REVIEW OF THE WEEK

(From 'City Watcher': Calendar Ten, Issue Fifteen)
It is only a week since citizens were laughing at, even ridiculing, the strange elderly figure of the Doctor and his friend, Dodo. They have bafflingly remained in the public eye and become intensely critical of Azmec, who we had assumed to be their paymasters. The increasing probability that they were not a scripted part of Azmec's launch of their new holoprobe leaves the question of who they are and where they came from. Cynics might say that it is beyond most of us citizens even to speculate, for so long have we allowed Azmec to do our thinking for us.

Then there is the holoprobe itself. It came as a surprise to no one that our Science Council would enhance one of the most precious holographic images our civilization possesses. The ancient vision of our Founder, Hal Simvoa, declaring his allegiance to Azmec and granting it the right to govern us in perpetuity is an obvious target for the new technology. The resolution was put to the Museum Board only three days ago and everyone assumed it would pass unquestioned. This is the committee that put preservation orders on the volumes of Garda when they were deteriorating. This is the committee that restored the Jewelled Head-dress of Princess Maxtra, the head-dress in which tradition has it the face of a screaming woman can be seen at certain times. Surely they would grasp the chance to computer-enhance what is at the same time our most important and yet shoddiest relic. The chance to see our founder in lifelike quality rather than the blurred vestige with which we have had to make do excited macrohistorians throughout the world beyond their wildest imaginings. The chance to absorb every nuance, to observe every flicker of Simvoa's face and to appreciate every inflection of his words represented a chance to get closer to history rather than to observe it from a distance.

So why did the board turn it down flat?

There are a number of popular explanations. The one favoured by most of the popular press is the official line. An ancient belief or superstition suggests that if the image is penetrated, the spirits of Tarron will emerge and smite all the interlopers. And that's us.

But this simply won't do. First, since when was the Museum bound up with ancient superstitions or be-liefs? The very suggestion appears ludicrous and reeks of a cover-up. Even more suspicious than that is the fact that nobody on our panel of researchers, least of all our History columnists, can recall ever hearing of any such credo.

Even stranger is a memorandum seen by the edito-rial team here at the *Watcher* from Azmec to the board of the Museum. In no uncertain terms, this memo instructs the Museum's principal to kill the proposal. We put this to Azmec's press people, who screeched back at us that it was a faked memo. 'You saw what the saboteurs did to our launch of the holoprobe,' they told us. 'This is simply more of the same.'

The Doctor, meanwhile – saboteur or not – is behaving as if he has all the answers. In next week's issue we hope to publish an in-depth interview with him on why he believes the holoprobe to be so important, in spite of calling it primitive only seven days ago. He

> will also, he tells us, explain why we are wrong to
> believe Azmec about the holoprobe, and why it could
> spell the end of our society as we know it. Melodra-
> matic? Certainly. But he sounds very sure of himself.

'Sounds like this Kronel Juslan's turned into quite a fan of yours,' Dodo said, smiling cheerily up at the Doctor.

'A "fan"? And what, pray tell, is a "fan", hmmm?'

'I mean he likes you. He's written about you in this *City Watcher* thing every day since we arrived.'

'Harrumph!' the Doctor snorted. 'If only they had taken me at my word, rather than doubting me, then this situation might well have been cleared up much sooner than it was, hmmm? When will people learn? If he had spent a little more time wondering about this holoprobe, and why the Azmec Corporation didn't want it used to clean up the holovid of their founder's speech, and a little less time writing about us then we might have avoided that nasty business at the Azmec Corporation Headquarters, mightn't we?'

Dodo shuddered. 'Those robots were creepy! I thought they might do us some serious damage. And then when that Vorassan appeared out of thin air...!'

The Doctor patted her shoulder. 'I know, my dear, but I had met the Azmec Corporation before, under a different guise. We had to break into their headquarters. We had no choice, but don't worry – it's all over now.' He glanced at the news digest. 'I wonder what they have said about it in here. All lies and misrepresentation, no doubt.'

But, despite his protestations, Dodo noticed his thumb creeping toward the touch-sensitive icon marking the next day's headlines.

STOP PRESS: KIDNAP AT AZMEC CORP

(From Watcher-Line News Feed: Calendar Ten, Issue Sixteen)

News has just come in of a frightening kidnap attempt at the headquarters of Azmec Corporation. The figure

known as the Doctor has lodged an official complaint
with the Enforcers surrounding the alleged attempted
abduction of his companion, Dodo Chaplet.

The mystery deepened as the old man was unable
to account for why he was at the Azmec Corporation in
the first place. He had no permit to be there.

A totchy Doctor told our reporter: 'It was fearful,
fearful, dear boy. The girl Dodo and I, we wanted to talk
to the people at Azmec, d'you see? So we went there
and that was all our intention.' Any citizen of Rotar
would have known, though, that the Azmec Corp sees
no one unless by prior arrangement.

'We are not citizens of Rotar,' the Doctor claimed
when we put this point to him. This claim appeared
more than ridiculous at first glance, and yet our city's
Enforcers were apparently unable to raise any data on
the pair. A breach like this must raise doubts as to the
adequacy of Rotar City's security procedures and the
Chief Enforcer announced a Public Review shortly
afterwards.

A reliable source close to the Enforcement agen-
cies tells us that the Doctor's statement to Officer Ragil
read as follows:

Doctor:	'We entered the main building not one hour ago.'
Ragil:	'Which was closed at the time. How do you explain that?'
Doctor:	'Don't bother me with trifles, young man. We went into the reception building and were greeted by one of those infernal computing machines. And the wretched thing told us we were denied access. Tch.'

What followed is not exactly clear. The Doctor's testimony becomes vague, he starts laughing to himself
and talking about 'confusing the dear metal fellow,
poor thing'. Whatever happened exactly, it appears the
logic circuits on the autoreceptionist jammed and the
Doctor and his companion entered the research and
development area.

It would count only as a break-in by persons unidentifiable if not for the Doctor's claims about what they saw when they entered. 'Technology, dear boy, technology,' he comments with a zealous gleam in his eye. 'But nothing to do with holovids, d'you see? No, this was temporal technology, aimed at extracting things from the past.'

The *Watcher* is not given to scaremongering and our first reaction, naturally, was to shelve any interest in the Doctor's claims. But Azmec Corporation has been acting a little strangely lately. And then there are his assertions about his companion's abduction, which she backs up.

'It was horrid,' she says. 'All these metal blokes came out to find what the fuss was about.' By 'metal blokes' she means the autosecurity robots, standard enough, and yet she appears to have been surprised. 'One of them tried to grab me so I clocked him one. But it didn't make any difference, just a clanging noise.'

The Doctor takes up the story again. 'Yes indeed, they tried to take the poor child away, can you imagine? But then they found something far, far darker than us to occupy their metal minds.'

It is at this point the Doctor claims the Vorassan appeared out of thin air.

It sounds ridiculous on the surface but somehow you can't help but identify with the sincerity of this slightly crotchety figure. He believes what he is saying. 'Materialized out of thin air, coloured with a vegetable dye and holding a handmade weapon! There's a mystery here, oh yes. Temporal machinery, some subterfuge about holovids... I don't like it. I don't like it at all.'

It sounds ludicrous. And yet the bloodstain on Chaplet's face where she says the Vorassan hit her is genuine enough.

And if the first part of the story is true, the rest might be also. The Doctor was able to use the machinery he had found to return the assassin to his rightful time. The robots apparently retreated, swamped by too much data that refused to fit into their preprogrammed preconceptions.

But why come to the press with this story? Wouldn't the Enforcers have been a better idea? The Doctor suddenly becomes very serious at the suggestion. 'We come to you because you are the only ones interested in the truth and your people need to be warned. The Enforcers, my good man, enforce what the Azmec Corporation tell them to. They are not interested in investigating their paymasters. And that is why I fear your world, your very civilization, may shortly be under threat of extinction.'

(Editor's Note: In view of the events related in the last news item, next week's general interview with the Doctor will be replaced with an in-depth analysis of his role in recent incidents. We are pleased to have secured the co-operation of the Doctor himself in this matter.)

The Doctor shook his head sadly. 'Shuttered minds, my dear, shuttered minds. They listened only to those things they wished to listen to.'

'Come on, Doctor,' Dodo exclaimed, 'you can't blame them, surely. I mean – telling them we were attacked by people from their past ...'

The Doctor stared down his nose at her. 'But that was indubitably what happened. We *were* attacked by people from their past – these Vorassans they've been writing about. It's as clear as the nose on your face. The equipment in the Azmec Corporation Headquarters was time travel equipment. These Vorassans had been *brought* to the present from the past to cause who-knows-*what* havoc?'

'Yes, but you can't expect the Tarronians to just accept your word. They wanted proof.'

'They treated me like a fool.' His thumbs slipped beneath the lapels of his jacket. 'Like a senile old fool.'

'They took you seriously enough to interview you,' Dodo reminded him. She pointed to the news digest. 'Look.'

CITY WATCHER INTERVIEW: A DAY WITH THE DOCTOR

(From 'City Watcher' Calendar Ten, Issue Twenty-One)

It is now two weeks since the stranger known as the Doctor entered our lives, at first mistaken for some sort of performer but since then proven to be more, so much more. City Watcher *went and met him but as staff reporter* CRAKAR LUND *found out, he did not want to be bearded in his den...*

The suns are up and the interviewee has arrived, but is late. Time has little relevance to him, he explains, rather crossly. He obviously doesn't work to deadlines, I reply. Yes he does, he snaps, and more deadly than any of the deadlines I am likely to have come across in my time. He has just learned to move between them. Smart answer.

The Doctor is a strange individual. He does not want to give this interview, oh no. That would be publicity-seeking. You gather he's above all that and wants everyone to know it. But we, he points out, are the only ones who listen to him and alert the masses as to what he is about. Why, thank you. We, it appears, are the only ones with the ear of the populace and sufficient clout to persuade them how serious their position actually may become.

Because he's about to make a discovery, this Doctor. He'll tell me what this afternoon, when he is sure. But he will need to use us, oh yes he will.

I start by asking him questions. Who is he? Where does he come from? 'That is of no interest, my good fellow,' he patronizes. And yet in his case you get the feeling that he means it. He dresses like something from ancient Earth, maybe in the European sector, first segment of time, if my history tutors knew their stuff. He has got the hair wrong, if the archives are to be believed. The hair should be short but it is long and white. He is speaking again.

'What you need to know is about the very real threat to your civilization, hmmm?' He hums a lot, this Doctor. So it's a universal threat. I sigh, sit back, sip my cup of stimular. Another universal-threat peddlar. I'm almost disappointed. I've heard it so many times. So we're about to get engulfed in an appalling battle, the like of which we have never seen before, and society as we know it is about to come to an end? My interest wavers.

'No, that's just where it's so clever, don't you see? You have already been engulfed, right from the start! From the very word "go", you might say.' He laughs. He tells me that everything I have ever believed in or held dear is based on a lie, then he laughs. You have to give him credit for audacity if nothing else.

His companion joins us, name of Dodo Chaplet. Short, young, short dark hair. Open-featured, no doubt aged somewhere between nine and ninety. It's one of those faces, impossible to tell. At least she has a name instead of a title. The Doctor isn't saying much more for the moment and I can't say I'm sorry. Is he always like this? 'Oh, the Doc will tell you what he has to say when he's good and ready. I'm used to it, myself,' she says. Has he told her what he thinks is going on, perhaps? 'No, not a chance.' She laughs. After bristling a bit at being called 'Doc', he laughs too.

For a couple who keep predicting the end of the world, they laugh a lot. I start to wonder whether he has anything to tell me at all.

Chaplet appears more forthcoming about her background than the Doctor, but when you listen you realize she's coming out with a load of hooey. 'I'm from Earth,' she tells you. Oh right, Earth. The one destroyed centuries ago by solar flares. 'Yeah, we saw that. It was gear.' Ten centuries ago it happens and now she's seen it. 'Went to Refusis and everything. But I expect I'll be going home one day, when the Doc can organize it.'

Ludicrous though it may sound, she has the sort of engaging personality that makes you want to believe her. Putting it down on paper, you start to see through it, you realize you were probably right about them being actors at best or lunatics at worst in the first place, but somehow she seems vaguely convincing. At least she is convinced herself, although what this says about her stability is open to anyone to speculate about.

The Doctor clears his throat. He wants to speak, and wants me to take careful notes so that I get this part of the report right. Yes sir, apologies in advance for getting the rest of it wrong, which as a reporter I undoubtedly will. He continues. He obviously does not realize others may find his attitude offensive. I ask

Dodo if he ever thinks of other people and she tells me
he thinks of nothing else, just not in a way we might
recognize. I feel like apologizing for being a mere
mortal.

'Now listen to me, young man. I believe I have had
dealings with these Azmec people before, although
they didn't use the same name.' Naturally not. All good
conspiracy theories are based on deception. 'You say
they have a mandate to rule in perpetuity from your
founder, many years ago.' OK, so I humour him. That's
right, grandfather, I say. Odd, he seems to react at
being called grandfather. 'Well then, tell me this. Did
you never pause to wonder why a world's founder
would give away such rights on behalf of future generations, rights that never belonged to him in the first
place?' Of course. We have all wondered about that
and never really found the answer. The people of the
time were primitive and made these gestures, is all. We
were lucky. It worked. Still does.

'But that's just my point, young fellow. The people at
the time were not primitive. They knew very well what
they were doing, they had their wits about them, don't
you see? They had mastered interstellar travel, survived invasions from outer space, fought off plague.
They were fully computerized in the way they lived,
they had a sophisticated society – it wasn't just a bunch
of cavemen rubbing sticks together, I'll have you know!'
He sits back and obviously believes he has made a
deeply important point. If he has it has shot past me and
Dodo's face suggests she is not quite there either.

'The Azmecs, child,' he tells her, as if teaching a
baby to read. 'The Azmecs were not given that mandate. They took it, or worse.'

This is the point at which I start to balk. The Azmec
Corporation has regulated this planet virtually since it
was first inhabited. Nobody has questioned them before and we have done well from it. 'And not had to do
any thinking for yourselves, hmmm?'

The old man is suddenly very stern indeed and I
don't feel as relaxed as I did an hour ago. Of course we
think for ourselves. And what we think is that things are
going very nicely, thanks, and we like to keep it that
way. He laughs somewhat dismissively, although as a

citizen he must have enjoyed the Azmec Corporation's bounty as much as anybody else.

'Going very nicely, is it? Is that what it's doing?' he laughs, then immediately the smile is gone. 'Going very nicely until the murders started, you mean. Going very nicely until these savages from your past, these Vorascans, made their return appearance!' I don't know what to say. He appears, by imputation, to be linking the spate of murders that has hit our city recently with the very foundation on which it is based. He's not the first. He's just damned good at it.

'The Azmecs, as they call themselves here, are colonists like yourselves,' he starts to say. But we're not colonists, I tell him. 'Your ancestors from Earth, I mean. Dear me, do I have to explain everything?' He looks genuinely exasperated. 'They take over societies, I've seen them do it before. They infiltrate their way into a group of people and get themselves invited to take charge, you see?' Not really, but I let him carry on. 'Before long everybody is doing everything the Azmec way, thinking, behaving, there are no individuals, just a solid lump of people following the same rules and doing what somebody else has told them, without question. And that is what has happened to you. And I can prove it.' At this point I start to feel uneasy. What can he prove? Dodo smiles sympathetically. The Doctor wants me to go with him. He promises it will be safe. I go.

'Such an irritating young man, this Crakar Lund,' the Doctor said.

'Oh, I don't know,' Dodo said quietly, 'I thought he was rather cute.'

The Doctor continued as though he hadn't heard her. 'Condescending, arrogant, smug and irritating –'

Dodo smiled. 'Don't know *who* he reminds me of,' she said.

The Doctor gazed at her for a moment, then turned back to the interview.

They say a criminal always returns to the scene of the crime. This may well be why the Doctor insists on returning to the spot where he made his first entrance onto our planet's soil, if he is to be believed. The Exhibition Centre.

An empty exhibition centre is an eerie sight. Fearsome, almost. Designed to house a lot of bustling, busy people, it loses its soul when it is empty. The Doctor appears not to notice that he is being watched by shadows, that the echoes seem to be talking back to him rather than simply mirroring what he has said. I start to notice things, the high ceilings, the derelict and dusty exhibition stands. What seemed so bright and polished such a short time ago suddenly has an air of decay I wish I had not seen. I ask if we can turn some lights on. The Doctor says the main circuit is probably off. He is probably right.

Then there's that odd blue box of his. He is reluctant to let me see it but says it's the only way I will ever believe him. So I look at it and don't feel any better. It looks slightly battered and has some ancient Earth inscription on the front. It looks primitive, non-technological. I say so, the Doctor and Dodo exchange looks and he does one of those high-pitched laughs of his. I don't know what is going on.

He goes into the box and she follows. It must get crowded in there. I wonder what they're doing and he comes out with some sort of incredibly sophisticated-looking gadget. It's on castors and it has a lot of flashing lights on it. He tells me it's a holoprobe, but I point out it's half the size if not smaller. 'Well then, well then, it's like a holoprobe but smaller, hmmm?' He prods me in the shoulder playfully and I start feeling like a child in a playground. He and Dodo exchange glances and I start feeling as though they have been toying with me all along. He starts setting this alleged holoprobe up, linking wires, pulling tiny levers. Nothing is touch-sensitive as it is with our holoprobe. 'More gadgets to go wrong, my boy,' he says. 'It's supposed to be a scientific instrument, not an *objet d'art*.' I lean against the box to watch him. I notice it is humming and vibrating. Somehow this does not surprise me.

He's finished and sends Dodo into the box, which he calls the Ship, asking her to switch the power on. He rubs his hands, he has a little laugh. He appears to have forgotten the gravity of the situation, although he was the one who insisted it was all so damned serious. He pulls a disk out of his overcoat pocket. It looks sort of familiar.

It is the holovid recording of our Founder's speech. The one the Board refused to enhance, the one that reaffirms the Azmec Corporation's right to run this planet as they see fit. I ask where he got it from, and he mumbles something about so many stupid questions, so little time, he has connections, journalists protect their sources and so will he. Now do I want to see the holovid or not? I do.

It starts. There is a solid image but it is not the Founder. It is a woman, young to middle-aged with curly brown hair, attractive. She is stooping over towards us, as if switching on a viz-screen. She seems to be wearing a nightdress. I ask the Doctor what it is. 'Looks like they used a genuine old hologram as a backdrop,' he says. 'That would solve the problem of testing the age of the recording, wouldn't you say? The distortion suggests a low power source. Perhaps they intercepted a wide-beam transmission from far away, hmmm? Ironic, hmmm? A hologram that old would be more valuable as an antique anywhere in the Universe. They were very lucky to find it.' I get no more out of him about the woman.

Then the Founder arrives and my heart sinks. The original recording, we have always been told, was in poor condition. The centuries have not been kind to it, they said, it has been battered. And that was why it was only ever seen in grainy, scratchy viewings witnessed by dumbstruck scientists wanting to get a little closer to the past. And here I am, watching it as the people watching it when it was new would have seen it, getting the first look at our so-called Founder.

I say so-called because the figure speaking such loud volumes about our debt to the Azmecs is not a real person. It is an animation, a cartoon against a backdrop of the talking woman and the room behind her – maybe an ancient holovid the forger found and used to give his or her own image some background depth. And it is not even a particularly good fake. It would have to be a dreadful copy to fool anyone, but then dreadful copies are all that had been seen until now and the Museum's Board sat on our chances of enhancing the original. I expect the Doctor to start that cackling again, but he doesn't.

'I'm truly sorry, young man,' he starts. 'I would give anything to spare you that, but I had to convince you, d'you see?' Dodo puts her hand on my arm. It's supposed to make me feel better.

Everything we have believed in. Everything we have done, every instruction we have followed in good faith. All based on orders from a people who hijacked an entire planet, using a deception a child should have seen through.

I don't feel any better.

'But –'

'But why?' the Doctor interrupted Dodo. 'A very good question, my child. As with most conspiracies, it probably seemed like a good idea at the time. The Azmec Corporation knew, all those generations ago, that if they faked a complete holovid then the forgery would be detected very quickly. They just didn't have the technology to do it, do you see? Not convincingly.'

Dodo frowned. 'So instead they used an existing hologram as their basis, blurred the image so nobody could make it out, then faked this Founder bloke on top of it.'

The Doctor beamed. 'Precisely! If anyone ever tried to authenticate the holovid, they would find it to be a holographic recording of indubitably ancient origin based on Earth technology of the period. The fact that the Founder – this Hal Simvoa – and his speech handing control of Tarron over to the Azmec Corporation for perpetuity had been added on *afterwards* would completely escape their attention!'

'So where did they get this ancient hologram signal from?' Dodo asked.

The Doctor shrugged theatrically. 'My dear child, how am I to know? Perhaps they brought it with them from Earth. More likely, perhaps they accidentally intercepted it when they were

concocting their plan. The woman looked human – perhaps it
was a message beamed out into the depths of space, accidentally and fortuitously intercepted by the Azmec Corporation.'

Dodo sighed. 'I wonder who that woman was. She looked so
worried.'

'It's not important,' the Doctor said firmly. 'What's important is what was added, not what was already there.'

'And,' Dodo agreed, tapping the news digest, 'what was
done with it.'

STOP PRESS: AZMEC CORP'S HOLD ON TARRON SHAKEN
(From Watcher-Line News Feed: Calendar Ten, Issue Twenty-Five)

In a shock move following the leak of the contents of the
above interview to the telecast news services, the
Board of Directors of the Azmec Corporation have
gone into some sort of retreat. Rotar City has witnessed some of the most violent scenes of civil unrest
since the original reign of the Vorassans, and we are
getting reports that the Corporation's headquarters
has been the centre of rioting. Early indications are that
some of the Board have already left the planet, possibly permanently. We will bring readers further reports
in our next issue when the facts are clear.

'And good riddance to them!' the Doctor crowed.
'Shh!' Dodo said. 'I'm trying to read.'

LEAD ARTICLE: WHAT HAVE WE GAINED?
(From 'City Watcher': Calendar Ten, Issue Twenty-Nine)

The last seven days have proven the most eventful of
our planet's history. If 'history' really means anything
any more. The question is where to start.

Following revelations made exclusively in *City
Watcher*, the entire populace came to understand that
the structure of their society was based on a lie. The

Azmec Corporation was not, as had been believed previously, a benevolent force originating on Earth and migrating later to Tarron, our own planet, but a group of humanoids with a history of taking over planets.

They did not appear malicious. Unlike many of the races encountered by mankind over the centuries they were officious if anything and not actually malign. They administered efficiently enough in an uninspiring sort of way and all in all we appeared to be doing OK out of the arrangement.

The confusion arises only when the holoprobe issue is raised. In itself it appeared a harmless enough idea. And the Doctor's protests that it could not plant things in the recordings that were not already there sounded like the hysterical ramblings of a person with their faculties less than intact. Nobody connected the Vorassan murders with the holoprobe; there appeared to be no link. But, as we have all found out, to the appalling cost of the citizens of Rotar City – the two sad victims and their families in particular – the one was indeed causing the other.

The so-called holoprobe was acting as a time-scooper, bringing our most feared assassins from history into the present. People speculated about the styles of the deaths of the victims, scarred as they were with the mark of the original Vorassan, Akha Vorass himself. Someone with a sick mind did that, we all said – and someone with a sick mind it was, but who could suspect it was Vorass himself? Vorass, say the history books, disappeared periodically and came back claiming to have seen the future. This reinforced our impression of his madness at the time. Now we know it was probably the only sane thing he ever said.

Azmec Corp's HQ now lies a deserted ruin. Three of the Executive Board were tried this week under emergency legislation provided by the Science Council, the nearest we have to an administrative legislature in the absence of Azmec. Dar Katin, science consultant, was left as the spokesman trying to excuse the company's actions. Here, for what it is worth, is a transcript of his testimony.

'We at Azmec, as you call us, also known as Kephras and sundry other names around the Universe, have been managing your planet since your ancestors settled upon it. We did this for two reasons. First, we believed it to be in your best interests. A psychosis had started to overtake the inhabitants of Tarron and this had led to the emergence of the so-called Vorassans, named after the first individual to be so affected. It was caused by low-level radiation from the planet's core activated by contact with certain chemical compounds and was easily treated. Our first action was to make the remaining inhabitants immune to this effect.

'It is in the nature of our people to serve others, and this we do through providing the wherewithal for a race to survive. Upon our arrival we noted that although your people had arrived on Tarron as an established grouping the administration, legislature and other vital components were not in place. Our histories of other planets demonstrate ably that this absence of infrastructure can lead only to races reverting to chaos. We therefore indulged in a standard deception to place ourselves in a position of authority, which over the centuries we believe we have used responsibly and for the good of the majority.

'Lately, over the last one hundred years or so, it has become evident to us that your technologists are evolving swiftly and would soon develop their own equivalent of the device we chose to name the holoprobe. This would have exposed our initial deception, in turn undermining our position on the planet. Whereas we act from no selfish motivation, we believed this would lead to high unemployment, social unrest and damaging uncertainty for your people.

'It was therefore with a heavy heart that we took the decision to cull the most advanced of your students in a bid to offset the damage they would certainly do should they develop such a device of their own, and ordered the Board of the Museum at Rotar City not to investigate the holographic image of your "Founder" any further.

'We genuinely regret the deaths of the two young people and the attempted termination of the Doctor and his companion, who were in danger of uncovering the truth. In the event, they did just that. However, as always we acted for the good of the majority. We compute that history will prove us right.'

And there the statement ends. The Doctor, for his part, has vanished along with his companion, Dodo. A lot of people have commented negatively on this and on his few statements immediately before his disappearance.

The Azmecs, in the meantime, have been banished from the planet permanently. A lot of people were for executing them in public, but to be honest our society had not got the stomach to do it. Instead they were turned out and the decision was taken to destroy the Founder's holovid and a number of other suspect artefacts. Prime among these was the head-dress known to us as the Jewelled Head-dress of Princess Maxtra. The Azmecs said this was an item from the extinct civilization that preceded us on Tarron; the Science Council decided that this, the holovid and the volumes of Garda, should all be disposed of. The Doctor, being the one with the most advanced technology among us, was asked to dispose of these safely.

It was here that the controversy started. The Doctor did not want any part of the destruction of any of our culture, false though we now know it to be. 'It's where you come from. You can't simply deny your past – where would that get us, hmmm?' he asked. The answer, very clearly, was that these items were not part of our past: they were part of a fiction concocted by those who wished to dominate us. Hours of argument followed. The Doctor maintained we should have at least something to show future generations regardless of its part in the deception. The Science Council disagreed. The Science Council being in charge, they won the day. Reluctantly the Doctor agreed to take the artefacts away and deposit them elsewhere. He then stormed off and neither he nor his companion has been seen since.

The Doctor gazed sadly down at the objects by his feet – the objects he had carried into the TARDIS. One of them was a head-dress made of glittering jewels. Another was a small set of bound books – the volumes of Garda. The last was a small data-block – the faked holovid of the Founder, Hal Simvoa, and his lies.

'What are you going to do with them?' Dodo asked.

'I will bow to the wishes of the Tarronians,' the Doctor said sadly, 'much as it pains me to do so. After the TARDIS has taken off I will cast them into the Vortex and let the time winds take them.'

Dodo patted his hand. 'You don't sound as if you want to,' she said softly.

He shook his head slowly. 'History is always a lie,' he said. 'Successive generations always embellish the facts and alter the truth. Nothing is ever the way it is remembered. The Tarronians' history was more of a lie than most, but better to base your civilization on a lie than on nothing at all.' He sighed, and laboured to push himself up from his chair. 'I fear, my child, that I may have done more harm than good on Tarron.'

As the Doctor walked slowly over to the console, Dodo's gaze fell to the news digest, and to the last few lines of the article.

All of this is a matter of record. The riots are, for the most part, quelled. Once the agitants saw they had destroyed their enemy's headquarters, they appeared to lose their ardour for destruction. But the Science Council has yet to restore order fully. The economy has taken a beating from which experts say it is unlikely to recover at any great speed – such experts as we have left.

There is this feeling that the Azmec Corporation was right. We do not have the infrastructure to maintain a viable society for any length of time. Our civilization is in danger of breaking down. Our initial outcry was over two murders, and there is no doubt that these were horrific; but there have been five more since the Azmecs left.

We have increasing levels of unemployment for the first time ever. We have street crime, we have violence. We have the humiliation of knowing that everything we did before, our beliefs and our ways of life, were based on a miserable piece of deception from a race that took us for fools – and did not find us wanting. Before he left, the Doctor told us it would not be easy, that we would have to make our own mistakes and endure our own knocks, but to appreciate that it would be real this time. Then he vanished. Created our new situation for us and lost interest.

Well, we at *City Watcher* certainly agree our position is 'real'. And we'd like to thank the strange Doctor figure, whose true identity we never really knew.

But to be honest, we're not sure what we'd be thanking him for.

Past Reckoning

By Jackie Marshall

'There it is. Trentillys Castle.'

Nyssa flipped up one hand to shade her eyes against the unremitting blaze of sunlight. Then she stared up to where red stone walls loomed above the forested slope like the craggy prow of a ship caught in a green leafy sea.

'It's big,' she said cautiously, not entirely sure what reaction was appropriate.

'Oh yes!' the Doctor enthused, fanning himself gently with his hat. 'The earliest part was built of local red sandstone in about 1300 by Roger Mortimer, one of Edward the First's warlords. The estate was sold in the Elizabethan period to Thomas Gosthorpe, a merchant adventurer, and it's been in the Gosthorpe family ever since.'

Nyssa nodded dutifully, although the precise meaning of some of the Doctor's terminology escaped her. She was beginning to regret that she'd ever mentioned in passing that she knew very little of the history of Tegan's home planet; her innocent remark had served to launch the Doctor on a mission to educate her. That didn't entirely account for why they were in the Welsh Marches, several thousands of miles away from Tegan's stamping ground of Brisbane, but, given the comments Tegan had made about that particular city, Nyssa thought that perhaps the Doctor was doing her a kindness by bringing her here instead.

'I met David Gosthorpe, the present owner, a few years ago,' the Doctor said, briskly leading the way up a winding gravel path arrowed and marked 'Trentillys Castle' at reassuringly regular intervals. 'Nice young chap, but a bit unsure of himself.

I gave a spot of advice on certain matters. It'll be interesting to see how he's turned out.'

'So that's why we're really here,' Nyssa deduced, rubbing surreptitiously at her heel and wondering if a transition from Traken clothing to some of the attire she'd found in the TARDIS wardrobes had really been such a wise move. She had a nasty suspicion that a blister of prize proportions was forming.

'Well, I thought we might look in on him.' The Doctor favoured her with his most ingenuous smile, the one he used to open doors into places most people wanted kept closed. 'If you don't mind, that is. Who knows, perhaps we can even persuade him to offer us a bite to eat and drink.'

'Tea and cake?' asked Nyssa hopefully.

The Doctor grinned broadly. 'Oh yes, tea and cake,' he said. 'Absolutely.'

Bill Hignett swatted a stray wasp away from his face and settled himself back down onto the chair in his stuffy little booth. In such hot weather he would have found it far more comfortable had he been able to position his chair outside the booth, but the narrowness of the path, surrounded as it was on both sides by high hedges, made that impossible.

The steep climb up to the castle from the car park and the village eventually rewarded the curious by ending here at the summit and branching in two directions. Beckoning one way was the castle entrance, slotted between two massive drum towers and leading into a grassy rectangular courtyard, while the other path led to Bill's booth and Trentillys Castle Gardens, where the formal terraces dropped away down to the landscaped garden and lake.

Bill's vantage point enabled him to see the castle entrance and he was studying it keenly now, hoping that Sally Thomas would remember her promise. She worked in the restaurant and had earlier agreed to bring him out a pot of tea – although right now a cold half of bitter would have been even more welcome.

There was no sign of Sally, so Bill sighed and turned his

attention to the path leading up from the village and the car park, following the progress of a solitary blonde. She walked by the entrance to the gardens, giving him plenty of time to admire the length of tanned leg as she passed him and the smooth fall of cornsilk hair under her wide black straw hat. Her eyes were invisible behind her dark glasses. A cool beauty, he decided, and one that wouldn't have looked twice at him even when he was thirty or so years younger.

The blonde was followed by a family, bickering loudly as they trudged up the path.

'I don't want to see a stupid castle!' The speaker was a girl aged about six or seven, long hair curling in dark snarls round her mutinous face.

'I don't neither.' A surly moon-faced youth, who looked about four years older than the girl, scowled blackly. His feet kicked moodily at the gravel. 'It's boring.'

'Shut up,' his father said irritably. 'The pair of you. I'm sick of you whining on. Anyway, it's your mam's idea, not mine.'

'Well, I wanted to go somewhere,' the woman complained, shoving a tendril of limp hair behind one ear. 'I'm sick of being stuck at home of a Sunday. Why shouldn't I get to go out sometime?'

'We're here, aren't we?' her husband demanded unsympathetically. 'What more do you want?'

'My legs ache and I'm starving,' the girl whined, tugging at her mother's arm. 'I want something to eat.'

'Yeah, that's a good idea.' Her father brightened. 'Do they sell beer here?'

To Bill's undisguised relief, the family passed by the garden entrance and headed – still squabbling – for the castle itself. A few minutes later a man and a young woman also passed him by on their way to the castle. The man was dressed improbably in a long beige coat and striped trousers – perhaps he was one of those re-enactment johnnies, Bill mused idly.

'It's open to the public!' the man exclaimed in startled tones.

'What do you mean?' the girl asked him.

'Look! It's no longer just a family home; the public are being welcomed in and paying to look around. Things have certainly changed; David told me he would never consider opening the castle up.'

'Maybe he needed some money,' the girl suggested.

'Shouldn't have done; the estate wasn't short of cash.'

The two passed by. Bill could have stopped them and enlightened them, but it was too much effort. They'd find out soon enough. Besides, he had other things on his mind: he'd just spotted Sally coming towards him with the promised pot of tea.

Ellen Carter paused before she went into the castle, staring up at the red-stone towers, the intensity of her gaze hidden by her sunglasses. To casual onlookers, she seemed merely another curious tourist. Only a certain tightness about the lips betrayed the strength of her emotions.

Quickly she crossed the grassed courtyard, moving from bright sun into cool shadows, and fumbled in her bag for the requisite fee that would buy her admittance into the castle itself.

Buy! She kept her sunglasses on as she paid, not wanting to show to the world how much she resented the transaction, slipping them off and into her bag only as she passed through into the lofty coolness of the hall. She blinked, paused a moment, and ran a hand lovingly over the curved oak bannister that swirled down at the side of the wide staircase. Then she snatched back her hand as though the touch of the wood had burnt it.

It did no good to indulge unhappiness. She, of all people, should know just how worthless a response it was. When that cute American student at Oxford had ignored her overtures in favour of a toffee-nosed bitch who played fast and free, when her husband Don had informed her after two years of marriage that she was a cold, obsessive shrew and that he wanted a divorce so he could marry his plump, pert secretary, she'd wallowed in self-pity rather than do anything about it.

Not this time, she told herself fiercely. This time it would be different.

'Another slice of cake, Nyssa?'

'Oh no,' Nyssa said quickly. 'I've had quite sufficient, thank you, Doctor.' More than sufficient, if the truth be told, but the delights of sticky caramel slices had, once sampled, proved hard to resist. She swallowed down the rest of her tea. She had been relieved to find that the opening of the castle to the public had necessitated the constructing of a tearoom in the buildings that formerly constituted the stables; the steep walk to the castle had left her parched as well as hungry.

'Well then,' said the Doctor, reaching for his hat. 'Let's take a look round the castle. Maybe we'll find out why David Gosthorpe changed his mind about opening it to the public.' The guidebook they'd purchased had been singularly uninformative in this regard, preferring to dwell instead on points of architectural interest rather than recent family history.

They paid their dues at the castle entrance and walked inside the cool, cavernous hall. To Nyssa it felt as though they had passed from one world into another, the cheerful warmth and light of the courtyard displaced by chill and gloom, by hushed voices and the musty smell of ages past.

'Neo-Gothic style,' the Doctor said authoritatively, thrusting his hands into his pockets and gazing round at the heavily carved oak wall panelling and staircase. 'Possibly Pugin ...' Then he frowned slightly. 'Curious, isn't it, how you can almost feel the weight of years pressing down on you. All the traditions and accomplishments of centuries past locked in one building. Perfectly splendid, of course, but also rather oppressive ... A demanding mistress, wouldn't you say?'

'Yes.' Nyssa understood exactly what the Doctor meant. 'It's hard to imagine anyone ever really feeling they owned this place; it rather gives the impression it would own them instead.'

The Doctor and Nyssa consulted their guidebook and followed the suggested route, up the Grand Staircase, then through the State Dining Room and Saloon. The Doctor paused frequently in their tour, not to exclaim over some historical gem as Nyssa would have expected, but to frown and look generally discomfited. Finally, in the Drawing Room, Nyssa felt constrained to ask him what was wrong.

'This is not as I imagined it,' he confided, gesturing around him in perplexity at the sparsely furnished room. 'From the way David spoke, the fixtures and fittings of Trentillys Castle were old and precious.'

'These aren't?'

'Well, old certainly. But not so very precious – those that are left. In here, only the ceiling plasterwork has any intrinsic value. And look over there, at those brighter patches of wall covering. Some paintings have been removed. Quite a few of them, by the looks of things.'

'Have they been sold?'

'Probably, which suggests that the family fortunes weren't quite so glorious as David painted them.'

They continued on their chosen path. Nyssa wandered down the rush-matted Long Gallery, eyeing the numerous portraits with an inexperienced eye. Sombre faces stared back down at her, but Nyssa knew nothing about Earth's artwork and couldn't judge whether the renderings were good, bad or merely indifferent. She noted one portrait that had been painted in pastels, the soft, warm colours catching her attention amid its gloomy oil-based companions, and leant forward to take a closer look at it.

'Doctor! Look at this!'

The portrait was of a fair-haired young man, the face and figure brought to life in bold strokes across the canvas. The gold plaque at the bottom identified him as David Gosthorpe, died 1987.

'So he's dead, then.' Although she had never known the young man, Nyssa felt a peculiar sense of loss. Perhaps it was simply that death of any kind left her forlorn; she'd seen too much of it.

'He collapsed with a stroke in Naples, and died there, penniless,' a woman's voice informed them.

Both the Doctor and Nyssa turned and found themselves

facing a strikingly beautiful young woman clad in a white shift
dress and holding a black straw hat. Her hair was sleek and
blonde, her complexion smooth as a porcelain doll, but her eyes
were fiercely alive, glittering in the half-light from the partially
screened windows.

'How tragic,' Nyssa said simply.

'How needless,' the woman returned, an edge in her voice.

'Penniless?' The Doctor drew his brows together, sounding
puzzled. 'That's strange. I understood David to have inherited
a considerable fortune.'

'Oh, he did,' the woman said. 'He spent it. Then the castle,
and what was left of its contents, was sold to a local entrepre-
neur who fancies he'll make money out of it.' Her dismissive
laugh at that suggestion owed nothing to humour. Then she
looked at the Doctor curiously. 'You knew David?'

'I met him a few years ago, at Glastonbury.' The Doctor
smiled, memories filling his eyes. Then he frowned. 'Of
course, I've changed a fair bit since then... I doubt he'd have
recognized me now.'

Nyssa allowed herself a slight and knowing smile. Knowledge of this fact had not, she noted, kept the Doctor from
proposing the visit in the first place. No doubt he would have
come up with an explanation to cover his altered appearance.

The woman nodded with a kind of bitter acceptance. 'Glastonbury,' she said with venom. 'Yes. He did waste some time
there when he was younger.'

'Oh I don't know about that,' the Doctor demurred. 'He was
quite a confused young man, feeling the weight of all this
responsibility.' He glanced around, at the cold faces of the past
generations of Gosthorpes staring sternly down at him. 'So
many expectations were being placed on him. I told him he
shouldn't let himself be bound by tradition, that he had every
right to take charge of his own destiny. Life should be about
living, not for propping up the past.'

The woman said nothing, her eyes lifting and fixing on
David Gosthorpe's portrait with an expression that was utterly
unreadable.

'Well,' said the Doctor, with a show of gallantry as the silence lengthened and it became clear that the conversation was over. 'Nice to have met you. Come along, Nyssa.'

They moved on and left the woman standing there, as stiff and silent as the painted faces on the wall.

'Rhiannon! I've told you half a dozen times already, you're not to touch anything!'

'Why not?' Rhiannon's face pouted sulkily through her dark curls at her mother as she jabbed one sharp finger at an elderly chair whose needlepoint upholstery was already badly frayed.

'Because I said so, that's why not. Look, just cut it out, Rhiannon, will you?' Beverly Cope snapped irritably. 'I've had enough of you today. Neil, tell her to leave off, will you?'

'What?'

'Tell her!'

'Do what your mam says, or I'll fetch you one,' Neil Cope said, in the bored tones of one who just might, if pressed, carry out his threat. Rhiannon stuck out her bottom lip, considered the likelihood of her father putting words into action, and then pelted off through the State Dining Room and into the Saloon in pursuit of her brother, Jason.

'It's your fault, Bev,' said Neil. 'You've got no idea how to deal with kids, have you? You let them run rings round you, you do.'

'Oh yeah? Why's it my fault all of a sudden? They're your kids too, remember?'

'Well I work, don't I? I haven't got time to be running round doing your job for you.'

'I have to work as well!' Beverly protested.

'Only part-time,' Neil returned with smug superiority.

'I do twenty hours a week at that supermarket, and then I still have to do the house and look after the kids!'

'So? It's my job that brings in the money to pay the mortgage, right?'

'Yeah, and it's my money that puts the food on the table, and pays for your beer and ciggies.'

'Suppose it's my fault now that the mortgage rates have gone up.'

'I didn't say that, you're always twisting what I say…'

Jason Cope gave the fat plaited red rope that screened off the State Bed a surreptitious tug and then watched in satisfaction as all the brass stands came toppling down in a pleasing domino effect. Then, before an irate warden could collar him, he raced off through the King's Bedroom and thundered down the narrow wooden Servants' Staircase.

'Jaa-son!'

Rhiannon caught him up on the ground floor at the exit. 'Where are you going?' she demanded.

'Dunno.' Jason scowled at her. 'Push off.'

Rhiannon stuck out her tongue. 'Shan't.'

Jason said a few words he wasn't allowed to use and Rhiannon pulled a gleeful face, skipping round him in mock outrage. 'You shouldn't say that! You'll get wrong!'

Jason ignored her and stomped off in the direction of the path towards the Castle Gardens. Rhiannon darted round him, like a malevolent Tinkerbell. 'I know, there's a lake down there, let's go see it!'

'What for?'

'There might be ducks.'

Jason's surly expression brightened a little and his eyes began scouring the gravel for any larger stones. 'Yeah. Ducks.'

'I've been wondering whether or not we should look up Tegan now that we're back on Earth,' Nyssa said tentatively as they reached the foot of the Servants' Stairs and stepped outside into bright sunshine.

'Have you?' The Doctor uncurled his hat and slapped it firmly on his head. 'And do you think that would be wise?'

'Would seeing her again be so very wrong?' Nyssa found herself frowning as she looked up into his face. There were times when the Doctor's expression gave the lie to who he appeared to be and this was one of them. Quite suddenly his eyes were alien, unfathomable, full of places she couldn't even begin to imagine.

'Why do you want to see her? For her sake or for yours?'

'Well, I …' Nyssa floundered and then gave a tiny shrug of confusion.

'You're not sure?' The Doctor raised an interrogative eyebrow. 'But you must ask yourself that question, Nyssa, and then think long and hard about the answer.'

Nyssa's eyes took on an abstracted look as she reflected on his words. Finally she said, 'I suppose I want to see Tegan for my own sake, but she chose to leave us. Therefore I have to ask – would *she* want to see *me*?'

'Now you understand.' The Doctor's expression was now one of wistfulness. 'They all leave, Nyssa. You will too, one day.' He glanced at her face and smiled. 'Come on now, there's no need to look so hangdog about the inevitable! What you must appreciate is that most of my companions choose their own time to depart because they know when that time has come. If I then actively sought them out, popped by from time to time to check on how they're doing, I would be diminishing that choice. Do you see?'

'I think so.' Nyssa considered. 'Your companions know that they can't journey with you indefinitely so they all choose when to leave and live their own lives. You have to respect their choices and accept that you're not part of their world any more. I do understand, but it's very bleak, Doctor. For you, I mean.'

'It's the way it has to be, Nyssa. I'm a Time Lord, I walk in eternity. And that means no going back, no regrets. Well' – the Doctor smiled a little sadly – 'maybe a few, for those who made the wrong choices.'

'Well, we've paid, haven't we?' Neil Cope said belligerently, waving the tickets under Bill Hignett's nose. 'My kids weren't lying.'

Bill Hignett tried not to look as intimidated as he felt. 'Yes, but that's not the point. Your children should've waited for you, not just shouted that you had the tickets and then gone running –'

'Which way did they go?' Beverly Cope interrupted. 'There's the lake down there and Rhiannon can't swim. Even if she doesn't fall in, she'll get herself all mucked up and covered in mud, knowing her.'

Then you should've kept a better watch on them, shouldn't you? Bill Hignett thought but, given the surly look on their father's face, dared not say aloud. 'I didn't see which way they went,' he returned shortly.

'Is there a problem?' The Doctor's and Nyssa's path had brought them to the entrance of the Castle Gardens.

'It's my kids,' Beverly said quickly. 'They've run off down to the lake.'

'Oh dear,' said the Doctor, knitting his brows together. 'How unfortunate.'

'They'll be all right,' Neil muttered. 'They can take care of themselves. You fuss too much, Bev. Come on, we'll catch them up soon enough.'

'The trail round the lake is a mile long,' Bill Hignett said with malicious relish. 'So you'll be in for quite a walk before you find them.'

'We're going to take a stroll round the lake ourselves,' said the Doctor. 'We'll keep an eye out for them.'

'Oh thanks a lot,' said Beverly. 'You'll know them if you see them. Jason's just like his dad, and he's wearing his *Ghostbusters*' T-shirt. Rhiannon has long dark, curly hair and she's got a pink sundress on. Just tell them to come back up here and wait, will you?'

'My pleasure,' the Doctor returned courteously.

Beverly Cope looked round, saw that her husband had already sauntered off on the path that led to the terraces, and took after him with a plaintive cry of 'Neil! Wait up!'

Bill Hignett shook his head as he looked at the Doctor's and Nyssa's tickets. 'Kids,' he muttered. 'Mind you, what can you expect when you see what the parents are like? Me, I wouldn't leave those two in charge of Sooty.'

The ducks had wearied of being on the receiving end of Jason's target practice and had wheeled off in screeching indignation. Various passers-by had not hesitated to give Jason a piece of their mind about his conduct either, and his face had become rapidly more sullen with each interference. If he'd had his mates with him, he'd have given back as good as he got, if not worse. But he was only ten years old, still just young enough to be intimidated by adults *en masse*, so he contented himself with muttering obscenities behind their backs.

Rhiannon danced across his path, her curls bouncing up and down across her shoulders. 'Let's play a game, Jason,' she demanded. 'Go on, let's!'

'No! Look, push off, will you?'

Rhiannon did no such thing, and Jason knew from long experience that nothing he said would come anywhere near close to cowing his little sister. He hit on an idea.

'Yeah, OK, let's play a game then. Let's play hide and seek. You hide and I'll find you.' Well, he might, if it suited him.

Rhiannon whooped with joy. 'You won't find me!' she taunted. 'I'll get the best hiding place ever!'

To Jason's relief, she charged off down the path to the lake and left him in peace.

Rhiannon skipped gaily round the lakeside, quickly dismissing the idea of hiding in the rhododendron bushes. That would be the first place Jason would look. She wanted somewhere much less obvious. Up ahead she saw what looked like a pile of rocks and raced over to investigate.

She found that the rocks had all been cemented together and arranged into something like a little cave. Inside there was a tiny pool, and in the water the statue of a half-dressed woman reclining beside a bubbling fountain. Several window openings set in the grotto walls looked out across the lake or the gardens. One opening was quite high up, but not high enough to deter Rhiannon, who had climbed into many supposedly inaccessible places in her short life, usually while in pursuit of her big brother. Her fingers and toes clinging to cracks and

crevices, she levered herself up into her chosen hidey-hole.
There was a sudden ripping sound as her dress caught and tore
on a rough piece of stone, and Rhiannon pulled a sulky face. Oh
well, Mum would just have to buy her a new one.

Once she'd reached the window slot, she pressed her back
against the side of the wall and drew up her knees. If she turned
her head to one side she could see straight across to the arched
bridge at the opposite end of the lake – and right into the clear
water if she cared to look directly down. When she turned her
head to the other side, she could see into the grotto itself. She
guessed she'd be spotted if anyone entering bothered to glance
up but she'd stay quiet as a mouse so that they would never
think of looking up and wouldn't see her. Anyway, Jason didn't
think she could climb that high. She'd said she'd show him, and
she had.

Smugly, Rhiannon settled herself more comfortably into her
hidey-hole and then lifted her head as she heard approaching
footsteps. Not Jason, she decided. His trainers had a rubbery
squeak. This was a light tapping noise, like someone in sandals.

A woman entered the grotto. Rhiannon guessed she was the
same age as her mum, only about a million times prettier. The
woman had long blonde hair, all smooth and shiny like in a
shampoo advert, and she was wearing a white dress. The only
time Rhiannon could remember her mum having a white dress,
Rhiannon herself had plastered raspberry lolly all down the
front of it and the stain hadn't come out. Mum had had a fit, but
Dad had just laughed – until he found out how much the dress
had cost. The pretty woman's dress looked like it had cost much
more than Mum's.

Which made it all the more surprising when the pretty
woman stepped into the pool, without even bothering to take
off her sandals, and let her dress get soaked in the spill of water
while she began tugging at the stones in the recess behind the
fountain.

The Doctor and Nyssa had negotiated the switchback terraces,
duly admiring the colourful, scented herbaceous borders and
avoiding the hosepipes, which lay curled like green snakes

across the paths ready to trip the unwary. At the foot of the terraced gardens, the Doctor had been firmly in favour of taking the Lakeside Walk. Nyssa had been more cautious, wondering how her feet would cope with the joys of a mile hike.

'Nyssa, Nyssa, Nyssa!' The Doctor wheeled round on her, shaking his head in mock exasperation. 'You could always take those sandals off, you know – ridiculously impractical things. I told Romana so, but she wouldn't listen either.'

'And go barefoot?' Nyssa was dubious, noting the stones and sharp twigs that littered the trail.

'Of course. Then you can dabble your toes in the water to cool them. Doesn't that sound appealing?'

To Nyssa, who'd noted that the banks of the lake were slathered in thick black mud, this idea was considerably less than appealing but in the interests of harmony she kept her objections to herself.

The blue-glazed lake itself lay smothered under the heat, as sleek and placid as a pampered cat. Ducks scarcely rippled the surface as they bobbed and dabbled in their ceaseless quest for food. The trail wound in and out of the glossy-leafed rhododendrons and sweetly scented azaleas pretty much as it would have done when it was first laid out. Every turn in the route led them to new perspectives; bridges, statues and follies were carefully placed to maximize interest. Nyssa began to forget her aching feet and to enjoy breathing the rich scents around her, lulled by the drone of the bees and the birdsong from the trees. There was no sign of any missing children, or indeed of many other visitors at all. In fact, it was all very peaceful until the Doctor remembered he had a duty to educate and inform her.

'Nothing like a brisk constitutional, is there?' he said breezily. 'We're treading in the footsteps of history, Nyssa. Gosthorpes have strolled along these paths since the lake was constructed in the eighteenth century. See how it's been landscaped so that one vista forms a vantage point for another?' The Doctor paused on top of the knoll they'd reached and indicated across to a white colonnaded structure at the other side of the lake. 'A Grecian temple,' he explained.

'A house of worship?'

'Not exactly. Just an architectural folly of a style that was very popular at the time. And up ahead we have a grotto which I think you will find a refreshingly cool place on a hot summer day…'

The Doctor's voice trailed off as he reached the entrance to the grotto and was able to see inside. Nyssa peered inquisitively over his shoulder.

'Well, hello,' the Doctor rallied. 'I'm delighted to see you again, Miss – er ? Though I will confess that the circumstances are not quite …'

The young woman they'd met in the Long Gallery was staring back at them. At first glance it seemed as if she'd observed the advice the Doctor had given to Nyssa and was busy dabbling her toes in the water of the pool. But, mystifyingly, her sandals were still on her feet, her white dress had been thoroughly soaked by the spray from the fountain, and her once immaculate glossy fall of hair hung in unbecoming rats' tails round her pale face. Still more curious was the fact that she seemed entirely careless of her appearance. She faced Nyssa and the Doctor with no trace of embarrassment. One hand was clenched determinedly round a stone which she'd evidently just prised out of the cavity behind the fountain and its recumbent statue.

'If you'll forgive me for saying so, I'd hardly expected to find you engaged in an act of vandalism,' the Doctor ventured in that mild tone of voice which meant that his mind was working overtime.

'Hadn't you?' she returned with sharp venom. 'But it's because of you that I'm reduced to doing this, Doctor.'

The Doctor's eyebrows shot up into his fringe. 'Me?' he said, puzzled.

'You are the Doctor, aren't you? It was your friendly advice to David that cost me my heritage.'

'You're related to David Gosthorpe,' Nyssa deduced with a sudden leap of understanding. Now she looked closer, there was a certain resemblance to the portrait of the last owner of Trentillys Castle: something in the eyes and the stubborn shape of the chin.

'I'm his sister, Ellen Carter,' the woman returned shortly, then seemed to make up her mind to offer a fuller explanation. 'As David died without an heir Trentillys Castle belonged by right to me. It would have been mine, if he hadn't had to sell it to pay off his debts.'

'So what are you doing now?' Nyssa asked, still not much the wiser about what was happening in spite of Ellen's disclosures.

'I'm taking necessary steps to recover what's mine by right,' Ellen said harshly. She turned her back on them and stepped behind the fountain to rip another stone free from the wall.

'If you plan on smuggling out the entire castle in your handbag, then I have to say that I think you're doomed to failure,' the Doctor remarked with a frivolity that Ellen didn't appreciate. She turned on him, her body shaking in fury.

'You're so damned . . . smug! You encouraged David to squander his inheritance chasing dreams! Do you know that thanks to your advice he spent every last penny he had hunting down lost historical artefacts? It ruined him. He had to sell the castle, and I lost my inheritance. Just what the hell gives you the right to barge in and mess up people's lives?'

'I didn't know that's what I was doing,' the Doctor returned quietly.

'Ignorance is a pitiful excuse as far as I'm concerned.'

'But you're ensuring that I remain in that state now,' the Doctor argued. 'So please tell us exactly what you're doing, unless you prefer that I inform the authorities –'

'I've already told you what I'm doing. I'm recovering my own property. David and I played here as children. We made a hiding place in the grotto and I know that's where he would have put it.' Ellen thrust her hand into the opening she'd made, fingers scrabbling urgently inside.

'Put what?' the Doctor prompted.

'None of your damned business! Now get out of my life!'

'Ellen,' the Doctor returned softly, 'you've just ascribed responsibility to me for the loss of your inheritance. I should say that makes it very much my business. Now, what have you found?'

Ellen had drawn a slick oilskin bag out from the cavity and

was cradling it in her arms as if she'd found the Holy Grail. A smile of triumph smeared her face, wiping away the bitter lines. 'I was right! He did find something after all.' She raised her eyes and stared at them triumphantly. 'You see, all David had left to leave me were some of his papers – research notes he'd kept. From those, and certain comments he'd let slip to me when we last met, I came to believe that in the last year of his life he had actually discovered something.'

'He'd finally found a lost artefact.' The Doctor frowned. 'But if that were so, then why did he make a secret of his discovery?'

'You never really knew David at all, did you?' Ellen's lips twisted resentfully. 'My brother wasn't in it for the glory or the money. He was addicted to the thrill of the hunt and, if he had succeeded in tracking down anything, all he'd have wanted to do was hoard it for his own personal satisfaction. He'd never have parted with it.'

'But why hide it here?' Nyssa asked. 'I mean, if he knew he was going to have to sell the castle –'

'It was far safer here than in the bedsits in which he lived out the last few months of his life,' Ellen said. 'And as I said, no one else knew about this hiding place. Only the two of us. And if he meant anyone to have it, it was me.'

'To have what? You haven't even opened the package,' the Doctor reminded her. 'How do you know there's anything in there at all, let alone anything of value?'

'Oh I know all right, Doctor,' Ellen said with absolute conviction. 'Like I said, David left me his research papers. That's how I pieced the puzzle together.' She stroked the sleek oilskin bag with possessive fingers, then ripped the seal open. 'Have you ever heard of the Jewels of Helen?'

Rhiannon tapped her fingers irritably on the stone, but no one below heard her. This was so boring. Grown-up talk was always dull. All her mother talked about was the telly, and what a pain Rhiannon, Jason and their dad were. This conversation wasn't much better. She didn't understand any of it and she was tired of sitting still. She'd jump down and scare them all silly, that's what she'd do.

Rhiannon turned her head and glanced through the window immediately opposite her into the gardens beyond. Much to her annoyance she could see Jason prowling about among the rose bushes. Rhiannon scowled. Now she'd have to stay where she was until he'd gone.

A bright fountain of gold spilt out over Ellen's eager fingers, a glittering diadem of gold pieces caught like fragments of sun on gold wire. Nyssa drew in a sharp breath of astonishment.

'Oh yes,' the Doctor murmured guardedly. 'I've heard of the Jewels of Helen. The head-dress which Heinrich Schliemann allegedly found while excavating the city of Troy in 1873, part of the so-called Treasure of Priam, which vanished in Berlin in 1945.'

'Allegedly? So-called?' Ellen mocked, holding up the diadem so that it swung and sparkled in her hands like a living thing. 'Are you blind? David succeeded in tracking it down. It's here, in front of your eyes, Doctor!'

'May I?' Without waiting for an answer the Doctor took the head-dress from Ellen's fingers. Startled at his action, she made no protest until it was in his hands. 'Oh, I just want to look at it,' the Doctor reassured her as he took his half-moon spectacles out of his pocket and peered through them. 'Don't worry, you'll get it back.'

'What do you intend to do with it?' Nyssa enquired of Ellen, observing the woman's tense face and the way her eyes remained fixed on the diadem as the Doctor carefully scrutinized it from every angle.

'Sell it to the highest bidder,' Ellen said bluntly. 'The proceeds will buy back my inheritance.'

'Your inheritance means a great deal to you,' Nyssa observed.

'Why wouldn't it? I was born at the castle – it's my home.'

'Most people grow up and leave home, Ellen,' the Doctor murmured.

'Some of us don't have any choice in the matter,' was Nyssa's quiet comment. Her eyes were suddenly full of pain.

'You can't buy back the past, Ellen. You can only let it go and move on from it.'

'I don't want to let it go,' Ellen said harshly. 'The past was the only place in which I was happy, and I want it back. I have no career, no lasting relationship. All I've done is lurch from one crisis to another, a disaster junkie enjoying wallowing in her misfortune. Poor little me!' Her smile was savage. 'But not any more. I'm tired of being the one who loses out. This time I'm going to get what I want, what I deserve to have. Trentillys Castle should have come to me, and now it will. Give me back what's mine!' She held out her hand.

The Doctor met her steely gaze with a shake of his head. 'I don't think you're wise to cling to the past like this,' he said, 'but it's your choice. Here.' He dropped the diadem onto her outstretched fingers.

'Is it genuine, Doctor?' Nyssa asked.

'It's undoubtably the same as the head-dress modelled by Sophie Schliemann – Schliemann's daughter – all those years ago,' he returned thoughtfully. 'Something about it seems familiar for another reason, however, but I can't quite ...'

Ellen raised the diadem, a look of almost childlike eagerness on her face. 'The Jewels of Ellen!' she mocked.

'It's alien technology,' the Doctor began. 'I wouldn't –'

'Alien technology?' Ellen laughed in his face. 'Don't be so ridiculous.' She set the diadem on her head.

The Doctor and Nyssa saw the golden pieces trickle into place around Ellen's face and watched her shake her head so that the cascade swung in the sunlight like a golden bell. Her expression was exultant. But then the diadem flashed suddenly brighter, almost as if something inside it had caught light. And Ellen shrieked in terror, raising her hands to her head as if to tear it away.

'Doctor!' Nyssa made an instinctive move forwards, but the Doctor gripped hold of her arm and stopped her. His expression was as horrified as hers.

'Don't!' he said sharply. 'It's too late …'

The light intensified, one burning wave after another washing over Ellen's face until it was suffused in a blazing halo of golden fire. Her mouth opened in one final soundless scream and then the light died and her body crumpled. She came to rest sprawled in the dust, stiff and silent. The diadem slithered free and lay curled in its own gleaming coils.

'Is she dead?' Nyssa whispered.

The Doctor knelt next to Ellen's inert body, his fingers fumbling for a pulse. 'I'm afraid so.' He raised his face to Nyssa and she saw the shadow the woman's death had laid upon it, how his eyes were suddenly heavy with the memories of choices made. And not just the choices made by others, she judged, but also the decisions he'd taken almost in passing with never a thought to their consequences.

She swallowed hard. 'How did it happen, Doctor? It looked almost as if the diadem itself caused it, as if it suffered a power surge of some kind. But it was only a piece of jewellery!'

The Doctor sighed, shaking his head. 'It was much more than that, Nyssa. It was living jewellery. The wearer completes a psychic circuit and their appearance is correspondingly enhanced.'

'But how could humans have created something that sophisticated so long ago in their past?'

'They couldn't, and they didn't.' The Doctor stood up, burrowing his hands into his pockets. 'I don't know if Helen of Troy ever wore that diadem, Nyssa – though if she had, it would explain a great deal about her legendary charms – but I do know that it wasn't manufactured on Earth. I recognize the technology now: I once saw something similar on Tarron.' He frowned. 'I always thought that the relics that I threw out of the TARDIS would be obliterated by time winds, but this one must have escaped destruction and somehow ended up on Earth.'

'But it was manufactured as an adornment, not as a weapon?'

'Probably, given that it was modelled by Sophie Schliemann when her father discovered it and she came to no harm.' The Doctor stared down at the diadem. 'This may have been a malfunction, or perhaps a more sinister subroutine was activated.'

'That poor woman,' Nyssa said, her face grave as she stared down at Ellen's body. 'How tragic.'

'How needless,' the Doctor returned, his voice a sombre echo of Ellen's own words.

'She was so adamant that the treasure belonged to her.'

'In the end she belonged to the treasure,' the Doctor said sadly. He prodded the diadem with the toe of one shoe. 'And now its power is spent. Nyssa, I think it's time we left.'

'Shouldn't we inform the police?'

'Somehow I don't think that would be a very good idea,' the Doctor demurred. 'The art of knowing when to make a discreet exit shouldn't be undervalued. The body will be discovered in due course, and our staying here really won't help anyone.'

'I suppose not,' Nyssa agreed reluctantly. 'But are you sure the diadem really is inactive now?'

'Oh yes. Well,' the Doctor amended, 'fairly sure.'

Nyssa eyed the glittering heap in revulsion. 'I don't think we should just leave it here, Doctor.'

'You want it as a keepsake?' He raised his eyebrows, startled at the idea.

'No!' Nyssa stepped forward determinedly, stooped and snatched up the diadem. 'I have a much better idea.'

She crossed to the nearest window and a ripple of gold slipped through her fingers as she dropped the head-dress into the water. 'There,' she said in grim satisfaction. 'Let it lie in peace.'

The scream that ripped through the still summer air startled Jason as he amused himself by idly pulling the heads off roses and shredding the petals. It wasn't his sister's voice, he decided at once. Rhiannon could shriek like a banshee when she was thwarted but the tone to this was much deeper. It was a woman's voice and it had come from the stone grotto by the lake. Jason set off to investigate.

Bill Hignett marched out of his booth, having heard the boy

yelling as he came racing up the path like a scalded cat.

'There's a dead body in the grotto! Come quick!'

'Don't talk such rubbish,' Bill snorted, eyeing the boy disparagingly. 'Here, aren't your parents looking for you?'

'Go see for yourself,' the boy panted. 'She's not moving and I bet she's dead!'

'Any more of your tales and I'll fetch you one, law or no law,' Bill threatened. 'Now push off, you little –'

'But there *is* a body!' the boy insisted. 'A woman in a white dress, just lying there...'

An image leapt into Bill's mind: a white dress, a black straw hat and a fall of sleek blonde hair. He hesitated.

'If this is a wind-up ...' he threatened.

'It's not, honest!'

Another visitor came running up the path to endorse the boy's story, telling much the same tale in between distraught gasps. Bill hovered, torn with indecision about the correct course of action, and then to his relief spotted Sally Thomas coming down the path from the castle to retrieve the tea tray.

'Sally!' he yelled. 'There's been an accident or something. Get hold of the police, and the ambulance, will you?'

'An ambulance won't do no good now,' said the boy derisively. 'I keep telling you, she's dead. Her face is all twisted up like –'

'Hey, where d'you think you two are off to?' Bill demanded, cutting off the boy's morbid description in full flow.

His words were addressed to the blond man and the girl who were attempting to slip unobtrusively past him.

'Who? Us?' the Doctor asked guilelessly.

'Yes, you. I hear there's been an incident down at the grotto. The police are on their way and they'll want to question everyone in the vicinity.' Bill was beginning to get into his stride now. 'So I'll have to ask you to wait here.'

'Ah,' said the Doctor, hands fishing in his pockets and then flourishing a pass under Bill's nose. 'Have you heard of UNIT? I'm a scientific adviser. They're expecting me, you see. Immediately.' The Doctor smiled his most winning smile.

'Of course I've heard of UNIT,' said Bill, insulted as only an ex-serviceman could be. He took a quick glance at the pass. It certainly looked official enough. And if the man was one of those science johnnies, well, that explained his eccentric appearance.

'Naturally we'd love to stay and be of assistance, but we've simply not the time for it. In any case, I think there's someone over there who might be able to help you.' The Doctor gestured vaguely down the empty path in a last-ditch attempt to divert the man's interest. It worked.

'Oh, there is, is there?' Bill made his mind up. After all, who was he to hold up someone on United Nations business? 'All right, off you go. But everyone else is to stay here, mind.'

As the Doctor and Nyssa departed, so staff alerted by Sally to the crisis began to flood out from the castle entrance. Emboldened by this sign of reinforcements, Bill felt it was his duty to go and check out what the Doctor had said. Accordingly he marched smartly down the path and, as he turned onto the terraces, was rewarded by coming face to face with the man he imagined he was seeking.

'Now then,' Bill said officiously. 'I hear tell you know something about a death.'

Now that the grotto was quiet, Rhiannon began to whimper slightly, a thin sound like a whipped dog. Her mind told her to jump down and run, but her body refused to obey, and her legs felt rubbery and useless. So she stayed where she was, shivering with fright, huddling back against the cold stones and staring down at the woman's body. Then finally, with a great effort, she managed to turn her head away from the corpse so that she was looking down into the water.

The grotto may have been quiet, but the water beyond it was not. Rhiannon watched in growing fear as waves began to ripple steadily from an underwater source. Then something gold blazed sharp and bright in the water and framed within it she saw the dead woman's face, twisted like a screaming angel.

UNITed We Fall

By Keith R.A. DeCandido

'How much longer do I have to wait?'

According to the nameplate on her cluttered desk, the young woman's name was Holly Roman. She didn't even look up at Brigadier Alastair Gordon Lethbridge-Stewart (ret.) as she answered his question with a lackadaisical 'As soon as Mr Fontaine's done with his meeting, Brigadier, he'll see you.'

Lethbridge-Stewart refused to let his annoyance at this tiresome American woman show through. Even after a decade and a half of retirement, he was too good a soldier for that.

He looked at his watch. It read, 9:27. His meeting with Stephen Joseph Fontaine III, Attorney-at-Law, had been scheduled for 0900 at the offices of Nissen Gibson Fontaine. Lethbridge-Stewart had always prided himself on his punctuality, and he found it particularly galling that these Americans refused to do likewise.

After what seemed ages, though Lethbridge-Stewart's watch insisted that it was only three minutes, the door to one of the other offices opened to permit several people to come out. One, a tall, dignified-looking gentleman in a light grey suit with hair to match, headed for the Brigadier while the others left the reception area. This had to be UNIT's American counsel.

As the Brigadier stood up from the reception-area couch, the man offered his hand. 'You must be Brigadier Stewart. A pleasure, sir. I'm Stephen Fontaine.'

'That's *Lethbridge*-Stewart,' he replied, returning the handshake.

'Oh, I'm sorry,' Fontaine said with a genuine look of regret. 'I obviously misread the files and missed a hyphen.'

'Quite all right,' the Brigadier said brusquely, not wishing to dwell on it.

Fontaine indicated the way to his office. 'In any event, we should get started. We do have a great deal of ground to cover before the hearings start up this afternoon.'

'In that case,' the Brigadier said plainly as he followed Fontaine into his office, 'perhaps we should have started this meeting on time.'

'You're absolutely right, of course, Brigadier. Again, I must apologize. The partners' meeting ran a bit longer than it should have. Please, have a seat.'

Lethbridge-Stewart followed Fontaine into a massive office. Shag carpeting lined the floor, bookcases stuffed with huge tomes decorated the walls to his left and right, and directly in front of him sat an oak desk that had to be at least two metres wide. Behind it, the entire back wall was taken up with a picture window that provided a magnificent view of the East River.

The middle of Fontaine's desk was festooned with wire baskets, and from one of them he retrieved a folder as he sat down. 'Now then, Brigadier, I assume you know why you've been summoned to New York?'

Summoned? the Brigadier thought, but let it go. The letters he'd received from the Secretary and from Brigadier Bambera were requests—strong requests, admittedly, but hardly a summons. 'I was told,' he said, 'that the oversight committee that monitors UNIT's requisitions has called a hearing to investigate some appropriations made by the British division over the years.'

Fontaine nodded. 'Particularly, I'm afraid, during your tenure as head of the British division.'

'I was also told by Brigadier Bambera'—and here Lethbridge-Stewart allowed a tiny amount of annoyance to creep into his tone – 'that her equipment has been impounded and shipped here and that her soldiers are on standby pending the results of this investigation.'

'I'm afraid so,' Fontaine said. 'However, I've been going over the requisitions that the committee will be asking you about, and I can say with confidence that you don't have *too* much to worry about. *Most* of them are just fine. In fact' – and at this Fontaine once again smiled his pleasant smile – 'at first, I began to wonder if this was all some kind of wild-goose chase to keep some bureaucrat from losing his job.'

'I'm glad to hear that,' the Brigadier said neutrally. He had thought much the same thing, of course, but saw no reason to say so outright.

'Although,' Fontaine continued, 'I can see why there might be a certain amount of trepidation on their parts. For example, your ammunition requisitions are quite extreme.'

'It is necessary for the types of threats UNIT faces to –'

Fontaine held up a hand, and again the smile returned. 'Easy, Brigadier, you're preaching to the choir. Of course, I understand the need for these requisitions, but I have to look at how the committee will react.' The smile then fell. 'Unfortunately, I was a bit concerned about a large number of items from your scientific branch. In particular'– and here he shuffled through several papers until he came across the one he obviously wanted – 'ones made by the British division's "unpaid scientific adviser" throughout UNIT's first decade or so. Computers, top-of-the-line scanning equipment – honestly, Brigadier, I can't even figure out who this adviser is; he's not listed on any of the payroll vouchers.'

'He wouldn't be, Mr Fontaine. He was, as you said, an *unpaid* scientific adviser.'

'A fair point,' Fontaine said, with a somewhat less pleasant smile, 'but I'm afraid I'm still going to need some kind of justification for this – well, exorbitance is the only word that comes to mind to describe these requisitions.'

Lethbridge-Stewart sighed. 'That will be difficult. The Doctor is a very unique individual.'

'This Doctor Whoever-He-Is is the adviser?'

'Yes. A type of freelance consultant, I suppose you could call him. Not the most reliable chap in the world sometimes, but he always came through in a crisis. In many ways, the Doctor is responsible for UNIT's existence.' Unbidden, images of the

hideous web that crippled London's Underground, courtesy of
the Yeti, and of a Cybermen invasion came to the fore of the
Brigadier's thoughts; even after all these years, the memories
of those terrible days remained strong. 'If not for the Doctor –
and his requisitions – I sincerely doubt there would be a planet
left for the pair of us to be discussing these issues on.'

'Mmm.' Fontaine did not look convinced. 'The fact remains, Brigadier, that we are discussing them, and frankly a
great deal of what I have in this file is, at best, an outrageous
abuse of this Doctor's access to UN equipment.'

'You can rest assured, Mr Fontaine, that, if the Doctor made
those requisitions, he had good reason.'

'Perhaps you and I can rest assured, Brigadier, but I doubt
the committee will buy that particular line of reasoning.'

Fontaine then hesitated. Lethbridge-Stewart got the feeling
that he was not going to like what the counsellor would say
next.

'These are much more – open times, Brigadier. In your day,
it was unlikely that word would get out that one of the UN's top-
secret divisions has been spending large sums of money.
Frankly, we can't count on that any more. And the outcry
against the British division's expenditures would be extreme.
Now our best course of action would be to get this Doctor
person in here to testify.'

Lethbridge-Stewart sighed. He had been hoping it would
not come to that, but he supposed it would be inevitable.
However, summoning the Doctor could prove difficult.

Before he could voice this objection to Fontaine, he noticed
a familiar sound, growing in intensity. The Brigadier allowed
the tiniest hint of a smile to play across his lips as he saw the
blue form of a police box slowly materialize approximately one
metre to Fontaine's left.

'What the hell's that?' Fontaine cried, his placid face
suddenly a mask of confusion.

'That, Mr Fontaine, would be the Doctor.' The Time Lord
always did know how to make an entrance.

The Brigadier was surprised to see that the Doctor who

emerged from the TARDIS was the tall one who wore the long scarf; he hadn't encountered this Doctor in almost two decades. Although of roughly the same height as Lethbridge-Stewart, this incarnation of the Time Lord always carried himself as though he towered over everyone. His presence discommoded the Brigadier, but only slightly. He'd encountered Doctors 'out of sequence' before, so to speak. Of course, both times it happened, the entirety of time and space was threatened.

Somewhere under his curly hair and large hat, a smile burst forth. 'Hello, Brigadier. So good to see you again. How are things with UNIT?' Without waiting for a reply, he turned to Fontaine (presently standing with his mouth hanging open in what Lethbridge-Stewart thought a most undignified manner), and said, 'Hello, I'm the Doctor. I'm very pleased to make your acquaintance. Now then, Brigadier,' he said, turning back to Lethbridge-Stewart without pausing for breath, 'what have you been doing with yourself all these years? I assume it is many years, since I can't imagine you ageing that quickly.'

'Quite right, Doctor. Since, ah, last we met, I've retired. Turned the British division over to new blood, so to speak. Still, I occasionally pitch in and help out, as I'm doing today.'

'Ah yes, well, that brings us nicely to the relevant point, that being what it is that is so urgent that you felt the need to engage the recall device.'

The Brigadier blinked. 'The recall device?'

'Yes. You know, I did instruct that it only be used in emergencies. Still, I was between engagements, as it were, and I'm always happy to visit old Earth again.' The Doctor turned to look through the window. 'Ah! New York! I won't have been here for several years ago now.'

Before Lethbridge-Stewart could say anything further, Fontaine exploded, 'What the *hell* is going *on* here? Who *is* this guy?' Gone was the urbane, collected Stephen Fontaine who had been calmly telling the Brigadier about public outcries and outrageous appropriations. In his place stood a man whose world had tilted somewhat sharply and who was trying desperately to regain his footing. Lethbridge-Stewart recognized the look, as he had often had it himself in his early dealings with the Time Lord.

'Mr Fontaine, this is the Doctor, UNIT's unpaid scientific adviser. Doctor, this is Stephen Joseph Fontaine III, UNIT's American counsel.'

'Ah, a member of the legal profession,' the Doctor said with a nod. 'That would explain the opulent office, the books on the bookshelf, and that rather unfortunate tie. In any case, Brigadier, what, exactly, is the emergency that brought me here?'

Fontaine pointed at the Doctor, and asked, 'This is the unpaid scientific adviser?'

Giving Fontaine a cautionary glance, the Brigadier said, 'Let me explain, Doctor. You see, UNIT's British division has been made the subject of an appropriations hearing. I'm afraid we're in danger of being shut down due to massive expenditures that the committee that controls such things is a touch wary of. Pending the results, the division's equipment has been impounded, the soldiers placed on standby.'

'An appropriations hearing? Brigadier, are you trying to tell me that the recall device, a device I gave you with the utmost reluctance and which is only to be used in the instance of a world-threatening emergency, was used to bring me halfway across the galaxy for an appropriations hearing?'

'No, Doctor, I am not telling you that.'

The Doctor frowned. 'You're not?'

'I didn't employ the recall device. No one did – it's one of the pieces of equipment that have been impounded. However, your coming is fortuitous. We'll need you to testify before the committee this afternoon.'

Fontaine, having finally regained some measure of his composure, came back into the conversation: 'I'm sorry, Brigadier, but this gentleman is not testifying.'

'I must agree with Mr Fontaine, Brigadier. I have better things to do with my time than babble in front of bureaucrats.'

The Brigadier set his jaw. This wasn't the first time he'd had to face down the Time Lord, and it probably wouldn't be the last, either. 'Doctor, the primary reason why it was deemed necessary to even call a hearing was the somewhat unusual requisitions made by the British division's unpaid scientific adviser, the vast majority of which were nonsensical, incomprehensible and impossible for anyone to justify.'

'Incomprehensible?' The Doctor faced the Brigadier nose-to-nose. 'Brigadier, anything I requested was important, no, *critical* to my continuing researches!'

'Be that as it may, Doctor, you are the only one who can justify these expenditures. And if you cannot, it is quite possible that the British division will be deemed wasteful and dissolved.'

Fontaine interrupted. 'Brigadier, I can't put this – this – this reject from the Harpo Marx lookalike contest in front of the committee!' Realizing he had lost control again, Fontaine took a breath, then continued in a quieter tone. 'Even if he can justify the expenditures, there is simply no way the committee will take him seriously. I mean look at him – *listen* to him. The man has just calmly stated he's from another galaxy.'

'This galaxy, actually,' the Doctor said, then turned to Lethbridge-Stewart. 'Very well, Brigadier, if you insist, I will testify before this committee. What time is the hearing?'

'Sixteen hundred hours at the UN building.'

'And what time is it now?'

'Approximately O nine fifty hours.'

'Excellent. I will meet you there.' The Doctor walked to the office door and opened it.

'Hold on a second, please!' Fontaine pleaded.

The Doctor stopped halfway through the doorway and turned back towards the attorney. 'Is there a problem, Mr Fontaine?'

'If you *are* going to testify, we have to review your testimony, examine the evidence, see what we can–'

'Yes yes yes yes yes, I'm sure there are a thousand things we can do to justify your no doubt exorbitant retainer, but it's completely unnecessary. The committee will ask about the equipment I requisitioned, I will answer the questions, and that will be that. Simple, hmmm?' the Doctor finished with a huge grin.

'No, it's not that simple. Do you have any idea of the legal complications involved?'

The Doctor resumed his walk through the door. 'Oh, I have a very good idea, Mr Fontaine. I simply choose to ignore them. Now, if you'll excuse me, since I am in New York, I'm going to take in the sights. I haven't been to the Metropolitan Museum of Art since fifty years from now.'

Fontaine stood with his mouth hanging open as the Doctor left, then cried out after him, 'What about this damn *phone booth* in my office?'

Robin Oemington looked at his watch. *C'mon, c'mon, dammit, Holly, call me. Tell me he's arrived.*

Calm. Calm down. Stay calm. Don't want your 'employer' to think anything's amiss now, do we? After all, that would blow my cover. And nobody's ever broken my cover before.

Strictly speaking, that wasn't true. But Robin didn't like to think about that. It just made him mad, and he couldn't afford to get mad, as he'd blow his cover.

It always came back to that, somehow.

Only blown my cover once. Just once, you bastard, and it ruined me. You'll pay for that. Oh, yes.

The phone rang. He pounced on it. 'Robin Oemington,' he said.

'Robin, it's Holly. Something's wrong. That doctor guy showed up – I don't know how he came in, he didn't come through the front door – but anyhow, he showed up after I pushed that button you told me to push, and then he left.'

'When?' Robin said anxiously. *He can't leave, goddammit, why did he leave?*

'About three seconds ago. Mr Fontaine and that brigadier are still here.'

'Damn, damn, *damn*! He wasn't supposed to leave!'

'That's what I thought.'

'How could you let him leave?'

'Whaddaya mean, "let him"? How was I supposed to –'

'Never mind.' Robin's mind raced. *Everything had been so perfect, how could it be messed up now?*

Then a thought occurred. 'Are you sure it was him?' he asked. 'What did he look like?'

'I didn't really get a good look at his face. He had on this big hat and coat, and this amazing scarf. It –'

'That's him, all right. One of him, anyhow. Dammit!'

It's been so much work to set this up, and now he's ruined it all. Again. He always messes things up.

'Holly, did he say anything – *anything* – that might've indicated where he was going?'

The other end of the line grew silent, presumably while Holly thought about it. *This could take hours*, Robin thought uncharitably. But then, Holly's inability to think was precisely why he recruited her for this mission. She had been willing to believe his convincing lies about why he needed to lure the Doctor here.

Finally: 'I think he was going to the Met.'

Why do I bother? 'They don't show operas at ten in the morning, Holly.'

'Not the Metropolitan Opera, silly, the Metropolitan Museum.'

Robin cursed himself. *Of course it wasn't the opera, you moron.* 'That's perfect. I'll be by in about fifteen minutes to get the recall device.'

'The what?'

'The blue thing I gave you that had the button to push.'

'Oh, that.'

'I'll see you in a bit.' And without waiting for her to say anything, he hung up.

He couldn't believe it. Everything had been set up.

Robin had stolen the Doctor's equipment from impound and given it to Betancourt to make into a bomb. Betancourt had questioned this – his own equipment was more reliable – but Robin didn't want the bomb to be traceable except to the Doctor himself. Not that Betancourt needed the protection; after all, the bomb maker's friends in high places had kept him out of jail thus far...

Robin then planted the bomb in the committee room. Holly had used the stolen recall device to summon the Doctor to Fontaine's office, so he'd be prepared to testify. Then he'd go to the UN building not suspecting a thing and die horribly.

Just like he deserves. Screwing me over and getting me stuck with low-level infiltration and surveillance. No promotions. No advancement. Stagnation. Purgatory. Misery.

And it's all the Doctor's fault.

But now, now the Doctor's going to the Metropolitan bloody Museum of all places. Which means he probably contrived some excuse not to testify.

Well, then, I'll just have to take care of it myself, won't I?

He opened his bottom desk drawer. In it sat the revolver he'd got his hands on as a backup. His superiors never issued him with a weapon. After all, his work primarily involved surveillance. The guns were left to others.

If not for the Doctor, I'd have my own gun. I'd be one of those others who get to carry them. But no, I'm just a low-level spook, and that's all I'll be, Doctor. You'll pay for that. Dearly.

Informing his titular supervisor that he had some errands to run before the hearings this afternoon, Robin left the UN building and made his way to the offices of Nissen Gibson Fontaine to retrieve the recall device. *Just like with the bomb – don't want to leave any kind of trail behind.*

'Ah yes, excellent,' Robin heard the Doctor say to no one in particular, staring at one of the carvings in the wall of the Temple of Dendur. 'You know,' he said to an elderly woman who happened to be walking by, 'they were talking about simplifying things by only displaying one foot in the side view, but I told them, "Don't be ridiculous – on a flat plane like this, with this style? You have to show both feet, one in front of the other, otherwise it'll look as if they've only got one foot!" '

Robin gritted his teeth as he read the card next to the alligator statue that sat in the moat that the museum had placed around the temple. It had been like this for almost two hours. From the

Lila Acheson Wallace wing, where Robin finally found the
Doctor carrying on about how he told Seurat not to use so many
dots, to the Arms and Armour collection, where he mentioned
that Charles V never wore anything that ornate when *he* met
him, to the American wing, where he explained to passers-by
that they should enjoy it now, as the whole wing would be torn
down in a little under seventy-five years.

Now he stood there going on about the advice he gave to the
ancient Egyptians who built the Temple of Dendur.

*I can't take this any more. No more. He's got to die now. This
second.*

But he held himself back. Drawing attention to himself
inside a crowded museum would be a mistake. Firing a gun
inside the Met would bring a whole heap of trouble down, and
escape would be damned near impossible.

*Listen to him go on and on like a gibbering idiot, wearing
that stupid scarf and not even sweating even though it's mid-
summer and there's all these people around, and he ruined
everything and he doesn't even care, he's just standing there
admiring the artwork...*

Maybe it would be a mistake. But right now, I don't care.

The Doctor stood near a sarcophagus that sat right under the
floor-to-ceiling window. That window, which led out to Central Park, took up the entire north wall of this ground-floor
exhibit area. Robin approached the Doctor slowly, knowing
that he would have nowhere to run except right at Robin
himself.

*Here. It ends here. No more waiting. No more planning.
Now he dies.*

At about ten feet from the Doctor, he unholstered the gun.

There was no room. There was no temple. There was no
sarcophagus. There was just the Doctor, Robin and Robin's
gun.

Sweat formed on his brow, but he ignored it.

He took aim.

His hands shook, but he forced himself to remain steady.

Someone screamed.

He pulled the trigger.

The bullet missed the Doctor, instead hitting the window behind him. It made an odd slamming sound, not at all the crashing noise Robin expected from cracking glass.

More people screamed and fell to the ground.

An alarm clanged in his ears.

One of the blue-uniformed guards – an older man who looked about as intimidating as a flea – ran towards Robin.

The Doctor turned towards him. He said something, but Robin couldn't hear for the alarm clanging over and over again.

Robin took another shot. This, too, missed, striking instead the stone sarcophagus and ricocheting into the window.

Another odd slamming noise.

This looks a lot easier on television, Robin thought as he tried to aim more carefully. His hands still shook, worse than before, but he had to stay steady.

All these years, I can't mess it up now.

The Doctor turned and ran straight for the window, specifically the part of the window that had been cracked by Robin's two shots, wrapping his hands in that stupid scarf as he ran.

Oh no! Robin thought, as he realized that the Doctor did have another way out – through the window! Robin started running after him, pausing only to knock the guard down with an elbow to the stomach.

The alarm kept clanging. People kept screaming. The sweat was starting to get in Robin's eyes.

His hands now protected by his scarf, the Doctor took a running jump right into the weakened glass. It shattered, and the Doctor ran into Central Park.

Cursing, Robin wiped the sweat from his eyes, took another shot – which also missed – then ran after his prey, several other guards on his heels.

Had he been chasing someone else, Robin would probably have lost him in the verdant park, full as it was of people sunbathing, walking, jogging, rollerblading, and so forth. But the Doctor's distinctive mode of dress made him easy to track down.

Robin chased the Doctor westward for a bit, then south down the paved road behind the museum. The Doctor cut right towards Cleopatra's Needle, then through to the Great Lawn, but Robin did not give up the chase. He could not. Not after all this.

Once they were out on the Lawn, Robin took another shot. It, too, missed, but Robin decided to blame that on the fact that both he and his target were in motion.

The various and sundry people around them took little notice of one man chasing another, but when Robin fired his gun, several decided either to scream or to run – or both. Robin ignored them.

The Doctor continued onward, running across the softball fields that dotted the Lawn (some of which had games in progress) towards Belvedere Lake. As Robin followed, one of the softball players tried to stop him, but Robin just knocked him over without breaking stride.

No one's coming between us, Doctor.

If only I can catch up. He had only two bullets left, and, as had been made abundantly clear, he simply did not have the skill to fire accurately from anything other than point-blank range.

The Doctor continued running towards the seaweed-choked lake. *Oh Christ, he's not going to jump in, is he?* But no, the Doctor cut left to run around the lake. Robin continued to chase him, wiping more sweat from his brow. *Shouldn't have worn the jacket in this heat*, he thought, looking down at his chest, *but I had to conceal the gun somehow. Complications, there are always damn' complications.*

His quarry ran around the circumference of the lake. If he kept going, he'd take the paved road that led up the hill to Belvedere Castle, a small edifice that sat overlooking the lake and the Great Lawn.

Perfect. This all started in a castle. Only fitting that I end it there.

Indeed, the Doctor did run straight up the tree-lined path that led to the castle, which these days served as a weather station, as well as providing a nice view of the park. If Robin was lucky, the Doctor would run into a cul-de-sac, and then Robin would finally have him.

Sure enough, the Doctor took a sharp right and found himself up against a small wall, beyond which sat a rather big drop into the lake.

Other people milled about, taking in the view and reading the plaques that described the tiny castle. Robin fired his gun into the air to get everyone's attention, then cried, 'Everyone get away from here, now!' He pointed the gun right at the Doctor. 'Except you.'

Most people got away from there. Two young men didn't seem to want to leave. 'Yo, what's up with this?'

Robin pointed his gun at the pair of them. 'I said get away!'

The two kids put up their hands, and moved slowly off, muttering curses to themselves.

'Excuse me, may I interject a word here?' the Doctor asked.

'If you want. Or you could turn around and jump – it'd save me the trouble.'

'I'd rather not. I've never been fond of falls from great heights. Well, that is to say, the falls themselves are quite fine; however there's this jarring stop at the end of it that's most unpleas –'

'Shut up! All you do is just talk and talk and talk.'

'Not all I do, no. Sometimes I ask questions. For example, one that springs to mind on this particular occasion is, "Why?" '

Robin's mouth fell open. 'Why? You have the gall to ask why?'

The Doctor shrugged. 'It is the first question that springs to mind when someone starts shooting at me for no good reason.'

'You don't remember me, do you? After you deliberately set the castle wardens on me?'

'This castle doesn't have any wardens.'

Robin rolled his eyes. He was as bad as Holly. 'Not this castle, you jackass – Trentillys Castle!'

'What, old David Gosthorpe's place?'

Robin's eyes widened. 'You *do* remember!'

'Remember what?'

Snarling, Robin said, 'The castle! That woman dying! Those guards being set on me! The little girl! All my surveillance work shot *completely* to hell!'

'Sorry, that doesn't ring any bells. Perhaps you're mixing me up with someone else. People tell me I have that kind of face, you know.'

'Shut up!' Robin cried, aiming the gun right at the Doctor's temple. 'It was you! You had a different face, but I've read your file. You've had repeated plastic surgery. And don't tell me you don't remember! You destroyed my entire career. Two years of work investigating David Gosthorpe's business dealings, and you ruined it by telling those guards that someone else around the corner could help them. They questioned me for an hour, and blew my cover.

'Do you have any idea what that *meant*? After that, it was nothing but crapass surveillance and infiltration. The kind of low-level garbage they give to the new recruits. It wasn't until they had me infiltrate the UN that I found UNIT's files – including one on you.'

'Unit? Do you mean a unit of measurement?'

Robin blinked. 'Don't pull this crap on me! You've been associated with UNIT for *years!*'

'Oh, you mean it's an organization of some sort,' the Doctor said, a look of realization spreading over his face.

But that's not possible, Robin thought. *He can't not know UNIT. He just can't, dammit!* 'You think you can play dumb, don't you? Well, it won't work. You think you're here by accident?' He took the recall device out of his jacket pocket. 'I'm the one who brought you here with this thing! I'm the one who drew the committee's attention to your stupid requisitions!'

'Requisitions? I'm afraid I've no idea what you're speaking of. Perhaps if you –'

Don't give me that, goddammit! 'I know you're here for the hearing with the UN because I brought you here for it! And I'm the one who used your old equipment to build the bomb and have it planted in the hearing room so you'd finally pay for what you did! But no, you couldn't just go to the damned hearing and get blown up, you had to go gallivanting off to the damned museum so you could convince everyone you're crazy. That's all you do, isn't it?'

'What, convince people I'm crazy?'

'No! You *ruin* things!' Robin's throat grew hoarse from all the yelling. His breathing became more rapid. *This is going all wrong. He's supposed to be begging me for mercy, not –*

'Freeze!'

Robin whirled around to see two uniformed police officers, each holding a gun on him.

'Don't move, son,' the darker-skinned cop, whose nameplate read 'Hawkins', continued. 'Just put the gun down, and nobody'll get hurt.'

The fair-haired one, who was named Drew, looked over at the Doctor. 'You OK, sir?'

'Oh, fine, merely having a bracing chat with this fellow here.'

Robin couldn't believe it. *I should've just shot him when I had the chance. But when he pulled that stupid act –*

And then it hit him. *Stupid act.* It was all an act. The Doctor had manipulated Robin into telling him everything, and stalled long enough for the police to arrive. *Oldest trick in the book, and I fell for it.*

His gun still aimed at the Doctor's head, he said, 'Officers, this is official government business. You're in over your head. This man is extremely dangerous.'

Hawkins said, 'This man has bad taste in clothes, but that don't make him dangerous. Now please, put the gun down.'

'You don't know what you're doing.'

'I'm telling you to put the gun down, sir. Now.'

Not now, not when I'm so damn' close.

'Sir, I'm gonna ask you one more time to put the gun down.'

Robin turned sharply towards the officer, still holding the gun.

Too late: Robin realized that he now had the gun trained on

Drew, and he knew exactly how the two officers would react.

Before he could lower the gun, both Drew and Hawkins opened fire.

Then everything went black.

The Doctor groaned inwardly as the two police officers fired on the man who'd been chasing him. As soon as he fell, the Doctor ran over to him.

'Sir, don't touch him he –'

'He appears to have fallen into a coma,' the Doctor said without looking up.

The man's gun was still in his right hand, the recall device in his left. The Doctor grabbed the device and put it in his own pocket.

The blond-haired officer grabbed the Doctor's arm. 'Sir, you just took evidence.'

'I took what is mine. I can assure you, you won't know what to do with it, and I might need it. Now this man has just told me that he's planted a bomb in the United Nations building.'

'What?' the other officer said. 'Look, I'm afraid we're going to have to take you down to the station so we can sort this all –'

'There isn't time!' the Doctor hissed. 'He said he made the bomb from my old equipment. Do you have any clue what that means? Hmmm?'

'Uh, no, I don't, I –'

'Look, officer' – he looked down at the man's nameplate – 'Hawkins, I don't have time to chat just now. There's a bomb I'll need to defuse. What time is it?'

Hawkins blinked and shook his head. 'What?'

The other one said, 'It's about twenty to four.'

'Then there's no time to lose. I must be off.' He turned and started to run off, then turned back when he remembered something. 'If you want to be useful, officer, contact your bomb squad and tell them to get over to the United Nations. It could be very important.'

'Wait a minute!'

But the Doctor ran off. He was worried that the two officers might give chase, but they seemed to have lent some credence to what the Doctor said, as the blond-haired one was yelling into his radio. This came as something of a relief to the Doctor, who half expected them to hold him at gunpoint until long after things had got out of hand.

Always good to get some variety once in a while.

He ran towards Fifth Avenue in search of a cab.

The Brigadier looked at his watch for the eighth time in the past five minutes while sitting on the bench outside the room where the appropriations hearings had begun. *Take it easy, Lethbridge-Stewart*, he admonished himself. *The Doctor will be here. Besides, Fontaine isn't finished with the preliminaries yet.*

But the Doctor was late. And that worried the Brigadier. The Doctor was capable of being punctual, but he also had a tendency to get distracted. Sometimes for days on end. And usually it was by something that threatened the very existence of humanity – or the entire Cosmos.

And then the Brigadier smiled. *I wonder how Fontaine would react to my telling him that the Doctor couldn't testify because he was fighting off a Yeti attack on the Empire State Building,* he thought. Retirement had given the Brigadier a sense of mischief he hadn't had since his school days.

Fontaine then came through the large oak double doors to the hearing room. He had on his smile, but this time it didn't quite make it to the counsellor's eyes. His eyes looked frightened. 'Well, Brigadier, the preliminaries are finished. I've called the Doctor to testify.' The smile fell, and the fright extended to the rest of his face. 'He's not here yet, is he?'

'I'm afraid not,' Lethbridge-Stewart admitted. 'But I'm sure he'll be here any minute.'

The smile returned to the bottom part of his face. 'Oh, good. Yes, that will be excellent. Most wonderful. Indeed.' Fontaine clapped his hands for no reason that the Brigadier could discern, then started pacing. He'd been like this all afternoon, ever since the Doctor had left. As they had looked over the various bits of documentation, every once in a while Fontaine would trail off and just stare at the Doctor's TARDIS, then resume in mid-sentence as if he'd never been distracted. It made for a most disjointed briefing.

'Ah, good, Brigadier, you're here. I was hoping you would be. Has the bomb squad arrived yet?'

Lethbridge-Stewart looked up to see the Doctor approaching hurriedly, several UN guards about four paces behind him.

Fontaine's eyes widened. 'Bomb squad?'

'What are you talking about, Doctor?'

One of the guards said, 'This man claims that there's a bomb in the hearing room, sir.'

'Then there probably is,' the Brigadier said.

'Of course there is,' the Doctor said testily. 'So we shouldn't waste time. I assume' – he continued, indicating the double doors – 'that the hearing room is through there?'

Fontaine began, 'Yes, the commi –'

'Excellent,' the Doctor interrupted, and made a beeline for the doors.

'Wait, you can't just go in there without being –'

The Brigadier sighed and turned to one of the guards. 'Is the front desk prepared to show the bomb squad through?'

'Yes, they are, sir, but –'

'Good. I'd suggest you start making plans for evacuation.' And with that, he turned to follow the Doctor into the hearing room.

A long desk took up the rear of the room, behind which sat seven men and women of varying nationalities. The Brigadier assumed them to be the oversight committee. In all his years with the organization, he had never encountered them. He, after all, reported to UNIT HQ in Geneva. However, UNIT HQ reported to these people. *Always someone higher up in the chain of command, isn't there?* he mused.

The Doctor stood in the centre of the room, holding a device of some sort in his right hand. The committee members were making noises of outrage.

Without looking up from the device, the Doctor said, 'Ladies and gentlemen, I do apologize for this inconvenience.

I'm the Doctor, and I'm supposed to be testifying before you today, but I'm afraid a more pressing concern has come up and I must – A-*ha*!' He interrupted himself when the device beeped. Then he approached a woman on the far left of the rear table. 'Excuse me, madam, but I'm afraid I'll need you to get up for a moment. You see, there's a bomb under your chair.'

The woman got up, quickly. The other six committee members did likewise with great dispatch.

The Doctor knelt and turned over the chair to reveal a strange piece of equipment. Just then a group of black-uniformed men and women entered, led by a tall man with curly blond hair sticking out from under a black cap emblazoned with the letters 'NYPD'. 'All right, I'm going to have to ask everyone to clear the room.'

The head of the committee, a short Indian gentleman who seemed quite befuddled by all of this, asked, 'Excuse me, but who are you?'

'Lieutenant Bottroff, NYPD Bomb Squad. We got a call that there was a bomb in the UN building, and the front desk directed us here. Said some military bigwig told 'em to expect us. Now my people are going to escort everyone out of here while we sort out the situation.'

'Very well,' the committee head said, and proceeded hastily to the exit, as did the other committee members, various clerks, the stenographer, Fontaine and others, led by Bottroff's men.

The Brigadier did not leave just yet; nor, unsurprisingly, did the Doctor. Indeed, the Time Lord had yet to acknowledge Bottroff's existence.

'Excuse me,' Bottroff said leaning over the kneeling figure of the Doctor.

'Unless it's quite urgent, I'm afraid I'm going to have to ask you to wait a moment. I'm in the midst of some very delicate work, here.'

'Sir, there may be a bomb in the room, and I have to –'

'I know there's a bomb!' The Doctor continued to not look at Bottroff, concentrating on what he was doing. 'What do you think I'm trying to defuse?'

Bottroff's eyes widened, and he grabbed the Doctor by the shoulder, turning the Time Lord towards him. 'Sir, I'm sorry, but I can't have civilians tampering in this.'

'Civilians?' the Doctor protested.

The lieutenant raised his gun. 'Please, sir, don't make me have to get violent. Mack,' he said to one of the other officers, 'check that thing out.'

'Yessir,' said the younger officer, who immediately knelt down next to the chair.

'You know, I'm rather getting tired of people waving guns in my face today,' the Doctor commented.

'That's enough,' Bottroff said. 'Now please –'

The Brigadier chose this moment to step in. Putting on the demeanour that had served him well through a lifetime of military service, he said to Bottroff, 'That will be quite enough, Lieutenant.'

Bottroff turned to the Brigadier. 'Who the hell are you?'

Indicating the ID badge clipped to the lapel of his suit jacket, he replied, 'I am Brigadier Alastair Lethbridge-Stewart of the United Nations Intelligence Taskforce. This man is the Doctor, one of our top scientists. Since we are within the confines of the United Nations, we are on international soil, and therefore out of your jurisdiction. As senior UN military officer present, I am taking charge of the situation.'

'Criminetly,' Bottroff muttered, rolling his eyes. 'Look, sir, all I want to do is defuse a bomb. If you and Toulouse-Lautrec over here want to watch, that's just fine with me. But –'

'Lieutenant?' This was the young officer who'd been examining the bomb.

'What is it, Mack?'

'Sir, I dunno what half this equipment is, but there's definitely an explosive in here. And sir – it's one o' Betancourt's.'

Bottroff winced. 'You sure?'

Mack nodded.

Lethbridge-Stewart asked, 'You know this Betancourt person?'

The lieutenant nodded. 'A real nasty piece of work. He's a

bomber, one of our biggest customers. Been trying to put him away for years, but he keeps getting away from us. I suspect he has some high-powered help.' The Brigadier frowned at that. He assumed Bottroff referred to the help of a government. He knew from experience that sometimes intelligence organizations employed people who built bombs, even if they had criminal records. He had never been happy about it.

Bottroff, meanwhile, turned to Mack. 'How long?'

'Till it explodes? Fifteen minutes.'

'I mean to defuse it,' Bottroff said impatiently.

'Hell if I know, sir. Like I said, I dunno what half this equipment is. Could take five minutes, could take three days.'

'Lieutenant,' the Doctor said, 'I *am* familiar with this equipment. I would strongly advise you to let me continue my examination of the bomb.' The Doctor's voice was quiet, and vaguely threatening. Lethbridge-Stewart knew that the Doctor resorted to that tone of voice only when things were grim.

'And if I don't?'

'Then the bomb explodes in fifteen minutes, and we all die.'

Bottroff sighed. 'Can't argue with that. Go.'

'Thank you.'

The Doctor knelt next to the bomb once again, examining it with the same device he'd scanned the room with. Bottroff, meanwhile, ordered the building evacuated; several of his people went off to carry that out.

Then the Doctor took out his sonic screwdriver (the Brigadier couldn't help smiling – he hadn't seen that particular contraption of the Doctor's in years). Its high-pitched whine caused all the police present to tense and grip their guns, prompting the Brigadier to reassure them that all was well. 'The Doctor is simply examining the bomb.'

'Uh-huh,' Bottroff said, unconvinced.

'Oh, dear.'

'What is it?' Lethbridge-Stewart asked.

The Doctor stood up to face the Brigadier and the lieutenant. 'It seems that Betancourt fellow did his work too well.'

Slowly, Bottroff asked, 'What do you mean, exactly?'

'This is equipment I used to try to reconstruct the dematerialization circuit during my exile. It's tied in to the explosive charge.'

Bottroff turned to the Brigadier. 'What did he just say?'

'What does it mean, Doctor?' Lethbridge-Stewart prompted.

'It means that when this bomb goes off, it will destroy the entire Solar System –'

'What?'

'– across a thousand years.'

Unbidden, the Brigadier's thoughts of that morning came back to him: *Both times I encountered Doctors 'out of sequence', so to speak, the entirety of time and space was threatened.*

'The fault in the dematerialization circuit was such that it could rend the TARDIS asunder and spread it across a one-thousand-year period. If I can't defuse it, this entire star system will cease to exist in the year 1000. And the havoc that would play with the space-time continuum is tremendous.'

'How does a simple American bomber manage such a feat?' the Brigadier asked.

'I doubt he realized what he was doing, Brigadier. But that hardly matters right now. I'm not sure I can defuse this with the equipment I have handy. And there's no time to retrieve the TARDIS from Fontaine's office.'

Inspiration struck the Brigadier. 'We could use the recall device! It's in impound, I'm sure we could –'

'Actually, I have it here,' he said, producing the device from his pocket. 'It was stolen by the same chap who put the bomb here. He used the recall device to summon me to Fontaine's office. In any case, it won't help now. The recall device broadcasts a signal to the TARDIS that it can home in on – but someone needs to be *in* the TARDIS for it to...' He trailed off, staring at the recall device, then looked up suddenly, his eyes wide, his mouth spread into a huge grin. 'That's it! Brigadier, you're a genius!'

And then he knelt by the bomb once again.

Bottroff turned to Lethbridge-Stewart. 'I lost track of this conversation about ten steps ago.'

'I'm afraid I'm not that far in front of you,' the Brigadier admitted. 'Doctor, what is it you are doing?'

'The recall device,' the Doctor explained while taking the device apart, 'transmits a signal throughout time and space to find the TARDIS. If I can calibrate it to a particular time and place, and hook up the device to the dematerialization circuit, I can send the explosion somewhere else.'

Bottroff looked at the Brigadier once again. 'Did that make sense to you?'

'As a matter of fact, it did.' So much so, he realized, that he even saw the flaw in it. 'Doctor, I thought that was a faulty dematerialization circuit.'

'Your problem, Brigadier, is that you're always letting inconsequential details get in the way of things.'

'That doesn't answer my question, Doctor.'

'A-*ha*!'

The Brigadier heard a wheezing sound – similar to that of the TARDIS dematerializing, but higher-pitched.

'A-ha what?' Bottroff asked.

'Take a look, Lieutenant,' the Doctor said, indicating the bottom of the overturned chair.

All that remained of the bomb were a few bits of wiring.

'Where did it go?' Bottroff asked with a frown.

'Ninety-second century. The far side of the Galaxy. An area of deep space that has remained uninhabited and untraversed for millennia. I assure you, no one will even notice the explosion.'

Bottroff blinked. He opened his mouth, closed it, opened it again, then finally said, 'The hell with it. Mack, give the all-clear. Let's get out of here.'

Within the half-hour, Bottroff and his people had left and the committee, Fontaine and everyone else had re-entered the room, assured that everything was under control.

Fontaine immediately announced that, unless anyone had any objections, they should pick up where they left off and have the Doctor appear before the committee.

Several committee members said they wished to adjourn for the day in the light of the bomb threat, but Fontaine said, 'If it please the committee, I think that would be unnecessary, and possibly dangerous. As we saw today, there are unique threats to this world cropping up every day. For every second that UNIT's British division is shut down pending the results of these hearings, that is one second that it can't halt one of these threats. In addition, the Doctor is an extremely busy individual, and to keep him waiting for twenty-four hours after he so kindly dismantled the bomb that endangered all of us would be discourteous to say the least.'

The Brigadier smiled, musing on how easily lawyers could take adverse circumstances and manipulate them for their own ends.

By nightfall, the Doctor was relieved to find that he had answered all the committee's questions. The committee members obviously understood only a small fraction of the details, but – combined with reams of paperwork, videotape and other material submitted by Fontaine – they seemed to accept the necessity of his requisitions.

Of course, he thought, *any rational person would accept that necessity without the need for hearings. Pity committees are rarely staffed by rational persons.*

At noon the following day, the committee formally announced its findings: there was no need to shut down the British division, as its appropriations were, though occasionally eccentric, more or less in order, certainly enough so that neither further investigation nor shutting them down was necessary.

'Well, goodbye, Brigadier,' the Doctor said shortly thereafter, standing outside his TARDIS in Fontaine's office and shaking Lethbridge-Stewart's hand. 'Glad I could be of service once again.'

'Always a pleasure, Doctor.'

Turning to shake Fontaine's hand, the Doctor said, 'And may I say, Mr Fontaine, that your work was impeccable.'

'I, uh – well, thank you.' Fontaine, the Doctor noted, was

having difficulty taking his eyes off the TARDIS. 'Glad to meet you. Yes.' He broke the handshake quickly, and stepped back.

Grinning, the Doctor stepped into the TARDIS and was off.

As his vessel moved away from Earth, he noted a signal. It seemed to come from a TARDIS! Then he realized that it was the signal from the recall device, moving forward through both time and space to carry the explosion to that far-off area of interstellar space. No doubt someone else might encounter it in the future.

He paused for a moment, considering the long-term consequences of what he had done. There would, of course, be consequences; there almost always were. But he was a Time Lord, not a lawyer – such consequences did not fall under his purview.

Or did they?

Shaking his head as if to brush off an insect, he set the coordinates for pastures new.

Aliens And Predators

By Colin Brake

The signal was still there, like a beacon illuminating the darkest night, pulsing out from the distant star system that was the giant ship's destination. Even in the heat of battle the automatic navigation system never lost its grip on that precious guiding signal. And the battle was hot.

The giant spaceship was called simply *Hope*. A simple four-letter word that said more about its purpose than any worthy mission statement but the qualifying adjective 'last' hovered like a ghost in front of the name, never stated, never necessary, its presence implicit.

After more than eighty years of constant travel the ship had reached an area of space far from the inhabited hub of the Universe. Out here the maps ceased to be very precise; areas were marked 'computer projection only' in exactly the same way cartographers on ancient Earth once wrote 'here there be dragons'. The star systems here were at the very edge of the rim-worlds, the frontier of known space.

But even here the crew of the giant spaceship *Hope* were not alone and far from safe. Here, as before on their long and lonely journey, predators were hunting them, seeking the many treasures carried in their enormous holds.

To call it a spaceship was an understatement. The craft was huge, vaguely insect-like, consisting of a number of linked spheres, each one hundreds of miles in diameter. Every surface of the craft was covered with extrusions and instruments, vents and engines. Larger than many a small planet or moon, the entire construct, a veritable complex of artificial mini-worlds, moved in a deliberate, steered vector, constructed and propelled by advanced technology.

The silence of deep space is tested most in war. Even without sound, a space battle is noisy: full of sound and fury, a beautiful orgy of destruction. The current assault was not the first that *Hope* had faced, and it wouldn't be the last. Fast enemy fighter craft, seemingly without number, had swarmed over the ship, from every vector, unleashing wave upon wave of deadly missiles. The defence grid of the spaceship, automated and deadly efficient, counted each and every bombardment, and answered the hostile fire with round after round from its own weapon mountings. Despite the overwhelming size of the attacking fleet the giant ship held firm – defiant and proud. Slowly, one by one, the fleet of raiders was being destroyed.

The crew of the *Hope* numbered only six, but they were equal to their task. Almost all of the defence systems were automated, leaving the crew to fulfil a supporting role, checking power distributions, overseeing running repairs, marshalling the data from the battle computers. The six-strong crew were guardians, honour-bound to protect their precious cargo. Whatever the cost.

On the bridge of the giant ship, the chief guardian, Nart, watched as the battle raged. Somewhere out there in the darkness of deep space was the mother ship that had given birth to this unending violent horde – a ship almost equal in size to his own. It had been pursuing them, hunting them, for years. The predators were one of the most evil, vicious and relentless races known in the Universe – more dangerous than the Daleks, more feared than the Sontarans, more ruthless than the Cybermen. They had no other name than the Other.

'Oh dear, oh dearie me!' The Doctor's voice, more agitated than normal, echoed down the TARDIS corridors. In what the Doctor occasionally called the galley Jamie McCrimmon looked up at the sound of the Doctor's voice. For Jamie the Doctor was more than just a friend and companion: he was part-father, part-brother, part-wizard, part-God. For all his elusiveness, vagueness and his annoying tendency to panic, the young Scot had complete faith in the Doctor's ability to survive any situation and to find the solution to any problem. In the end.

In the short term Jamie favoured the age-old philosophy that what can go wrong will go wrong and at the first anxious cry from the Doctor Jamie dropped the chocolate-like bar that the food replicator had produced in response to a request for roast beef and ran toward the console room. The Doctor might need his help.

Elsewhere in the unending corridors of the TARDIS, Zoe Herriot the brilliant astrophysicist from the 21st century also reacted instantly to hearing the Doctor's cry.

Zoe had less experience of travelling with the Doctor than Jamie but had the advantage over the young Highlander in two key areas. First, she had a reasonable level of technological sophistication and was able to appreciate and understand more of the wonders of the Universe that the Doctor and the TARDIS took them to than Jamie. Secondly, although she trusted the Doctor implicitly, she secretly thought that much of the time it was he who needed her assistance rather than the other way round.

She dropped what she had been doing – reprogramming a data pad she'd found somewhere – and ran for the console room.

The crew of *Hope* were known as guardians because they were custodians of the cavernous holds of the planetoid-like craft. The ship's contents were a museum of the last remains of the once-great human race. Humans had been major players in the Universe with a wide spread of influence for tens of thousands of years but now they were all but extinct.

The last humans had felt a need, a duty even, to preserve what they could of their extensive culture. With the last resources of the race they scoured the Universe collecting, rescuing, restoring and cataloguing relics of human achievement. Works of art in all manner of forms, books, historical records, buildings and other constructs from the long-lost homeworld, Earth, and the many other worlds that had been home to the human race had been collected. All of these relics were carefully placed into the holds of *Hope*, which then launched on its long and desperate journey. Their destination was a subject of much heated argument until the detection of the mysterious radio signal from deep space. Computer analysis of the signal was only partially successful; the alien physics that had generated it was almost completely incomprehensible but part of its message was clear. It showed the way home, back to long-lost Earth, where a fresh start might be made.

If they managed to get there safely.

The battle raged on, the defence grid spitting deadly fire to destroy the fighter craft of the Other's fleet. The area of space surrounding the giant ship was riddled with the fruits of war: corpses and debris. Unnoticed by any sensor, some of the debris drifted, apparently innocently, towards the outer hull of one of the spheres. In normal circumstances such space junk would be instantly obliterated by the defence grid but, with the battle computers locked into responding to and destroying the fighter craft, no systems were free to track flotsam and jetsam. Hidden in the shattered remains of a fighter ship, the real assault squad of the enemy floated ever closer to the ship. When contact was made, they appeared, emerging from stasis tubes, like butterflies from the cocoon, latching onto the outer hull of *Hope* with clawlike hands, adapted especially for the purpose.

Moving swiftly, the three creatures who made up the real assault squad began to make their own entrance to the ship.

The aliens were loosely humanoid, but their mammalian features were clearly augmented by reptilian and other alien DNA. Their eyes were protected by a double layer of finely scaled skin, the mouths housed fierce-looking sharp teeth and a long forked tongue. Chitinous panels cloaked the shoulders and lower torso like a shell. They were a race built, literally, for battle. For races throughout the known Universe in this time period they were the very definition of alien: the Other. Inspiration for a million nightmares, the Other were conquerors of a thousand planets which they had invaded, raped and finally discarded.

The silicon-enhanced senses and the sophisticated computer/mind interface surgically inserted into the hippocampus of each of the Other enabled them to absorb data directly from their warship computers at machine speeds. They were formidable opponents and wasted little time in battle.

Forty-two seconds after their initial contact with the outer hull of *Hope*, they were inside.

In the TARDIS console room the Doctor was dancing round the six-sided central control console, plucking nervously at the odd switch or button, stopping occasionally to tap at a readout and generally acting like a prehistoric chimp confronted with a big black alien obelisk.

'This can't be right!' muttered the Doctor to himself, his normally well-lined face heavy with concentration and concern. From the corridor to the rest of the ship Jamie skidded into the room, followed seconds later by Zoe.

'What is it?' Jamie asked bluntly.

For a moment it looked as if the Doctor was just going to ignore him but then he looked up and took in the fact that his companions had joined him.

'Ah well... That's a very good question Jamie,' he said slowly, as if needing the time to think more fully about what he might say next.

'Aye, so perhaps you could give me an answer then?' Jamie retorted, not a little angrily.

'Have we materialized somewhere dangerous? In the Vortex or something?' Zoe's concerns, as usual, were practical in nature.

'No, no, nothing like that.' The Doctor absent-mindedly patted his forehead with the dirty spotted handkerchief that often trailed from his jacket pocket. He attempted a reassuring smile. 'It's just the rather peculiar signal I've picked up.'

'A signal? Like an SOS or something?' asked Zoe.

The Doctor shrugged.

'So what's odd about it?' Jamie demanded.

The Doctor looked a little sheepish, like a child caught raiding the biscuit tin in the middle of the night. 'Well, that's just it Jamie. It is very odd. Very odd indeed.'

Zoe and Jamie exchanged concerned looks. Neither of them had seen the Doctor quite so worried before. The Doctor looked up at them, his blue eyes shining with anxiety and his voice loaded with confusion. 'You see, as far as I can make out the signal comes from another TARDIS.'

On board *Hope* Guardian Nart was on duty on the bridge of the ship. With most systems automated bridge duty was a formality rather than a necessity. Nart sat for hours on end with the great patience he shared with the other guardians, watching the various consoles and readouts and scanning the communications channels. The signal was still there. Their beacon. Their goal was the planet that had originally given birth to humanity, abandoned over one hundred generations in the past, after the coming of deadly solar flares had forced a planet-wide evacuation. In the panic and speed of their departure much had been lost and forgotten, including the most precious knowledge of all – the galactic coordinates of Earth. Many had searched for the home world over the millenia but no one had ever returned claiming to have found it. Finally when the inevitable onward march of time had reduced the idea of Earth to the status of childhood fantasy, believed only by the youngest and most romantically minded of people, an ancient coded message was received.

For a further forty-two years the message remained a subject of intense academic argument and study until a public announcement declared partial success at decoding the primitive signal from the past – it contained the long-lost coordinates of legendary Earth. Once this discovery was known there was no more argument about a destination for the giant ship *Hope*. Where better for humanity to start again than their original home world? With the precious DNA material that was the vessel's most precious cargo, the guardians hoped to clone a new human race.

Nart let his gaze fall onto the external sensors, taking in the latest battle status of the ship's defence against the Other. So far it appeared that the defence grid was holding – and slowly they were winning this battle. And, he hoped, the war.

Suddenly Nart's train of thought was derailed by a klaxon-like alarm which erupted into the still air of the bridge, with a banshee wail. Hull breach!

Unlike the multiple space dog-fights, which had raged for hours, the assault squad's attack lasted a mere 83 seconds and cost the lives of three guardians and all of the Other's raiding party. Their deep scans had long ago mapped each square centimetre of the cavernous interiors and their point of entry had been chosen with care. They used neutron-cutters to sear through the four-inch thick toughened metal with almost nonchalant ease. That act, finally, alerted the guardians to the attack.

Three guardians reached the scene – by vacuum tube – within 23 seconds of the alarm sounding. By this point the raiding party had breached internal doors and arrived at the long corridor leading to the third of the linked spheres that made up the main body of the giant spaceship – the biosphere. Here various artefacts of a biological nature were secured, including the most precious treasure: the human DNA material destined to seed the reborn human race on Earth.

The three guardians took position to defend the corridor – aware instantly of the aliens' goal. Despite their heavy arma-ment and battle armour two of the guardians were annihilated by the time a further twelve seconds had passed.

A fair exchange perhaps, since, in the exchange of fire, two of the raiding party were also blasted into their component atoms.

The third raider was quicker. Taking advantage of the carnage caused as his companions messily lost their lives, he fired his own weapon and unleashed a blinding controlled micro-thermonuclear explosion, mere microns across. Despite its tiny size the flash from this explosion flared brighter than a star for a moment, blinding the last defender, Nart.

The alien leader, his eyes shielded by thick filtering eyelids that he had grown to order, ran on towards the biosphere.

Nart, his eyes still non-functioning after the nuclear flash, his body already beginning irrevocable system breakdown, made a final desperate decision and ordered immediate separation of the fourth sphere.

The Other ran at impossible speed towards the door to the third sphere as massive explosions rocked the entire corridor. With a wrench of tearing metal the corridor disconnected from the rest of the ship, triggering the automatic self-destruct in the fourth sphere. The guardians were determined to destroy all of their cargo, if necessary, to prevent any of the treasures of mankind falling into the wrong hands.

Like a small nova, the destruction of the fourth sphere filled the area with light and debris, buffeting the rest of the ship and sending wave after wave of excess energy.

Then, all was silent again.

Silence also reigned in the TARDIS control room, save for the ever-present and rather reassuring hum of electrical activity. Zoe and Jamie watched, as patiently as they could, as the Doctor continued his interrogation of his instruments. His face dark with puzzlement, the Doctor grappled with the controls on the mushroom-shaped console, trying to push the TARDIS instruments to new limits.

Jamie cast an enquiring sideways glance at Zoe, who merely shrugged in reply to the lad's unspoken question. With the Doctor who was to know what was better: to ask and risk having your head bitten off or to remain in ignorance while the Universe died around you? Zoe was tempted to let Jamie make the first move, on the basis of his longer association with the Doctor. For his part Jamie felt only confusion: if the signal came from another TARDIS that must mean another member of the Doctor's own race, a subject on which the Doctor rarely spoke.

Jamie tried to remember what, if anything, the Doctor had told him about his own people and came up with very little. He knew the Doctor had fallen out with his home world in some way and had taken off in the TARDIS but that was about it. Victoria, the girl from a Britain a hundred years older than his own who had travelled with them for a while, had once told him about a conversation she'd had with the Doctor on the subject of families. The Doctor had spoken of his own family with some sadness, Victoria had remembered, but Jamie could not recall the Doctor ever revealing any such vulnerability to him.

Now it seemed as if some of the mystery surrounding the Doctor might be revealed and Jamie found himself almost saddened by the notion, as if the Doctor might lose something by being known a little better. Jamie shook his head, dismissing his own strange thought, and decided to take the bull by the horns. 'Doctor?'

'Hmmm, yes Jamie. What is it?' muttered the Doctor without raising his eyes from the set of dials on the console which he was currently studying.

'This other TARDIS… Is it in trouble?'

Encouraged by the response Jamie's question had received, Zoe joined in. 'Is it a distress call? From one of your own people.'

The Doctor looked up and smiled, making an arch of his two hands, fingertips to fingertips. 'Well, I'm not sure Zoe. The answer to your question is yes… and no.' Zoe frowned, and the Doctor's smile widened a little. 'You see, as far as I can make out that signal is indeed coming from another TARDIS but, more than that, the TARDIS sending the signal is *my* TARDIS.'

Now Jamie was frowning. 'You're talking in riddles, Doctor.'

Zoe, however, thought she may have understood. 'Of course, we travel in time in the TARDIS don't we? So theoretically we could meet ourselves at another point in our own timeline…'

The Doctor nodded, pleased at Zoe's quick thinking. 'Yes, exactly. In theory. Although it breaks every rule of Time, and they wouldn't like that, would they?' The Doctor's words hung in the air for a moment as he drifted off into thought. 'Unless it suited them of course,' he muttered, almost as an afterthought. His brow furrowed, and a peculiar expression crossed his face, a fleeting look of... fear?

'They? Who?' demanded a curious and confused Jamie.

'Who?' asked the Doctor, clicking back into the conversation as if he'd been a million miles away. 'Never mind, never mind... we'll just have to investigate and get to the bottom of this ourselves. Hold on – I'm going to make an emergency materialization.'

The Doctor operated the necessary controls and the familiar sound of the TARDIS engines filled the console room, groaning and wheezing, as the craft left the space-time vortex and re-emerged into the normal three-dimensional universe. The sound roared and soared in their ears in fury, and the TARDIS rocked from side to side, as if protesting at the suddenness of the landing. Inside the console room Zoe and Jamie were flung to the floor, landing in a tangled heap together. Miraculously the Doctor managed to stay rooted to the spot, standing by the console, despite the manic gyrations of the space-time craft.

Suddenly it was over and, with a loud and satisfying thump, the engines completed their task and the craft materialized. Jamie helped Zoe up, a broad grin on his face. 'At least that was just like normal!'

Zoe laughed, but standing at the console the Doctor remained grim-faced.

The surviving three guardians did not waste time in recriminations or debates. What had happened was in the past – done, finished, over; their only concern was with the future. If they had one.

The last raider had died in the destruction of the fourth sphere, his last act to grab defiantly at the door to the next sphere, a grip so strong that it held even in death.

The guardians had recovered the remains of the creature's inert body, curious about the beings who had staged such a desperate and yet nearly successful attack. The bits and pieces

of the corpse lay in the lab, as yet untouched. The very fact that
it remained recognizable as a once-living creature in the face
of the powerful explosion that had robbed it of its life was
testament to the incredible strength of the alien's physical
form. In fact, the alien physiognomy had raised more questions
than answers in the brief examination that the guardians had
given it thus far; no doubt a more detailed autopsy would unveil
more useful data in the future. For now they were happy merely
to confirm that the creature was indeed dead and no longer a
threat.

The Other, *en masse*, however, remained a positive and
urgent threat to the guardians, to *Hope* and to the success of
their mission. No doubt they would raid again, and although the
crew of the giant ship were now alerted to their proximity, the
creatures had reached the ship's hull without detection once
and there was no reason to suppose they could not do so again.

For their part the guardians were now reduced in number to
half the size of their original complement. Another raid like the
first could remove them all. Earth's treasures would be the
Other's for the taking. That could not be allowed to happen.
From now on the guardians would be on a constant state of
alert; any intrusion, no matter how apparently innocent, would
be met with the deadliest force.

The TARDIS had materialized in what appeared to be a
massive museum room.

That was Zoe's first thought as the picture from the TARDIS
scanner appeared on the small screen set in the wall of the
console room.

The walls of the chamber disappeared into the far distance
in every direction, and the vast space in between these infinite
walls was packed with... well, stuff. Huge containers and
boxes of a thousand materials, all different shapes and sizes,
some transparent, some opaque, some locked with multifarious security devices, some open, displaying their contents in
part, teasingly, like an inventive window display in a department store. And on and between these boxes other things lay in

deep piles: clothes from every period of Earth's rich history, fabric samples, carpets, wall-coverings, furniture, utensils.

Zoe felt a strange excitement as she looked out at this vast and bizarre collection, every inch of space offering up some new marvel. The more Zoe looked, the more she saw; here and there something would glint with surprising familiarity: a computer console of the design used in her own time; a Biba chair from the 1960s Zoe recognized from her visit to the London of that period with the Doctor; a bust of Napoleon hauntingly like the one she'd found abandoned in a broom cupboard in the corridor outside the console room in the TARDIS just the other day.

From his expression Zoe could see that Jamie was as impressed as she was by the sight, perhaps more so. To his more primitive eyes it must have appeared like some fairy-tale treasure trove.

The Doctor seemed to be regarding it with less awe. He nodded as if it were the kind of sight he saw every day, as if it were almost what he would expect to see on the scanner screen. Zoe almost sighed out loud in frustration – she was sure the Doctor acted with such coolness merely to infuriate her.

'It looks like some kind of museum,' she said, tentatively, hoping the Doctor might have a better idea of what it could be.

'Not a very organized one I should say,' remarked the Doctor with a smile. 'Maybe I should take a closer look, see if I can find the curator, give them a little advice on creating order…'

The Doctor's soft tone made it sound like an innocent walk in the park, but Zoe and Jamie had travelled with the Doctor long enough to realize that appearances could be very deceptive.

The Doctor operated the door control and the TARDIS doors obediently swung open for him. 'I think it might be best,' the Doctor began slowly as he moved towards the open doors, 'if you two were to stay in the TARDIS for now.'

Jamie immediately started forward, complaining. 'But Doctor –'

'No arguments Jamie.' The Doctor held up his hand like a policeman stopping traffic and his uncharacteristically raised voice had the desired effect: Jamie stopped in his tracks.

Zoe found the moment a little frightening, unusual – this uncharacteristic desire to be alone. The Doctor preferred to explore a new landing place with his companions by his side, not left in the TARDIS. Normally.

'*Is* there something dangerous out there Doctor?' Zoe asked, a little quietly.

The Doctor turned to her and gave her one of his warmest smiles, offering as much reassurance as he could in the circumstances. 'I really don't know, Zoe, but something's telling me to take every precaution. Just to be on the safe side. Now you and Jamie stay right here – and I'll be back before you know it.'

The Doctor quickly slipped out into the museum outside, swiftly closing the door of the TARDIS behind him.

In the console room Jamie and Zoe just looked at each other in surprise, both equally worried by this unexpected event. In unison they both turned to look at the scanner. If they were to be denied being with the Doctor the least they could do was keep an eye on him.

On the screen they could see the Doctor making his way down one of the clear pathways marked between the rows of artefacts. For once the Doctor seemed less interested in stopping and looking as he moved. Although neither Zoe or Jamie could see it from the angle presented by the TARDIS scanner, the Doctor's face was once again both grave and dark.

On the main bridge of the good ship *Hope* another scanner monitor was also showing a picture of the Doctor, this one from an automated security camera mounted high in the chamber in which the TARDIS had landed.

Merik, the new chief guardian, examined the new intruder carefully. He had a humanoid form, and his clothing certainly made him look harmless but Merik was inclined, on experience, to mistrust such appearances. The most alarming fact about this newcomer was the manner of his arrival. Without tripping a single alarm the alien's craft – an unusually compact blue box – had materialized within the second sphere, passing through the defence shields effortlessly and solidifying as if transmatted into place but without the need for a transmat-receiver.

Frica and Uri, the two remaining guardians, stood nearby, waiting for Merik to reach some conclusion. Unlike the Other, this alien had made no offensive moves so far, and appeared not to be armed. This gave the guardians a little time to consider their move; with their decreased numbers they were biased towards even greater caution than normal. They dared not risk their continued existence by reckless, hurried action.

'Get to the second sphere and capture the alien,' ordered Merik after a few seconds' thought.

'Capture?' queried Uri, and his weaponry seemed to twitch in his hand.

'Capture,' confirmed Merik. 'I want to question it.'

With no further discussion Uri and Frica ran from the room. Merik watched them go for a split second, considering amending the order, but then he turned back to the bank of monitors and asked the system memory to rerun its audio-visual recording of the materialization. He watched it a couple of times, at various speeds of playback, and initiated a search of the main databanks for anything similar. Surely in the entire history of the human race something like this had been experienced before, by someone.

In the second sphere the Doctor had reached a set of doors which, he concluded quickly, must lead to whatever high-speed method of internal transport was used on board this craft. Almost as soon as he reached this conclusion an instrument panel placed adjacent to the doors flashed with life. The Doctor realized that this could only mean one thing: company.

With no working hypothesis about the nature of the ship and its inhabitants – although part of his brain was already busy developing and testing out various scenarios based on the evidence he had seen thus far – the Doctor felt that a direct confrontation with the creatures who were approaching might be a mistake. He looked about him quickly for a suitable hiding place.

The rows of human relics stretching for miles in every direction offered a multitude of choices. The Doctor quickly climbed into a large elaborately carved seventeenth-century chest, which lay not too far from the doors, hoping that the aliens would not have heat-seeking or other similar sensors which would make their job easier and his concealment temporary. The Doctor decided to cross his fingers. Both hands. Just in case.

In the TARDIS Zoe and Jamie continued to watch the monitor. As usual the TARDIS seemed to have a near-magical ability to amend the scanner's view to show the occupants exactly what they wanted to see. The picture had zoomed in a number of times, managing to keep track of the Doctor even though he had travelled quite some distance from the TARDIS.

They had watched with confusion as the Doctor disappeared inside the chest. 'Now what's he doing?' complained Jamie. 'Playing hide and seek?'

On the screen the doors the Doctor had discovered suddenly slid open and two creatures appeared from the vacuum-lift cab beyond. Zoe heard herself gasp in amazement at the look of the newcomers. Even allowing for the distorted perspective of the scanner image the two guardians were clearly big – seven or eight feet tall – humanoid but not human.

'Androids,' breathed Zoe.

Jamie frowned at her. 'Wee robots? Like the Yeti?'

Zoe shook her head. 'Those things are about as much like a Yeti as the TARDIS is like a bicycle.' Jamie, wisely, let Zoe continue, rather than question this. 'From the look of them, these are quite sophisticated androids, probably constructed by humans, to resemble themselves. They're artificial life-forms, mechanical in the strictest sense of the word, but not in a nuts-and-bolts way; the technology is a long way from the basic robotics of the Yeti.'

'And I suppose those things they're carrying are weapons,' muttered Jamie, who had learnt a thing or two in his travels with the Doctor – mostly about the many diverse ways creatures could inflict pain on other creatures.

On the screen the two android guardians moved towards the area in which the Doctor had hidden himself, as if drawn by some knowledge of his whereabouts.

Jamie reached for the door control and activated it. The TARDIS doors swung open. 'They're heading straight for the Doctor. Maybe we can distract them,' he suggested, heading for the door.

'But the Doctor said…' started Zoe in reply, but Jamie had already gone. Zoe tutted in anger, hesitated for a beat. The sight of the androids frightened her but she couldn't let both Jamie and the Doctor go off and leave her. She quickly followed Jamie out of the TARDIS.

Frica and Uri approached the aisle in which, according to their inbuilt sensors, a life-form was hiding. The signal was indistinct, as if shielded somehow, but there was a definite reading coming from this direction. The two androids moved with maximum caution, their pulse-energy weapons drawn and set on standby.

Inside the chest in which he was hiding, the Doctor had wrapped himself in a metallic cloth that he had found in it. He thought the metal content of the fabric might confuse any sensors. In addition he had tried mentally to shut down some of his body activity, lowering his internal temperature and generally trying to make himself appear non-organic or inert.

Suddenly the two androids stopped dead, as new life-form signals appeared in their sensor field, some distance away. Two life-forms, clear distinct signals, moving swiftly.

The androids hesitated for a split second then ran off in the direction of the latest signals. If these newcomers were the Other, it wouldn't matter what or who the original intruder was. The Other were infinitely more dangerous than any other creature could possibly be.

Inside the chest the Doctor heard what sounded like two creatures running away from his position. How many were there of the aliens? He had thought only two had emerged from the vacuum-lift, but could he be certain? The Doctor decided to risk it. The lid of the chest cracked open an inch or two and he peered out, cautiously. All seemed clear.

Moving swiftly the Doctor climbed out of the chest and ran to the doors leading to the lifts. He hit what could only be a call button and was rewarded by the doors sliding open to reveal the lift-cab, still waiting for the return of the androids. The Doctor entered the lift and studied the internal control panel. Taking a guess that the topmost control would return the lift to the main bridge the Doctor prodded it with a finger. Instantly the doors closed, and the lift silently began to move at high speed.

Jamie and Zoe ran, as if their lives depended on it – and they probably did. It was not a new experience for them: travelling with the Doctor seemed to involve an inordinate amount of running, normally from unpleasant alien monsters and/or heavily armed opponents.

Consequently they were both fit and fast.

Unfortunately the androids were better built, hence fitter and faster.

The Doctor's companions ran without any particular plan, changing direction at random, doubling back where possible, desperately trying to keep ahead of the pursuing aliens, who encouraged them with intermittent blasts from their wicked-sounding weapons. In running in this fashion Zoe noticed that they were moving ever further from the sanctuary of the TARDIS. Despite her fear of the pursuing androids she kept a steady head.

'We'd have been safer in the TARDIS,' complained Zoe as they turned yet another corner. Jamie paused for a moment, to let his friend catch up. 'Aye – and the Doctor would have been caught. Then we'd be stuck. Come on.'

Jamie resumed running, any fear he might have known swallowed up by the sheer excitement of the chase. Zoe

watched as he quickly disappeared around another corner.
With her own lungs threatening to burst in her chest, her ribs
aching with the effort, the muscles in her legs failing her, Zoe
somehow forced herself to follow him.

A blast from one of the androids' pulsed-energy weapons,
narrowly missing her, inspired a new burst of adrenalin in her
system. The androids were getting closer. Now pure terror
drove her on.

Jamie suddenly cried out in surprise. Zoe ran on, worried;
had the androids found him? She slid round the corner she had
seen him take and came to a complete stop. Jamie was grinning
at her wildly. In his hands was a laser-rifle; a belt of some kind
of hand-grenades was wrapped around his waist; a second
projectile weapon hung over his shoulder. He gestured to the
cabinets open behind him. 'I think I've found the armoury of
this museum!'

The lift doors opened and the Doctor hopped out, finding
himself on the main bridge of the craft, as he had planned.
Striding forward the Doctor quickly took in as much information as he could from the various monitors and screens, com-
pleting his construction of a working hypothesis as to where he
was. Seeing that the bridge contained only one of the androids
– who appeared not to be armed – the Doctor decided on a
straightforward approach.

'Hello, I'm generally known as the Doctor. I wonder if I
could take a look at that signal you're following...'

The android turned round to face the Doctor, without
answering, revealing that he was in fact armed after all. A
dangerous-looking projectile weapon was clasped firmly in the
android's hand, pointed directly at the Doctor.

'If that's not a problem, of course,' continued the Doctor, a
little less confidently.

At least we're not running, thought Zoe, a little bitterly. She
crouched in her hiding place, squeezed between two huge
boxes of body armour. She tried to slow her ragged breathing

down to a more normal pace but her heart continued to beat erratically in her chest, so loudly that she feared it alone would give away her hiding place. She wished she'd had time to climb into one of the suits of armour but with the androids so close she hadn't had the chance. Instead she'd managed to identify and activate a personal protection force-field but with no great confidence that it would be strong enough to withstand any prolonged attack. She had refused to take a weapon. Although she could rationally see the need for violence on occasion, she had little stomach for it herself and preferred to avoid the use of weapons whenever possible. It was something she knew she shared with the Doctor and she was secretly proud of the fact.

Jamie was less squeamish but, given his cultural and temporal background, this was understandable. Despite this heritage Jamie was not fearless in war: instead he relished his terror. For Jamie fear was a part of war, a part of life, something to be embraced and welcomed like an honourable death on the battlefield.

Having quickly ransacked the armoury-like collection of offensive and defensive weapons Jamie had started to climb up the shelving of this particular aisle, looking to get himself into an advantageous position, from which to counter-attack against the androids. Soon he was twenty or thirty feet above the ground.

Down below Zoe hoped his plan would work. Climbing high above the androids might put Jamie in a commanding position. On the other hand, it might make him a clearer target.

In the control room the Doctor was relieved that thus far Merik had not found reason to fire his weapon in anger. So far the Doctor had convinced him that he probably was not one of the Other – whatever they were – but he had not yet convinced him of his true identity. Which was a shame, since the TARDIS was known to the ship's database.

'Your craft is known to us. Owned by a time-traveller named the Doctor.'

The Doctor couldn't conceal a small smile at this. 'Oh it is nice to be known. I suppose I do have a little reputation in some quarters…'

'According to our records, you should have a companion.'

'I normally do. I do like company.' The Doctor was smiling broadly. This was going better than he could have hoped.

'Is Benny with you?'

A frown creased the Doctor's forehead.

'Benny? No I don't know any Benny. There was Ben, but he left me some time ago. They do come and go you know.'

This didn't appear to be the answer his interlocutor required.

From his vantage point high above the floor, Jamie had a perfect view of the androids as they turned into the aisle in which he and Zoe had stopped. Jamie held his breath. This was the closest he'd been to the giants and, at this distance, they were a fearsome sight, larger and colder even than the Cybermen.

Trying to ignore the beads of sweat that had begun to break out on his forehead and pour down his face into his eyes, Jamie looked through the viewfinder of his energy weapon and took aim. With one hand he found what he guessed, correctly, to be a power setting, and moved it to maximum. He didn't know what effect, if any, the weapon would have on the androids but if what Zoe had said about their construction was correct he knew he would need all the power he could get to stop them.

And he knew that he *had* to stop them. They had already demonstrated a willingness to fire at them without warning. If they had questions they seemed unlikely to seek answers first.

With an unspoken prayer to a God he'd long stopped believing in Jamie pulled the trigger. Impossibly fast, a bolt of energy streaked from the barrel of the weapon and impacted against the android's chest.

The hit android, Uri, jerked in reaction, lightening-like daggers of electricity arcing all over his body. His own weapon slipped from his hands but he did not fall. In reaction his companion, Frica, raised her own weapon in the direction the attack had come from.

From her hiding place Zoe could only watch in horror as the

second android fired her own weapon up in the direction of Jamie's vantage point.

A fierce explosion, accompanied by a shower of vicious electrical sparks, erupted in the general area that Jamie had taken up position in.

As if in slow motion Zoe watched as the unconscious body of the brave highlander fell out of the damaged shelving. With a sickeningly loud thump, he connected with the metallic floor and lay unmoving.

The two androids, one still reeling in shock from the direct hit Jamie had scored before his fall, advanced on the stricken Scot, guns raised, ready to fire.

Zoe knew they would kill her friend if she didn't help him. She reached back in the depths of the armaments case beside her, looking for something, anything, that she could use against the androids. Her hands found something cold, deadly and spherical.

Without daring to stop and think, afraid that fear itself would strike her immobile, Zoe leapt out into the aisle, and started running at the two androids. In one swift movement she lobbed the spherical device she had found into their path, dived in the direction of Jamie and restored the power to her personal protection device, enveloping her friend within its force-field. The sphere – a pulse grenade – bounced once, then exploded, unleashing its deadly charge: a massive pulse of electromagnetic energy which completely disrupted the internal systems of the androids. Unable to contain their own power source, they simply exploded, hurling Zoe and Jamie, semi-protected in the force-field, away down the aisle, like a runaway ball.

The remains of the two androids burnt quietly at the end of the aisle. Nothing else moved.

On the main bridge klaxons sounded, interrupting the Doctor's interrogation by Merik.

Merik and the Doctor had been ignoring the monitors but now they both turned to look, and found that the pictures told the whole story. Both took in the sight of the smoking remains of the two androids and the Doctor's two companions some distance away. The Doctor could see that Zoe had turned off her protective force-field to attend to her friend. Jamie lay ominously still but not dead, the Doctor noted with relief; Zoe was trying to revive him.

On another screen a digital clock had appeared, counting down from three minutes. At the same time a computerized voice filled the room with a simple but terrifying message: 'Auto-destruct armed.'

'Oh no. That won't do. Turn it off!' exclaimed the Doctor instantly.

'I'm afraid that's not possible. After the last attack by the Other, we reprogrammed the system to destroy *Hope* if any of us were to be killed. We cannot let the treasures of the human race fall into their hands.'

The Doctor was amazed and appalled in equal measure.

'So your solution is to destroy it all? What kind of custodians are you?'

'We are the last, the last of the human race. If we cannot complete our mission and use the DNA material we have to seed a new flowering of the race then it is better that we, and all that the human race created, are obliterated.'

The Doctor shook his head, firmly.

'No, no, no. This is all a mistake. We aren't your enemy. Zoe was just trying to protect Jamie. You don't need to self-destruct the ship on our behalf...'

The Doctor moved forward to the computer console nearest to the screen showing the auto-destruct countdown, now at two minutes, twenty-two seconds.

'Tell me how to access your base computer code – there must be something I can do.'

'Jamie, wake up please. Jamie?' Zoe's voice trembled with anguish. For all her scientific knowledge her grasp of basic first aid had always been weak. If only she'd found the time to sit down and read one of the manuals on the subject; with her computerlike memory she'd have learnt all she would ever need in a matter of minutes.

Jamie groaned and opened his eyes, bringing a hand up to his forehead, which he massaged. Blinking rapidly he took a few deep breaths before trying to speak. 'Did I get them?'

Zoe decided a white lie might do less damage to her friend's ego: the truth – that she had been the one who had destroyed their enemy – was better left unstated. 'Yes, Jamie. Thank you. Do you think you can stand?'

'Aye I'm fine.' Jamie sat up and got to his feet, wobbling ever so slightly as he did so, causing Zoe to wonder if he might be putting on an act for her.

'Are you sure?'

Jamie glared at her. He'd just said so hadn't he? 'We McCrimmon's bounce well. Now let's see if we can find the Doctor, eh? If there are more of those android things about he may need our help.'

On the bridge Merik and the Doctor worked in silence at separate consoles, their fingers flying over the keyboards. On the screens, reams of machine code scrolled by at incredible speeds as they tried to reprogram the self-destruct circuits.

On the countdown screen the digital figures reached 60 seconds. One minute to total destruction of the entire legacy of the human race, not to mention the Doctor, Zoe and Jamie. The Doctor glanced up briefly to note the time he had left to pull off this miracle, determined not to fail.

The vacuum-lift doors opened and Zoe and Jamie arrived on the bridge. Jamie started forward on seeing Merik, energy blaster in hand. The Doctor looked up and shook his head.

Zoe put a restraining hand on Jamie's arm.

'What's going on Doctor?' asked the Scot, confused as ever.

'Not now Jamie – please. I'm trying to disarm this auto-destruct.'

Zoe realized the implication of the Doctor's words and took in the countdown display. It now read less than 30 seconds.

Merik, the android, turned to the Doctor, despairingly. 'It's no good Doctor, get your companions and yourself to safety.'

The Doctor noted that Merik had obviously decided that he was who he claimed to be but didn't comment on the change of heart. There wasn't the time. 'No. I can't give up yet. You see – this little crisis is all our fault... so I really have to try to make amends.'

'When we – I mean you destroyed the others it must have triggered the auto-destruct,' explained Zoe for Jamie's benefit.

'Oh aye, so it's my fault as usual, is it?'

'Now, now – this isn't the time for blame, Jamie,' the Doctor said, clicking a final sequence of commands on his console with a flourish. 'More a time for congratulations,' he concluded, stepping back.

On the countdown screen the figures read 00:00:13, then 00:00:12, then stopped.

'Doctor! You did it!' exclaimed a happy Zoe.

The Doctor smiled modestly, and indicated Merik. 'Well, I did have some help, you know...'

He came over to his companions and grasped them both warmly by the hand in turn. 'I am so sorry I asked you to stay in the TARDIS. I'm afraid we've handled this whole situation rather badly.'

'But it's ended all right, hasn't it?' asked Zoe, optimistically.

'I think so, Zoe, I think so...' The Doctor turned back to Merik. 'You said you'd recovered the body of one of the Other which attacked your ship?' Merik nodded. 'Perhaps I could take a look at it? I'm curious as to exactly what it is they want from you.'

'Isn't it obvious, Doctor?' replied Merik. 'They want the human DNA material we carry. That's what they were heading for. If they just wanted the treasures they could have taken them from any part of *Hope*. But they made straight for the DNA storage area. That's their goal.'

'Yes, I'm sure it is,' agreed the Doctor. 'But the question is: why?'

On board the mother ship of the Other fleet the commander

examined the sensor input with surprise. The bridge hummed with controlled, regimented activity. It was a bleak place with no personality, just machine-like order. Here design was submerged under function, every console, screen and panel plainly set for maximum clarity, minimum clutter, the entire bridge a tribute to cold, emotionless rationalism. Some kind of crisis had occurred to the internal systems of the prey's ship – some crisis that had happened after their own aborted attack.

The commander had no idea what could have caused such a complete change in the prey's status but he wasn't about to look a gift horse in the mouth. According to the sensors the entire defence system of *Hope* had been shut down and an auto-destruct sequence initiated. The auto-destruct had subsequently been frozen, halted but not completely rescinded. The defence systems remained in a similar state of suspension.

For now *Hope* was blind and defenceless. At last the long hunt might be over. Now was the time to attack in force.

The commander gave the order.

The final battle was about to begin.

The Doctor returned to the main bridge with a strange expression on his face. Neither Zoe nor Jamie had fancied assisting the Doctor with the examination of the Other but both were eager to hear his findings. Merik was also keen to learn what the Doctor had discovered. Now he was the last guardian, he knew that only he stood between the Other and their goal. Any extra data he could receive on the nature of his enemy might give him the edge he needed.

'Well, Doctor?' asked Zoe, impatiently.

The Doctor looked up, an infinite sadness in his eyes. He seemed reluctant to speak for a moment but knew that he had to. 'Well, I've examined the body and I now know all I need to know about the Other.' He paused, as if considering his next words very carefully. Then, after a heavy sigh, he continued. 'The Other are incredibly mutated, evolved, aggressive humanoids...'

'Mutants?' Zoe asked. 'Mutant what?'

'Human mutations, I'm afraid, Zoe,' replied the Doctor sadly. 'Humans like you and Jamie. The Other are the *real* final descendants of the human race.'

Neither Zoe nor Jamie had ever heard such a despairing tone in the Doctor's voice. For a long moment there was silence.

'So why do they want the DNA?' asked Zoe finally.

'My guess is that the Other plan to use the "pure" human DNA to regain some of the things their race has lost: compassion, humanity if you like. But I rather think it's too late for them. Their efforts to regain some vestige of humanity is doomed to failure; they've gone too far down their evolutionary cul-de-sac. Too far for any hope of return. They'll just get more and more aggressive and evil until either they've destroyed and killed all living things or been destroyed themselves.' The Doctor stopped. There seemed little more to say.

'I'm sorry, Merik. Your makers must have been some of the last "pure" humans. When they died that was probably the end of the human race.' Again the Doctor let silence punctuate his statement, clearly upset at coming to this conclusion.

Jamie glanced around the room, not knowing how to respond to any of this or how to lighten his friend's mood. What he saw only made things worse.

'Doctor! Look!' exclaimed Jamie, pointing in horror at the monitor screens showing the exterior of the ship. A huge number of boarding craft were slipping through the blackness of space and landing on the many surfaces of *Hope*.

'The defence system is down; while the auto-destruct is in limbo it cannot be reset,' explained Merik.

On the screens thousands of the Other could be seen pouring out of the assault craft and cutting through the outer hull with powerful lasers.

'This time you must go, Doctor,' continued Merik. 'Run now. I'll reactivate the self-destruct sequence when you've reached the TARDIS – that way you can get away and I can complete my mission the only way I can now and destroy the Other.'

The Doctor started to complain but Merik held his hand up

to silence him.

'There's no time to argue Doctor. I was built in the hope of taking mankind to a new beginning but now I can see that my destiny, my duty, is to ensure the destruction of the evil that mankind has become. Go now.'

The Doctor turned to his companions and nodded. 'Go on, Jamie, Zoe. Get to the TARDIS. I'll be there in a moment.'

Zoe and Jamie entered the lift and disappeared from view.

The Doctor turned back to Merik. 'Are you sure there's no other way?'

Merik shook his head. 'There is something you could do for me, though,' he began.

'Something I can take from your collection, perhaps?' guessed the Doctor.

By way of an answer Merik moved to a secure door and punched a security code into the small keypad. The door opened to reveal a picture resting on the shelf within.

The picture was about three feet square, a representation of two human faces, one of each sex. The image was picked out in tiny raised metal rods, a form of art the Doctor recognized as having been popular on Earth in the 21st century, itself a revival of a 20th-century toy in which people were able to make an impression in a frame containing similar rods.

Merik handed the artwork to the Doctor.

'Encrypted into the rods is a recording of the signal we are following; this artwork was commissioned and executed in honour of our mission. If nothing else of the human race is to survive, I'd like this to. It's called "The Faces of Humanity".'

The Doctor nodded gravely and took the artwork. 'I'll do what I can.'

On the screens the two could see that the Other were already gaining access to the inner hull. It was time to go.

'You could set the auto-destruct and come with us, in the TARDIS...'

'No Doctor. I was built for a purpose and when the ship dies that purpose will be over. Leave me to my fate.'

The Doctor nodded again, an infinity of sadness in the

gesture, and ran swiftly to the lift.

Behind him the android, the last almost-human, turned back to the computer console and cancelled the hold command on the auto-destruct.

Seconds after the Doctor had run through the waiting open doors of the TARDIS and secured them, the ship exploded in a massive ball of destructive energy, which filled the system it was flying through with the bright light of a sun going nova.

The entire complex ship called *Hope*, the thousands of the Other attacking the ship and the android guardian Merik were all instantly reduced to their component atoms.

Only the TARDIS, slipping sideways into the space-time continuum, survived.

It was some time later – insofar as a term like 'later' had any meaning in a time-space machine – and, according to the Doctor, the TARDIS had travelled many millennia chronologically backwards to a period long before the Other had evolved from humans.

The TARDIS had materialized on a populated planet right in the heart of the inhabited universe and the Doctor and his two companions had enjoyed a pleasant rest in one of the leisure resorts. During their visit the Doctor had arranged to leave the last artefact of the human race in one of the many art galleries in the city. He didn't bother to explain exactly what it was, or what it signified, just passed on its title and left it at that, letting it speak for itself as an *objet d'art*.

Back in the TARDIS Jamie asked the Doctor if he'd had any luck deciphering the odd TARDIS signal that had taken them to the museum ship in the first place.

'Oh yes, Doctor,' added Zoe, her brow wrinkled a little as she recalled – with exact precision thanks to her remarkable memory – what the Doctor had reported Merik saying about the artwork. 'Merik said that a version of the signal was encoded in the picture. Did you find out where it came from?'

The Doctor shrugged absent-mindedly, as if his mind were elsewhere. 'No, I never did. Sometimes it's best not to look too closely at the future. Especially one's own.'

'Doctor – I've been thinking…' said Jamie, unexpectedly. Zoe bit her tongue to stop herself injecting some rude remark. 'Most of the Other were destroyed when *Hope* self-destructed weren't they?' continued Jamie.

The Doctor nodded.

'Aye, but that couldn't have been all of the race, could it? Somewhere out there, in the far future there's probably a whole lot more of the creatures. Human monsters doing terrible things.' Jamie sounded appalled by the idea.

The Doctor nodded, gravely. 'I'm afraid that you're right, Jamie, I'm very much afraid you're right.'

Suddenly, the console room felt a little colder and a little darker for just a moment, as if the TARDIS itself was reflecting her owner's thoughts, and then things returned to normal and the ship spun on through the impossibility of the time-space continuum towards their own unknowable future and the unimaginable excitement of new adventures.

Fegovy

By Gareth Roberts

Miss Monodine hobbled onto the small, cluttered bridge of the *Phaethon*, supporting her broad-beamed bulk with her stick, whispering crossly and shaking her head. Her gaze settled on a half-empty bottle of rye and a tumbler resting on the navigation panel and she made a fearsome, disapproving noise, a sort of volcanic rumble, at the back of her throat. 'Willchook!' she bellowed. 'Willchook!'

The pilot's chair whipped round guiltily. Its occupant's eyes were wide with fear, but he knew better than to scurry away and he sat still, transfixed, as she advanced. 'I told you,' she said, drawing out each word, 'no drink, not on this trip.' He bowed his head, and her ire grew. 'How dare you just sit there! Are you man or mouse?' She raised the flat of her hand and batted him about the head in rhythm with her admonishment. 'This is not a joyride, Willchook!'

Now satisfied – she liked to start the day with an act of violence and it was often difficult to find a suitable excuse – she pulled back. Her hand was pink and it stung. She brought it up to her lips and kissed herself better.

Willchook spoke. 'But Miss Monodine,' he spluttered, 'there is simply nothing out here.' He waved a hand in the direction of the forward scan display. The way ahead was unremittingly black and blank. 'No traffic, no planetary systems, no debris.'

She hissed. 'Idiot. Do you imagine we're the only ones to have been summoned by this Fegovy? There might be any number of other bidders. I ordered you to keep a constant watch!' She felt anger returning.

'I've been on watch for eighteen hours,' he said drowsily, with a longing look at the bunk built into the bridge's wall. 'And there's nothing but void. I was bored.'

Miss Monodine landed him another slap, brutally, under the chin. 'I'll give you bored. You're a drunk, Willchook. I wonder why I picked you.'

'I'm cheap, Miss Monodine,' he muttered.

Her face flushed beetroot-red. 'Shut up! Shut up!' She lunged for the whisky bottle and raised it menacingly over his head. 'I told you never to speak of money in front of me!' She threw the bottle into a corner, where it sparked a small electrical fire, then reached out and grabbed his jaw, clamping it with her raw fingers. 'When I was a child,' she rumbled, 'I watched my father flay a man that crossed him. He peeled off the fellow's skin from head to toe' – at this point in the telling she increased the force of her squeeze – 'and forced him to carry it, over his shoulder, out into the vacuum. If I didn't need a pilot, I'd do much the same to you!' She released him with a shove that sent him crashing into the navigation panel. 'From now, you keep a clear head!'

She expected more apologies, but something had caught Willchook's eye, a light flashing on the forward scan display. He raised a finger. 'That's impossible. Something's registering.'

Miss Monodine squinted at the display. 'Too small for a ship.'

Willchook shrugged. 'Could be a nipper.'

She cuffed him once more. 'This far into the dark zones, with the nearest refuelling satellite on the far side of Abarantikos? Don't be a fool. It must be an asteroid.' The trace shifted to the centre of the display and began to grow, spreading outwards along the grid-lines. 'It's right in our path!'

Willchook blinked his bleary eyes, and sat dazed, like a frightened animal caught by a bright light. 'Well, compensate, man, compensate!' Miss Monodine urged him, her own alarm getting the better of her. The asteroid was now horrifyingly close, the details of its irregular, sharply jagged outline picked out by the *Phaethon*'s battery of scans. One puncture and they would be torn apart, sent spinning, as aimless and lifeless as any piece of cosmic flotsam.

Willchook's hands fluttered nervously over the flight controls.

After several months, reckoned by her own relative experience, of travels aboard the TARDIS, Mel was beginning to understand more of the Doctor's character. He was, she had decided, almost impossible to pin down, and his personality was as vibrant and varied as his colourful coat. Whenever she thought she had the measure of him he'd reveal a totally unexpected side to his nature, a tactic he employed against friends and enemies alike. He might brush aside the death of a galaxy with a flippant remark and then descend into depression at the sight of a diseased tree; be extolling the wonders of some distant constellation one minute and claim never to have heard of it the next. On first meeting he could appear rather brusque and egotistical, but there was more than a hint of self-mockery in his boastings, and she'd seen him perform acts of forgiveness and compassion which gave the lie to any accusation of heartlessness. Put simply, if anything about the Doctor could ever be simple, he was always thrilling company, despite his erratic exterior.

His present craze had come about purely by accident. The TARDIS had jerked in mid-flight, dislodging a book from a high shelf that landed right on top of his curly head. The book turned out to be a scientific text so abstruse as to be meaningless to Mel, and the page at which it fell contained what the Doctor called a 'fascinating thesis' on a phenomenon known as interstitial bias. Immediately he was consumed by a desire to test out the theory, to which end he had materialized the TARDIS inside a floating asteroid, set up a laser device, and proceeded to drill for a particular mineral.

Now Mel stood in the centre of the asteroid's largest cavity, hands on hips, her head tilted up to take in the grandeur of her surroundings. Rust-red stalactites hung from a mighty arch, like a curtain raised over a spectacle. Beneath were formations of rock, hundreds of them, twisted in unfamiliar patterns. Mel was overwhelmed by the beauty of the scene, and felt humbled by a sense of timelessness. Even the Doctor's nine hundred-plus years paled when compared with the geological ages of this lonely fragment. 'Doctor, this is fantastic,' she called over her shoulder. 'To think, we're the only beings that have ever stood here, or ever will.' She sighed. 'What an incredible privilege.'

The Doctor left his laser cutter and strolled over to her, waving the beam of his torch about nonchalantly. The light threw up two shadows on the cavity wall: her own, slender and petite, and his, tall and wide. 'Mere *son et lumière*, Mel.' She watched as he lifted a hand and made a bunny-rabbit shadow, which then started to bounce along.

She slapped his hand lightly, giggling in spite of herself. 'You're spoiling the atmosphere.'

'No atmosphere to spoil,' he reminded her. 'Not within this desolate crag.' Their oxygen came from cylinders brought out from the TARDIS. 'Anyway, I wouldn't get too comfortable. I'm nearly ready to go.'

'You've got what we came for?'

'Yes, Mel.' He shut away the miniature cutter he'd been using for the finer points of the job and returned it to his pocket. 'Do you know, this experiment is going to be fascinating. Could herald an astounding breakthrough in the field of inter-stitial physics.' His eyes glazed over, which she recognized as a bad sign. He was going to get lyrical. 'Did I say break-through? Too meek a word. No, our work will be a positive confutation to the sceptics. A bold charge through the flum-mery, a vital strike against the purist hordes!'

Mel sniffed. 'That's as may be. But you still haven't ex-plained exactly what we're meant to be doing.'

For a moment she thought he was about to explode with temper. He gaped at her as if she had said the most astonish-ingly stupid thing. Then, seemingly with an effort, he brought himself under control. 'Doing? Doing? Mel, we are going to be "doing", as you so quaintly put it, an experiment that will revolutionize the sphere of bias-related studies!'

Mel took a deep breath, and was about to point out that she had no idea what bias-related studies were, but before she could, both she and the Doctor were hurled off their feet. It was like being caught in the middle of an explosion. The asteroid shook around them, and they were thrown up and down. At the same time there was an enormous sonic boom. Mel shrieked, lost her balance and was sent tumbling over and over. Thinking quickly, she brought her arms and legs up into a crash position, and waited for the vibration to subside.

To her relief, stability returned after only a couple more seconds. She sat up slowly, shaking grit from her hair and checking for injuries, but apart from a few cuts and bruises she was unscathed. She looked about, but the Doctor was not in sight. She called his name, and her brow furrowed. Where could he have disappeared to? They'd been standing right next to each other when the upset struck. She called out again, her voice tinged with fear. 'Doctor, where are you?'

'Where do you think?' To her astonishment his reply came from above. She looked up and had to stifle a guffaw. For the Doctor's ample girth was sandwiched between two outcrops of rock halfway up the cavity wall. He held a hand down and wiggled his fingers. 'I seem to have got myself wedged between a rock and a hard place. Help me down, will you?'

Mel folded her arms and smiled sweetly. 'I don't know whether I should. You look almost angelic up there.' Her point scored, she relented, and aided his release. 'What caused the tremor?'

He dusted himself down, and an icy glint appeared in his eyes. 'Tremor? Nothing so natural. Something knocked into us. From the sound of that bang, a spacecraft.' He held out a shirtcuff, ripped in the tumult. 'Look at that, ruined.'

'A spacecraft?' Mel was confused. 'I thought you said this place was located far outside the space trade routes?'

'It is,' he replied. 'Nevertheless, a spacecraft came knocking into this asteroid.'

'And we ended up doing a very good impression of a couple of jumping beans.' Mel sighed. 'Still, not to worry. No bones broken.'

'That is hardly the point,' fumed the Doctor. 'I'd like to know what a spacecraft, and one presumably piloted by a suicidal maniac, is doing out here. It takes true incompetence to bump into something as large as this. A mystery indeed, and one worth the solving.' He nodded to the TARDIS and set off in its direction.

'Hang on, Doctor,' Mel protested. 'What about the experiment?'

'Never mind that,' came his reply. He was already through the doors of the police box. 'Obviously this incident takes precedence over such an abstract endeavour.'

'Obviously,' sighed Mel. Resigning herself to his eccentricity, she quickly scooped up the laser cutter and followed him in.

'Only very minor damage sustained,' Willchook reported, in a voice heavy with relief. 'Scratches on the right rear fin.'

Miss Monodine glanced over the report supplied by the ship's computer and took a deep breath. 'A metre or two either way and we could have been ripped apart.' She reached out and gripped Willchook's shoulder, hard.

'I still can't believe it was there,' he babbled. 'There's no way I could have foreseen it.'

She dug her nails into the flesh of his neck. 'Apart from keeping your eyes on the forward displays, cretin.' She let go and flexed her fingers. 'You get us on, lad. Not far now to the rendezvous point.'

Willchook consulted a chart. 'Should be there in about half an hour, yes. Barring any' – his eyes flickered with fear as he caught sight of her expression – 'any unforeseen circumstances.'

Miss Monodine growled and left the bridge.

The Doctor squinted at a display on the TARDIS console. Over his shoulder Mel saw a spiral pattern shrieking through space. 'That's an energy trace, isn't it?' she asked.

He nodded. 'The energy trace of that ship's badly shielded engines. They're a health hazard in more ways than one.' A similar, but larger, pattern appeared. 'Ah! More traces. More ships. But what are they all doing out here?' He bustled Mel around the console and reached for the scanner control. 'Let's see, shall we?'

Mel turned to face the scanner screen as the shutters parted. The image revealed was startling. A large space platform was floating before them. Its long runway reminded Mel of aircraft carriers back on Earth, but this was three times the size, and looked rather run-down and overused; there were bare metal patches between the landing strips. Arranged at equal distances around the dock were circular pads, fourteen in all, and all but one were occupied. The variety of designs was intriguing. One of the craft resembled nothing so much as a giant crystal cube, in which a statically charged blue fluid swirled. Another was squat, black and many-faceted like a crystal; its neighbour was a space yacht, its tall white sail billowing in the winds of a self-generating ion stream. 'Those ships are all totally different,' she pointed out. 'Recognize any of them?'

The Doctor grunted. 'I'm afraid to say I do. That' – he pointed to the squat black craft – 'belongs to a Chelonian.' Mel shuddered to recall her previous meeting with that savage reptilian species. 'And that' – now he indicated the crystal cube – 'is the property of an Eyspeer. They're bleach-like creatures, from the Vesperus series. I can't see what those two would have in common, let alone any of the others.' He tapped his chin with a finger. 'That's the really curious thing.'

'Hmmm,' agreed Mel. 'Why would such a diverse bunch come together like this?' An unpleasant thought struck her. 'They couldn't be meeting in an unholy alliance, could they?'

'What, war council?' The Doctor dismissed the notion with a shake of his black-and-yellow-striped cuff. 'Unlikely. Besides, look again at the state of that place. Dark, lonely, gone to seed. And not remotely military.'

'Perhaps that's what we're supposed to think,' said Mel.

'In this isolated spot there'd be no need to camouflage. After all -' The Doctor broke off as another spaceship appeared on the screen, zooming into the picture from above. Mel caught a blurred glimpse of a tattered grey craft, its fins blackened and cracked. 'There's our reckless driver,' said the Doctor. 'Going in for a landing.' He fiddled with a control on the console and the scanner image zoomed in to pick out the details of the space dock. In the centre, Mel now saw, was a pentagon-shaped block, featureless and windowless, into which ran narrow tunnels from the landing pads.

'Let's materialize down there,' she urged the Doctor. 'It must be their base, whoever they are.'

But the Doctor's face wore an unexpectedly cautious expression. 'Hang on, Mel.'

She was puzzled. 'Come on, Doctor. You're not normally so reticent. I thought you wanted to unravel this conundrum.'

'And so I do,' he replied. 'But new puzzles keep presenting themselves. Look at these readings.' He beckoned her forward and indicated a panel on the console that Mel recognized as an interface with the TARDIS's environment sensors. She glanced at the flickering display and frowned.

'That's incredible,' she said. 'There's an enormous energy build-up around that space platform.'

The Doctor sighed. 'I know. But what kind of energy?'

Mel examined the readings once more. 'That's strange. The sensors won't specify.'

'Won't?' the Doctor mused. 'Or can't?' He looked out at the platform. 'And there's no sign of any power store or the like. Certainly nothing large enough to cause a disturbance of that magnitude.'

'All the more reason to investigate,' Mel enthused.

The Doctor smiled. 'Mel, you are indefatigable.' He reached for the materialization controls.

Varzlad the Pitted viewed the other occupants of the hall (except, of course, for his trusted reptile-at-arms Jerlot) through eyelids narrowed in suspicion. Though his hydraulic joints needed extra oiling these days, he remained hardy as a beast of the field, and was ready to react with violence to any opposition, whenever it was met. Proximity to these strange creatures made him wary. Nowadays, dealings with humanoids were unavoidable, almost commonplace, although secretly Varzlad fantasized about the days of empire: it was the stranger lifeforms that most unsettled him. The Eyspeer, for example, a wisp-like entity, half gas and half liquid, encased in a hovering opaque cube. Then there were the two Moroks, tall and bipedal, with grotesquely enlarged upper bodies and dome-shaped craniums. And he could barely bring himself to look upon the slimy, matted fur of the Grimyr, its odorous body buzzing with bright blue flies. In spite of decades spent adventuring and travelling across wide reaches of space, Varzlad still found it difficult to read the non-verbal signals of other species. But somehow he could tell that his own anxiousness was shared by all of the others.

Jerlot hissed in his ear, 'Sir, it's coming up to noon.'

Varzlad grunted. 'Good. Enough time has been wasted. I don't like this waiting.' He leant closer to his comrade and whispered, 'These others. None can match our bid, I am certain.'

'Agreed, sir.' Jerlot nodded eagerly. His one remaining yellow eye swept around the gathered group. 'I don't think we'll have much of a problem with these, sir. Milksops all, eh?'

'Never underestimate your opponents,' warned Varzlad. His shell sagged slightly. 'That is how the empire was lost, you will recall. Forethought is essential in all conflicts. You should –'

He was interrupted by the big blue door at the end of the hall, which swung open automatically to admit another delegation. All eyes turned to face the new arrivals. Even the Eyspeer, Varzlad noticed, swivelled about for a look.

These ones were almost certainly pure-bred humans. There was one male, pink and round with yellow curls of wool about the head, and one female, much smaller and possessed of orange wool. They advanced into the hall, looking around them. The male nodded his head and said brightly, 'Evening all.' Then, to Varzlad's astonishment, he walked briskly up to the Chelonian party. 'Hello.'

Jerlot hissed and Varzlad reared up on his back feet slightly.

'Quite pleasant here, isn't it?' he went on, looking around the big hall. 'A bit too blue for my taste. Sorry, I'm forgetting myself.' He held out one of his adaptable appendages. 'I am known as the Doctor.' He paused, as if expecting a reaction from them, but the name meant nothing to Varzlad. He indicated the female. 'This is my dear friend and constant companion, Melanie Bush.'

'Known as Mel,' the female put in brightly.

Varzlad supposed some reply was expected. 'Varzlad,' he said gruffly.

'Jerlot,' said Jerlot, equally gruffly.

There was a potent silence.

'Ah,' said the Doctor. 'Well, if that's how you feel ...' And he walked away, the female tagging along behind. Varzlad's eyelids narrowed even further as he observed his departure.

As soon as they had found themselves a secluded corner, Mel tugged the Doctor's sleeve and whispered fiercely, 'Did you have to antagonize them like that?'

'I wasn't antagonizing them. Merely testing a theory.'

'Mind letting me in on it?'

He sighed. 'Well, they've never heard of me, have they? Added to that, no Chelonian worth his salt can resist bragging about his rank.'

Mel nodded. 'I get it. They're not with the military?'

'Well, at this stage of their history the Chelonian military won't be how you remember it. But no, to all intents and purposes, you're correct. Those two have no official status. And what really clinches it are those markings.' He pointed to the older Chelonian, Varzlad.

Mel looked more closely at his shell and saw, among the dents and scorchmarks, a painted symbol, an inverted red cross overlaid by three green dots. 'What does it mean?'

'Escaped convict,' said the Doctor. 'Such markings are used in penal institutions all along the Pelopennese borders. Now, I wonder what that says about the rest of this lot?' He gestured vaguely about the big blue hall. Mel had learnt in her time with the Doctor not to judge by appearances, yet such was the variety of alien life about her that she couldn't help but feel alarmed.

'I've an inkling we've stumbled upon some nefarious enterprise,' said the Doctor. 'These ne'er-do-wells are all waiting for someone. But who?'

Mel might have hazarded a reply, but the entranceway slid open once again, and two extraordinary, although mercifully human, figures entered. First was a rotund, wheezing elderly woman who supported herself painfully on a silver-topped cane. She wore a plain black suit and skirt and had an angry, red, scrunched-up face. In close attendance came a man, much younger, with a hesitant and shady look to him. He wore a dishevelled one-piece tunic and reeked of engine oil and rye whiskey. She guessed he might well have been the cause of their earlier accident.

So, plainly, did the Doctor. He stepped forward, clasped his lapels (a sure sign he was about to deliver some of his crushing wit), and said, 'Hello. I think we may have bumped into each other before.' The heads and analogous organs of the other creatures gathered in the hall turned to witness the exchange. 'My young friend and I happened to be aboard that asteroid you so carelessly knocked into. It was a good job neither of us was injured.'

The young pilot smirked. 'Who the dark mine are you?'

The Doctor introduced himself and Mel again. 'It is common practice,' he went on, 'for parties involved in a collision to stop at the scene and discuss terms.'

The old woman hobbled up. She was becoming angrier and redder by the minute. 'And what,' she bellowed, in a voice so loud and deep it hurt the ears, 'were you doing inside an asteroid in the first place?' Her gnarled hand curled around the silver knob of her stick. 'One can hardly be damned for supposing it a most unlikely place to be.' As she spoke small particles of dribble flew from her mouth and adhered to the Doctor's shirt collar. 'And as you say you are neither of you injured in any way.'

Mel spoke. 'That turn-out was pure luck. We could have been killed.'

The old woman snorted. 'It's of no importance to me.' She nodded to her assistant. 'Willchook.'

'Yes, Miss Monodine?'

'I've no time to waste on these two clowns. Let us take up our positions. It's nearly noon.' She teetered off, and Willchook followed. They joined the mixed assemblage at the far end of the hall, and fell into line between the Eyspeer and one of two New Alexandrians.

'I think you're right,' Mel whispered to the Doctor. 'They're a fishy bunch, all of them.'

The Doctor seemed lost in thought for a few moments. When at last he spoke it was quietly and calmly. 'Mel, why don't you sneak out and see what you can discover from their spaceships? There might be any number of clues to be turned up.'

The suggestion was welcomed by Mel, who was inquisitive by nature. 'OK. What about you?'

'Oh, I think I'll stay and keep an eye on' – he nodded towards the aliens and smiled –'on things here.'

The scanning mechanisms reported that the final delegation had arrived in the hall. Everything was ready. Proceedings could commence. It was noon.

Fegovy activated.

Miss Monodine's mind was racing. She glanced back at the other humanoids in the hall, and the frown she wore habitually deepened. 'Who can they be?' she muttered. 'Why are they here?'

Willchook had overheard her. 'For the same reasons as us, surely?'

She slapped him. 'Of course not. Think, man. People with our position in life dress down, keep themselves in the shadows. Draw attention to yourself and you're dead. But just look at that ludicrous coat.' She indicated the Doctor. 'He likes the whole Universe to know he's around.'

'Yeah,' said Willchook. 'A real ponce, isn't he? And the girl's just unreal. Could they be the law?'

'No. But they –' She caught Willchook's arm tightly and hissed, 'Look.' The red-headed girl, after snatching a moment's whispered conversation with her mentor, was slipping out the back way. 'Where's she off to, I wonder?'

Willchook's eyes widened. 'You don't think they might–'

'– have had the same idea as me?' finished Miss Monodine. 'It could be. Get after her.' Willchook nodded and slipped away.

Jerlot nudged Varzlad in the side. 'That Doctor's coming back over, sir.'

Varzlad looked up. The yellow-wooled human was sauntering across, hands in pockets. He nodded towards the big blue door. 'Taking their time, aren't they?' He blew out his cheeks. 'You could cut the atmosphere in here with a thermic lance.'

Varzlad narrowed his eyes in suspicion. 'That is not possible. And why should I wish to?'

The Doctor sighed. 'It was a joke. A witticism.' Varzlad stared blankly at him. 'I was speaking figuratively.'

Varzlad shook his head slowly. 'I do not understand, nor do I wish to. Please do not talk to us. It is inappropriate.'

'I was only trying to be friendly,' the Doctor protested, sounding rather hurt. He stooped to address Varzlad more easily. 'So, what were you in for, then?'

Jerlot spoke. 'Is this another witticism?'

'Of course not.' The Doctor nodded to Varzlad's penal identification mark. 'I mean, we've all of us served time. Sometimes I think I must have spent most of my life in custody.' Varzlad glowered at him. 'I was merely being sociable.'

'I have no wish to socialize with a human,' said Varzlad. Then, with a flourish, he whipped out a keen-bladed knife from his shell and held it to the Doctor's fleshy throat. 'Ask any more of these questions, make any more of your witticisms, and I will assuage your curiosity by granting you a second mouth. Ironically, you should then never prattle again!' He gurgled, then pushed the Doctor away.

'That is a good witticism, sir,' said Jerlot.

The Doctor rubbed his neck. 'Yes, very amusing. I was wondering why one sees so few Chelonian variety turns.'

Varzlad might have responded to this, but there was a sudden musical chime and the big blue door at the far end of the hall opened at last. Whatever lay beyond was shrouded in darkness. The gathered company fell into silence, and there was a moment of hushed expectation.

The moment was broken when a ball of sizzling bright green light whooshed into the open. Varzlad flexed his muscles, alarmed, but the ball settled before them, hovering about two metres off the ground. The brightness of its core made it difficult for him to examine it closely, and its constant sparkling and wobbling were dazzling to the eye.

A voice came from the ball. 'Welcome.' The voice was high-pitched, metallic, distorted, polite and strangely inflected. 'I'm so glad that you could come. I trust your journeys here were smooth and free of trouble.'

The elderly human female with the support-stick hobbled forward. 'Dispense with the pleasantries. None of us can spare the time. Where is your master? Where is Fegovy?'

'I am Fegovy,' said the ball.

There was a ripple of surprise around the company. Varzlad glanced up at the Doctor, and was surprised to see his previously foolish face set hard in an entirely different arrangement.

Jerlot edged forward. 'It doesn't matter what he looks like. When is the auction to begin?'

'Yes,' said the Eyspeer, its cube vibrating slowly, tilting the fluid within. 'I am anxious for bidding to start.'

'All in good time,' said Fegovy. 'I am sure you would like

to inspect the lot.'

'Obviously,' growled Varzlad. 'Bring it out, now.'

There was a raucous chorus of approval at his words, a rustling of scales, feathers and other physical parts.

'I can do better than that,' said Fegovy. 'Observe.'

A thin tendril of light flashed statically from his core, snaking back through the still-open door through which his entry had been made. Seconds later it returned, carrying in its grip the Face of Humanity, the male and female faces rippling in its pin-cushion effect. Varzlad shuffled forward for a closer inspection, as did the elderly human female. Fegovy reacted to their advance by angling the Face so that its surface glinted under the powerful lights of the hall.

'As you can see,' said Fegovy. 'I was not exaggerating in my claim. The Face of Humanity has been restored to perfect condition. Missing for centuries. Its value is almost incalculable.' He paused, then added significantly, 'Almost.'

The Doctor stepped forward, a frown etched deeply into his forehead. His lower lip trembled. 'I feel as if someone's just walked over my grave. In a pair of hobnail boots. May I ask where you came by that?'

Fegovy hesitated. He dipped and bobbed at the sight of the Doctor, and for a moment Varzlad thought he detected a flicker of activity at the heart of the strange being's electric core. Then that assured voice replied, 'You may ask. I will not answer.'

The Eyspeer was getting impatient again. 'Bidding to start. I have no wish to linger here.'

'Very well.' Fegovy crackled, and a second tendril split from its body. On this second occasion it formed a large, roughly circular surface suspended in mid-air. Across this surface appeared a series of symbols in Galactic standard notation. 'Let bidding commence,' said Fegovy, 'with a starting price of forty thousand mega-credits.'

One of the New Alexandrians bristled. 'Forty thousand!'

'A fair amount, surely?' said Fegovy. 'This item is certainly one of the rarest, most special, most valuable, in the known Cosmos.' The tabulator clicked up, displaying the starting price. 'Let bidding commence.'

The Eyspeer grated, 'Forty-five thousand.'

'Fifty,' slurred the Grimyr.

'Fifty-five,' said Miss Monodine, rapping at the metallic flooring with her stick.

Varzlad and Jerlot exchanged a knowing glance.

Fegovy's recognition membrane quivered at the sight of the tall male humanoid. Mechanisms connected to his ident interface clicked and whirred, struggling to interpret the meaning of this stranger's arrival. A precision study of the man was collated, and this referential material checked against a coded index stored in Fegovy's backup core. Seconds later a series of images flashed into the frontal cortex: a distorted and much-copied two-dimensional recording that showed the stranger, arms gesticulating wildly, shouting soundlessly up at an unheeding chamber of stiff-collared dignitaries. This was exchanged for a bewildering array of other faces, each man displayed in some unfeasibly heroic pose.

Fegovy's sensors twitched with excitement. The Doctor!

Mel found her way to the docking chambers with ease. The hallways of the platform were featureless, metallic and spotless, and as she walked at her usual brisk pace on her errand, her sense of unease increased. 'I've a feeling I'm missing something,' she said to herself, stopping to rest at a corner and cradling her chin in one hand. Since emerging into this environment with the Doctor she'd felt an unaccustomed alarm. It wasn't the sight of the aliens in the main hall – she was no stranger to bizarre company – so much as a creeping sensation of unreality. These drab corridors reinforced the impression. It was as if, despite the platform's obvious age, nobody had ever used it before.

Still, speculation wasn't any use. She carried on, and came eventually to a wide white terminal, its concave surfaces host to fourteen entrance locks. She chose one at random and peered through the transparent panel built into it. The short passage-

way beyond ended in a buckled and much-scarred grey metal
hatch. 'That'll be the old woman's ship,' she surmised. 'Looks
like it's been in many a scrape.'

The next door along was of the same design, and through the
clear porthole Mel saw the familiar irregularly edged chassis of
the Chelonian ship. Third along the line was the New
Alexandrians' vessel. There was nothing out of the ordinary,
nothing that could be pointed out. But still she felt uncomfort-
able, troubled by something she couldn't name.

'Standing about here isn't going to help the Doctor,' she
sighed. Then she put her eye to the fourth door, deciding this
investigation might as well be conducted thoroughly. She
squinted through the porthole, and was forced to blink to check
her vision.

There was nothing on the other side of the door. Beyond the
panel was a short passage, and at its end only empty space and
distant stars winking coldly at her.

She thought quickly, and brought back into her mind the
mental image of the platform as seen from space on the
TARDIS scanner. The next ship in the sequence should have
been the Eyspeer cube. 'Perhaps it's undocked,' she whispered. Curiosity aroused, she slipped to the fifth door, where
her memory told her the Grimyr craft was located. Again,
nothing.

She stepped back, and contemplated the puzzle. 'Why
would they leave?' she wondered aloud. 'Clearing off like
that's totally out of character for cut-throats.'

Her musings were interrupted rudely as a grimy male hand
gripped her suddenly about the waist, and a warm stubbled
cheek, reeking of alcohol, pressed itself against her face. 'Do
you always talk to yourself?' asked her attacker. 'It makes you
look mad.' The voice belonged to the pilot of the Earth ship.

Mel writhed and kicked. 'Get your filthy hands off me!'

But his grip was firm. He reached up and clamped his dirty
fingers around her neck. 'Don't struggle, little doll,' he whispered. Mel felt something pressing into the small of her back.

Fearfully she asked, 'What's that thing digging into me?'

'It's a blaster,' he hissed. 'So don't think of screaming for help, all right?' He started to drag her away, towards the first of the docking ports, where his mistress's ship was docked.

'I wouldn't dream of it,' sighed Mel.

The auction was proceeding apace, and too quickly for Varzlad's liking. His pulses pounded in his head as the price spiralled ever upward. The start-up value had now been doubled.

'I have ninety thousand, ninety thousand,' said Fegovy, ducking slightly to indicate the Grimyr leader, who in turn bowed his own flea-infested head. 'Any advance on ninety?'

'One hundred,' said Miss Monodine.

Varzlad bared his teeth. 'One hundred and twenty.'

'One hundred and forty,' said the Eyspeer.

'Two hundred,' Varzlad barked, stomping one of his front feet down so heavily that sparks flew from his outstretched claws. A silence descended over the gathering. The Grimyr shuffled, dislodging several flies; the fluid in the Eyspeer cube bubbled furiously, signalling a fierce internal conflict.

Jerlot edged closer to his commander and whispered, 'Sir, you are approaching the credit limit agreed by the God Mother!'

'Thank you for reminding me,' Varzlad snapped back.

'Two hundred and one,' said the Eyspeer.

'Two hundred and ten,' said Varzlad.

'Sir, the God Mother,' Jerlot protested.

'Damn him,' Varzlad hissed. He gestured to the lot. 'That is the Face of Humanity. Constructed out of phizlomium. Neither the God Mother nor the idiots here realize its worth. I know of a collector in the Valence sector who'll pay five times as much for it. So be silent!'

Fegovy hovered over. 'There is some dispute, gentlemen?'

'No dispute,' Varzlad said promptly. 'Now, where do we stand again?'

'You lead the bidding on two hundred and ten,' said Fegovy.

'Make it two hundred and twenty, then.' Varzlad sneered up at the ball of light.

'Two hundred and twenty.' Fegovy's voice was rich with

delight. 'Any advance on two hundred and twenty thousand mega-credits?'

There was silence; the Eyspeer and the Grimyr were immobile, their appendages cast down. Miss Monodine stood rigidly, her face imperturbable.

Fegovy crackled, and swooped to place himself next to the Face. 'Very well. Going once, going twice –'

'Wait!'

Varzlad's head turned abruptly to trace the source of this interruption. It came from the Doctor, who had retreated to the back of the hall at the start of bidding, his arms folded, forgotten. He stepped forward, pushing through the crowd until he stood directly before Fegovy.

'I bid three hundred thousand mega-credits,' he said.

Mel had never felt so helpless. With a length of rope, Willchook had secured her to a chair in one corner of his ship's bridge, and a quick tug at her bonds confirmed that she was held fast. Her surroundings were markedly unappealing. The small flight cabin was cramped and out of repair, with lengths of wire exposed along several surfaces and fault-warning neons glowing above half of the functional system panels. The air was thick with grease and alcohol fumes, and the grinding throb of a motor sounded every couple of minutes.

She watched Willchook as he busied himself at the flight panel. 'This place is pretty grim,' she remarked. He made no answer. 'It's falling apart,' she went on. 'Even if you had come a cropper on that asteroid I don't think it'd have made much difference.'

'Why don't you just shut that squeaky little mouth of yours, china doll,' Willchook grunted as he wrestled with the controls.

Mel was used to people rejecting her advice. It didn't bother her; more often than not later events proved her right. She sighed. 'If I'm to be your prisoner, at least you can tell me what you're planning.'

He grinned and shook his head. 'Slow, aren't you?' He nodded to the ship's flight screen, which displayed the vista of empty space. 'We're going to be heading back homeward, one hell of a lot better off. Miss Monodine will return from the auction soon, with the Face.'

'I don't understand,' said Mel. 'Auction?'

Willchook sneered. 'Of course. She got the summons from Fegovy last week. She's been lying low of late. Lost out in a big deal, fallen on hard times. This Fegovy character obviously don't know that, though. She'll lift it, all right.' His eyes misted over and he lost himself in the screen's image. 'I get half a per cent of the sale price.'

Mel sniffed. 'Half a per cent? That doesn't sound like much of a deal.'

He grinned. 'It'll set me up for life on one of the planets of exotica, which is all I want. I'll never have to slave for anyone again.' He lost himself in reflection. 'Another couple of weeks and I'll be bathing in the crystal springs of Uffe...'

'Then what do you want with me?' Mel asked. She shrugged the best she was able. 'I mean, look at me. I'm hardly a threat to your scheme.'

'We may need a hostage,' he replied. 'And that's a role you'll play very well.' He crossed over and stroked her hair gently with a dirty finger. 'And I might not be able to wait for my pleasures. The anticipation might be too much for me, you see. You're not too revolting, I suppose.'

Mel shuddered at the vile suggestion. 'Hadn't you better continue those flight checks?'

He smiled and withdrew his hand. 'You're right. We'll have to get away very quickly.' She sensed apprehension in his manner. Most likely, she thought, he feared his formidable-looking mistress. He pressed down a row of switches on the panel, and frowned. He flicked them up and then down again. Still there was no discernible result.

'What's wrong?' asked Mel.

'Docking clamps,' he answered. 'They're not retracting.' He fumbled at the screen controls and a computerized diagram flashed up. It showed the innards of some sort of locking mechanism, presumably that connecting the ship to the space platform. Mel made a mental note of the three heavy clamps securing the ship's hatch to the airlock. Willchook depressed the switches for a third time, and for a third time there was no response. The locking bars remained in position on the schematic.

Willchook cursed. 'We're held fast!'

The Doctor's pronouncement had stunned the occupants of the auction room. Even the inscrutable Fegovy had seemed, for just a second, to fizzle with shock. Varzlad shuffled anxiously. Out of the corner of his eye he saw Jerlot muttering and cursing. The only other attendee to show a marked reaction was Miss Monodine, who had puffed up her chest like a scavenger bird and whose wrinkled face was turning deep purple.

'Well, Doctor,' said Fegovy. 'Three hundred thousand mega-credits it is. We must now settle payment.'

The Doctor bit his lip. 'Ah,' he said. 'Will you accept a postdated cheque?'

Varzlad growled. 'Ridiculous! The terms set out by the summons specified an instant cash payment via credit-coil!' As he spoke, he raised one of his front feet and rotated it three times, a movement that all but Jerlot would take as a natural expression of his exasperation.

'That is true, Doctor,' Fegovy concurred.

The Doctor bristled. 'A cheque from the Bank of Pantorus is automatically guaranteed.' He narrowed his eyes. 'By the way, I don't remember telling you my name.'

'The payment, Doctor,' said Fegovy.

'Ah, yes,' said the Doctor, patting his pockets and giving an embarrassed smile. 'Do you know, I think I may have left my cheque book in my other coat. Silly of me.'

'Not good enough,' rumbled Miss Monodine. She addressed Fegovy. 'This fellow's clearly an idiot. His claim is invalid.'

'Clearly.' Fegovy retreated from the Doctor's side and turned to face Varzlad. 'Mr Varzlad of the Chelonian party must inherit the prize. Was it two hundred and twenty-four thousand?'

'Two hundred and twenty,' Varzlad said quickly.

'Let us settle the matter, then,' Fegovy said smoothly. 'Your credit-coil card, please.'

Varzlad took it from a pouch on his work-belt and held it up. A thin tendril of sparkling light took it from his grasp and brought it to rest next to the tabulator. Instantly the display altered to show Varzlad's credit coding juxtaposed with the final fixed price of the Face.

'Credit transfer will now take place,' said Fegovy. A fierce buzzing and humming erupted from him and the tabulator's sparkling green border blurred.

Varzlad exchanged a glance with Jerlot. In several seconds they would be wealthier than could be imagined. But there was a look of alarm and fear on his deputy's face. This was to be his final vision of Jerlot. For a moment later a flaming red haze settled over the boy. He screamed, once, horribly, but nothing could be done. The red haze did its work, stripping away his shell, burning away his flesh. In the second before he crumbled away to ash his skeletal frame was visible, outlined in a ghoulish yellow glow.

'Jerlot!' screamed Varzlad, his body wracked with rage. He looked up at Fegovy. 'Why kill him? You knew he could not harm you.'

Fegovy flickered and spun, as if confused. 'I didn't kill him.'

The Doctor spoke. 'I think, Varzlad...' He completed the sentence with a gesture over his shoulder.

Varzlad turned slowly. Miss Monodine was no longer using her stick as a support. Indeed, her straight-backed frame fairly glowed with vigour, and her red cheeks bloomed health where only minutes before they had signalled decrepitude. Also glowing with a fierce light was the end of her stick which she had raised to cover what remained of the gathering. She angled it towards Fegovy.

She spoke firmly and clearly, her temper implicit for once. 'This is an ion-converter,' she announced grandly.

'And what does that do?' asked the Doctor.

'It converts ions,' snapped Miss Monodine. 'All forms of energy can be converted.' She waggled the stick at Fegovy. 'All forms.' Fegovy drew back a little, and dwindled, as if scared.

Mel sighed as Willchook, now desperate, activated the release mechanism for what must have been the fortieth time. Yet again the clamps held firm. 'This can't be happening,' he breathed, and his hands hovered over the controls once more.

'Perhaps there's a technical fault,' Mel suggested helpfully.

'Shut your mouth,' barked Willchook. He reached under the flight console and moved aside a section of metal panelling, reached inside and withdrew a whisky bottle. Fumbling, he unscrewed the cap.

Mel raised her eyes heavenward. 'Drink's no solution! You'll need a clear head if a crisis occurs!' He scowled at her over his shoulder and took a swig from the bottle. Mel assumed a more plaintive tone. 'Look, I may appear useless, but I do happen to be a computer programmer. If you'll set me free, I may be able to help.' He viewed her with suspicion and drank again. 'I give you my word,' she added. 'I mean, as I see it, we're all in the same boat, and I don't fancy being trapped here.'

Willchook stood up and grunted. 'No tricks?' She shook her head, and he set to work untying her bonds. As soon as she was free she rubbed her chafed wrists and leapt over to the flight panel.

Swiftly she called up the backup programs on the locking systems. An array of perfectly aligned code digits scrolled up. She bit her lip, puzzled. 'Strange. Everything seems in order.' A flashing blue light on the display caught her attention. 'But wait a moment...' She tapped in more commands and the screen altered. 'I've reconfigured the sensors to scan the immediate area,' she told Willchook. 'There's an odd energy profile registering around the hull. Could be an exterior influence.'

'Like a force beam?' suggested Willchook.

'Possibly.' Mel drummed her fingers impatiently on the console as the computer struggled to comply with her request. At last the screen changed, to show a continuous looping design.

'What's that?' asked Willchook. Mel looked briefly at him

and saw that already he'd nearly downed the bottle's entire contents.

'It's an energy pattern, all right,' she explained. 'And not a natural one, the shape's too regular.'

'And thatsh…' Willchook burped and shook his head. 'That's what's got a hold of us?' Mel straightened. 'I think so. Thing is, it's too big for such a simple task. We noticed it from the TAR – from our own ship, as we were coming in to dock. It's generating a huge capacity.' She pointed to the exit. 'I suggest we bury the hatchet, pool our resources and try to get out of this place.'

Willchook laid down the empty bottle and brought up his gun to cover her. 'What do you mean?'

Boldly, Mel turned to go. She suspected that Willchook was too much of a coward to shoot anyway. 'Somebody's trying to keep us here. All of us. Staying on opposing sides will just be playing into the hands of that enemy.' She gestured impatiently for him to follow and flounced from the bridge of the *Phaethon*.

The Doctor looked anxiously around the auction hall. The moment Miss Monodine had lifted her weapon he'd expected a grand fight to begin. After all, he was surrounded by representatives of some of the galaxy's most aggressive species. But strangely the majority of the delegates appeared rather cowed, with only Varzlad and the two New Alexandrians registering the slightest reaction to the death of Jerlot. The Eyspeer cube hung motionless; the Grimyr merely extended its long barbed tongue to catch a fly; and the Moroks looked on with an air of polite disinterest. Frankly, the prospect was baffling.

Miss Monodine gestured again up at Fegovy. 'Release the Face of Humanity. Release it to me now!'

Fegovy bobbed slightly. The Doctor noticed that, each time it did so, it was moving slowly and steadily, back to the door through which it had made such a sparkling entrance. 'I am afraid,' it said coolly, 'that you have transgressed the terms of our agreement. This auction is hereby terminated.'

'Give it up now,' thundered Miss Monodine, her face growing purpler by the second, 'or I'll destroy you and take it for myself!'

'I really cannot countenance –' Fegovy began, fluttering, and then seized its chance. It whizzed back, and the doors of its hidey-hole swished apart to take it back. Miss Monodine lunged forward with a speed that belied her great age, and fired as the doors closed. The Doctor stepped forward to get a clearer view, and saw the ion-conversion beam strike its target with deadly accuracy. The dazzling red of the beam hit Fegovy right at its centre. It spluttered and fizzed, and then the doors finally closed. At the same moment, the lighting flickered, and both the tabulator and the Face of Humanity disappeared.

There was silence for a second. Then Miss Monodine snarled and hobbled forward. Holding her stick awkwardly under one arm she attempted to prise open the door. Her thick red fingers scrabbled uselessly at the thin seam linking the door's slats.

The Doctor harrumphed. 'I really don't think that's going to do you much good.'

Varzlad essayed a bitter chuckle. 'Foolish Earth woman. Your scheme has come to nought. Now, we shall –' He broke off suddenly. A little surprised at this, the Doctor turned. Immediately he saw what had stunned the Chelonian to silence.

The auction room was almost empty. The only occupants were himself, Varzlad, Miss Monodine, the smoking remnants of Jerlot and two very confused-looking New Alexandrians. The Moroks, the Eyspeer, the Grimyrs and all the rest had simply vanished.

Miss Monodine was herself struck by the sudden quiet, and turned from the door. 'Where are they all?' she blurted, her rage temporarily forgotten.

The Doctor walked over to where the Grimyr had stood, surrounded by its entourage of smelly flies, and thought for a moment. Then he smiled broadly and clicked his fingers. 'Of course! So obvious, I should have realized.'

Before any of the others could request clarification, the sound of footsteps came from the outer companionway. The Doctor smiled in recognition. 'Ah, the stalwart Melanie.'

Sure enough, she very soon came bursting into the hall, the

bedraggled Willchook panting to keep up with her. 'Doctor,' she began with wonted ebullience, 'that energy trace we picked up in the TARDIS, it's somehow suspend –' She too broke off, and looked about confusedly. 'Hey, what happened to that Eyspeer, and the Moroks, and –'

'Uncle Tom Cobbleigh and all?' the Doctor completed on a sly note. 'A very good question.' He moved to centre stage, and addressed the remaining attendees confidently. 'Well, I suspect our "friend" Fegovy has indulged in some guileful chicanery of his own.'

Varzlad inched forward. 'You mean to say that none of the others were corporeal? They weren't even present?'

The Doctor nodded. 'Exactly so.' He turned to Mel. 'That explains the energy trace. To maintain the illusion of the others, their ships, and quite probably the goods themselves.'

Mel frowned. 'But they were real, I pushed past them. I even smelt them!'

The Doctor waved a hand airily. 'Child's play to one skilled in ultragraphic hologistery.'

Miss Monodine slammed her stick down on the floor, making a resounding clang. 'All through the auction they were upping the bidding.'

'Until it had reached a quite unseemly amount,' put in one of the New Alexandrians.

Varzlad uttered a curse in broad Chelonian dialect. 'An amount I was prepared to pay. From the funds of the God Mother himself.' He hung his head in shame, and quickly tucked his credit-coil card back in his shell. 'I would have bankrupted them, all for nothing.'

One of the New Alexandrians twitched nervously. 'The powers of this Fegovy are too strong. We must leave immediately.'

The first response to that suggestion came from the drunken Willchook. 'Some hope of that,' he said bitterly. 'Our ships are trapped here.'

'But Fegovy has been weakened, if not destroyed,' said Varzlad.

The Doctor shook his head and grasped his lapels. 'Weakened, yes. But he'll recover soon enough, I'm sure.' He raised a significant eyebrow to Mel. 'I rather think that our "ship" will be trapped here as well. We'll just have to muck in together to get out of here.' There was no reply; the gathering seemed to regard the offer with scepticism. 'It's the only offer you're going to get, and I suggest we get moving, fast.' Varzlad shuffled uneasily, although the New Alexandrians seemed to be on the brink of accepting.

'No!' The interruption came from Miss Monodine, who had once again raised her ion-converter to cover them. She spun around, bringing its glowing end inches from the Doctor's face. 'You seem very well informed.'

The Doctor sighed. 'Mere guesswork, I assure you, madam. Any brilliant mind could have formed the same conclusions. Now please put that thing away.'

Miss Monodine edged closer. 'If you're so clever,' she spat, 'why don't you open that door?' She nodded to Fegovy's bolthole.

'I really don't think that would be wise,' said the Doctor.

Miss Monodine raised an eyebrow. 'Ah. So you could do it?'

'I could jump from a cliff,' the Doctor said, exasperated. 'It wouldn't be a very good idea, would it?'

'I don't know about that,' Varzlad muttered.

Miss Monodine's answer was to prod him towards the door. 'Open it. This holo-whatever technology. I want it. It'll be worth a great deal at the nearest spaceport, when I go there. Alone.'

'Really, I–' began the Doctor.

To emphasize her point, Miss Monodine swung the stick casually, and blasted Varzlad. He squawked in suprise, bubbled for a terrible moment, then simply evaporated into dust and ashes, making an identical little heap of carbonized material alongside his compatriot.

Mel was appalled. 'There was no need to do that!'

Miss Monodine scowled. 'You've a big mouth for such a little girl. Shut it or you'll be next.' She prodded the Doctor again. 'Open it!'

'Doctor, don't do what she says!' Mel protested.

'I've no choice,' he said simply, and reached in his pocket. He produced the small, but powerful cutting tool he'd used on the asteroid, and set to work on the door.

At the centre of his lair Fegovy twittered with excitement. The loss of the Chelonian was a cause of little regret. Two hundred and twenty thousand mega-credits was as nothing compared with the reward on the Doctor's head! And in combination with the bounty posted for Miss Monodine, it would make an even prettier packet. The New Alexandrians were a small added bonus.

He watched on a sensor screen as the Doctor sliced through the door. Sections of the metal sheeting melted away in buttery gobbets. Mel watched as the Doctor switched off the cutter. 'There we are. Very easy. Suspiciously easy, I'd say.'

Miss Monodine snatched the cutter from him, then jabbed her stick meaningfully into the darkness of Fegovy's lair. 'You lead the way.'

The Doctor did as bid, and stepped through the still-smoking gap. The New Alexandrians followed, herded through by Miss Monodine. Willchook was next, but he blanched, and shook his head. Miss Monodine grabbed his collar. 'You've been drinking again!' she thundered. 'Through you go!' She made to throw him bodily through the hole, but he struggled and kicked feebly. Her response was to throw back her head and then butt him brutally. He staggered back, dazed, and fell backwards into the hole, blood streaming from his nose.

Mel squared up to Miss Monodine and followed the others, without saying a word.

She found herself in a small, dark antechamber. From up ahead came a faint light, and she could hear the Doctor's muffled voice. She used it as her guide in the dark, and a few moments later she tumbled out into a room that took her breath away.

The Doctor and the others were surrounded by glittering jewels, heaps of banknotes of wildly various currency, works of art of unparalleled variety and beauty, and several stacks of books. There was an overall lack of symmetry or thought to the display, and Mel was reminded of the careless clutter of her younger brother's bedroom back home on Earth. Each precious item looked as if it had been tossed casually aside.

The Doctor was holding up what appeared to be a very large ruby. 'Ah, Mel, what do you make of all this?' He tossed it to her.

She examined the stone's perfect cut. 'It feels real enough, but I suppose this is another illusion.'

'No no.' He took it back and held it up to the light. 'All this is genuine. A veritable treasure trove. Strange it should be kept away in here, though. As an old friend of mine once said, the chief enjoyment of riches consists in the parade of riches.'

'Forget the Adam Smith rhetoric,' said Mel. 'Where does all this come from?'

The Doctor looked about. 'That's an early Galostophus, and if I'm not mistaken those are a fine pair of Sissoroan serving spoons. Yes, several of these items have been missing for centuries, whisked from under the very noses of the most ardent collectors and gallerians.'

'By this Fegovy?' Mel inched closer, lowered her voice. 'That's what I can't figure out. I can see why Fegovy would want the Chelonians here, if they were prepared to hand over that money. But why summon them' – she indicated the New Alexandrians –'and Miss Monodine? From what I've seen, the latter has barely a penny to her name.'

The Doctor put a finger to his lips. 'I suspect all will be made clear shortly,' he whispered, just as Miss Monodine barged in.

For a moment her eyes glazed over at the sight of the treasure, but she soon regained her composure. 'More clever tricks.' She hammered the stick on the floor three times. 'Fegovy! Show yourself!'

Straight away, from an unseen cavity, Fegovy emerged, shining brightly once again. 'I see I have uninvited guests,' he said smoothly. This was Mel's first sight of the odd creature, and she was impressed by its brilliance and its calm demeanour.

Miss Monodine turned a control on her stick and raised it. 'I don't intend to go back empty-handed,' she said sternly. 'You know what this weapon could do to you. Give me whatever you're using to fake all of this'– she gestured to the scattered jewels –'or I'll destroy you and take it anyway.'

Fegovy came closer, and there was something about its spattering core that suggested bad temper. 'You are wrong there. These items are pieces of my collection.'

The Doctor raised a finger. 'I have to ask. What pleasure can an overgrown Catherine wheel such as yourself take in this hoard?'

Fegovy turned to address him. 'My purpose is to accumulate wealth, Doctor. As you will shortly discover.'

Miss Monodine shook her stick to regain his attention. 'Listen to me! Do you hand over the trick, or do I kill you to get it?'

Fegovy extended a thin tendril of light. 'Before I answer that question, I think you should see another part of my collection.' The tendril brushed over a concealed wall panel, and the far section of the treasure room was suddenly brightly illuminated.

Mel gasped. For Fegovy had revealed line upon line of tall inverted glass domes, similar in shape to those used to house carriage clocks, and many were occupied by apparently dead creatures. Her mind reeled at the startling array of alien beings imprisoned there; she recognized several, including a Glasseater and a distant Kroton.

The Doctor whistled in admiration. 'A rogues' gallery indeed.'

'Every one,' said Fegovy, 'suspended in half-life. Until my task is completed.' He bobbed away from Miss Monodine to address the entire party. 'Your addition to their ranks will swell the total prize money by millions.'

'So that's why these unfortunates were lured here!' said Mel. 'That's despicable!'

'Steady on, Mel,' said the Doctor.

Fegovy crackled disdainfully. 'Time enough has been wasted on talking.' He brought the tendril round, and before Miss Monodine had time to cry out it had encased her. 'Rhona Beatrice Monodine, you are wanted on fifty-eight worlds for offences too numerous to list here. The total sum of reward money exceeds forty million mega-credits. Welcome to your new home.' The tendril flickered; Miss Monodine yelled and pressed furiously at the activator stud on her stick. It had no effect. Then she simply disappeared.

Mel blinked; and when her eyes opened it was to see the elderly antagonist in the front row of Fegovy's collection, features for ever frozen in mid-scowl.

Willchook was the first to react. He put his hand to his mouth. 'Oh mercy, no, no...'

To Mel's astonishment Fegovy chuckled. 'Fear not. I have no need to add you to the gallery. A most inferior specimen.' He turned to the Doctor. 'This is a much more tempting prospect.'

The Doctor raised his hands placatingly. 'I am honoured, although unenthusiastic. I also have a few questions.'

Fegovy came closer. 'Yes?'

'I was wondering,' said the Doctor, 'who precisely you're amassing all this wealth for?'

'The Syndicate,' replied Fegovy. 'I travel the Universe on their behalf.'

'I see,' said the Doctor. 'But for how long? I mean, some of this stuff is very old. That Quark looks positively motheaten. Won't your Syndicate be anxious for their cut?'

'The Syndicate homeworld is dead,' said Fegovy simply. 'There is nothing to return to. I am simply continuing my original program.'

Mel sighed. 'Typical immutable computer logic.'

Fegovy crackled at her disdainfully. 'Excuse her,' said the Doctor, 'she likes to spell things out.' He narrowed his eyes at the ball, and said, 'Your databank contains all information on me, I presume?'

'Oh yes. A renegade Time Lord, a grand prize.'

'Quite.' The Doctor rifled through his pockets and produced a pencil and a scrap of paper. 'Fegovy,' he said grandly, 'I propose a deal. As a Time Lord, I can offer you greater riches than my humble self could bring.' He started to write.

Fegovy came closer. 'What is that?'

The Doctor pushed it to his chest. 'No peeking.' He completed his work and folded the paper in half. 'My bargain is this: spare the lives of myself, my companion and these gentlemen, and I give you this piece of paper.'

'What can you possibly offer me?'

The Doctor blew out his lips. 'Well, how about the galactic coordinates for Gallifrey, eh?'

Fegovy buzzed excitedly. 'Gallifrey? Planet of the Time Lords?'

'The very same. Just think of the pranks you'll be able to play there. The secrets of time-space travel could be yours.'

Fegovy bristled. 'Give me that piece of paper, Doctor!'

The Doctor shook his head. 'I'll throw it from the door of my TARDIS if you let us go, and not a moment before. Agreed?' He wagged a finger up at Fegovy. 'And I wouldn't try to snatch it. Consult your files and you'll know my reflexes are lightning-quick. I'll simply eat the paper.' There was a pause. 'Well, what do you say?'

Fegovy considered. 'Gallifrey… yes, yes. Go, Doctor, and take your friends with you! Go now! But remember… no trickery or I increase the energy field, and you will be trapped here.'

'Done.' The Doctor beamed. 'I'd offer to shake on it, but you appear to lack the necessary extensions.' He beckoned to the others and led the way out.

With a last glance back at the frozen form of Miss Monodine Mel obeyed him. Ten minutes later she was saying goodbye to Willchook at the door of the *Phaethon*. 'I'd wish you good luck, but really we're enemies.'

'I can't believe we're getting away,' he said. 'But I'm glad to be free of Monodine.' He turned to the airlock of the ship. 'I suppose this hulk is mine now.'

'Just try and fly straight in future,' said Mel, and forced a smile as they parted. She watched as the airlock closed; a couple of moments later the clamps snapped back and the ship was gone.

She hurried to rejoin the Doctor, who was bidding the New Alexandrians farewell. 'And remember,' he was telling them, 'if you keep things on your own world better organized you'll be a less easy target. Never mind just stockpiling everything you collect and learn – set up a big library. Do it properly, and you'll have people paying to look at your goodies.' Their ship's door swung shut, and they were likewise gone.

'What was all that about?' asked Mel as the Doctor led her to the door of the TARDIS.

'The New Alexandrians are famed for their magpie habit of collecting just about anything,' he told her. 'Especially books, as it happens, which I suppose shows some leanings to learnings. But the information they collect so avidly is never actually catalogued or compiled. Fegovy was after their great stockpile of knowledge, which would be worth a great deal on the open market. I was merely suggesting they should pull themselves together and start storing their data correctly. Then they wouldn't again accept so dubious a summons as Fegovy's.' They were now at the door of the TARDIS. The Doctor raised a suggestive eyebrow. 'Your new friend got off safely? You seemed to be getting along nicely.'

Mel rolled her eyes at the suggestion. 'No way, Doctor! Even if he'd been a musclebound Adonis with a penchant for pocket-sized redheads. I'd much rather travel with you.' She looked around. 'But that's neither here nor there. Where's Fegovy?'

As if on cue, Fegovy appeared. The Doctor slammed the TARDIS door hurriedly shut. 'Keep out. Remember the deal.'

'Of course. You are free to go. But you must remember your part of the bargain.'

The Doctor waved the folded note up at Fegovy. 'As if I could forget. My thanks.' He shooed Mel through the door, then shot in himself.

A moment later came an unearthly grinding noise, and the police-box shell of the craft started to desolidify. Fegovy hovered warily. Then, the folded note, now reshaped as a paper dart, flew elegantly through the closing door.

Honouring the agreement Fegovy withdrew the energy field, and the TARDIS turned transparent, the blue beacon flashing on its roof, and then it was gone.

Fegovy zoomed to intercept the dart.

Mel watched as the Doctor pottered about the TARDIS console, humming happily to himself and flicking at the occasional control. The glittering central column rose and fell smoothly. 'That was a close one,' she said, collapsing into a chair. 'Well?'

'Well what?'

'Aren't you going to set a course for Gallifrey?'

'Why would I want to go there?'

Mel leapt from the chair. 'To warn the High Council, of course.'

The Doctor smiled infuriatingly. 'Warn them about what?'

'Fegovy!' Mel shouted, driven to exclamation. 'Your artful manoeuvring may have saved us from him, but what about your peers? They won't thank you for leading such an immoral creature up their garden path!'

The Doctor clasped his lapels again and suddenly looked extremely pleased with himself. 'But Fegovy isn't going to Gallifrey,' he said smugly.

'But –' Mel protested, confused. 'I saw you give him the coordinates.'

The Doctor shook his head of blond curls. 'No, Mel. You saw me give him a piece of paper. I may have mentioned the coordinates, but that piece of paper was all I agreed to hand over.' He tilted his head at a proud angle. 'It struck me that a machine such as Fegovy might very well have been designed to exploit the gullibility of organic races, but wouldn't be equipped to expect equal cunning from its victims.'

Mel had one more question. 'So what did you write in that note?'

The Doctor smiled. 'Rather childish, really. Still, "childhood shews the man, as morning shews the day…" '

Mel tugged his arm. 'Doctor!'

He thumbed his nose, wiggled his fingers and said, 'Nyah-nyah-nyah-nyah-nyah!'

Continuity Errors

By Steven Moffat

The Luna University, The Hammerstein Building, smaller lecture theatre. 2643.

The little man on the podium plucked his watch from his waistcoat and glanced quickly round the lecture hall. Around fourteen million, he estimated. Almost half full. Ten minutes more would probably see the rest of the virtual attendees downloaded from the…thingummy. Never any good at technobabble, he reflected. All those consonants.

As his hand reached for the scroll button (on his Notematic Whatchamacallit) he noticed he was shaking, if only very slightly. Nerves, of course. Understandable. He wasn't just giving a speech, after all: today he was going to change history. And a great deal was hanging on his getting things exactly right.

The lovingly prepared speech (eight weeks of actual writing, thirty years of research, a lifetime of serious resentment) spun silently across the Vidtronic Whatsit.

Ten minutes. Just time for one quick readthrough…

Extract from Professor Candy's lecture notes.

Doctor Who?

(Notes for Franklin lecture)

Doctor who? Nice guy or utter bastard? (*Look round the audience sternly. Ignore gigglers.*) With the wealth of historical evidence now unearthed, few people still doubt that the time-travelling Doctor is more than simply a myth or, as has been claimed, a conspiracy of historians on drugs very late at night. He's real and he's out there. The question is – do we want him?

The sole surviving Morthoid from the Dark Planet once remarked, 'Never argue politics with the Doctor. He'll just nip down a ventilation shaft, destabilize your political infrastructure, and blow up your solar system.' (*If get laugh, smile knowingly. If don't, look serious.*)

The Daleks of Skaro, of course, know him as the Ka Faraq Gatri. Traditionally this is translated as 'Bringer Of Darkness' though Professor Lyttle has established beyond reasonable doubt that this translation was, typically, the work of the Doctor himself. More accurately, and with that wonderful Dalek sense of irony, Ka Faraq Gatri means 'Nice guy – if you're a biped.' And that perhaps sums up the Doctor better than anything. He just never knows when the Daleks are kidding.

Do we want him then? Do we need this one-man crusade crashing round our history, patronizing our ancestors and kidnapping young women? Oh, yes, kidnapping them indeed! And simply discarding them wherever and whenever he chooses, the moment they grow too old or cease to be amusing. Consider, for a moment, the plight of the grieving parent whose daughter is not dead, nor in any conventional sense missing, but is a Warrior Queen on Thoros Beta. Can you imagine explaining that while the police are digging up your garden?

Incidentally, on the subject of the young women who have, seemingly voluntarily, become the disciples of the Doctor, the sponsors of today's lecture have released a special, full colour pictorial tribute to these many unfortunates, which is available in the foyer for any students who wish to continue their studies on their own. I've been asked to tell you that it includes never seen before holographs of Jo Grant, Tegan Jovanka, and...

*   *   *

The New Alexandria Library, 2668.

'Excuse me, does your Archaeology section have a minibar?'

For a moment the Librarian didn't even want to look up. She wanted to keep looking at her screen, concentrate very hard, and hope that this very stupid person who was asking this very stupid question at the end of this very long and stupid day would take a hint and combust. She gave it one whole second – no sudden blast of heat, no falling ashes. The trouble with people these days, thought the Librarian bitterly, was that they simply had no manners. She left it two more seconds (precisely calculated – any longer you look deaf, any shorter you look interested) and looked up. Good face, bad earrings; could those clothes be on purpose?

Bad Earrings smiled (rookie mistake) and repeated the question (had this woman ever *met* a librarian before?).

'Yes, of *course* it has a minibar. This is a *library*, you know!'

Bad Earrings slapped the counter triumphantly and turned to a little man with a worse sweater. 'You see. Academically, I've had an effect!'

Worse Sweater was frowning. He tapped his chin thoughtfully with the handle of a simply appalling umbrella – dear God, the umbrella and the sweater *matched* – and said, 'All right, you can go. But any books you wrote, you're not allowed to read!'

'Can I run copies? It'll save me time when I get around to writing them.'

'Absolutely not. They come down very heavily on that sort of thing.'

'Time Lords?'

'Critics.'

She nodded soberly. 'Better behave, then.'

As she turned to go, Worse Sweater pointed his umbrella at her. It looked like a warning. 'Particularly not your diary!'

'My diary gets published?'

'You may already be here sticking Post-Its over it.'

Bad Earrings sighed. 'So I keep doing that, do I?'

'Sometimes there's a queue of you.'

With a grimace, Bad Earrings turned and headed through the cavern of the Reception Hall to the TransBooths. The Librarian decided to dislike her intensely, which was the twenty-eighth time that day she'd made roughly that decision. She noticed, with a complete lack of curiosity, that just as Bad Earrings reached the Archaeology TransBooth she glanced furtively back at her companion as if to check he wasn't looking. She then quickly changed direction and slipped into the TransBooth two along. Literature department, noted the Librarian, still without the slightest flicker of interest.

Oblivious of this, Worse Sweater – whom the Librarian decided to dislike intensely (twenty-nine) – remained where he was, now leaning on his umbrella and frowning ferociously at the floor, as if he thought he could burn through it just by staring. The thought slipped into her head that if he really wanted to he probably could and she felt herself blinking in surprise. She hadn't meant to think that! Where had that thought come from? Abruptly she found herself thinking that there was no point in worrying about the odd random thought pottering around in her head unexpectedly and she should get on with thinking about something else immediately. So she did.

She forced her attention back to the catalogue screen and assured herself it would take a great deal more than some transplanted garden gnome in a stupid hat to hold her interest.

Suddenly the little man stopped ignoring her (Damn! Why was she staring at him again?) and looked up. The frown was gone, flicked off as if he'd just thrown a switch, and in its place the gap-toothed smile – no, *grin* – of a seven-year-old delightedly showing his mother some worms he'd found in the garden.

'I'm looking for a book,' he said.

She held eye contact and risked the full four-second pause, raising an ironic eyebrow halfway through the third second so there could be no confusion about her faculties. 'Well in view of the fact that this is a library,' she replied with precision-judged tartness, 'indeed not only a library, but the single largest, most comprehensive library anywhere and at any time;

given that our catalogue department itself crosses two international datelines and a HyperSound Monorail pass is essential simply to get around the detective fiction section alone; considering that any book of any type ever written in all of history, in all the known Universe, is stored on these premises; with all that in mind, may I venture to suggest that you have come to the right place?'

The idiot-child grin grew broader – not just some worms, probably a dead mouse in a milk bottle too. 'In that case you'll have David Hittenstall's *Massacre On Deltherus 5: The definitive account of the Drakoids' extermination of the last of the Deltherons*?'

'You'll forgive me, I hope, if I haven't memorized the entire stock, consisting, as it does, of every word ever written by a sentient being. I had yesterday off.'

'David was sentient most of the time. Which means you must have his book.'

'Block 4300B, floor 2348, cabinet 45, second top shelf. It's right on the pole so take a coat.' Gratifyingly he looked surprised. 'I said I hadn't memorized the *entire* stock. Try me tomorrow.'

He smiled again, doffed his hat (did he do that without taking his hands from the handle of his umbrella? No, that would be silly!) and spun smartly on his heel. She let him raise one foot in the direction of the TransBooths. 'Of course it's a restricted text. So there's no possibility of you being allowed to read it, see it, or even stand around in its general vicinity.'

The foot stayed raised. Then, with comical deftness, he whacked it with his umbrella and spun himself back round to face her. It was like watching some kind of music hall routine, she reflected – except she didn't know what a music hall routine *was*. Just where were these thoughts coming from? 'I wonder,' he said, 'if we can come to some sort of understanding concerning the word "restricted".'

'We have an excellent dictionary department. I believe it's very pleasant there this time of year.'

'I was thinking more in terms of perhaps some arrangement

we could come to. Just between the two of us.' The grin again and a wiggle of the eyebrows. Absurdly, his hat seemed to wiggle in sympathy. In other circumstances she might have thought she was being propositioned but the quirky, fidgety little cartoon character in front of her seemed more likely to suggest they bunk off school together and raid an orchard.

'Restricted,' she intoned, with relish, 'means restricted.'

'Ah! I see you've also memorized the dictionaries.'

'I was bored one day – I worked through lunch.'

'It really is of vital importance that I see a copy of this book. I happen to know you have the only copy in existence.'

'Correct.'

'And that your security systems are such that even *I* could not penetrate them.'

She arched an eyebrow to the perfectly judged angle for maximum irony. 'Not even you.'

'Unless, of course, I had your specific permission and the necessary security codes.'

'Which is absolutely out of the question.'

As he leant forward his face slipped into shadow (what shadow? where was the shadow coming from?) and for a moment his eyes seemed to burn. 'Lives,' he said, almost growled, 'are at stake.'

'The Deltherons were entirely wiped out by the Drakoids a hundred years ago. I think it may be a little too late to do anything about it now.'

'The information in that book –'

'Is restricted.'

'Is vital to me.'

'I don't see why.'

He smiled again, but it was a sad kind of smile this time. 'Let's just say I'm a doctor of history.'

She smirked, in a way exactly calculated to inform people when they were being pretentious. 'You mean you study it.'

'I mean I make it better.' And he held her look. Funny thing about those eyes...

For a giddy, plunging moment she *believed* him. She knew

he really needed the book, knew that she could trust him absolutely, knew that lives hung in the balance and only this improbable-looking music-hall reject could make a difference. She found herself reaching to punch in the authorization codes and the complex protocols that would pluck the book from its shelf half a world away, suck it through a HyperTube, and thump it down on the desk in front of her. As her fingers flickered over the sensor pad, she only hoped it wasn't too late, prayed she hadn't cost this strange little man too much time...

Her hand froze before she even knew why. Music hall? Music hall *again*? What the hell *was* a music hall and why should she be thinking about...

Oh God! She snatched her hand from the sensor pad. Oh dear God! Frantically, she cancelled the Text Release, reversed the protocols. She felt herself trembling with the sudden shock of understanding, with the fear of what she now knew was standing across the counter from her. She made herself look back at the little man with the terrible sweater and the appalling umbrella.

She'd never met him before, of course, and he didn't look at all as she'd imagined. But it was him. And, God help her, she almost hadn't noticed!

'Something wrong?' he was asking.

She forced down the surge of panic. OK, so it *was* him. What the hell! she thought. She always knew he might turn up here – it had always been a possibility. She could handle this if she just got a grip. Just look him right in the eye, she told herself, and think, 'So what?' Better yet, imagine he's your husband – your husband on the very night he left!

She looked at him again, right in those burning eyes, and she didn't flinch at all. 'I want you to understand,' she said, and her voice didn't shake in the least, 'that whatever you do, whatever you try, whatever little plan you have in mind, there is not the slightest chance of you ever being allowed anywhere near that book. Is that entirely clear?'

He stared back at her, gloriously surprised. Hurt even.

She enjoyed the moment to its full, then added in a low voice, 'I know who you are.'

'You do?' asked the CSTE.

Extract from Professor Candy's lecture notes.

You think this guy can talk his way from a detention cell to the captain's chair on any given starship in under twenty-five minutes because he's cute? You've seen the pictures. He's not big on cute! According to every report we've got, he comes across as erratic, arrogant, rude, reckless and quite possibly insane. So you've got to start wondering why any military outfit he comes in contact with hands him the keys to the gun cupboard, not to mention supreme command, before they've even cleared him of the murder they've usually just arrested him for.

Why? Understand this. The Doctor is not a person in any sense we understand. He is what I like to call a CSTE – a Complex Space-Time Event. In fact, I believe he is the most complex space-time event there has ever been anywhere. And like all such events he cannot easily be studied because his very presence alters the way you think.

Consider: this man has telepathic abilities that can automatically translate every language in the Universe – not only for himself but for all those in his immediate company. Each of his so-called companions seems to have wandered the Universe in the happy belief that the entire Cosmos speaks their language and, somehow, not considered this even mildly surprising. The conclusion is inescapable. He not only translates for those around him but he uses the same remote telepathic control to suppress any curiosity on the point.

Consider also: if he routinely alters our perceptions to this degree, how else are we misled? How comforting that he appears humanoid. But is he truly? How reassuring that he even seems to wear our clothes. But is that even probable? Most troubling of all, everyone on record as having known the Doctor insists that he is a good man, a hero in fact. But did they think that for themselves?

Or did he think it for them?

The New Alexandra Library, 2668

The Librarian stood stock-still at the counter and felt her breathing slowly return to normal. She had managed to say no and he had stormed off, seemingly to sulk about it. So far, so good.

'You OK?' Walter was hovering at her shoulder – naturally – and she wondered for the thousandth time why she tolerated an assistant who was not only impossibly wet but had the most supremely irritating crush on her.

'I'm fine. Difficult customer, that's all.' She nodded in the direction of the CSTE just visible at the far end of the Reception Hall, pacing up and down with almost comic rapidity and muttering fiercely to himself. Not so much difficult as extremely dangerous, she reflected. Still, no reason to alarm Walter.

'Oh, you mean the Doctor!'

For the very first time she could recall, she looked at Walter in surprise. 'You know him?'

'Sort of. All your predecessors were old friends of his.'

She frowned. '*All* of them?'

'Every last one. Funny that, when you think about it.'

More than funny. In fact, deeply troubling. Out loud she said, 'Might explain why he marches in here expecting special terms. He was after the Hittenstall.'

'*Massacre On Deltherus 5: The definitive account of the Drakoids' extermination of the last of the Deltherons*? Block 4300B, floor 2348, cabinet 45, second top shelf?'

'The very one.'

'Bit boring in the middle.'

She hesitated, tried to sound casual. 'My predecessors... did they give him special terms?'

Walter looked evasive. Or rather, since he invariably looked evasive, he looked marginally more evasive than normal. 'Well as I say – they were friends of his.'

'You mean they allowed him access to restricted texts?' she persisted.

Walter performed a spectacularly evasive shrug that seemed to involve at least three shoulders and changed the subject. 'Why is the Hittenstall restricted anyway?'

'Because the Drakoids are our friends now. Which makes any minor social infractions they were responsible for in the past a tad embarrassing.'

'They wiped out an entire species!'

'And people will keep casting it up.'

'It was genocide!'

'You see?'

'Andrea, I cannot believe that even you...'

Andrea! She almost flinched at the name. Typically, Walter was the only one who ever used it; to herself, and to everyone else, she was always simply the Librarian. She interrupted before he could get through any more indignant spluttering. 'A judicious amount of fact suppression was part of the treaty.'

'It's disgusting, dishonest, and completely amoral!'

'Sure. But they let us use their beaches.'

'And what about the Deltherons?'

'No planet, no beaches.'

Thin-lipped with disapproval, Walter turned to go. 'Incidentally,' she added to his back, 'I was thinking of staying late after work and having dangerous sex with you.'

Walter's neck did extraordinary things as his head jerked round to look at her. 'You were?' he croaked, in naked wonder.

She smiled benignly. 'No.'

Walter, she considered, did quite the best facial crumple she'd ever witnessed. 'Oh,' he said. 'Right. Joke. Good. Got that. Fine.' He turned to go again but almost immediately he swung back round on her, flushed and blinking rapidly with that special kind of hyperventilating rage of the far too sensitive. 'You know,' he said – and she could tell he could hardly believe he was saying it – 'sometimes I just wonder how you managed to turn out this way!'

She shrugged. 'My daughter was murdered, my husband left

me. Just lucky, I guess.'

For a moment he seemed to agonize between continued rage and his more traditional raptures of apology, before he settled for storming off into the back office and slamming the door.

Almost adorable, she thought, in a thoroughly tiresome sort of way. She wondered vaguely what he could possibly see in her and for a moment she almost wanted to check in a mirror. Not possible of course. She grimaced, remembering the morning she'd become so sick of the occasional glimpse of her own face that she'd banned all mirrors from the Library. Not the healthiest impulse and possibly indicative of autophobia, she found herself thinking – and froze! Just where had that pithy little diagnosis come from?

He was back at the counter, barely three feet from her and she hadn't even heard him approaching – as if *that* was any kind of surprise! 'You know,' he said, 'I really can't tell you how important it is that I see that book. A short loan wouldn't hurt anyone, would it? Not really. And with the information in that book you've no idea how much suffering I could prevent.'

She looked at him and abruptly realized that saying no to this man was made so much easier simply because she disliked him so very much. Detested him in fact. She regarded him with artful coolness for a moment. 'Lives are at stake, I think you said,' she remarked, finally.

'Many lives. Innocent lives.'

'Innocent? Is that a fact?' She remembered her daughter, looking up, trustful and imploring, clinging to her and asking if there really were monsters in the world. Five years old, entirely beautiful, and ten seconds from death. With an effort she suppressed the memory. 'Well you tell those innocent people with their innocent lives,' she said, more forcefully even than she intended, 'that life, innocent or otherwise, isn't fair.'

A frown like thunder. 'Final word?'

'Amen.'

'I see.' He considered for a moment. He pulled a pocket watch from his jacket and flipped it open, revealing rows of buttons in place of a watch face. His fingers danced across them in what appeared to be a series of complex calculations. 'If my companion gets back before I do,' he said without looking up, 'tell her I won't be gone long.' He fixed her with a look and suddenly his eyes seemed very dark indeed. 'I have to go on a little errand.'

Extract from Professor Candy's lecture notes.

How far would he go? If someone got in his way – someone he couldn't influence by the normal means, someone who stood between him and his need to impose his will on the Universe – just how far would our heroic, benevolent Doctor be prepared to go?

The New Alexandria Library, 2668.

From beyond the shelves there was a momentary flash of blue and a screeching, grinding roar, somewhere between an enraged elephant and a protesting asthmatic. There was a chorus of 'shh's from the reading area.

The Librarian felt a knot of tension she had barely realized was there slowly unravel in her stomach. According to all reports it was the sound that invariably accompanied the arrival and departure of the CSTE by whatever arcane means of travel he employed (there were tales of an old-fashioned telephone kiosk, but that was just silly!). So he was gone then, out of sight and, thank God, out of her mind. But not, she reminded herself, gone for long. So what now? she considered, drumming her fingers nervously on the counter top. There was little doubt he would try again and the next time the gloves would be off. He would mean business and that was most definitely not a comforting thought. In her mind she ran through the current security protocols and safeguards. Flawless! And for that matter, quite deadly if the need arose. She was confident the CSTE knew that too; he didn't seem the sort of man who would ever bother to ask for something if he knew he could just take it.

So what could he do now? What could he possibly try? The answer, she thought exultantly, was nothing. Absolutely *nothing*! For a moment she almost glowed. It couldn't be often the little man encountered someone he couldn't simply manipulate in any way he chose.

As she turned back to her work, she noticed her little smirk of triumph in the mirror behind her desk.

From the other end of the hall came the whir of a TransBooth. She glanced round to see Nice Earrings sparkle back into existence from the Literature department. She stepped from the booth and gave that oddly furtive look round that had so intrigued the Librarian earlier. Whatever Nice Earrings was up to, her friend, the CSTE, didn't know about it. Probably not a very common situation, the Librarian thought, sardonically – and probably not a very safe one. By the look of her, Nice Earrings didn't think so either. Clutching a book tightly to her chest, she walked quickly over to the reading area. 'Excuse me,' called the Librarian.

Nice Earrings did an absolutely wonderful caught-in-the-act startle and turn and the Librarian instantly felt rather guilty. She attempted a reassuring smile. 'Your friend had to pop out for a minute. On an errand.'

'An errand?' Nice Earrings nodded soberly. 'Well just you let me know if the Universe ends.'

Nice line, thought the Librarian as Nice Earrings headed off to find a table. Thing was, she sounded as though she meant it. For a moment she was tempted to follow her, strike up a conversation, maybe even find out a few things about the CSTE – not least why anyone would ever choose to travel with such a person – but from behind her there was an impatient little cough. Standing at the counter was the perfect summation of a difficult customer, right from the drumming fingers to the pursed lips and the querulously raised eyebrow. For the eighteenth time that day, the Librarian decided to dislike someone intensely.

It was another hour before the Librarian got a chance to stroll casually past Nice Earrings's table. She had her book open in front of her and was carefully copying one of the pages into what looked like her diary – which, if nothing else, was a good cue. The Librarian leant politely over her shoulder. 'We could arrange to have that copied for you, if it would help.'

Nice Earrings jolted as if she'd touched a live terminal and slammed the book shut. 'Thanks, no, doesn't matter, finished copying anyway.' It was spoken all in a rush and accompanied with the worst attempt at a casual smile the Librarian had seen in at least a month. Quite definitely, this woman was doing something behind the CSTE's back. But did that make her an ally? Find out, she decided. Provoke her a little.

'So! You've been abandoned by your friend, eh?'

An ironical smile. 'Trust me, he's done a lot worse.'

'Really?'

'With bells on.' She looked back to her diary. The Librarian held her ground, thinking frantically of how to prolong the conversation. Her gaze held for a moment on the woman's earrings. She had a confusing sense that at some previous moment she hadn't liked them so much, but that wasn't possible. Her first thought had been how nice they were.

'I just had to turn him down on a book request. He wasn't very pleased.'

'I can imagine.'

'He went storming off and marched up and down, muttering to himself.'

'That's the Doctor for you. He usually ends up talking to himself because no one else can understand what he's saying.'

OK, time to push it a little. 'Too smart for his own good?'

'No. Terrible diction.'

They laughed together – good, they were bonding – and there was a 'shh!' from the next table. The Librarian threw a dagger look in the general direction. She was a librarian, dammit, they weren't supposed to do that to *her*! A hatchet-faced woman glared right back at her. Someone else to dislike intensely, she decided abruptly, which made a total of twelve today. 'Men all over, isn't it? Disappearing when you least expect it.'

Nice Earrings raised an eyebrow. 'Voice of experience?'

'Divorced,' she admitted. 'Well sort of divorced. He just sort of nipped out one night to go to the shops. But I could tell he wasn't coming back from the shifty look on his fat, stupid face!'

Nice Earrings smiled at the description. 'You still miss him obviously,' she said, ironically.

Time for a moment of disarming candour. 'Yes,' she said simply.

The other woman just looked embarrassed and quickly changed the subject. 'With the Doctor it's not quite like that. He's not really interested in all that stuff.'

The perfect opportunity! 'What stuff *is* he interested in?'

'Oh, monsters for the most part.'

The Librarian felt her hand grip suddenly onto a chair back and she clung till her fingers hurt. The memory surged as it always did when it took her unexpectedly. Damn her augmented recall! Twenty years ago her daughter, held tight in her arms, asked why she kept dreaming about monsters if there weren't really any monsters in the world. Outside the vines thrashed and tore at the windows but there wasn't any wind.

Hush, now, Gwenny, of course there are monsters. But they're not so bad. Monsters have nightmares too, you know.

The little round face looked up in solemn wonder at the very idea then frowned as she started to frame a question. In three seconds her spine would snap and she would die. From the window there was the sound of splintering wood...

'Andrea?' Walter was next to her and Nice Earrings was frowning concernedly. With the usual sickening effort she fought down the memory.

'Sorry, I'm fine. Mind was wandering, that's all.'

'OK, sure.' Walter didn't look convinced. 'Just letting you know – I'm popping over to Science and Technology. Shouldn't be long.'

'I'll cope till you get back.'

'And, um...' He glanced awkwardly at Nice Earrings who realized she wasn't supposed to be listening any more and buried her head in her book again. Walter leant closer. 'What you were saying about dangerous sex tonight.'

She smiled. 'Yes?'

'Turns out I'm available after all.'

Sometimes he was so cute! She touched his nose with her finger. 'You're not cancelling anyone for me, are you? Because I think it's about time you were seeing someone your own age.'

'Thanks but I'm happy seeing you.'

So *cute*! 'OK. But be warned, I'm feeling particularly dangerous today.'

'Great!' He did his worried look again. 'Now are you sure you're OK?'

'I told you, I'm fine.' He was always so concerned about her! Almost tiresome in a thoroughly adorable sort of way. 'So what's happening in Science and Technology?'

'A complaint.'

'Remember: the customer's always right.'

He shook his head bemusedly at her. 'After all you've been through, how come you've turned out so nice?'

'Tibetan thought control techniques,' she replied, and wondered if he realized she wasn't joking. By his smile, evidently not.

'See you!' he said and headed off towards the TransBooths.

'Ginger Wig!' said the Librarian, suddenly remembering.

Nice Earrings looked up in surprise. 'I'm sorry?'

The Librarian frowned. 'Temporary teacher at my school years ago. He took over for a couple of months and taught us Tibetan mind control – said it would make us nicer people.'

Nice Earrings was looking at her in confusion, obviously wondering what this had to do with her.

'And I'm just realizing,' continued the Librarian, as her frown deepened. 'He was rather like your friend the Doctor!'

And for a moment she remembered him so vividly: the odd little figure in the hopelessly obvious ginger wig (what was it supposed to be? they'd laughed – a disguise?) and the old-fashioned black gown turning from the TeachScreen and grinning like a kid with some tadpoles in a jar. 'Hello, class,'

he'd said in that funny accent of his. 'Mr Rooney's decided to take a bit of a holiday so I'm taking over for a while.'
Extract from Professor Candy's lecture notes.

The Doctor is a time traveller. Never forget that because it is central to an understanding of what makes him so terribly dangerous. Most of us, in our tiny, individual ways, are involved in the writing of history. Only the Doctor is out there rewriting it.

The New Alexandria Library, 2668.

Extraordinary! thought the Librarian. Quite extraordinary! Old Ginger Wig and the CSTE so hauntingly similar – the quirky, nervy mannerisms, the sudden grins, the often impenetrable accent – and it had taken her this long to realize! For a moment it occurred to her, in a vague sort of way, that she might be missing something obvious here, but the thought seemed oddly difficult to keep hold of so she dismissed it. Anyway, she reminded herself, she had her responsibilities! However charming she personally found him, the CSTE had to be denied the Hittenstall! She glanced over to where his companion still sat at her table. She'd finished copying from the book and seemed to be sticking Post-Its in her diary. That woman was the key, she thought. If she could just find out some useful information.

A TransBooth whirred and her assistant returned from Science and Technology. 'Dealt with the complaint,' said James, briskly, 'I'll file a report and give you the details.' He disappeared into the back office. Always so formal, thought Andrea. With a real pang, she remembered shy, charming Walter. Had he really been gone a year already? It would never have worked, of course, the two of them lusting after one another the whole time, and it was the right decision that they stopped working together. After all, she thought, there were some things too good to jeopardize.

She looked fondly over to the Returns desk where the broad-shouldered, bulky figure was diligently tapping away at his console with his huge, labour-calloused hands. On a mischievous impulse she walked over, leant into him, and nibbled her husband's ear. 'I think you ought to know,' she whispered, mostly because she knew it would make him blush, 'I'm feeling very dangerous today.' She was looking pretty dangerous too, she thought, noting her reflection in the mirror wall behind the counter (how everyone had laughed when she had that installed – they thought she was so vain!). Freddy grinned back at her and squeezed her hand. She noticed a man glance disgustedly at them from the reading area so she stuck her tongue out at him and for the first time that week decided to dislike someone intensely.

Oddly enough Super Earrings was staring at them too, but she looked more surprised than disgusted. Very surprised, in fact. Almost confused. Deciding this was as good a reason as any to restart their conversation, Andrea walked over to her. 'Problem?' she asked.

Super Earrings looked troubled. 'None of my business, of course, but exactly who is that man you were, ah... nibbling on?'

'Freddy. My husband. I mentioned him, didn't I?'

'Actually, you were telling me how he left you.'

'Left me?' she laughed. *'Freddy?'* Actually, she reflected, it wasn't as inconceivable as all that. In fact, one night in that terrible year after Gwenny had been killed, it had very nearly happened. He'd fallen silent for days and then one evening, avoiding her eye, he announced he was nipping out to the shops. She'd known – she'd absolutely *known* – that he wasn't coming back. But a few hours later he did. And he was a changed man too, excitedly full of new plans, determined they could start afresh. It was a full month into a glorious new beginning before he admitted what had really happened.

He *had* been leaving of course, intending to hitch-hike to the spaceport and just go anywhere, and he'd thumbed down an enormous blue lorry right outside their house. Entirely blue, he'd said, covered in strange blue-painted wood panelling with a blue light flashing on top of the cabin. Oddly, the words 'Call

Here For Help' were emblazoned in huge letters along one side. The driver, a strange little man, had offered him a lift all the way to the spaceport and he'd gratefully accepted. It was a long drive and the driver didn't stop talking the entire time, though to this day Freddy couldn't seem to remember about what. The odd thing was, though, when he jumped from the cabin at the end of the journey and waved the blue lorry goodbye, he found himself back outside his own front door. What was even odder was that he went straight back inside, knowing he would never want to leave again.

'Are you aware,' Super Earrings was saying, 'that your hairstyle has changed in the last five minutes?'

What an odd thing to say! Of course it hadn't! She checked in one of the many reading area mirrors.

'Or that suddenly you're wearing make-up and you weren't before?'

What on earth was she talking about? 'I can assure you, I've had the same hair and make-up all day.'

Super Earrings regarded her thoughtfully, tapping her pen against her chin. 'This teacher of yours,' she said finally, 'Ginger Wig. His name wasn't Smith by any chance?'

Andrea stared. 'How did you know that?'

'I've had some of the same education.' There was an ironic twist to Super Earrings' mouth. 'Listen,' she continued, 'the Doctor is my friend and in most respects he's a very fine man, if something of an utter git most of the time. But be careful of him, OK?' She hesitated, as if she was saying more than she should. 'He messes with people.'

Andrea smiled. 'I think I probably know more about your friend than you realize.'

'I don't think anyone knows more about the Doctor than he wants them to.' She hesitated again, then pointed to her diary still open in front of her. 'Do you know what I'm doing here?'

'You appear to be sticking Post-its in your diary.'

'Sometimes, when the past gets tough to deal with, I go back and rewrite it. I change things.' She looked hard at Andrea. 'The Doctor does that too. But with better equipment.'

Rewriting the past! Andrea felt a chill but didn't quite know why. OK, time to ask the big question! 'So what were you doing here today that you didn't want the Doctor to know about?'

Super Earrings looked momentarily startled and glanced at the library book lying next to her diary. 'I was that obvious?'

'I don't think he noticed anything.'

Another hesitation, longer this time. 'A while back,' she said at last, 'I had a nifty little computer which could do a remote access on practically any database anywhere. And once, for the hell of it, I did a search for references to the Doctor. He's had quite an effect on history in his own little way but he's usually careful about not letting it get written down. I didn't turn up much – obviously – but I did find this.' She pointed to the book. 'I couldn't access the text itself because it was only held in print form, but I did find out the Doctor was mentioned. So when the Doctor said we were coming here today I thought I'd have a look.' She slid the book across to Andrea. 'Page one – the prologue. I think you ought to have a look too.'

With a sudden thrill, Andrea saw the title of the book.

Extract from Professor Candy's lecture notes.

The consequences of having the Doctor crashing around our Universe can be colossal. For instance:

Two men are talking political theory and the Doctor walks past and overhears. Hardly breaking stride he lectures them on where they're going wrong and where they ought to be going right. As a direct result those two men change their thinking and their plans and in the years that follow lay the foundations of a new civilization in the Kantrassi Solar System. Today, the entire Galaxy-spanning Kantrass Empire is the direct consequence of the Doctor's casual interference – or so Professor Lyttle believes in his paper on the subject, and knowing how exhaustive his research was I see no reason to disagree.

A lot of Kantrassi thinking is profoundly affected by the Doctor, of course, though few of them realize it. One who did, their most celebrated poet and philosopher Orcnell, only mentioned the Doctor once in his writings, and then merely in the prologue to his collected works, *Four Seasons And A Wedding*. Unfortunately it is impossible to get hold of this work as, prudently, the Doctor bought all the copies. It would be fascinating to know what Orcnell actually wrote.

The New Alexandria Library, 2668.

Four Seasons And A Wedding! It had been here all this time and she'd never thought to look. Quite possibly she was holding the only copy in the Universe the CSTE had not succeeded in purchasing himself.

She opened the book on the counter and turned quickly to the prologue.

'On the planet Destrus,' she read, 'where astrology is the highest form of science, four of the oldest and wisest astrologers of their time went to consult an astrologer even older and wiser than they.

'"We're worried about the future," they said. "It keeps changing. First it is one thing, then it is another. First there is war, then there is peace. First there is love, then there is heartbreak. Frankly, we just wish it would settle down a bit. What," they begged to know, "does it all mean?"

'"It means," said the old man as he looked to the stars and smiled, "that the Doctor is planning something."'

That was it? That was all? She closed the book, confused and disappointed. It was interesting enough, she supposed, and a curious idea that somewhere that little man was busy rewriting the future while his friend sat with her diary rewriting the past, but it didn't tell her anything she didn't know already. Rewriting the past, she mused. The phrase had chilled her again but she couldn't quite work out why. If only, she thought sadly, you really could rewrite the past.

And the memory was upon her and this time she couldn't fight it. This time, as happened every day – every *single* day for the last twenty years – she would live it all again. She gripped the counter to keep from falling and she was back in the house on Argolia 4 on the night the plants came alive and consumed the town. The vines hissed and thrashed at the bedroom windows and Gwenny clung tight and asked about the monsters in her nightmares.

Hush, Gwenny, of course there are monsters. But they're not so bad. Monsters have nightmares too, you know.

(In the library, an oddly familiar woman was walking towards her.)

The rescue choppers were already on the way, she knew, but they would be too late – far too late. In a moment there would be the sound of splintering wood. A second later a vine would smash through the window, whip round Gwenny, and delicately snap her in half. Three seconds from death, Gwenny frowned and started to ask that last question, the one that was destined never to be answered.

('Are you OK?' asked the oddly familiar woman.)

'What,' asked Gwenny, 'do monsters have nightmares about?'

'Me,' said a voice from the doorway.

The whole library spun. Andrea felt herself falling. The young woman caught her, held her. 'Mother?' she said.

For one fleeting moment Andrea felt the change. She felt a whole new past unfolding in her mind, old memories melting away. She gasped with the shock of it and clung to the entirely beautiful young woman who was her daughter.

'What's wrong, Mother?'

'The Doctor,' said Andrea, 'is planning something.'

'Andrea!' grinned the CSTE delightedly. 'You look wonderful. Even more wonderful than you looked three hours ago. Very clever of you. Love the mirrored ceiling, by the way. Most unusual in a library!'

Andrea smiled. Whatever you said about him, he was damned hard to dislike – not that she ever felt much inclined to dislike anyone. 'Hello, Doctor,' she said.

'I meant to ask before. How is that equally wonderful daughter of yours?'

'Fully qualified doctor as of two days ago.'

'Dr Gwendoline Talwinning,' said the CSTE, sounding very pleased with himself. 'It has a certain ring.'

'They say her final-year project is going to revolutionize medical science. She wants to talk to you about it actually. Do you know anything about nanites?'

'They're very cute,' he replied solemnly, 'but they're not just for Christmas.'

She laughed and then turned serious. 'We owe you so much, Doctor,' she said. 'If you hadn't been there that night... '

He did that comical little shrug of his. 'I just happened to be in the neighbourhood – with some industrial-strength weed-killer, a spray gun and a crack team of gardening experts.' That adorable, impudent grin again. 'By the way,' he continued, 'that restricted text we were talking about earlier. Do you think you could find some way of releasing it to me?'

Andrea smiled fondly at her old friend, wondering how he could still ask that. She took one of his hands in both of hers, squeezed it, and looked at him for a long moment. 'No,' she said.

Extract from Professor Candy's lecture notes.

He's not your friend. Remember that if you remember nothing else. He has the control and power to make virtually anyone he chooses like him, but if he does so, it is for a purpose. It is part of a complex agenda we cannot hope to understand. It is for that reason if for no other that we, as a species, must learn to do without our self-appointed guardian angel.

(*Look around them all, long pause before the big finish.*) Perhaps in this hall today we have taken the first step towards learning to say 'no' to the Doctor.

The New Alexandria Library, 2668.

'No?' It was the face of a four-year-old urchin who'd just been told his holidays were cancelled after he'd been good all week. 'But…' he continued, and didn't seem to find anything else to add.

She smiled sadly at him. 'I've been thinking about my life this afternoon. It's funny, isn't it, that I decided to come and work on a library planet to get over a heartache when I've never had one. It's also pretty funny that I work with my husband when there's a specific rule here against married couples working together. It's especially funny since he is, by trade, a farmer. Actually, when I thought about it, I realized there's quite a lot about my life which doesn't really add up. It makes me wonder,' she added, looking very directly at him, 'if there's someone I can complain to.'

There was a long silence. 'I know what you did,' she said in a low voice.

'Andrea –' he began but she cut right across him.

'At least I have a vague sense of what's happened. I've got no idea what my life was like before you rewrote it. I imagine it wasn't much fun and I'm pretty sure my daughter wouldn't be here –'

'Andrea,' he persisted, quiet and serious now, 'there were three key tactical errors the Deltherons made in their battle with the Drakoids. I need to know what they were.'

She ignored him. 'I'm grateful for what you did – of course I am. In fact I love you for it. Which, of course, is the general idea, isn't it? But anyone capable of doing what you've just done to me simply to withdraw a library book is very dangerous. And I really don't think I could justify releasing a restricted text to a man as dangerous as you.'

Another long silence. She glanced over at the reading area. Daft Earrings was watching their confrontation, riveted. She looked back at the CSTE. 'But thanks,' she said, 'for everything.' And she turned, walked over to the catalogue screen and sat down to work. After a moment she heard Daft Earrings's voice.

'Is this the bit where you shout "back to the TARDIS"?'

'I'm afraid it's looking that way.'

'Met your match this time, I think.'

'Hmmm!'

Their footsteps receded across the floor. She heard the CSTE's voice, surprisingly clear from such a distance. 'I wonder what possibly could have turned her so against me.'

The Luna University, The Hammerstein Building, smaller lecture theatre. 2643

As the little man on the podium finished reading through the lecture notes, he glanced up to see that the full thirty-million audience had finally downloaded – virtuals at the back in the folded-space gallery, corporeals at the front. He looked along the front row, which was barely ten feet away. Right at the centre, staring up at him, was a young woman. She had sharp, intelligent features and a hint of challenge in her dark eyes. On her lapel was a blue badge, indicating that she was undergoing memory augmentation, probably for a career in one of the larger libraries or InfoCentres. A side-effect of the process, of course, was that during the initial stages of the treatment she would become extraordinarily susceptible to received ideas. Whatever she heard in the lecture today would stay with her for ever. Except, of course, he reminded himself again, he wasn't giving a lecture – he was changing history. He hit the erase button, deleted the entire lecture from the Notematic and turned his full grin on the audience.

'Professor Candy can't make it today as he's unexpectedly taken a holiday,' said the most complex space-time event in the history of the Universe, nervously fingering his false moustache, 'so I thought I'd come along instead.' He fixed the eighteen-year-old Andrea Talwinning with his most serious look. 'I'm going to give you a little chat on the importance of lending library books to your friends.'

Extract from the New Alexandria Library log.

M. On Delth. by Hittenstall.

Text no 12256834750485009 – Restricted Access Grade 1
Current status: Just returned from two-week loan to the Doctor, no fixed abode.
Authorization: Andrea Talwinning
Full text title: Miracle On Deltherus 5: The definitive account of how the Deltherons repelled the Drakoid invasion.

Timevault

By Ben Jeapes

Purser Xo'ril of the vaultship *Collateral Security* was clutching his clipboard and tapping his foot, staring down at the two feet sticking out from the innards of the ship's recycling plant. Like their owner, the feet were ludicrously outsized.

'How much longer, Doctor?' he said.

'One moment.' The voice was muffled by the machinery. 'There.' Suddenly the Doctor slid out from the plant and jumped to his feet in one, fluid movement. 'Try that,' he said, dusting his hands.

Xo'ril nodded at Engineer Ra'lan, who turned to his keyboard. The Doctor busied himself wrapping a length of knitted wool several times around his neck. Ra'lan studied the instruments, then studied them again, and finally turned back to Xo'ril and the Doctor.

'The Doctor has increased the efficiency of the plant by two per cent,' he said.

Xo'ril looked up at the Doctor – and up, and up. Xo'ril was of the Lorq, and the tallest Lorq Xo'ril had ever met would barely have come up to the Doctor's chest. He looked quickly down at the clipboard he was holding with two hands and tapped numbers into it with his third, while the fourth scratched his head absently. 'Well, Doctor,' he said. 'Two per cent... you say you require no bunk?' *Collateral Security* primarily carried cargo and passengers slept in a single dormitory.

'Correct.'

'And that item in the hold is your sole luggage?'

'It is.'

'Then let us see...' Xo'ril's fingers were a blur as he made his calculations. 'Assuming you eat two meals a day –'

'Unlikely,' said the Doctor, with a grin that faded at Xo'ril's frown.

'Every passenger is rated for two meals a day, Doctor,' Xo'ril said. 'It is a fixed item of my budget.'

'Oh, well, if it's fixed . . .'

'Two meals a day, standard consumption of shipboard resources for a mammalian being of your – ahem – size and metabolism... and you have contributed to said shipboard resources by... Doctor, you have earned yourself passage on board *Collateral Security* for a period of one week and three days, thirteen hours and seven minutes as of now.' Xo'ril entered the figure into his clipboard with the feeling of a job well done.

The Doctor's face fell. 'Oh, is that all?'

Xo'ril scanned the figures again quickly. Surely... Then it seemed to jump out at him. He had calculated for a reptile. 'I do apologize, Doctor, I should have said, seventeen hours and nine minutes. Now, Doctor, I must advise you against trying to stow away on any other Lorq ship. Other pursers might not be as forgiving as I am.'

'I assure you, I didn't –'

'I don't want to hear it, Doctor, please.' Xo'ril had heard all manner of excuses in his time but as far as he was concerned it all came down to the same thing: anyone who didn't have a valid ticket was a stowaway. The clipboard extruded a chip which Xo'ril handed to the Doctor. Numbers on it were already ticking down. 'When this reaches zero, you will be required to pay for further passage or earn your keep in another way. Naturally, the count can be updated before then. Good day.'

K9 came trundling forward to greet him as he stepped into the console room of the TARDIS. The Doctor dropped down into a chair and leant forward to fondle K9's antenna ears.

'We're in the safest place in the Universe,' he said.

'Master?'

'We're on a Lorq vaultship,' the Doctor expanded.

'Master?'

The Doctor smiled a wry smile. What should have been a brief reconnaissance had taken slightly longer, having to modify that recycling plant of theirs before an enraged Xo'ril had him and the TARDIS ejected into space (*Stowaway! Huh!*). That was what you got for trying to freeload the Lorq; a man of his years should have known better. Nothing was for free with the Lorq.

'We're on a Lorq vaultship,' he said again. 'You've never heard of the Lorq?'

'Affirmative.'

'Remarkable race. They've cruised the spacelanes for billennia. Not much to look at, four-armed teddy bears, but... They look after things for people, indefinitely, as long as payment is received. Out there in the hold there are crates stacked as far as the eye can see. They'll carry passengers, goods, works of art, foodstuffs, data, all with absolute security. No questions asked. Whole civilizations and cultures will leave their most valued items with the Lorq and the Lorq will defend them with their lives. The weapons on this ship could take a solar system apart, but they'll only use them to maintain their neutrality.'

K9 was not designed for small talk and made no reply.

'They'll even put long-term cargo into stasis for you, for a small extra fee. Bung it into a vault, turn on the stasis field and you can retrieve it any time, make your withdrawal thousands of years, a million years, later...' The Doctor shook his head. He was rambling. 'Come on, I'll show you around. It'll be a valuable part of your education.'

Xo'ril hurried into the *Collateral Security*'s medbay. It was a large room as the facilities were designed for the passengers, and even to Xo'ril the Lorq medteam looked small next to the equipment. 'I came as soon as I could. You said it was an emergency.'

'Yes, thanks for coming.' Dr Shr'crue led the purser over to one of the isolation pods. 'Take a look.'

Xo'ril peered in and recoiled. At a second glance, he was

able to see that the isopod held a Draconian. The shape of the face and the capital crest were the clues. The Draconian's scales had vanished and his body was covered in festering green sores.

'I was treating him yesterday,' said Shr'crue. 'He had a rare Draconian condition where they grow new scales before the old ones have moulted. He was being driven mad by itching.'

'You solved the scale-loss problem,' Xo'ril commented.

'I didn't have the required medication so I dosed him with Aesculac.'

'A bit excessive?'

'He was desperate and prepared to pay.'

'Ah.' Xo'ril shrugged the objection off. 'And now he's overreacted?'

'More than that. He came in like this this morning, and if I didn't know better I'd say it was Anlerrian rash. It's not a nice condition. First the epidermis peels away, then the dermis, then everything right down to the inner organs. It's lethal, it's not fussy about which carbon-based species it attacks and it's highly contagious. The virus gets carried on the flaking skin cells.'

Xo'ril paled at the word *contagious*. 'But you're not sure, then?'

'No. Anlerrian rash has never been reported in this sector and the patient says he's never been exposed to it, or even been in a part of space where it's been known.'

'So it's something else?' Xo'ril was grasping at straws.

'I hope so, because it's been known to wipe out half a planetary population.'

'Ah, excuse me...' The two Lorq turned round to face the doorway. Two adult humans and a child stood there, and a vivid red rash covered half the child's face. 'Our daughter woke up this morning like this,' said the woman. 'And my husband... Show the doctor, dear.' The man held up a hand and a small patch of rash glared out from his wrist.

Xo'ril and Shr'crue looked at each other. Shr'crue shouted, 'Nurse!'

'Doctor?' One of the nurses hurried up.

'Get these humans into isopods now. You three, we're going down to the passenger quarters. Purser, we'll keep you informed.'

Shr'crue and her entourage left the medbay like a small whirlwind, leaving the humans and Xo'ril blinking after them.

'Merciful Cosmos,' Xo'ril whispered.

The Doctor's footsteps and the whining of K9's drive mechanism echoed away into the depths of the hold. The Doctor sauntered along with his hands in his pockets and K9 followed at his heels. Rows of crates and containers stretched away on either side like a miniature Manhattan.

'Of course, this isn't the half of it,' the Doctor said. 'This is only temporary storage for transit. The stasis vaults will be far bigger. Goodies from civilizations no one's ever heard of, held against the day when –'

'Master.' It was the first thing K9 had said since leaving the TARDIS.

'What?'

'Single life-form at twenty-three degrees to the course of our current perambulation.'

The Doctor paused to listen. He could make out a slithering noise, punctuated every few seconds by a faint 'splosh'.

'So there is,' he murmured. 'I've known plenty of slitherers in my time, but sploshers are more rare.'

They came to where a small side aisle intersected the main aisle through the cargo, and they peered around the corner. A male Lorqling was mopping the deckplates listlessly. Slither, slither, slither. Then he would dunk the mop in the bucket with equal listlessness. Splosh.

'Hello,' the Doctor said cheerfully.

The Lorqling jumped. 'I'm not supposed to talk to the passengers,' he said. His mopping noticeably increased in tempo, all four arms applied to the job.

'Oh, you can talk to me, I'm a doctor,' said the Doctor. He delved into his pocket and produced a crumpled paper bag.

'Jelly baby?'

'No thanks.'

'As you will.' The Doctor popped one into his own mouth. 'You know, if you keep mopping that same patch of floor you'll wear a hole through to the gravplates. And even if you start mopping other bits of the deck it'll take you about twenty years just to do this hold.'

The boy stopped altogether and leant on his mop. 'It's a punishment from my senior dad.'

'Now that's what I call a chore. What did you do? Kill someone?'

'No.' The boy's voice trembled and the mopping resumed, *con brio.*

'We still haven't been introduced,' the Doctor said. No reply. 'Well, I'm the Doctor, this is K9 and these' – he held the bag out again – 'are just jelly babies. I've always resisted giving them names. It doesn't do to get too attached to something you might have to eat.'

'I asked him if he had a nice day,' the boy blurted. 'I saw someone on the vids do it once so I thought I'd try.'

'And had he?' said the Doctor, before he realized. 'Ah. A Lorq who asks questions?'

'That's what he said.'

The Doctor tried not to smile. 'You know, you're never alone with a jelly baby. They're renowned all over the Galaxy for their therapeutic value in combating black moods.'

The boy half smiled, and finally took one. 'I'm Ts'ril,' he said shyly.

'So now everyone knows everyone. Your father... are there many of the ril'ar on board?' Crew duties on a Lorqship were generally hereditary within a clan and whole families would travel together, the younger generation shadowing the old.

'Just my parents and my broodmates.'

'So your senior father must be my friend Xo'ril?'

The boy looked alarmed. 'He's your friend?'

'A figure of speech.' The Doctor drew himself up to his full height. 'We didn't really see eye to eye.'

The mental image made Ts'ril giggle, which was the effect the Doctor had hoped for, and they parted on good terms. The Doctor left Ts'ril the bag of jelly babies, and he and K9 resumed their journey.

They reached the hatch between the hold and the habitation module, and the Doctor began to step through it.

'Gangway!'

He pulled back quickly as a couple of Lorq in medbay uniform scuttled by, small legs pumping, pushing a stack of isopods on an agrav trolley. The Doctor gazed after them. 'Were those what I thought they were?'

'The design was consistent with a standard multispecies isolation pod,' said K9.

The Doctor scratched his head. 'Well, old chum, this is a poser. To our left, we have the unexplored delights of the habitation module. To our right we have something involving a lot of isopods and some very agitated Lorq.'

They turned right.

It was a landscape to be found nowhere in the Cosmos, put together from the merged minds of the Crialans to remind them of what was lost. The twin suns shone through the purple haze of the sky but what should have been a shimmering plainland, covered with the blue fauna and flora of Crial, was a bleak and barren desert.

Crial no longer existed physically in any form at all, but the desolation was a more effective picture.

A humanoid figure stood in the middle of the desert. Crial had been destroyed by a humanoid race and taking their shape was another way of reminding the Crialans of their past. Preserver himself hadn't existed at the time of the war; only his fellows could remember it. His eidolon was taller than average and his skin rippled with muscles; his duties involved the safety of his fellows and the Plan, and he found this Adonis-like figure a useful focus for his thoughts.

Come together, he pulsed. *We must speak.* Two more figures appeared around him. *I have interesting news. The ship has an outbreak of plague on board.*

Are the crew able to contain it? Conceiver appeared as a slight, wiry androgene, long fingers twining together as he explored possibilities. His job was to develop and maintain the Plan, incorporating all contingencies and altered circumstances and revising it as necessary.

Unknown as yet. The medics are baffled as to how the plague was carried. All passengers were scanned before embarking and there has never been a case of it before on board.

That is interesting. Guider, who appeared as a bearded old man, was the most senior of the three. He approved policy and directed their actions. Nothing could be done without Guider's say-so. *A vector that can carry an organism through all detection systems... Preserver, you must see that this vector is identified. Then we will see whether it is suitable for our needs.*

I am hardly qualified, said Preserver.

Then stay close to those who are. Guider was abrupt and Preserver knew why: after so long and after so many false hopes, it would be foolish to raise expectations too high. But the prognosis was good.

'The captain would like a report,' Xo'ril said. He was having to trot behind Dr Shr'crue as she moved around the medbay, directing and ordering. The place thrummed with activity and her small team was plainly stretched to the limits.

'Three fatalities, including the Draconian,' she said. 'Every passenger has it, and four of the crew.'

'It's what you said it is?'

'Anlerrian rash? Can't be anything else. Five,' she added, as a Lorq tech staggered in through the hatch. One of the nurses intercepted him and guided him to an isopod. 'We're keeping the emergency cases in quarantine and the less severe ones are back in their dormitory. We've converted it into an emergency ward.'

'What can we do to treat it, doctor? Can we inoculate the rest of the crew?' Shr'crue was already on the other side of the medbay, in conversation with a nurse, and didn't hear. 'Doctor?' Xo'ril called.

'Yes?' said a voice behind him. The Doctor rose up from behind a monitor which had blocked him from view. He had taken off his coat and scarf, and rolled up his sleeves. 'Oh, sorry, you must have meant her.' He began to sit down again.

'Doctor!' Xo'ril exclaimed.

The Doctor looked wary. 'Which one?'

'You! What are you doing here? You might infect someone!'

'Infect? I'm very clean-living. I volunteered my services to Dr Shr'crue and she was glad to accept.'

'You're medically qualified?'

The Doctor patted a strangely shaped item of machinery on the desktop next to him. 'The original K9 model was developed by a man who knew a thing or two about combating nasty bugs, and I'm not altogether ungifted in that area. Isn't that right, K9?'

'Affirmative,' said the machine.

'It's a robot?' By instinct Xo'ril pulled out the clipboard, though he already knew the Doctor's details and possession of a robot was not down.

'Oh, relax,' the Doctor said. 'He's got an on-board power supply, he's entirely self-maintaining, he won't consume any shipboard resources and, besides, he's paying his way by helping me.'

'Here you are, Doctor.' The biggest surprise yet: Xo'ril's senior male progeny Ts'ril hurried up with a tray of blood samples. The boy stopped, aghast, when he saw his father.

'And what are you doing here?' Xo'ril growled.

'I... I...'

'I asked him,' said the Doctor, not looking up. He had put one of the samples into the analyser and was studying it through the eyepieces. 'Shr'crue was short staffed and I needed someone to run errands. He's been a great help. A credit to his upbringing.'

Ts'ril put the tray down next to the Doctor and scurried quickly away.

'So when will we have a cure?' Xo'ril said.

'Shr'crue's synthesizing the serum now.'

'Wonderful! Excellent!'

'It's well documented. It just takes time to make.' The Doctor's gaze hadn't moved.

'Then what are you doing?' Xo'ril said.

'Tracing the vector. Somehow it came on board unnoticed, and preventing a second wave is just as important as curing the first, wouldn't you say?'

'Master.' K9 broke into the conversation. 'Analysis of the Draconian's blood sample indicates that the quantity of Anlerrian rash viruses is increasing at a rate inconsistent with documented growth rates.'

'Increasing in the samples themselves?' said the Doctor.

'Affirmative.'

'Any idea why?'

'A possible cause is –'

– *Aesculac*, pulsed Preserver. *The Galaxy's wonder drug.* The Crialans met again in the virtual mindscape of lost Crial.

Explain, pulsed Guider.

It was developed at the Gwendoline Talwinning Memorial Institute, Preserver pulsed, *and it's based on nanotechnology. It is generally used in extreme cases. It makes an on-the-spot analysis inside patients and develops its own antidote to whatever ails them. A condition of use is that blood samples from cured patients are returned to the institute so that the information which the drug picked up is encoded in the next batch. Each generation of Aesculac is smarter than the one before.*

Conceiver was puzzled. *Aesculac caused this plague?*

Correct, pulsed Preserver. *Every so often a sample of Aesculac goes wrong. Every consignment has details of all the diseases that previous consignments have been used to fight, and sometimes it cures something nasty by manufacturing something even nastier.*

So, Guider pulsed, *something is on board that has been*

designed to manufacture organisms within a living body.

There is more. Preserver radiated smugness and knew it. *Given sufficient skill and facilities it can be directed to manufacture specific organisms. One of the passengers used the medbay's nanolathe to manufacture a specific against the rash virus from the drug, and it has been pumped throughout the ship. The apparatus used for this operation is still in place.*

Conceiver spoke in his official capacity. *The Plan requires that this passenger be apprehended and brought to our cause, immediately.*

Guider spoke likewise. *The modification to the Plan is approved.*

Gladly, pulsed Preserver, and vanished.

Dr Shr'crue writhed under the Doctor's gaze. 'It's so rare,' she said, 'so rare. One in a million! One in ten million cases goes wrong!'

'You gave the Aesculac to the patient yourself,' the Doctor said, 'and you still didn't guess?'

'Why should I?' Shr'crue wailed. 'The chances of the rash being caused by the drug were still lower than the rash being caused by something natural, however unlikely –'

'The entire medical establishment knew about this possible side-effect and *they covered it up?*'

'The benefits are so much greater than the disadvantages. The probability of any one individual being dealt a faulty sample is minimal –'

'Oh, don't talk to me,' the Doctor snapped. 'Talk to the relatives of your fourteen fatalities.' He headed for the door. 'If I'm wanted, I'll be in the hold. Come on, K9.'

He had a near collision as he stormed out of the medbay and almost sent Xo'ril's small form flying. 'Doctor, you're going somewhere?' the purser said.

The only answer was an angry yell.

'They knew! They knew! The stuff can kill and they knew!' The Doctor hadn't stopped talking to himself as he paced through the ship back to the hold. He wished he could find something small and light lying in his path so he would have the satisfaction of kicking it, but the Lorq were too tidy. 'Unethical, underhand, venal, immoral, corrupt – *gaah*!'

The lights went out and something launched itself at him from a side-passage. The Doctor was knocked to the floor and in the dim emergency light he saw the glint of something metallic in one of his assailant's several hands. It was a Lorq, and that was the hand the Doctor concentrated on. The Lorq race had evolved on a high-gravity planet and his attacker was very strong, pinning the Doctor down. The metal thing came closer and closer –

A red flash of energy struck the attacker and sent him sprawling. K9 fired his nose blaster again, and again. Each bolt hit the attacker in the chest and knocked him further backwards, and should have put him down permanently, but each time he tried to get to his feet and come at the Doctor. Eventually he was sufficiently discouraged to turn and run.

'Interfacing with local systems to restore illumination to corridor,' K9 reported. The lights came back on and K9 retracted his blaster.

The Doctor sat up slowly, rubbing the back of his head. 'Thanks. Did you see who it was?'

'Negative. Targeting software was operating by radar alone. I was only able to determine that the assailant was an adult Lorq.'

'That narrows it down.' The Doctor looked down the corridor, back towards the medbay and the direction in which the Lorq had run. Another mystery, another puzzle –

No.

'I've had enough of this place,' he said. 'We're leaving.'

His hand was on the door of the TARDIS when he heard the call.

'Doctor!'

Any other voice he would have ignored. He would have gone on inside and given whoever it was a brief, unexplained introduction to Gallifreyan technology as the TARDIS vanished before their eyes. 'Hello, Ts'ril.'

The boy came hurrying up, panting. 'Doctor, please can you come to the medbay?'

'Why?'

'I don't know! I was just told it was urgent.'

'You ran all the way here?'

'Yes! It's urgent!'

'Just this once, then,' the Doctor said. 'And I've got a complaint to make to your senior father. Lead on.'

Preserver steeled himself as the Doctor, Ts'ril and the robot entered the medbay. For as long as he had been alive he had stayed hidden on board the vaultship, watching and planning, the eyes and ears of Guider and Conceiver. He had always yearned for action and this was it, but the old instincts to stay concealed were screaming at him. And yet his first attempt to get the Doctor had failed and now Guider ordered him to proceed, even though it would mean revealing himself. He walked towards the newcomers.

Shr'crue had noticed them too. 'Doctor, what are you doing here?' She sounded pleased.

'I was told it was urgent. Ts'ril?'

Ts'ril pointed at his father. 'Dad said –'

Preserver reached out and grabbed the boy's pointing hand. Ts'ril yelped. Preserver pulled him round and backed into a corner with one arm round Ts'ril's neck. Ts'ril writhed but Preserver held him in front of his body and a pocket staser was pressed to the boy's throat.

'First, Doctor,' Preserver said, 'disarm the robot's weapon. Remove it.'

'Dad,' Ts'ril moaned, 'you're hurting –'

'Quiet.' Preserver tightened his grip round the boy's neck, briefly, just to make his point. 'I mean it, Doctor.' He pressed the barrel into Ts'ril's skin and Ts'ril wailed.

'K9,' the Doctor said quietly. 'Disengage your blaster.' He pulled a slim sonic instrument from his pocket and crouched down next to the robot's head to detach the weapon.

'Shr'crue,' Preserver said. 'While he's doing that, clear the medbay. Everyone except you and the Doctor, out.'

'Xo'ril,' Shr'crue said, 'this is most irregular –'

'He's not Xo'ril.' The Doctor didn't look up from his task. 'The discerning eye can pick up the clues.'

Shr'crue hesitated, then gave the order. The med staff shuffled out.

'Now, shut and lock the door,' Preserver said. 'And the pressure bulkhead.'

The airtight bulkhead, designed to protect the medbay if the ship was ever holed, came sliding down with a thud. Shr'crue locked that, too. They were alone.

'Who do I have the pleasure of addressing?' the Doctor said.

'I am Preserver.'

'And how long are you going to hold that boy?'

'That depends on you, Doctor,' Preserver said. 'I want your help.'

'You had only to ask.'

'That Aesculac stuff can make anything, can it not?'

The Doctor nodded. 'Any microscopic organism, yes.'

Preserver nodded towards a nearby monitor where he had already drawn up the gene specs for what he had in mind. 'Make that. When it's ready we're going to pump it through the ship, just like the anti-rash specific.'

The Doctor studied the monitor. 'It's a bacterium.'

'Correct. It's quite harmless. I've got it,' Preserver said.

'K9,' said the Doctor, 'scan and verify.'

'The statement is correct,' said K9 after a pause. 'A strain of bacteria of unknown classification is endemic throughout Purser Xo'ril's body. It has suppressed his immune system and yet he appears to suffer no ill effects.'

'Except that he can withstand your stun bolts and he shows a distinct change of character,' said the Doctor. 'Xo'ril, Preserver, whoever, once I've done what you want, you'll let Ts'ril go?'

'I will,' said Preserver.

'Then I'll start.'

'Security will be on their way right now!' Shr'crue said.

'They'll cut their way in. You can't stop them.'

'Then get the captain on the com and tell him that if they try anything, I kill the child,' Preserver said calmly. Ts'ril whimpered.

'Do as he says, Shr'crue,' the Doctor said. 'K9, over here. I need your help.' He sat down in front of the nanolathe and got to work.

Preserver felt a thrill he was careful not to show when the Doctor sat back slowly and cracked his knuckles.

'That's it. Would you care to check it?'

'There is an easy way to find out,' said Preserver. 'Take a sample and inject it into the child.'

'No-o-o!' Ts'ril screamed.

Preserver tightened his grip against the boy's renewed wriggling. 'It will be painless,' he said quickly. 'You will not suffer. Look at me! It will be the most wonderful thing that has ever happened to you. Do it, Doctor.'

The Doctor didn't move. 'Will the old Ts'ril still be there?'

'He will,' said Preserver. 'I promise. We are not murderers, Doctor. Ts'ril will still be there, just as Xo'ril is still here. They will learn to live in symbiosis, sharing the same body. All we have ever wanted is to share in the life of this galaxy on an equal basis with other races.'

'I've heard that before, but I believe you believe it,' the Doctor said. He took a hypo and applied it to the valve of the nanolathe's culture tank. Pale fluid appeared in the hypo's chamber. 'I'm sorry,' he said over Ts'ril's sobbing, and injected the boy in the arm.

After about thirty seconds, Ts'ril stopped squirming and a blazing light appeared from nowhere in the Crialans' mindscape. A Crialan child. Immature, ignorant, unsure; relying on adults for its safety and information. Preserver had never known anything like it. He smiled and let the Lorqling go, supporting him as he staggered. Ts'ril's expression was blank, then slowly changed to a look of wonder. He gazed about him.

I live, he pulsed. He turned slowly about in a circle, stopping when he faced Preserver. *I am the same as you.*

You are a Crialan newborn, Preserver pulsed back. *I and the other Crialan adults on board will help you become accustomed to this life. It will not take long. Soon you will know your name and your function. Now, wait, because there is more I must do.*

He pulled out the staser again. 'Now, Doctor, we're almost there, and I still have Shr'crue.'

'Consistent, if nothing else,' the Doctor said. 'What now?'

'Make preparations for pumping the bacteria through the air-conditioning, as you did with the anti-rash. Then inject Shr'crue. Last of all, inject yourself.'

Shr'crue's reaction was similar to Ts'ril's: a new light in the mindscape, a childlike awe on her face. Meanwhile the Crialan in Ts'ril was growing fast: it was already showing signs of character and learning to speak orally, picking up the ability from Ts'ril's own memory.

'It's ready,' the Doctor said. A thick tube led from the culture tank to the fan mechanism of the medbay's air duct. Preserver entered Xo'ril's priority code, which turned off the air scrubbers.

'Now inject yourself,' Preserver said. The Doctor shrugged, rolled up his sleeve and did as he was told.

It wasn't right. No light, no child. The Doctor seemed unaffected. 'What is wrong? What have you done, Doctor?' Preserver said.

'Me? I haven't done anything. We've always had a natural immunity to the Crialans.'

The surprise made Preserver step back. *He knows us! He knows the Crialans!* he pulsed urgently, and got immediate signs of distress from the two children, frightened at his worry.

Hush, children. Don't be scared. It is under control. Conceiver immediately began to soothe them while Guider addressed the problem.

The answer is obvious, he pulsed. *He is a Time Lord.*

'A Time Lord?' Preserver said out loud. Unlike Guider and Conceiver, veterans of the war, he had never met a Time Lord, and he felt a thrill of fear and power at having one of the old enemy under his control.

'Yes. I must say, I thought you were all dead,' the Doctor said.

'Dead?' Preserver shouted. 'Worse than dead, Doctor.' The Doctor shrugged. 'You set yourselves up as moral guardians of the Universe but what you did to us was a crime against nature!'

'What you did to your hosts was a crime against nature,' the Doctor said. 'The life-forms on Crial were evolved for symbiosis with you, but you had to spread out into the Cosmos. You had to infect other life-forms with no regard for their dignity, their rights –'

'I have told you, we do not harm our hosts. We never have. We share bodies.'

'Then put your money where your mouth is,' the Doctor said. 'Let Xo'ril out and we'll ask him what he thinks of it.'

You are wasting time, Guider pulsed. Preserver wasn't going to give up so easily.

'Admit it, Doctor,' he said. 'You were scared of us.'

'Scared of bacteria?'

'No, scared of our knowledge. You couldn't bear the thought of rivals.'

Another shrug from the Doctor. 'Perhaps we overreacted. Even the Time Lords were young once, and what we did then is a matter of great shame to us, but that doesn't excuse what you're doing now. You're just up to your old tricks, aren't you? You're going to infect everyone on *Collateral Security* whether they like it or not. And other vaultships, after this one. And their passengers. And their worlds. And –'

'Our culture should have spread across the Universe millions of years ago, Doctor. We have earned the right.' Preserver had believed this for his entire existence and wasn't going to change now.

The Doctor sat down and put his feet up on a table. 'Let me guess. A couple of survivors – not many, maybe just one or two – hid out in a stasis vault on this ship for a few millennia, booking a wake-up call from the purser a few generations hence. He took them out of stasis and got infected by you for his efforts. The survivors went back into stasis and you've passed yourself from purser to purser ever since.'

'Clever, Doctor.'

'It's what I would have done. How many are there in the stasis vault?'

'Just two. They're in a culture tank – Now what is it?'

The Doctor's look was triumphant. 'You've just proved my point. You've given me details of something in the vault. Xo'ril would rather have died than give me that information.'

Preserver, you are wasting time! Guider pulsed again. *Let the infection of the rest of the ship begin.*

'We must continue this conversation, Doctor,' said Preserver. 'But not now.'

The Doctor gazed at the machine that was pumping the bacteria throughout the ship. Already the medbay air was full of the stuff.

Preserver crossed to the bulkhead that sealed off the medbay and tapped out the code that made it slide open. Then he unlocked the door, opened it and stood back with his hands raised as security guards rushed in, their guns levelled.

Thirty seconds later there were five more new Crialans.

Preserver communed silently with them. Then the new Crialans and Shr'crue gathered by the door, and Preserver handed his pistol to Ts'ril.

'We are going out to counsel the new arrivals,' he said. 'This child will stay to guard you. You might conceivably harm an adult host, but I don't think you will harm a child one. I have told him how to use the gun.'

Then the Doctor and Ts'ril were alone. They looked at each other for a while. Ts'ril's Crialan was still nervous and jittery; it startled when the Doctor's hand went to his pocket.

'What are you doing?' it said. The gun in his hand wavered.

The Doctor flashed his most brilliant smile as he pulled out his reserve bag of jelly babies. 'I was going to offer you one of these,' he said. 'Your host body has quite a taste for them.'

'Jelly babies,' said the Crialan, delving into Ts'ril's memory.

'That's right. Like one?'

'No.'

'Suit yourself. Do you have a name yet?'

'No.'

'Well, doubtless they'll think of one.' The Doctor leant forward suddenly. 'You're young, you're not quite sure what's what, you rely on Preserver for protection, isn't that right?'

'Yes.' The Crialan tightened Ts'ril's grip on the gun and the barrel trembled.

'Your host's young as well, did you know that? He's frightened too. He doesn't know what's going on. You don't mean to harm him, do you?'

'No.'

'But you are,' the Doctor insisted. 'You're doing it now. Let him out. Let me talk to Ts'ril so that I can reassure him.'

The Crialan paused for a moment, then: 'Preserver instructs me to say that he is in constant touch with me and can hear what you say. I am to say, "it won't work, Doctor". '

The Doctor shut his eyes. 'My compliments to Preserver.' He opened them again. 'Oh, well. Pass me that hypo, will you?'

'No.'

The Doctor stood up and retrieved the hypo himself from a nearby desk. Then he sat down at the desk with the nanolathe.

'What are you doing?' said the Crialan.

'Experimenting.'

'What on?'

'I'm a scientist,' the Doctor said, with another of his smiles. 'I'm always experimenting.' He pressed the hypo to his own neck and the chamber filled up with red blood. He squirted it into the sample chamber of the nanolathe, pulled the eyepieces down and got to work. His fingers flew over the keyboard and he hummed merrily.

After a while he took another hypo and drew a sample from another valve on the nanolathe. This time the liquid was clear and he beamed at it with satisfaction. 'Well, that should –' His whole body stiffened. 'Good lord,' he said. 'Well I never.' He looked back into the eyepieces, then up to frown at the Crialan, then back again. 'That really is remarkable.'

'What?' the Crialan said, nervous.

'Quite unprecedented. Certainly a case of *amo amas amat*, quite probably *nemo me impune lacessit* and maybe even *e pluribus unum*. You should look at this.'

The Crialan was straining to do so. The Doctor sat back so that it could look down the eyepieces.

'You see?' the Doctor said. 'Lymphocytes, leukocytes, building sites and caravan sites, all apparently co-existing, which the best authorities will tell you is impossible.' He brandished the hypo. 'And yet they're all in one sample! This is serum synthesized from my own blood, which is to say, they're inside me too, and that is also to say, notwithstanding and wherewithal and all that, inside you as well.' He casually reached out and injected the sample into Ts'ril.

The Crialan shouted and staggered back, raising the gun, but then Ts'ril's whole body went limp and the Doctor had to catch him. It lasted for only a moment before Ts'ril's eyes opened again.

'Are you all right?' the Doctor said.

Ts'ril looked dazed. 'It was horrible, it was...' he said faintly.

'Can you remember it?'

'It was inside me.' Ts'ril's voice began to rise. 'It was in charge of me, I couldn't do anything, I couldn't move –'

'Ts'ril!' The Doctor gave the boy a shake. 'Preserver was in touch with the Crialan and he'll know something's happened. We don't have much time. Can you get us to the hold without anyone seeing?'

Ts'ril drew himself up with a trace of pride. 'I've lived on this ship all my life.'

'Then get us there. K9, come.'

The howls were mental and vocal – a physiological reaction of the host bodies to their masters' grief. By the same token, Preserver felt tears pouring down his cheeks.

Quiet, children. Quiet. He leant against a bulkhead while the former bridge crew of *Collateral Security* milled about.

We do not understand what has happened, said one of the children; its host body was the captain of the ship. *There was a light, then there was no light and we felt such a wrench –*

The child is dead, Preserver pulsed. *A martyr. Now, quiet, my child, I must consult. Guider? Conceiver?*

We, too, felt it, Guider pulsed. *How did the Time Lord do it?*

He injected the child with something, then contact was lost. Preserver winced at the memory. *Counselling the children must now take second priority to tracking the Doctor down. I ask permission to concentrate my resources on this problem.*

Granted, said Guider.

Preserver? Conceiver pulsed. *There is a significant probability that the Time Lord has a TARDIS on board and will head for it. When we fought the war the Gallifreyans were experimenting with shape-shifting technology, so it may be of any shape or size.*

Preserver consulted Xo'ril's memory concerning the Doctor. *He has something in the hold. That may be it.*

There is also a good chance that this TARDIS will be impervious to anything currently on board the ship, Conceiver added.

Then the question becomes, Preserver mused, *where will he take it to?*

Ts'ril stopped dead just inside the TARDIS doors, and drew in a breath as he looked around him.

'Yes, isn't it?' The Doctor gave the boy a shove so that he and K9 could get in, and crossed to the console to shut the doors. 'There, safe at last.'

'Doctor?'

'Yes?' The Doctor was poring over the TARDIS controls.

'Thank you.'

'Don't mention it.'

'What did you do?'

'My race is naturally immune to the Crialan bacterium, so I synthesized the agent from my own blood that would make you immune too.'

'It was good of you.'

The Doctor pulled a face. 'Was it?'

'Why, yes...' said Ts'ril. 'Um... wasn't it?'

'One moral point to the Crialans,' said the Doctor. 'They spared the life of a Lorq child, to wit, you. I killed one of theirs to get you back.'

Ts'ril opened his mouth, then shut it again. He waited all of thirty seconds before his next question. 'Doctor?'

'What?'

'What are Crialans? Why did your race fight them? Who –'

'You do ask questions, don't you?' said the Doctor. 'The Crialans are... were... are composite telepathic intelligences. The bacteria grow a crystalline network inside the hosts which acts as a parallel nervous system and a Crialan intelligence is created spontaneously, and, as you know, it can do with that host what it will.'

'But it won't harm the host, will it?'

'Not out of compassion, believe me. Only out of self-interest.'

'Doctor, if your race was immune –'

'They still frightened us.' The Doctor was staring at the walls of the console room but his eyes were unfocused. 'The Universe was young, so were the Crialans, so were the Time Lords. Before my time, of course. The irony is, being non-corporeal, the Crialans have a distinctly abstract slant to their thinking. It was a race between us to develop time travel, and we picked up several hints from them.'

'Who won?' Ts'ril was fascinated.

'It was a draw. That wasn't the problem, though. Yes, the Crialans' habit of infecting everyone they met had us worried, but we could live with it. But some Crialan factions wanted to go back in time, using time vessels like this one, and infect the Universe from the start. We couldn't allow that.'

'So you had a war?'

'Worse. We did some time-editing of our own and we made the Crialans never to have existed in the first place, except in our own history books.'

'But these ones are still here,' Ts'ril said.

'They went into stasis before we got to work. That's the only way they could have escaped, by leaving the timestream altogether.'

'What are you going to do now?'

'That's just what I was wondering. I can't inject everyone.' Another silence.

'I know,' Ts'ril said after a minute. 'This is a time machine?'

'Yes.'

'Then go back to yesterday and stop it happening!'

The Doctor smiled and shook his head. 'Blinovitch,' he said.

'Who?'

'Nice chap but he had his limitations. Won't work.'

'Oh.'

More silence. The Doctor began to pace round and round the console.

'I know,' Ts'ril said.

The Doctor raised his eyes to the ceiling. 'What?'

'Are there more of your people?'

'Some would say a planetful too many.'

'Then ask them to help you.'

'Never again!' the Doctor snapped. 'Not after last time.' He stopped pacing. 'Besides,' he said, and now his tone was more thoughtful, 'they'd just want to finish the job and wipe the lot out. I want to stop them, but I've found out the hard way that I'm just not a xenocide. K9!'

'Master?'

'See if you can interface with *Collateral Security*'s main computer. I want to get a schematic of the ship.'

'Interface is under way.'

'Doctor, couldn't we–' said Ts'ril.

'No!' the Doctor said. Ts'ril looked hurt.

'Security overrides on *Collateral Security*'s computer will take approximately twelve hours and nineteen minutes to bypass, master,' said K9.

The Doctor tapped his fingers on the console and looked at

Ts'ril. 'Let's hear it, then.'

'Well, the stasis vaults are just normal vaults with a stasis field thrown over them. We could get to the generator room and extend the field to cover the whole ship. Then we send an SOS out to the medical authorities and they can deal with it.'

'Now, that's a good idea.' The Doctor wagged his finger. 'It won't work but it's a good idea.'

'Why won't it work?'

'It's too dangerous. Anything that might expose more people to the Crialan bacteria is too dangerous.'

'But if they take precautions –'

'Something will go wrong. The authorities would have to retake the ship, the Crialans would fight, people would get hurt... but... if...' The Doctor was staring into the distance again and his face was beatific. 'The stasis generators,' he said. 'Ts'ril, you're a genius. Where are they?'

'You're using my idea?' said Ts'ril, delighted.

'Yes. Where are they?'

'That's brilliant! I thought my ideas didn't work.'

'Ts'ril –'

'Wait till I tell my dad! When he's better, of course –'

'*Where are they?*'

'Oh. Um, between the hold and the drive compartment, deck two.'

The Doctor moved his hands rapidly over the console. 'That'll be about half a mile aft?'

'Um, yes, I suppose –'

The console came to life and the time rotor began to move. Ts'ril looked about him with wide eyes and the Doctor chuckled as the dematerialization sound filled the console room. It didn't take long. The rotor settled down again and Ts'ril frowned. 'It's stopped.'

'We've arrived,' said the Doctor. He activated the monitor. 'Is that it?'

Ts'ril looked. 'Yeah, that's it. The stasis generators. You mean we've moved?'

'We've moved.' The Doctor opened a locker set into the

wall of the console room and began to rummage inside it. He was always pleased with himself when the TARDIS went where he wanted it to. At first, he had been like a novice driver with the TARDIS, never quite sure what it was going to do; increased skill had come with practice, but even so...

He looped several lengths of interface cable around one shoulder, then crossed back to the console and made some final adjustments to the controls. 'I'm going out. You stay here –'

'Aw!'

'– and whatever you do' – the Doctor jabbed a finger at the largest, most inviting control he could see – 'don't touch that.' He opened the doors.

The generator room was like the boiler room of an old-time Earth steamer: dimly lit, with six massive generators rising from the floor in two rows of three and vanishing into the gloom above. The TARDIS had landed between two of them. They hummed, it was hot and there was an acrid smell of static in the air. The generators between them were producing the field presently centred on the stasis vaults, where the process of Time itself was slowed down. The ultimate cold-storage system.

The Doctor peered up at the nearest generator. 'Primitive but adequate.' He looked around him, located the entrance and quickly crossed to it. He shut and locked the pressure bulkhead, then looked about him again. 'Now...'

Where you get generators you also get control panels. This one was at the end of the room between the two rows. The Doctor stepped towards it and a small figure emerged from behind the nearest generator. 'Doctor.'

The Doctor grinned. 'My dear friend Preserver. What a pleasant surprise.' Preserver stepped into the light and raised the gun. 'Oh. Perhaps not.'

'Raise your hands,' said Preserver. The Doctor complied. 'I was hoping to use your expertise, Doctor. You would not have found us ungrateful. We could have worked together. I was a fool to think we could ally with a Time Lord.'

'You were a fool,' said the Doctor, 'to think I'd let you get away with imposing your will on other intelligent life-forms.

Non-intelligent, perhaps. In fact, why not? I know most of your activity takes place on the mental level. The intelligence of your host isn't important to you. Preserver, I can take you anywhere you want. I'll take you to an empty planet, no cognizant life but plenty of animals. You can build your own thriving civilization there and the Time Lords need never know –'

'Shut up,' Preserver said.

'But you prefer it this way, don't you?' the Doctor said. 'Take over cognizant life-forms, use their memories and skills as a short cut to developing your own. The easy way out.'

'We have that right! We were the earliest form of life in this Cosmos, Doctor, and –'

'No thought without your say-so. No freedom without your say-so. Nothing without your say-so,' said the Doctor.

'You're wasting time again, Doctor. You killed one of our children and for that there's only one answer.' Preserver raised the gun again and sighted down the barrel.

The dematerialization sound of the TARDIS boomed around the room. Preserver jumped and looked about him for the source, and just had time to look back at the Doctor before the Doctor's foot kicked the gun out of his hand, and the Doctor's fist connected with his jaw.

The Doctor had forgotten that, under the influence of a Crialan, Xo'ril's body could absorb K9's stun bolts without effect. Preserver merely staggered back, then hurled himself at the Doctor. The Doctor sidestepped quickly, at the same time removing his scarf but keeping it looped. He lassooed Preserver while the Crialan was still trying to regain his balance, and wrapped several more lengths around him as Preserver struggled to get loose. Finally he bodily picked up the firmly trussed and wriggling Lorq, and hung him off a projection on one of the generators. The Doctor stood back and grinned as he admired his work.

The TARDIS noise was reaching a tortured crescendo, though the TARDIS itself sat obstinately there. 'About time,' the Doctor murmured. He pushed the door open.

Inside, Ts'ril had his back pressed against the wall. He was staring at the shuddering console with eyes like saucers, all four hands stuffed into his mouth, and the racket was deafening. The Doctor flicked three switches on the console and the anguished noise died away.

The Doctor scowled at the boy. 'What did I just tell you?'

'You… you said, don't touch that –'

'And did you?'

'No!' Ts'ril said, indignant. 'I touched that.' He pointed at a more innocuous control on the other side of the console, directly opposite the control that the Doctor had forbidden.

'And I touched that,' the Doctor said, waving a hand at the coordinate controls. 'I zeroed us in time and space so that wherever the TARDIS tried to go it would just stay put.'

'So what did I touch?'

'The launch controls, as I hoped you would. You took your time, you know.'

It took a moment for Ts'ril to understand. 'You wanted me to?'

'I didn't know who might be waiting for me, did I? I had to have some advantage.' The Doctor smiled and ruffled the boy's hair. 'A sense of curiosity is a wonderful thing, Ts'ril. Now, this time you can help me.

It took ten minutes. Cables ran from the control panel to the TARDIS, where they vanished inside the doors.

Preserver still dangled powerless from the generator. 'Go on, Doctor. Throw that switch. Do whatever you're going to do and finish the job your people started.'

The Doctor's hand hovered over the switch. 'Traditionally,' he said, 'you're meant to try to make a last-minute deal with me. But I'll do it the other way round if you insist.'

'Get on with it.'

'It won't hurt my dad, will it?' Ts'ril whispered. The Doctor didn't look down as he answered.

'No, it won't. Xo'ril and the other infectees will be back to normal. Preserver, I meant that bit about taking you all somewhere safe and out of the way.'

'I should trust a Time Lord?'

'You should trust this one.'

'Get on with it,' Preserver said again.

'No. You can link telepathically. I want to talk to the Crialan in charge.'

Preserver's expression smouldered, but the next time his host opened his mouth it was to say, 'I am Guider.'

'Guider, hello. Can I tempt you with my offer?'

'A planet, Doctor? You offer us a planet when the Cosmos is ours by right?'

The Doctor sighed. 'Not this again. How about a quick vox pop? Ts'ril, did you enjoy being possessed by a Crialan?'

'No!'

'Would you do it again?'

'Never!'

'Not even to timeshare your body?'

'No way.'

'Well,' the Doctor said, 'one hundred per cent of corporeal beings queried said they wouldn't like to be possessed by a Crialan. Of course, we could broaden the sample a bit. I once challenged Preserver to let Xo'ril out so we could canvass his opinion. Would you care to try it now? Or how about everyone else on this ship who you've infected?'

'Doctor,' said Guider, 'your race wiped ours out in a deliberate act of xenocide. More than that. You stole our heritage, our history, our entire existence. No, Doctor, we will not be happy with just a planet. The Cosmos is ours; the Plan demands that we retake it. We will not rest.'

There was a look of tragedy on the Doctor's face. 'Then, I'm sorry,' he said, and his hand came down on the switch.

Nothing seemed to happen, but then Ts'ril felt what was like a low, subsonic rumbling deep in his guts, which grew slowly to a high-pitched scream that keened throughout his body. His vision began to blur and there was a tightness, a tension all over him that made him feel he would burst, but he couldn't open his mouth to scream. Colours flashed across his vision and, dimly, above the cacophony in his mind he thought he heard the TARDIS noise again, as agonized as he himself felt.

Then the noise stopped. The pressure was still on his body.

No, it was on one side of his body, his left side, from his left foot and up his left leg and left arms and left ribs to the left side of his face. His left eye was blind; something vast and grey floated in front of the right one.

He was lying on his left. He rolled over and pain stabbed into his brain. He moaned.

The Doctor helped him stand up. 'If it's not hurting it isn't working.'

'What happened?'

'Hopefully I cured everyone. Let's see.' He strolled over to the still form of Ts'ril's father. The scarf that had bound him seemed to have rotted away and Xo'ril lay sprawled on the floor. The Doctor checked under an eyelid. 'Alive. That's a good sign.'

Ts'ril could still feel that all-over tightness. He raised a hand to scratch his head and felt the pressure around his elbow. He frowned at it, then at his sleeve, then looked down at his feet. His trousers were an inch too short. His belt was too tight. His wrists strained at the cuffs of his tunic. 'Doctor, my clothes have shrunk!'

The Doctor gave him a quick up-and-down. 'No, you've grown. About a year, I'd say.' He picked up one of the strands of his scarf and looked mournfully at it. 'Well, expecting it to hold an adult Lorq for a whole year was a bit much.'

'Did you put us in stasis for a year?'

'If I had you wouldn't have grown, would you?' the Doctor chided. At his feet, Xo'ril groaned. 'Ah! K9, come out here please.'

'Master.' K9 rolled out of the TARDIS and came to a halt at the Doctor's feet.

'K9, scan Xo'ril for the Crialan bacteria.'

K9's single eye probe extended downwards. 'The bacteria count in the patient's body is falling rapidly. The patient's immune system is now fully active.'

'Just what I wanted to hear. Purser Xo'ril, how are you?'

'Doctor?' Xo'ril sounded parched. 'I feel terrible.'

'Are you better, Dad?' Ts'ril said nervously.

'I am perfectly well.' Xo'ril shook off the Doctor's hand to stand on his own two feet. 'Don't waste time with idle questions.'

Ts'ril grinned.

'Purser,' the Doctor said, 'everyone else on board will be as disorientated as you. Some leadership may be called for.'

'Cosmos, you're right,' said Xo'ril, and he hurried off.

'Doctor, what did you do?' Ts'ril said.

'I had the TARDIS interface with the stasis generators.' The Doctor put a hand on Ts'ril's shoulder and they strolled at a more leisurely pace towards the hatch. 'Normally they slow time down. I used them to speed it up again. And down. And up. And –'

'How did that help?'

'The first thing the Crialan bacteria do is take control of their host's immune system,' the Doctor said. 'Then they grow their surrogate nervous system to match the host's. As the host changes, so does the system, but if the host starts changing rapidly, say, growing, or getting younger, or both, the bacteria can't keep up. They have to concentrate. They spend all their time on keeping the network in order –'

'– and they let go of the immune system!' Ts'ril was delighted and the Doctor smiled.

'They let go of the immune system,' he confirmed, 'which, having been suppressed for so long, has a lot of catching up to do. I'm sorry I made you a year older, but think of it as a side-effect. It's a good cure if the patient can walk away from it.'

They strolled in silence for a moment, just a moment.

'Doctor?'

'What?' the Doctor said with a sigh.

'The two original Crialans. They aren't in hosts.'

The Doctor winked.

Under the Doctor's guidance, two Lorq were pushing a silver cylinder half the size of the Doctor down the corridor. The Doctor turned when he heard Ts'ril call his name.

The boy hurried up to him. He was in his overalls again. 'Not still mopping the hold, are you?' the Doctor said.

'Hmmm? Oh, no.' Ts'ril looked down at his overalls. 'No, I'm scrubbing out the medbay – what's that?'

'That, Ts'ril, is the culture tank containing our friends Guider and Conceiver. The ultimately absolutely finally last of the Crialans.' Ts'ril looked at the cylinder as if it was poisonous. 'Don't worry, it's safe and self-contained. Your father offered me a lifelong passenger ticket but I commuted it to this.'

'To what?'

'Perpetual storage for these two in the stasis vault, with a large sign attached saying "do not touch". Xo'ril was going to space them for gross violation of contract, but I thought otherwise.'

'So you're not going to stay, then,' Ts'ril murmured, eyes downcast.

'Stay? Well, I don't know… of course, I still have a little over a week's passage already paid for. Can't guarantee I'll stay all that time, but –'

'I want to ask you things,' Ts'ril said in a rush. 'There's so much you know, and I don't, and I want to find out –'

There is such a thing as pushing gratitude too far, and the Doctor thought he might have found the limit as he imagined Xo'ril's reaction to the unsolicited tutoring of his son. 'Well, there's no such thing as a free lunch,' he said. 'You as a Lorq should know that.'

'Yes, but –'

'I mean, you saw the size of my console room? It's never been cleaned as far as I know, and you're dressed for the job… and of course, once I've seen this safely put away, I'll want to come and supervise personally to stop you pressing things, and who knows what I might happen to think out loud?'

Ts'ril seemed to glow from within. 'I'll be right there!' he said, and ran off.

The Doctor turned back to the two Lorq just in time to see them bump the cylinder into a wall. 'Hey, careful with that! It's rare, very rare…'

Zeitgeist

By Craig Hinton

'Behold our deliverance,' intoned the High Priest, throwing his arms wide to receive the prayers of his acolytes. In a very few moments, their Lord and God would extend His benevolence to them all, as He had done since the dawn of time. But these were newcomers; they had to be shown the beneficence of the Spline. As long as they continued bowing their heads, of course.

On cue, the wide, white altar behind him suddenly burnt with blinding white fire, accompanied by a shrill whine which was underpinned by a throbbing roar. The priest didn't need to turn round to know what was happening; indeed, to have done so would have been a supreme blasphemy. When the Spline gathered its manna, it was forbidden to watch.

And then it was over; the sound and light just a memory. He turned to the altar and inspected the latest offering, and was pleased to see that it contained a large proportion of food this time; the last three manifestations had mainly been odd metal artefacts and trinkets – absolutely nothing of use to the priest-hood. But the ten translucent crates which covered most of the altar clearly contained food of some sort, and this made the High Priest extremely happy; there was nothing like a banquet to keep his servants satisfied. And therefore obedient.

As far as the High Priest of the Heracletes was concerned, the Spline had delivered. As all gods should.

Enryk Ullius checked his watch, but it was only half-nine. He sighed; it felt as if it had been half-nine for the last four hours. That was the problem with time, he decided ruefully. Unpredictable.

Another heartfelt sigh later, he stood up from his cramped and untidy desk and ordered a cup of spice tea from the replimat. As he waited for the antiquated machine to dredge up something palatable, he thought about his current problem: for the last three hours, he had been trying to make some sense of the equations that danced on his monitor, but he was no closer to understanding them than Ullius had been when they had been transmitted to him a week ago. Which was worrying, because the Ambassador reckoned that Ullius was the only person on the entire planet capable of understanding them.

Picking up his drink from the dispensing slot, he sauntered back to his desk. The Ambassador was due at ten o'clock, and Ullius's professional pride was mortally wounded by the fact that the equations meant absolutely nothing to him at all.

How had it happened? A fortnight ago, he had been a junior researcher at Hotampa University, trying to put the subject of his doctorate – equation networks – to some sort of applicable use. And now here he was, working directly for the Ambassador at the very limits of his knowledge. Even beyond those limits, to be truthful.

Trying to avoid looking at the monitor for as long as possible, he leant back in his chair and gazed at the ceiling. Life had been so much easier when he had been a student; the only problem had been finding the time between the endless parties and drunken evenings to write his dissertation... And then he understood.

He'd been trying to interpret the Ambassador's equations in isolation, but what if they were all aspects of one larger equation, each one a slice of a polydimensional equation network – the subject of his final dissertation? No wonder the Ambassador had selected him – there were only about three people in academic history who knew anything about the subject, and two of them were dead. With renewed vigour, he began typing away.

Half an hour later, he reached down to shake one of the diminutive Ambassador's four hands and greeted him warmly.

Because he now knew what he was being offered. And what it meant for Heracletus.

Turlough entered the console room and was puzzled: it was empty. For some reason, he had expected the Doctor to be standing there at the console, scowling at the controls and screens as he had been scowling at everything and everyone since Tegan had left. That had been weeks ago, but nothing that had happened since – not Sontarans and Rutan, not the so-called holiday on the Matasian Pleasure Rings, not their expedition up Mount Gysis, none of it – had done anything to improve the Doctor's demeanour. Even when he had been involved in the Black Guardian's machinations, the Doctor had always had a cheery grin and a sense of optimism. Nowadays, life in the TARDIS felt more like one of those lessons at Brendon with a particularly dreary teacher like Peterson or Dribb.

It just wasn't any fun any more.

His musing was interrupted by a series of chirps and bleeps from the console. Turlough stepped forward to investigate, but the blue arc of electricity that leapt from the nearest panel to just in front of his feet made him freeze.

'Doctor!' he yelled, moving back from the console with careful steps. 'Doctor, come quickly!'

'What is it?' Turlough jumped again; the Doctor was standing right behind him. 'Why the urgency?'

'It's the console. It's... it's bleeping.' Yes, it sounded feeble. But what else could he say? Oh yes. 'And I can't get near it.'

'What?' The Doctor walked past him towards the hexagonal console, but received the same greeting. Rubbing his chin in confusion, the Doctor looked around the white-walled room as if searching for the answer. And then he cocked his head. 'I recognize that sound. Of course! Of all the duplicitous, underhanded...' He trailed off, seething. His eyes were narrow slits of unbridled anger.

'What is it?'

'Gallifreyan machine code, Turlough. We're listening to the unmistakable sound of a cyber-psionic argument. Psi-bit versus psi-bit.'

'The Time Lords?'

'Who else? There are only two things in the Universe which can influence the TARDIS: another TARDIS and the Matrix. And there are enough safeguards built into this ship to prevent another TARDIS from unduly influencing her.' He closed his eyes. 'Only the Matrix could "persuade" the TARDIS to change course.'

'We've changed course?'

'Of course we've changed course!' he snapped. 'We weren't heading anywhere. I'd moored the TARDIS in the Vortex to make some adjustments to the dynamorphic relays. But from what I can see from over here, we're now preparing to materialize. It looks like one-nil to the Time Lords, the high-handed, sanctimonious, two-faced –' He growled in tune with the TARDIS. 'I'm the President, for Rassilon's sake! What are they doing, ordering me around like a messenger boy?'

Turlough tried to calm him down. 'You ran away from them, didn't you? What was it? "After all, that's how it all started"? Did you really expect things to be any different after you left them again?'

'I left them because I have no taste for their antiseptic way of life,' he snapped. 'All that power, all that knowledge, and they never dirtied their hands to help anybody. I hate to think what I would have become if I'd stayed on Gallifrey. Some dried-up scholar without compassion, no doubt, just like the rest of them.' He shook his head as the TARDIS began to materialize. 'Why do you think I couldn't face becoming Lord President again?'

Something suddenly occurred to Turlough. 'Aren't you missing the point? If the Time Lords have taken control of the TARDIS, they want you to do something for them. So they *are* getting their hands dirty.'

The Doctor arched his eyebrows. And then frowned. 'By proxy, but you're right. And after my complaints about their lack of action, who am I to argue if there's work to be done?'

But Turlough could see the anger, barely restrained, behind the words. 'Still, I shall have strong words with Acting President Flavia when I next see her. She could have at least asked me politely.' As he spoke, the console chimed to indicate that the TARDIS had landed. *Wherever* it had landed. Turlough reached out and opened the scanner.

'Very scenic,' he commented as the shutters parted. The view on the scanner was less than inviting: an endless vista of dark green sand and an uninviting burning sun, incandescent orange in a lilac sky. He frowned. 'And we're supposed to go out there?'

The Doctor retrieved his panama hat from the pocket of his beige frock-coat and thrust it on his head. 'Time for a recce, I feel.' Turlough smiled; most of the Doctor's anger had now dissipated. There was a mystery outside the TARDIS, and the Doctor's scientific curiosity was overriding his resentment at being manipulated. Perhaps this was the impetus he needed to put the past behind him and get on with life.

'Is it safe?'

The Doctor peered at another monitor. 'No radiation or atmospheric pollution to speak of.' He raised an eyebrow. 'Actually, there's nothing at all to speak of: according to the instruments, this planet is lifeless – not even a solitary bacterium. So why have the Time Lords sent us here, I wonder?' And then he reached for the red, inset door handle. 'Still, only one way to find out…'

The huge roundelled doors opened onto the mystery that lay beyond. 'Ready?'

Turlough shrugged. 'What choice do I have?'

The Doctor grinned for the first time in ages. It was like the beatitude of some ancient human saint. 'That's the spirit, Turlough.'

The Doctor blinked. Instead of a desert, he was confronted by the turmoil and confusion of a busy city. He turned back to the reassurance of the TARDIS, but it was nowhere to be seen. And nor was Turlough.

Puzzled, he studied his surroundings: he was on a black

tarmac pavement which ran alongside a wide road, frantic with
motor cars, which darted in between one another at alarming
speed. Looking up at the skyline, he saw that it was populated
with dark grey tower blocks interspersed with drab little shops
and dreary little offices. And, about a mile and a half away, the
lilac sky was broken by an imposing grey cube of a building
which must have been over half a mile high, adorned with
spires on all four corners. A sickly green glow hovered just
above the roof, as if something was decomposing up there.
Decidedly unpleasant, when all was said and done.

In a way, it reminded the Doctor of an Eastern Bloc city on
Earth in the middle of the twentieth century, or maybe one of
the Utilitats towards the end of the sixtieth. Even the people
who milled around him were indistinguishable from human
beings, save the preponderance of bright red hair.

But the orange sun in the purpling sky proved that it was
definitely not Earth, not in any of its multifarious eras. And nor
should it have been: although the Doctor hadn't recognized the
coordinates when the TARDIS had materialized, he knew that
they were about as far away from his favourite planet as it was
possible to get and still be in the same galaxy.

So where were Turlough and the TARDIS? Trying to think
logically, he attempted to locate his ship through the psychic
link that existed between them. Slowly, with measured mental
steps, he reached out… and the backlash of pain that assaulted
him drove a stake through the centre of his mind.

As he crumpled to the pavement like a dismembered mari-
onette, his last coherent thought was of concern for the TARDIS
– nowhere to be seen. Because, according to his Time Lord
senses, the vessel was standing two feet behind him.

And a universe away.

'This isn't –' He stopped as he realized that the Doctor was no
longer at his side. And the TARDIS was no longer behind him.

Not only that, but his surroundings were subtly different
from the image he had seen on the TARDIS scanner. Green
sand was underfoot, it was true, but it wasn't the scorched and

barren sand of the scanner image: there was a large lagoon, fringed with exotic palm trees, about half a mile away, with a medium-sized settlement leaning over it. A collection of corrugated metal sheeting and brightly coloured blankets, it seemed to make a defiant yet pathetic statement against the difficult landscape.

But the biggest difference was the square grey building that stood about a mile beyond the settlement, a half-mile-tall grey cube with a sharp spire on each corner. Turlough was confused; the level of development needed to build something like that was so far beyond that of the settlement... And then he thought of the Trion shanty towns that had sprung up around the Palaces and decided that it wasn't impossible for a planet to end up like this.

But where was the Doctor? And where was the TARDIS? With both missing in action, it was time to make the best of a bad job, and the settlement looked like the best place to start: it looked far friendlier and more approachable than the big cube. Resigned, he set off over the moist sand, hoping that the ramshackle chaos of sheet metal and rainbow fabrics would provide some answers.

The Doctor realized that he was awake. His last memory was of a rather unpleasant acquaintance with the pavement, but he was now lying on a comfortable couch with a duvet over him. And he was inside someone's house.

That someone walked into the room and grinned. 'So, you're awake.' The man was red-haired, a tubby individual with a friendly face and a short ginger beard. He was wearing the drab grey clothing favoured by the locals. 'You worried me,' he said in a concerned voice.

The Doctor sat up on the sofa and untangled himself from the duvet. Thankfully, there didn't seem to be any after-effects of his psychic trauma; all his neurons appeared to be in the right place and doing the right things. But although the symptoms had abated, the cause was worryingly clear to him: the TARDIS was on the planet but displaced in some way; and he had to find it. And then there was Turlough. 'I'm feeling a lot better, thank you. I'm the Doctor, by the way.'

The man proffered a hand. 'And I'm Festle Caloon. This is my apartment.'

'What happened?'

'I was on my way home from work, and I saw you collapse. Everyone else ignored you, but that's typical nowadays; nobody gives a damn about anybody apart from themselves.' He suddenly looked a little bashful. 'Although I like to think I'm a bit different. I called an ambulance, but my credit-rating was too low, so I brought you back here. I hope you don't mind.'

What a wonderfully caring society, thought the Doctor. 'Thank you for that, Mister Caloon. But – and excuse me if this sounds odd – where exactly is *here*?' A question easily explained by partial amnesia, he reasoned.

Caloon laughed. 'That must have been some bump on the head. You're in Hotampa, of course.'

Not quite enough information. 'And which planet?' the Doctor asked tentatively. A question most certainly not covered by partial amnesia if the planet had had no contact with other life-forms.

Caloon grinned. 'Which planet? Then you're another alien. Brilliant! You're on the planet Heracletus, Doctor.'

An interesting reaction. 'So you've had... visitors?'

Caloon nodded. 'We used to have an alien Ambassador, but he's dead now.' Suddenly, Caloon checked his watch. 'Excuse me a moment; my boss is on the television, and I can't really afford to miss it. Brownie points, you understand.' He picked up a small grey cube and aimed it at the wall. A flat screen lit up, and then an image appeared. A television.

'Your boss?'

Caloon nodded. 'I work for Professor Ullius.' He said it as if the Doctor should know who he was talking about. 'He's on the news.' Caloon pointed towards the screen, where a dull-looking man sat behind a desk.

'And now we go over live to our Hotampa studio for an exclusive interview with Professor Enryk Ullius. The creator of the Spline, for those of you who've been on another planet,' the newsreader added with a smug grin. 'Over to you, Yug.' The picture changed to a familiar image of interviewer and interviewee on either side of a low table.

'That's Professor Ullius on the right,' Caloon pointed out. Ullius was in his early thirties, a slight individual with receding red hair and thick glasses.

Creator of the Spline? Why did that sound so ominous? Puzzled, the Doctor settled back in the sofa to watch.

'And there it is,' said Ullius. 'The Spline.' He nodded at the large monitor on the wall behind. It showed a turquoise room, speared through the centre, from floor to ceiling, by a scintillating column of emerald light. 'Our salvation.'

Over one billion people were watching this broadcast, and Ullius could feel his message reaching out to each and every one of them. And why not? He held their futures – and their pasts – in his hand. They ought to listen.

Tubos leant forward in his chair and gave his famous oily smile. 'But Professor, this "Spline" of yours has cost a lot of taxpayers' money. What benefit will it give us? Why is it our salvation?'

Ullius leant away from his slimy interrogator and templed his hands. 'The Spline is a stream of coherent temporal energy which runs from the very beginning to the very end of time – reverse-spin imaginary chronons for the technical among you – flowing from Big Bang to Big Crunch. And, through the Spline, we can access any era and take all the resources that we need to maintain the present.'

'But isn't that rather dangerous?' asked Tubos in his oleaginous manner. 'If you change the past, don't you change the present?'

You, you, you – all of the blame was landing at Ullius's feet, and the bloody thing hadn't even been activated yet; only the tau-meson carrier wave was currently working. But he had the perfect answer to Tubos's attack.

'The Spline will only interact with the future, Yug – the

software will not allow any interaction with our past. It's as simple as that. And I wrote the software.'

'What about the late lamented Ambassador, Enryk?' Oops. One below the belt there – typical of Tubos's belligerent interviewing technique. Ullius leapt onto the defensive, his counter-attack primed and ready. It had to be. Ts'ril's death wasn't a subject he really wanted to discuss.

'The Ambassador died as a result of an unfortunate accident, but his knowledge has given us access to the future. The Spline was his dream, and it will stand as a testament to our first contact with alien life.' Actually, their only contact; as Ullius and the Ambassador had worked together and become firm friends, the Heracletan scientist had learnt the unfortunate truth, a secret that the alien had kept from his adopted home planet for fear of causing hurt and distress. It had only served to fuel Ullius's ambition.

Heracletus was actually so far away from any other life-bearing planets that it was unlikely that anybody would ever visit them again. And, without nearby planets, the crucial first steps towards interstellar travel were impossible. They were absolutely, totally alone, with no chance of escape, and the Ambassador's death had only served to cement their isolation.

Trapped on their own planet, the Heracletes were doomed to drown in the effluence of their own excesses. Unless some method could be found to renew their dying world.

Something like the Spline.

The majority of the Heracletes weren't ready for the truth. Only the Cabal of the Presidium knew that it was the Spline… or death for all in less than fifty years. And, when the Spline was operational, the population would never have to know the dreadful reality of their situation. Their future would be assured. In all senses of the word.

Ullius turned to face the camera, ignoring Tubos in favour of the people watching at home. 'The destiny of our race is now ours for the taking, an inexhaustible cornucopia of possibilities that will give each and every Heraclete the best of every possible future. And we have the Ambassador to thank for it.'

His voice rose. 'Our first encounter with alien life has safe-guarded the future for all of Heracletus!'

Turlough wandered through the street market that lay at the heart of the settlement. Sauntering past stalls offering trinkets, food and clothing, he tried to get a feel for the culture that he was stranded in. Was it the decaying ruins of the civilization that had built the enormous structure a couple of miles away, or an emergent one growing among the remains of an earlier attempt?

And then he saw him. On the far side of the market, examining some trinkets from an overflowing stall with his trademark curiosity.

The Doctor.

Calling out, Turlough pushed past the crowds of shoppers, trying to keep sight of the blond head in the bobbing sea of redheads. But the Doctor seemed to be paying him no attention whatsoever, more interested in the trinket than his companion.

'Doctor?' he shouted from only feet away.

The Time Lord turned and stared at him with a look of utter contempt. 'Where did you hear that name?' he hissed.

'What?'

'I renounced that name a very long time ago,' the Doctor continued. 'After I realized where my best interests lay. So, who are you?'

Turlough couldn't believe the conversation. It was as if the man standing in front of him was a complete stranger. And then he noticed the Doctor's clothes: gone were the beige frock-coat and cricketing jumper, replaced by a brightly coloured poncho. Was it the Doctor, or a native whose similar appearance was purely coincidental? But no, the man had recognized the name. Was the Doctor suffering from some sort of amnesia?

'I'm Turlough,' he replied. 'Your companion.'

'Companion?' the man repeated disdainfully. 'Companion? My dear boy, the Savant travels alone.'

'The Savant?' Now that was a name to conjure with. It just wasn't the right one.

'Indeed. Now go away. My mission here is extremely delicate, and I can do without bunglers interfering. What are you? An acolyte on a field trip? If you are, I want to know the name of your mentor; I shall have sharp words with them when I return home.'

Turlough realized that it didn't even sound like the Doctor; the tones were arrogant, conceited and condescending, without a trace of the compassion and friendliness of the real Doctor.

'Please,' he begged. 'What's going on? And where's the TARDIS?'

'That's it,' snapped the other. 'I've had enough of this pestering. Give me your time ring and the name of your mentor. I'll have him struck off the Academy register for this ineptitude.'

'My what?' Turlough started backing away. The argument was already attracting stares from the crowd.

'Your time ring. Your mentor's name,' he said slowly and coldly. 'Now, boy.'

'Doctor, what's happened to you?'

And then a commotion began a few metres away. Turlough looked round, and saw a group of white-jacketed men forcing their way through the crowd. In his direction. On any planet, in any time zone, people like that were undoubtedly guards of some sort. Not people that Turlough fancied being captured by.

He turned back to the Doctor, but he seemed wholly unconcerned. 'Your problem, boy. Your mentor should have briefed you better on field etiquette. Would never have happened in my day.' He pulled out a small golden disc and squeezed it. And disappeared.

An unexpected tug on Turlough's wrist pulled him away from the approaching guards. Seconds later, he was behind one of the stalls, concealed by curtains. Through a chink in the heavy drapes, he saw the guards pass by. Sighing, he turned to his rescuer.

A thin man, with a ginger goatee beard and dressed in an orange poncho, was smiling broadly. 'That was close. If the

Militia had got you, that would have been the end of it. The High Priest enjoys interrogating strangers.'

'Thank you. I'm Turlough.'

The man accepted Turlough's outstretched hand and grasped it warmly. 'And I'm Festle Caloon. Welcome to Hotampa, Turlough.'

As Caloon switched off the television, the Doctor's mind raced at what he had heard. *A stream of coherent temporal energy which runs from the very beginning to the very end of time.* Although that was fairly primitive as time technologies went, it would surely have been enough to attract the attention of the Time Lords. A race that developed something like that, simply to plunder their own future… The Time Lords would be honour-bound to intervene.

Was that why he was on Heracletus, he wondered? To prevent the Spline from being activated, to prevent Ullius's discovery from polluting the time lines? To be a good little Time Lord and do his duty? 'Tell me about Professor Ullius,' he asked Caloon. Before he barged in and did something unpleasant, he wanted to know exactly what he was up against.

Caloon, on the other end of the sofa, shrugged. 'What do you want to know? He invented the Spline; he and the Ambassador started designing it about ten years ago. He presented the idea to the Presidium two years ago, and they stumped up the money. And we've all been working flat out since then to build it.'

'And it does what the Professor claims? It can reach into the future?' Con men were only too common where time travel was concerned.

'Oh, definitely,' Caloon replied enthusiastically. 'We've been testing it for the last six months. It really is everything the Professor says it is: our salvation.'

Races that preferred to usurp the efforts of others – even their own descendants – rather than solve their problems with more conventional methods were another common feature of the Universe. The Earth Empire was a marvellous example of

that, with planets such as Solos being raped for the benefit of
the human aristocracy. True, Heracletus might have problems,
but that didn't give them the right to mortgage their own future.

'Do you think I might be able to see this Spline, Mister
Caloon? I'm very interested in time technology.' If the
Heracletes had had one alien ambassador, they could have
another.

Caloon frowned. 'I'd have to ask the Professor, Doctor.
Tomorrow's Activation Day; things are understandably a bit
hectic at the Temple.'

'The Temple?'

'That's what we call Spline Control. A bit of a joke, you
know.' He smiled wanly.

Not much of a joke. 'I'd very much like to have a look.'

'I'll tell you what. We'll take a wander over to the Temple;
I'm due back at work in half an hour. If you're up to it, that is.'

'Right as rain, Mister Caloon, right as rain.' He leapt to his
feet. 'Shall we go?'

Turlough sat on an overstuffed cushion in one of the corrugated
huts, sipping a cup of some herbal drink. Caloon sat opposite,
grinning.

'So,' he began, 'whereabouts are you from? Mistelee?
Pontahoon? You're definitely not from around here.'

And that's not the start of it, thought Turlough. 'No, I'm
from quite a way away.'

'So, what do you think of Hotampa?'

'Unfriendly?' ventured Turlough. Although he didn't want
to offend his rescuer and host, being arrested for being a
stranger wasn't the warmest of welcomes.

'The High Priest sees Hotampa as his private recruiting
ground for acolytes, Turlough, and strangers are prime acolyte
material. So, what brought you here? Surely not the reputation?'

To say 'I arrived in a space-time machine which then
vanished' wasn't even an option. 'I tagged along with a
caravan.' Turlough had seen a couple of ox-like animals

dragging a wagon away from the settlement, and hoped it was a satisfactory cover. 'So, what is the reputation?'

Caloon sipped his drink and sighed. 'A dwindling community trying to eke out a living from the lifeless soil, while the High Priest and his acolytes feed their faces in the Temple. That's the general opinion around these parts.'

'The Temple? That big building?' It didn't look very religious.

'That's the place. For the last five hundred years, we've been dying in its shadow; between the people who leave Hotampa for a better life, those who die of starvation or illness, and the ones who are "recruited" by the High Priest... well, Hotampa will be nothing more than an abandoned pile of rusting metal in less than two years' time, I reckon.'

'What's in the Temple?'

'The Spline,' said Caloon simply. 'All powerful, capricious, dangerous... Nobody has ever seen it and lived to talk about it. But Ullius – that's the High Priest – has got it by the throat. It does his bidding: people disappear, crops wither and die – all of it due to the High Priest and his Spline.'

'And that's why you don't rise up against him? Because you're afraid of some mysterious bogeyman?' An idea was forming in Turlough's mind, despite the alarms that warned him that it was this sort of rebelliousness that had had him exiled from Trion.

'What?' said Caloon.

'A society in this position has only two choices: to rebel, or die. Obviously there's nobody in Hotampa brave enough to stand up against this High Priest.'

Caloon leapt to his feet. 'What are you implying, Turlough? That we're all cowards?'

'Well, I may have only been here a short time, but that's what it seems to me.' There, that should get a reaction.

Being grabbed by the throat was slightly more than Turlough had expected. 'There's a group of us who aren't content to sit and watch our community die,' Caloon growled. 'We go on regular recces to the Temple, looking for weak spots, ways in.

We're more than a match for the High Priest.' He let Turlough go.

'So when's the next recce?' asked Turlough hoarsely.

Caloon smiled. 'Tonight. Fancy joining us?'

Dusk made Hotampa even more gloomy than earlier, if that were possible. Gloomy, cold and empty, an unloved carcass of a city lit only by the feeble illumination of the small twin moons that occasionally broke through the smoggy night sky.

'What powers the Spline?' asked the Doctor as he and Caloon walked towards the Temple, taking advantage of Caloon's natural openness to do a little brushing up before his meeting with Ullius. 'Forewarned is forearmed' was a sensible tenet, something the Doctor knew only too well.

'Something called a tachyon decelerator; have you heard of it?'

The Doctor most certainly had, and its presence on Heracletus was as impossible as that of the Spline, although it would explain the green glow: a Cherenkov backlash. The late Ambassador had obviously played merry hell with the normal development of this civilization, giving them techniques and equipment centuries beyond anything they were capable of discovering for themselves. Then again, he could have been coerced; the Doctor remembered how poor old Erato had been used on Chloris. 'Indeed I have. Very handy.'

Turning a corner, they came up against a huge set of grim gates, topped with razor wire. A stocky Heraclete in a brown uniform strode from the shadows, hand outstretched.

Handing the guard a security pass, Caloon pointed at the Doctor. 'I'm taking in a visitor, Crooce.' The guard simply grunted, and opened the gates.

Even this worried the Doctor; the Heracletes simply had no idea of the magnitude of the Spline's importance if they allowed visitors just to wander in on the say-so of a junior technician. A strike raid by Sontarans – who would trade their inefficient osmic projectors for the Spline without hesitation – wouldn't even cause them to break into a sweat. Not that

Sontarans sweated, of course.

A short journey through the bleak grounds later, the Doctor and Caloon walked into the Temple itself. A wide tunnel broke the monotony of the grey stone wall, its interior sparsely but regularly lit with wall-mounted lamps. Unsurprisingly enough, there were no guards.

'My station's on the thirteenth floor,' said Caloon as they entered the tunnel. 'The tachyon-chronon flux relays,' he added. The Doctor could only conclude that the man's open nature was due to his excitement at the Doctor's alien nature; if Ullius's association with this 'Ambassador' had made him saviour of Heracletus, who was to say that a similar destiny didn't await Festle Caloon?

'And Ullius?'

They reached a lift, and Caloon inserted his card into a badge-reader. 'The Professor's at the very top; his office is right next to the Spline Chamber itself.'

That figures, thought the Doctor. Mad scientists always liked to be able to gloat about their imminent triumphs surrounded by their latest invention. And from the clues he had picked up so far – mysterious deaths of technologically advanced aliens, a callous disregard for the laws of cause and effect – Ullius would probably feel right at home with Davros, Greel and Whittaker.

As they waited for the lift to arrive, the Doctor pondered his course of action. The more he learnt about the Spline, the more he knew that he had to stop Ullius. This was time travel for deliberate gain, a direct violation of the Time Lords' codex. And, even though Ullius had probably never even heard of the Time Lords, such a violation was something that even a lapsed Gallifreyan like the Doctor couldn't ignore.

To use Tegan's phraseology, it was time to get heavy.

The increasing darkness made Hotampa even more depressing than earlier. Turlough and Caloon had been joined by another eight Heracletes; all of them were dressed in black, with black scarves wrapped around their faces so that only their eyes showed.

'We're looking at how well defended the dump area is,' Caloon explained. 'It might offer us enough cover to get inside before the Militia notice us.'

'And what's the dump?' asked Turlough, ignoring the instant stares from the others. Being an outsider was hardly unusual for him.

'Just what it sounds like,' said Crooce, another of the raiding party. 'When the Spline's offerings turn up, they aren't always useful. Anything that the priests can't use is thrown on the dump.'

Caloon had explained about the offerings. Items apparently materialized in the inner sanctum: food, clothing, and things that the High Priest considered unimportant. The food and clothing was used to keep the lesser priests happy, the rest was discarded. To Turlough, such technology was commonplace – transmats were in use on all of the civilized worlds. But to a primitive race like the Heracletes, it would seem like a miracle.

It took about half an hour to reach the dump. They had taken a wide arc around the Temple, bearing left to about five hundred metres behind it, and then doubling back. A twenty-metre-high mound glittered in the wan double moonlight. Ten metres beyond it, the clear sky was blocked out by the Temple.

Turlough walked over to the dump and was flabbergasted. From Caloon's comments, he had imagined that it consisted of junk. In reality, it was anything but. There were books, items of furniture, scientific equipment – and items that could prove considerably more useful. Plasma rifles, laser guns, stasers – a positive armoury of high-tech weaponry was mixed in with the rest. Turlough carefully extracted a matter-disruptor from underneath a plastic chair.

'Have you any idea what this is?' he said quietly, well aware that Militia were lurking nearby.

'A trinket,' muttered Tubos. 'Whatever it is, it's useless; why else have the priests dumped it?'

'Really?' Turlough pointed at the sand in front of Tubos and squeezed the trigger. A beam of purple light lanced out and turned the ground to smooth obsidian. 'A bit more than a trinket, eh?'

Caloon came forward. 'What is that? Witchcraft?'

'High-energy photon beam laced with anti-quarks. With this, we could get in without any problems.' And then, realizing how bloodthirsty he sounded, Turlough grabbed another weapon from the pile. 'But this is a neural stunner; it'll just send the Militia to sleep.'

Caloon looked at Turlough. 'How many more of these stunners can you find?'

Turlough rooted around the dump, but there were only about three more stunners to be found in the tip. Unless they went in armed with plastic chairs, or with guns that had only a 'kill' setting, that was their lot. But where was the Spline grabbing these things from?

Distributing the stunners – Caloon took one and indicated that Turlough give one to Estribus and Crooce – Turlough looked beyond the dump. A wide tunnel broke the monotony of the grey stone wall of the Temple, its interior sparsely but regularly lit with wall-mounted lamps. 'That's the way in? Isn't it a bit obvious?'

Caloon answered. 'The Militia are convinced of their own superiority, Turlough. With these' – he held up the stunner – 'we have the advantage.'

'This is… astonishing,' said the Doctor. And it was.

Once they had reached Caloon's workstation – nothing more than a desk and a computer in a cramped and untidy office – they had discovered that Ullius was far too busy to see anybody. Then again, Caloon had refrained from telling his superior that the Doctor was an alien; was this because Caloon wanted to save the glory for himself, or because he feared that the Doctor would meet the same fate as the Ambassador?

So Caloon had taken him directly to the Spline Chamber. The chamber was square, approximately twenty metres across, the walls, floor and ceiling a metallic turquoise. Banks of complex instruments lined those walls, streamlined metal consoles and workstations with flickering surfaces. Just like the image on the television. But that image hadn't done justice to the centre of the chamber, which was the most impressive part of all: a hole in the floor, about ten feet across, enclosed by a chest-high metal rail. A beam of coruscating green light streamed through the hole, casting its flickering brilliance across the chamber before being swallowed up by a similar hole in the ceiling. Presumably, this was the tau-meson carrier wave; when the Spline was activated, the reverse-spin imaginary chronons would populate the beam, turning it a brighter shade of green as the Cherenkov backlash increased. Harmless radiation from something that was far from harmless.

The Doctor sighed: this wasn't a fumbled attempt at time travel, a bungled arrangement of barely thought-out theories and equipment. The Spline was a polished model of an efficient time machine that impressed even the Doctor. Whoever the Ambassador had been, he must have had a firm grasp of temporal mechanics; the Spline was far beyond the time scaphes and scoops built by the early Time Lords. Indeed... But something caught the Doctor's eye, and he wandered over for a closer look.

And froze.

The tall thin block that stood in one corner was nothing less than a helmic regulator, a stabilizing device vital to the operation of TARDISes, and a perfect way of stabilizing the beam of chronons as it penetrated the time vortex. The Ambassador's knowledge could only have come from a detailed inspection of a TARDIS, and there were very few Time Lords willing to show off their vessels. The Master and the Rani weren't renowned for their hospitality, and the Doctor doubted that Drax's TARDIS even had helmic regulators. That left only one option, and it wasn't one that he cared to entertain. But a sudden shout from behind him interrupted his reverie and made him turn around.

'Who the hell are you, and what do you think you're doing in here!'

Professor Ullius stood in the doorway. And he didn't look

very pleased.

They reached the end of the tunnel without incident, but that didn't surprise Caloon; he had always suspected that the rumours of the Temple's impregnability were just that: rumours, generated by the Militia to frighten people off.

'Which way now?' asked Turlough. Caloon had already decided that the boy was undecipherable – a curious mixture of cowardice and bravery. He just hoped that the latter overrode the former in their current situation.

'There's a door just over there, apparently.' Turlough looked along the corridor and saw an inset rectangle. 'The divine will of the Spline propels the occupants from here to the inner sanctum.'

'Divine will?' said Turlough cynically. He walked over to the rectangle and touched the wall; the door immediately slid open. 'It's a lift.'

'A lift?'

'A mechanical device, Caloon. A box that is winched up a shaft. No godlike powers required, I'm afraid.'

Caloon's response was aborted by a cry from Tubos, dropping to the floor with a crossbow bolt through the chest. Crossbows: chosen weapons of the Militia.

'Don't move!' snapped a voice from the shadows.

'Use the stunners!' screamed Turlough. He raised his own to fire, but Crooce knocked it from his hand. And then pulled a knife.

'What are you doing?' shouted Caloon.

'It's over. We've been waiting for you to make a move, to identify all of your fellow heretics. And this is it.' As the Militia stepped from the darkness and grabbed the others, Crooce smiled. 'You'll be a lesson to those in Hotampa who defame the glory of the Spline and his High Priest.'

And then Caloon was frogmarched away from the traitor, his arms pinioned behind his back. But he had one last thing to say to Crooce: 'Burn in hell, you bastard!'

'You must be Professor Ullius,' stated the stranger, holding out his hand. 'I'm the Doctor.'

Ullius ignored the hand. 'A Doctor of what?' With only hours to go until the Spline was activated, the last thing he wanted was a stranger wandering about the Spline Chamber itself. He glanced at Caloon; once the Spline was working and Ullius had some spare time, he would have strong words with the junior technician about security procedures.

'Given the current circumstances, temporal physics would be a good start.' The Doctor opened his arms to encompass the chamber. 'This is all most impressive, Professor. Would you care to tell me where you got the idea?'

Activation in hours, and he was still being dogged by journalists. 'Technician Caloon will escort you back to main reception and get you a press pack, Doctor. I'm extremely busy at the moment; the Spline comes on line in less than six hours –'

'I don't think that that would be very sensible, Professor. This device could have disastrous consequences if switched on; catastrophic, even. Time isn't like a glorified ocean that you can sail across at will; there are certain... considerations.' The Doctor's anger was clearly rising. 'Now, will you listen to reason?'

Ullius laughed. 'Reason? Half-baked drivel, more like. I know every circuit of the Spline, Doctor; it's perfectly harmless.'

'You're not in a position to guarantee anything as far as time is concerned, Ullius. You're playing with –'

'Forces beyond my comprehension?' How many times had he heard *that* argument? 'What gives *you* the right to lecture *me*?'

The Doctor stepped forward. 'The fact that I am Lord President of the Time Lords. We cannot permit this tinkering.'

'The Time Lords?' Ullius frowned in recollection. Ambassador Ts'ril had mentioned them frequently: near-omnipotent beings who policed the timestream, travelling in vessels called... 'Prove it, Doctor. Show me your TARDIS.'

Shaking his head, the Doctor slammed his fist on the metal railing that surrounded the Spline conduit. 'My TARDIS is temporally displaced, and I can't help wondering whether your precious Spline is responsible.'

'But the Spline isn't even on line yet!' Ullius protested.

'Where time travel is involved, the laws of cause and effect don't always behave as expected.'

The Doctor's constant whingeing was getting irritating. It had been the same holier-than-thou attitude that had led to the Ambassador's unfortunate accident; it had been a pity that the primary displacement board of the helmic regulators had short-circuited while Ts'ril had been working on it. Ullius wouldn't allow anyone to stand in the way of his race's future. 'Come over here,' he ordered the Doctor. 'If this doesn't prove that the Spline is harmless, nothing will!'

The status board was capable of showing every aspect of the Spline's operation, from power feeds to the tunnel through the Time Vortex itself. Ullius tapped a sequence of touch controls and brought up an image of the tau-meson carrier wave. 'There you have it. A perfectly safe, perfectly harmless means of time travel, a beam of coherent time stretching from the very beginning to the very end of time, to quote the press release.'

'Really?' asked the Doctor, barging Ullius out of the way and taking over the station. He tapped away for a few seconds, and then stepped back. 'So, how do you explain that?' He stabbed a finger at the screen. The Doctor had reduced the magnification, showing a much larger portion of the Time Vortex.

The thin bright line of the carrier wave stretched back and forward from Heracletus's current time – but only two years in both directions. Heracletus was surrounded by a sphere of... of something, a something that curtailed the Spline from eternity to four years. Where the hell had that come from? And then Ullius realized that he hadn't run a scan for weeks – more than enough time for these high-and-mighty Time Lords to emasculate his invention.

'What is it?' he asked the Doctor. His voice was guttural.

The so-called Time Lord tapped the keyboard again, bringing up a slightly different picture. He groaned. 'It's a time loop.

And a Time Lord time loop, come to that. So why am I here?' He pinched the bridge of his nose. 'There's something not quite right about this, you know. Not right at all.'

'You're telling me!' growled Ullius. 'You come in here, going on about meddling with time and how the Spline is a danger to the Universe, while your Time Lord subjects have already made damned sure that the Spline won't work anyway.'

The Doctor tried to calm him down. 'I can assure you, Professor, I'm as concerned about this time loop as you are. Perhaps you'd care to assist me?'

That was it. Breaking point. Pushing past the Doctor, Ullius marched over to the main control station, a flat surface with only one button, the melodramatically bright-red activator. 'Perhaps you Time Lords aren't as all-powerful as you'd like to think, Doctor. Let's see whether your loop is strong enough to handle the Spline at full power.' He slammed the activator.

Immediately, the column of light deepened in colour as the reverse-spin imaginary chronons streamed up from the generator in the basement, ready to penetrate the Time Vortex and put the Time Lords and their bloody loop to the test.

But the initial setting for the chronon rate was only a quarter of the maximum; reaching out to another panel, Ullius violently twisted a large dial.

Within seconds, the column was almost black with temporal energy.

'Ullius!' screamed the Doctor, trying to make himself heard over the thundering growl that filled the chamber. 'You have no idea what this could do. The feedback could be disastrous!'

Ullius shook his head. 'I built the Spline to save this world, Doctor. If Heracletus is going to die, I'd rather it died at my hands than wither away in agony because of you.'

'So, this is Caloon the rebel?' said the High Priest quietly. He was sitting on a large throne in front of a pillar of sparkling green light, its radiance bouncing off the turquoise walls.

'Why bother asking, Ullius?' he replied defiantly. 'In fact, why bother with an interrogation at all? I'm sure your lapdog Crooce has told you everything.'

'Indeed he has.' Ullius looked over at Turlough, and held up one of the stunners. 'You will show me how to operate this, or I will have Caloon killed. And believe me, the Spline can draw out a man's death longer than you could possibly believe.'

Turlough sneered. 'Oh, I can believe it. From the look of this room, the Spline is a fairly advanced temporal transfer device. Is that the source of your power, Ullius? Plundering the time lines for food? With this, you could rebuild this entire planet, make Heracletus fertile again. Instead, you squander what little control you have over it on keeping your priests happy and the locals under your thumb. You're sitting in the middle of all this technology, and all you're worried about is a stunner?'

The High Priest frowned. It was clear to Caloon that Ullius hadn't really understood a word of Turlough's explanation. And, being the narrow-minded head of a narrow-minded faith, he reacted predictably. He ignored him. 'I ask you again: how does it work?'

Turlough's sneer changed to a slight smile, and Caloon suddenly wondered what he was up to. As far as he could see, there weren't too many options left, considering that six armed Militia surrounded them.

'Press the first stud three times; that powers it up.' Ullius did as instructed, and smiled like an excited child as the weapon started to hum. 'Once you've aimed it, press the second stud to fire.'

Ullius stood from his throne, and turned. He lifted the stunner, and aimed it at the far wall, where there was only plain turquoise metal. His thumb came down on the stud...

And Turlough took advantage of the guards' distraction and shoved Ullius's arm. The beam of sizzling white fire missed its intended target... and seared through the column of light and hit one of the complex boxes against the far wall. The box exploded, sending burning fragments in all directions.

But that was only the beginning. The pillar began to flicker, and, simultaneously, the lights in the room began to dim.

'What have you done?' screamed Ullius. 'Guards – kill them both!'

But the guards didn't have time to act. The pillar became an incandescent tower of cold fire, whiting out the room and forcing everybody to close their eyes. At the same time, a terrifying scream rose up to assault them, a wail of pain that seemed to come from the pillar itself.

Caloon swallowed. Was this the vengeance of the Spline, the divine retribution that Ullius had promised for so long? That was Caloon's final thought as his body dissolved in fire and ice.

'You fool!' shouted the Doctor, frantically pressing buttons and levers as he scurried round from station to station. 'Unless I can shut this down, you could rupture the Time Vortex.'

But Ullius seemed unmoved by the Doctor's plea. He stood with his back to the chronon beam, his arms folded, his face impassive. 'Do what you damned well like, Doctor. I won't try to stop you.'

Caloon stepped back from the chronon beam, which was now an unfathomable, soul-sucking black column. The growl was now so deep that he could feel it through the soles of his feet.

'It's no good,' muttered the Doctor. 'The initial feedback from the time loop has fused the control systems. The only option is to shut down the tachyon generators. Caloon – can you do that?'

Startled at hearing his name, Caloon froze for a second. And then nodded. 'I'll get right onto it.'

But he never reached the door. The darkness from the beam suddenly expanded, its shadowy substance spilling out in black tendrils which thrust outwards from the centre of the room, caressing walls, floor and ceiling as though alive.

'Get out of here!' yelled the Doctor, ducking as a tentacle of darkness engulfed the station he had been working at. 'Quickly, both of you!'

Caloon tried to move, but couldn't. To his horror, he saw that both his feet were rooted to the floor by a pool of liquid blackness. As he watched, it slithered up his body, numbing and freezing him as it progressed. He called out for help, but soon realized that he was alone in the chamber; the Doctor and Ullius were already lost to the shadows.

And then so was he.

Turlough opened his eyes cautiously, but the blinding light had gone. Then again, so had the control room. He was now in a vast scientific complex, the level of technology so sophisticated that it was on a par with the TARDIS itself. At the far end of the huge chamber, a much larger version of the energy column stood encased in a faceted crystal cylinder.

And Turlough wasn't alone. There were over a hundred people there, including the reassuring figure of the Doctor. Turlough ran over to him, but his smile dissolved when he realized that it wasn't the Doctor.

It was the Savant.

'You again,' the Time Lord spat. 'And I suppose this is all due to your incompetent bungling? I intend to hold a full review of academic standards when I return to Gallifrey –'

'Turlough?' Spinning round at the familiar voice, Turlough was face to face with the real Doctor. He hoped.

'You're all right,' said the Doctor breathlessly. And then he cast a dismissive look at the Savant. 'Although I'm not too keen on the company you're keeping.'

'Would you mind telling me what's going on? Where are we?'

'We're still on Heracletus,' the Doctor explained, pulling Turlough away from the Savant. 'Or rather, *a* Heracletus. There do seem to be rather too many of them, don't there?' He gestured around the complex. Turlough frowned for a second, and then realized that all the people in the complex were Caloons, Ulliuses, Doctors and Turloughs. Dressed differently, perhaps, but all variations on four familiar themes.

'Parallel universes?'

'Not exactly. I was putting together a theory about it before the Spline overloaded, but that reality's equipment wasn't up to the task. Then again, this place looks like it is.' With that, he sauntered over to a large desk, its turquoise surface covered with a criss-cross pattern of thin dark blue lines, not unlike a circuit diagram. As he did so, Turlough told him about his experiences in his version of Heracletus.

'And what do you think you're doing?' came a recognizable voice. Ullius was behind them. But it was a very different Ullius from the High Priest. The cruelty and self-importance had been replaced with intense scientific curiosity. 'I presume you're something to do with this?' He waved his hand at the assembled crowd.

'Professor Ullius,' said the Doctor, pumping the man's hand. 'I'm the Doctor, and this is Turlough. The others… well, I'm sure you recognize them. I'm afraid there's been something of a malfunction with the Spline. I'm a Time Lord and I'm here to sort it out for you.'

'The Time Lords?' Ullius grinned. 'The Ambassador mentioned them.' He smiled sadly. 'It's such a pity that he died before the Spline was completed; he would have been so proud. Then again, how was a Lorq to know that the pollution on Heracletus would have given him cancer?'

'Lorq?' The Doctor frowned. 'Small race, look a bit like four-armed teddy bears?'

Ullius nodded.

'I didn't know they'd developed temporal technology.' He rubbed his hands together and grinned. 'Still, perhaps someone left a time machine in one of their vault ships for safe keeping. Anyway, I'm very pleased to meet you. Perhaps we could sort out what's happened.' The Doctor's fingers danced across the surface of the desk, eliciting a stream of bleeps and whistles as he did so. After a few minutes of concentrated effort, he looked up. 'Oh dear. This really isn't what I expected at all.' He steepled his hands. 'Professor, what I'm about to tell you may prove distressing; for that I must apologize. You see, it's all to do with the Time Lords…'

As the Doctor began his story, Turlough watched the colour drain from Ullius's face, the spark of hope guttering. Then again, it was hardly the most cheerful of tales to tell.

For a whole minute after the Doctor finished, Ullius remained silent, obviously digesting the Doctor's explanation. And then he spoke, his voice empty and bitter.

'Four years? We're condemned to spend eternity reliving a four-year period?' Ullius seemed on the verge of tears. 'All my work, all of it, for nothing.' And then he scowled. 'So how does that explain all of these people?'

The Doctor spread his hands over the desk. 'As I said, the Time Lords made a mistake. It would appear that the surface of the time loop wasn't smooth; like a mirror with an imperfection, the reflection wasn't perfect. Over the centuries since the loop was created, your planet has been reaching the end of its allotted four years, and then bouncing back at an angle, so to speak. The result has been another, parallel version of Heracletus. And each bounce has deviated further and further from the original.'

He opened his arms to encompass the complex. 'Events in the realities that Turlough and I occupied – and presumably the realities of these others – must have momentarily broken down the barriers between the pocket universes and deposited us here. Actually, the barriers must be riddled with weak spots; that's where your offerings were coming from, Turlough. Flotsam and jetsam crossing the boundaries.'

'But if the Time Lords acted before the Heracletes had developed time travel, how was the Spline developed in the first place?' asked Turlough.

The Doctor shrugged. 'Now there's a question to which I really would like the answer. There's something else going on here... I can feel it.'

A commotion from the far side of the complex drew their attention. The Savant version of the Doctor was arguing with one of the Ulliuses.

'Trouble,' muttered Turlough, rushing over. And then another problem occurred to him. Where the hell had the Savant come from? If Heracletus was sealed in a bubble of time, and all the alternatives were versions of that planet, how had a Doctor from a parallel Gallifrey arrived there?

The Savant was attempting to reach another control desk, but one of the Ulliuses – a man dressed in a silver suit – was trying to stop him.

'The Lorq Ambassador claimed that such a setting would overload the primary systems!' he shouted.

'Out of my way, imbecile! I can easily rectify this situation.' Shoving the Ullius out of the way, the Savant began operating the circuit-like control surface. Turlough helped the discarded Ullius to his feet. 'Thank you. But he doesn't know what he's doing; the Ambassador committed suicide when he discovered the consequences of his discovery. This man must be mad to consider this course of action!'

'No!' protested the Doctor to the Savant. 'You don't know the entire story. There are other forces at work here. Without knowing all the facts, your actions could prove disastrous.'

'Nonsense,' replied the Savant. 'By re-routing the subsystems, I can convert the Spline into an interstitial matter transmitter –'

'Of course! I should have realized!' exclaimed the Doctor, staring at the chronon beam. 'The Spline isn't real!' Even the Savant paused at the Doctor's revelation. 'This entire situation is an unstable fantasy. The Spline is simply a reflection of another time machine, trapped in the loop and unable to escape.'

'Another time machine?' whispered Turlough. 'You mean –'

The Doctor nodded gravely. 'The TARDIS. That's why the technology has all seemed so familiar. The TARDIS was caught in the loop and reflected back and forwards, so its technology appeared in every subsequent reality.' He tapped his nose. 'We must have traversed the loop time and again without realizing it! The Heracletes never developed time travel – the TARDIS gave it to them. *I* gave it to them.'

'Utter nonsense!' The Savant continued his attempts at the desk.

'Listen to me!' insisted the Doctor. 'The only way to escape this loop is to find the TARDIS – we have to do that before we do anything else.'

But it was too late. The Savant straightened and pointed at the chronon stream which was now pulsating with a regular beat. 'You see? Very little is beyond me.'

The explosion from behind them came as something of a surprise to everyone. When Turlough looked round, he could see that the control desk by the far wall was now on fire. It was all happening again, he realized, and freely admitted – to himself – that he was absolutely terrified.

'You've unbalanced the time loop!' exclaimed the Doctor. 'The realities are collapsing into one another!' He pushed past the Savant and began frantically to operate the controls. 'Despite your insufferable arrogance, you were on the right track. If I can just locate the TARDIS's temporal signature, I should be able to transport us to that reality. The TARDIS will have landed on the original Heracletus, and that reality will be safe. Actually, it will be the only one left.' He paused to look up at the erratic flickerings from the chronon stream. 'If I can do it in time.'

'Allow me to help,' said the Savant in a humbled tone. 'If you will allow it?'

'Many hands make light work,' muttered the Doctor. 'See if you can find the TARDIS; I'll open up the dimensional barrier.'

Turlough looked beyond them to the column of light: it seemed to be expanding with each flicker, threatening to break out of its crystal prison. 'Found it!' shouted the Savant. 'Open up the barrier.'

The Doctor tapped the surface with a flourish. 'There!' A large cubic space inset into one of the walls lit up. 'All of you – onto the transmitter!'

A horde of Caloons, Ulliuses, Doctors and Turloughs filed into the cramped space and vanished as a further series of explosions rocked the complex. As Turlough stepped onto the transmitter, he looked back at the chronon stream, but it was too bright to look at.

As he felt his body lose substance and cohesion, Turlough

just hoped that the TARDIS was waiting for them.

The orange sunlight was only marginally less bright than the chronon stream had been. Turlough and the Doctor were standing on the green sand of the arid and empty desert that the TARDIS scanners had shown, however long ago that had been.

Turlough broke into a grin when he saw the TARDIS about a hundred metres away, but the grin faded when he realized that he and the Doctor were alone. There was no sign of the hundreds of others who had travelled with them.

'Doctor?'

But the Time Lord said nothing. Pulling the key from his pocket, he trudged through the sand and opened the TARDIS door.

As the TARDIS began to dematerialize, the time rotor rising and falling in time with the raucous groaning, the Doctor peered intently at one of the monitors on the console. He sighed. 'As I predicted, the Savant's tampering has collapsed the loop. What's left shows all the signs of developing into a rather spectacular temporal rift. A fitting memorial for the Heracletes,' he added bitterly. 'I'll leave the Time Lords to deal with that.' A stray thought crossed his face. 'Unless they already have,' he murmured. 'Unless *I* already have. I seem to remember…'

'Remember what?' Turlough prompted.

The Doctor shook his head. 'Nothing,' he said. 'For a moment I had the strangest sense of *déjà vu.*'

'Why didn't the others make it?' asked Turlough quietly.

When the Doctor finally looked up, there was a haunting emptiness behind his eyes. 'They weren't real, Turlough. They were all three-dimensional illusions created by a combination of the loop and the TARDIS. The desert that we've just left is Heracletus as it would have been without the loop – time has reasserted itself, and it suddenly has an entry in the TARDIS database. It's what really happened.' He prodded a button and then stood back. 'I've just looked it up; whoever this Ambassador was, his attempt to give the Heracletes time travel was a disaster. The final Ullius was nearest to the truth, it seems – the Ambassador apparently died of natural causes before the loop was established, and that's why he wasn't around in any of the parallel dimensions – but his work simply accelerated the collapse of their civilization and the desert is all that remains. The Time Lords needn't have bothered,' he said sadly.

Turlough sighed. Even though the Ambassador hadn't been present, he had still been a figure in the history of all the realities, his death varying from murder to suicide to natural causes in each one, it seemed. What an epitaph. 'But one thing still puzzles me, though. Why did the Time Lords send us to Heracletus if they had already acted? Or did they discover that the loop was malfunctioning?'

The Doctor shook his head. 'Oh no, Turlough; the Time Lords had nothing to do with our arrival on Heracletus.'

Turlough was puzzled. 'Then who was it?'

The Doctor hung his head. 'It was us, Turlough. The loop broke the laws of cause and effect; we were already in the loop before we arrived. What we heard was the TARDIS begging herself for help.' He stepped back from the console. 'But the experience has taught me one thing. I was absolutely right to leave Gallifrey.'

As the Doctor left the console room, Turlough pondered his words. Was it the actions of the Time Lords in imprisoning Heracletus that had made the Doctor say that? Or was it the presence of the Savant, a figure presumably dragged from the Doctor's deepest fears by the TARDIS's telepathic circuits?

Whatever the reason, Turlough knew that he was just as glad that the Doctor had left Gallifrey. Even if he was a little grumpy.

From time to time.

Afterword
By Professor Arthur Candy
(as dictated to Steven Moffat)

The Doctor, of course, knows that we are watching. And when, as has happened more than once, a culture extrapolates his existence from his multiple interventions in their history, the Doctor has a favourite 'panic button'. He simply slips back in time and introduces himself as a fictional character in the popular mythology of that particular world. As a consequence, there are now millions of races all over the universe following his adventures in one form or another without ever realising their deadly significance. Naturally, it becomes all but impossible to explain to the Intelligent Tree Spores of Xandar 6 that the hero of their popular weekly bark carvings is a real and dangerous phenomenon when they're too busy complaining that the carving looks a bit cheap and sniggering at the space ships.

But why am I telling you? By buying this book you have colluded in the Doctor's careful self-erasure from history. Truth is, I'm not talking to you at all.

Doctor, I know you're reading this. Joke's a joke – I want to go home now.

Prof. Arthur Candy
Birmingham
1996

About The Contributors

PETER ANGHELIDES has written for a diverse range of publications, including *Starburst*, *QuarterBack*, and *The Listener*. His previous *Doctor Who* stuff includes articles in *DWM*, two other drabbles, a wild-haired appearance on BBC television's *Did You See..?*, numerous rambling postings to rec.arts.drwho, and co-editing the reference series *IN*VISION*. He works in the documentation and localization group of a big computer company in Hampshire, where he lives with his toddler son and wife Anne Summerfield (Benny's glamorous older sister). He loves writing about himself in the third person, and spent longer producing this rather conceited biography than on the actual story.

STEPHEN BOWKETT was born and brought up in South Wales. He began writing at age thirteen, soon after *Doctor Who* first appeared on television. Much of his early work was fan fiction, published in magazines such as *Capitol*, *Arc of Infinity*, *Axos*, *Gallifrey*, *Frontier Worlds*, *Moonbase* and *Spearhead From Space*. Recent published output includes poetry, SF, fantasy and horror stories for children and teenagers, and, under the pseudonym of Ben Leech, horror novels for adults. After twenty years of teaching English, Steve is now a full-time writer and hypnotherapist. He lives near Leicester.

COLIN BRAKE is 34 years old and not very tall. Colin spent a number of years as a Script Editor lurking in the BBC Drama Department and had high hopes of being Andrew Cartmel's successor on *Doctor Who*. In 1989, in an act of desperation, the BBC thwarted this ambition by cancelling the series.

As a freelance writer Colin has written scripts for *EastEnders* and *BUGS*, and the book *EastEnders – The First 10 Years*. He lives with his wife, Kerry, who is *slowly* coming to appreciate Doctor Who.

GUY CLAPPERTON has contributed to several radio and

television programmes on the light entertainment side. He has a long-standing fondness for *Doctor Who* and was only too pleased to step in and write something when the other fifteen choices turned the editors down. He is married with two cats.

KEITH R. A. DeCANDIDO was first exposed to *Doctor Who* at a very young age when he stumbled across Part 2 of 'The Horror Of Fang Rock' on the tiny black-and-white TV in his bedroom, and has remained a big fan ever since. His one desire was to see a story wherein the Doctor gallivanted around his hometown of New York City; imagine his surprise when he found he had to *write* it. His other short fiction has shown up in *The Ultimate Spiderman*, *The Ultimate Silver Surfer*, and the *Magic: The Gathering* anthology *Distant Planes*; he also co-edited the anthologies *OtherWere*, *The Ultimate Alien* and *The Ultimate Dragon*, as well as the forthcoming *Alligators in the Sewers: Tales of Urban Legends*. He still lives in New York with his wife and an ever-growing collection of books, CDs, videotapes, stuffed animals and percussion.

CRAIG HINTON lives in London, and regularly contributes to *TV Zone* and *Cult Times* magazines. When he isn't writing, he delays executions to pull the wings off flies. To his eternal shame, he was at Warwick University with both of the editors, but he still had to bribe them both to get them to commission his story.

BEN JEAPES's childhood ambition was to take the lead role in *Doctor Who* when he grew up: he abandoned it because the Krynoids were so scary on screen he thought they must have been ten times worse in the studio. By day he works in Oxford and is Managing Editor of various academic journals; by night he is an aspiring science fiction writer, with several sales notched up to *Interzone* and other publications. Since selling 'Timevault' he has revised his views on shared world authors.

ANDY LANE lives three separate lives. On the one hand he has a degree in physics and works for the civil service. On the other hand he writes TV tie-in material: four *Doctor Who* novels and one *BUGS* novelization for Virgin and various articles for *Star Trek Monthly* and *Star Wars Magazine*. On the third (Venusian) hand, he is the author of various serious SF and fantasy short stories in anthologies such as *The Ultimate Witch*, *The Ultimate Dragon*, *Full Spectrum 5* and *The Ultimate X-Men*, as well as in the British magazine *Interzone*. He is still waiting for Craig Hinton's bribe to arrive.

JACKIE MARSHALL lives in Norfolk and teaches at a primary school. She is notorious for co-producing (along with Val Douglas) the fanzines *Space Rat*, *Queen Bat* and *Rats Tales*. This story took shape on the back of hospital advice to patie ·s recovering from an appendectomy while the author convalesced at the seaside. She is deeply grateful for the monies received for penning this tale as it enabled her to have her two kittens neutered.

STEVEN MOFFAT wrote the popular teen drama series *Press Gang* (for which he won a BAFTA and a Royal Television Society Award) and *Joking Apart* (which won the Bronze Rose Of Montreux). He is also a regular contributor to Dawn French's award-winning *Murder Most Horrid*. His hobbies include mentioning his awards rather more often than is strictly decent.

JUSTIN RICHARDS started writing for *Doctor Who* fanzines in the nineteen eighties. He was co-editor of the first 'alternative' *Doctor Who* fanzine, *The Black and White Guardian* (*BAWG*), and more recently edited all the Tom Baker issues of the definitive reference work *Doctor Who IN*VISION*, together with Peter Anghelides.

Justin wrote, edited, and supervised the writing of dozens of software user guides and technical manuals when he worked as a technical writer for several years. Having thus established an interest in producing fiction, he turned his hand to novels and is the author of three of Virgin's *Doctor Who* novels – including the recently published Missing Adventure *The Sands of Time*. Justin currently divides his time between (in order of increasing priority) writing, working for a multinational computer company to define the way people will work with computers and software into the next millennium, and his family. He lives in Warwickshire, and likes that.

GARETH ROBERTS was born in 1968 and raised in Chesham, Buckinghamshire. He has been a perfume packer, an Inland Revenue assistant, an envelope stuffer, a playscheme supervisor, a clerk at the Court of Appeal, a sticky-label affixer, a drama student, a film critic, an editorial assistant, a performer and a writer. He has written six *Doctor Who* books and novelized two stories from the *Cracker* TV series. He likes pop music, has never married and lives in Cricklewood.

ALSO AVAILABLE:

DECALOG
Edited by
Mark Stammers & Stephen James Walker

TEN STORIES SEVEN DOCTORS ONE ENIGMA

Into the office of a private investigator walks a mysterious little
man with a story that's out of this world. He says he's lost his
memory. He wants the PI to help him. When he turns out his
pockets, he produces a pile of bizarre objects, each of which
restores a memory and solves a part of the puzzle. And the memories seem to belong to seven different people.

£4.99
ISBN 0 426 20411 5

DECALOG 2
LOST PROPERTY
Edited by
Mark Stammers & Stephen James Walker

TEN STORIES SEVEN DOCTORS NO FIXED ABODE

In this second volume of Doctor Who short fiction the theme is the
Doctor's home – inasmuch as a peripatetic Time Lord can be said to
have a home. Among many other unexpected occurrences, the
Doctor meets a pretender to the English throne, Nyssa meets a
ghost, Zoe gets lost in time, Brigadier Lethbridge-Stewart is
dismissed from UNIT, and K9 is in electrifying form. And to cap it
all, the Kandyman is on Tara in a verse play in Iambic pentameters.

£4.99
ISBN 0 426 20448 4

All books in the Decalog series feature a galaxy of star writers – many of
whom will be known to the readers of the New and Missing Adventures – as
well as contributions from new writing talent.

Already published:

THE PIT
Neil Penswick

One of the Seven Planets is a nameless giant, quarantined against all intruders. But when the TARDIS materializes, it becomes clear that the planet is far from empty – and the Doctor begins to realize that the planet hides a terrible secret from the Time Lords' past.

ISBN 0 426 20378 X

DECEIT
Peter Darvill-Evans

Ace – three years older, wiser and tougher – is back. She is part of a group of Irregular Auxiliaries on an expedition to the planet Arcadia. They think they are hunting Daleks, but the Doctor knows better. He knows that the paradise planet hides a being far more powerful than the Daleks – and much more dangerous.

ISBN 0 426 20362 3

LUCIFER RISING
Jim Mortimore & Andy Lane

Reunited, the Doctor, Ace and Bernice travel to Lucifer, the site of a scientific expedition that they know will shortly cease to exist. Discovering why involves them in sabotage, murder and the resurrection of eons-old alien powers. Are there Angels on Lucifer? And what does it all have to do with Ace?

ISBN 0 426 20338 7

WHITE DARKNESS
David A. McIntee

The TARDIS crew, hoping for a rest, come to Haiti in 1915. But they find that the island is far from peaceful: revolution is brewing in the city; the dead are walking from the cemeteries; and, far underground, the ancient rulers of the galaxy are stirring in their sleep.

ISBN 0 426 20395 X

SHADOWMIND
Christopher Bulis

On the colony world of Arden, something dangerous is growing stronger. Something that steals minds and memories. Something that can reach out to another planet, Tairngire, where the newest exhibit in the sculpture park is a blue box surmounted by a flashing light.

ISBN 0 426 20394 1

BIRTHRIGHT
Nigel Robinson

Stranded in Edwardian London with a dying TARDIS, Bernice investigates a series of grisly murders. In the far future, Ace leads a group of guerrillas against their insect-like, alien oppressors. Why has the Doctor left them, just when they need him most?

ISBN 0 426 20393 3

ICEBERG
David Banks

In 2006, an ecological disaster threatens the Earth; only the FLIPback team, working in an Antarctic base, can avert the catastrophe. But hidden beneath the ice, sinister forces have gathered to sabotage humanity's last hope. The Cybermen have returned and the Doctor must face them alone.

ISBN 0 426 20392 5

BLOOD HEAT
Jim Mortimore

The TARDIS is attacked by an alien force; Bernice is flung into the Vortex; and the Doctor and Ace crash-land on Earth. There they find dinosaurs roaming the derelict London streets, and Brigadier Lethbridge-Stewart leading the remnants of UNIT in a desperate fight against the Silurians who have taken over and changed his world.

ISBN 0 426 20399 2

THE DIMENSION RIDERS
Daniel Blythe

A holiday in Oxford is cut short when the Doctor is summoned to Space Station Q4, where ghostly soldiers from the future watch from the shadows among the dead. Soon, the Doctor is trapped in the past, Ace is accused of treason and Bernice is uncovering deceit among the college cloisters.

ISBN 0 426 20397 6

they wreak havoc and destruction. United, they threaten every sentient being in the universe.

ISBN 0 426 20437 9

SANCTUARY
David A. McIntee

The Doctor and Bernice are stranded in medieval France, a brutal time of crusades and wars of succession. While the Doctor investigates a murder in a besieged fortress, Bernice joins forces with an embittered mercenary to save a band of heretics from the might of the Inquisition.

ISBN 0 426 20439 5

HUMAN NATURE
Paul Cornell

April, 1914. In the town of Farringham, a teacher called Dr John Smith has just begun work. Struggling to fit in, he finds himself haunted by memories of a place called Gallifrey – somewhere he knows he's never been. Can it be true that, as his niece Bernice claims, creatures from another planet are invading the town?

ISBN 0 426 20443 3

ORIGINAL SIN
Andy Lane

The last words of a dying alien send the Doctor and Bernice to 30th-century Earth in an attempt to avert an unspecified disaster. There, Adjudicators Roz Forrester and Chris Cwej are investigating a series of apparently motiveless murders. And their chief suspects are the Doctor and Bernice.

ISBN 0 426 20444 1

SKY PIRATES!
Dave Stone

Join the Doctor and Benny for the maiden voyage of the good ship *Schirron Dream*, as it ventures into a system which is being invaded by the villainous, shapeshifting Sloathes. Watch Chris Cwej and Roslyn Forrester have a rough old time of it in durance vile. Who will live? Who will die? Will the Doctor ever play the harmonium again?

ISBN 0 426 20446 8

ZAMPER
Gareth Roberts

The planet Zamper is home to a secretive organization that constructs the galaxy's mightiest warships. The TARDIS crew are intrigued by

Zamper's mysterious rulers. What is their true agenda? And why have they invited the last remnants of the Chelonian Empire to their world?

ISBN 0 426 20450 6

TOY SOLDIERS
Paul Leonard

The Doctor and his companions are following a trail of kidnapped children across a Europe recovering from the ravages of the First World War. But someone is aware of their search, and they find themselves unwilling guests on the planet Q'ell, where a similar war has raged for the last 1,400 years.

ISBN 0 426 20452 2

HEAD GAMES
Steve Lyons

Stand by for an exciting adventure with Dr Who and his companion, Jason. Once again, they set out to seek injustice, raise rebel armies and beat up green monsters. But this time, Dr Who faces a deadly new threat: a genocidal rogue Time Lord known only as the Doctor and his army of gun-slinging warrior women.

ISBN 0 426 20454 9

THE ALSO PEOPLE
Ben Aaronovitch

The Doctor has taken his companions to paradise: a sun enclosed by an artificial sphere where there is no poverty or violence. But then the peace is shattered by murder. As the suspects proliferate, Bernice realises that even an artificial world has its buried secrets and Roz discovers that every paradise has its snake.

ISBN 0 426 20456 5

If you have trouble obtaining Doctor Who books from your local shops, a book list and details of our mail order service are available upon request from:

Doctor Who Books
Virgin Publishing Ltd
332 Ladbroke Grove
London W10 5AH